W9-BMO-896

THE SISTERS SWEET

A NOVEL

ELIZABETH WEISS

BK00691147

"A beautifully told coming-of-age story that embraces life with a galloping energy and irresistible curiosity."
—MAGGIE SHIPSTEAD, AUTHOR OF *GREAT CIRCLE*

THE SISTERS
SWEET

"Elizabeth Weiss's debut novel, *The Sisters Sweet*, is an elegant, immersive family saga set within the duplicitous culture of early-20th-century vaudeville. . . . An intimate exploration of sisterhood, identity, ambition and betrayal. It forces us to ask who we are if the very thing that should make us unique—our face—is shared by another who takes it and becomes famous in the process. The novel does a fine job of answering that question and gives us plenty of surprises along the way."
—*The New York Times*

"A fascinating coming-of-age novel . . . *The Sisters Sweet* is fiendishly well imagined, a powerful family story about selfishness and duty, sacrifice and freedom."
—*The Star Tribune*

"Weiss's writing is flawless."
—*Pioneer Press*

"Beautifully written, immersive . . . *The Sisters Sweet* is a story about family and sisterhood, about talent, about hardship and hard choices, and Weiss is a talented writer, evoking time and place seemingly effortlessly."
—*Historical Novel Society*

"A beautifully told coming-of-age story that embraces life with a galloping energy and irresistible curiosity."
—Maggie Shipstead, bestselling author of *Great Circle*

"*The Sisters Sweet* will charm you into another world. Weiss has conjured a lost America with wit, sorrow, and beauty—a book like a favorite old movie."
—Andrew Sean Greer, Pulitzer Prize–winning author of *Less*

The
SISTERS
SWEET

A
NOVEL

ELIZABETH
WEISS

THE DIAL PRESS

NEW YORK

2022 Dial Press Trade Paperback Edition

Copyright © 2021 by Elizabeth Weiss

Book club guide copyright © 2022 by Penguin Random House LLC

Published in the United States by The Dial Press, an imprint of Random House, a division of Penguin Random House LLC, New York.

THE DIAL PRESS is a registered trademark and the colophon is a trademark of Penguin Random House LLC.

RANDOM HOUSE BOOK CLUB and colophon are trademarks of Penguin Random House LLC.

Originally published in hardcover in the United States by The Dial Press, an imprint of Random House, a division of Penguin Random House LLC, in 2021.

LIBRARY OF CONGRESS CATALOGING-IN-PUBLICATION DATA
NAMES: Weiss, Elizabeth, author.
TITLE: The Sisters Sweet : a novel / Elizabeth Weiss.
DESCRIPTION: First paperback edition. | New York : The Dial Press, [2022]
IDENTIFIERS: LCCN 2020047449 (print) | LCCN 2020047450 (ebook) |
ISBN 9781984801562 (paperback) | ISBN 9781984801555 (ebook)
SUBJECTS: LCSH: Twin sisters—Fiction. | Vaudeville—Fiction. | Identity (Psychology)—Fiction. | Psychological fiction.
CLASSIFICATION: LCC PS3623.E455225 S57 2022 (print) |
LCC PS3623.E455225 (ebook) | DDC 813/.6—dc23
LC record available at https://lccn.loc.gov/2020047449
LC ebook record available at https://lccn.loc.gov/2020047450

Printed in the United States of America on acid-free paper

randomhousebooks.com

randomhousebookclub.com

2 4 6 8 9 7 5 3 1

Book design by Barbara M. Bachman

For
Riley

THE

SISTERS

SWEET

PROLOGUE

A YOUNG WOMAN IS PACING UP AND DOWN THE FRONT steps of my house, her briefcase bouncing against her knees. She's muttering to herself, steeling her resolve to ring the bell, I think, as I watch her through my study window. I've been staring at the blank page in my typewriter for an hour. I'm not exactly sorry to abandon it.

When I open the front door, she scrambles up the steps, pushing her sunglasses back into the nest of her pale hair.

"Harriet Szász?" she asks.

"Yes."

"You're Josephine Wilder's sister? Her twin?" She blinks at me expectantly.

"Who are you exactly?"

"I'm Linda Delaney? I'm working on a story? For *Vanity Fair*? Well, it's on spec. But in light of your sister's passing. I took the train up from the city." And then she shakes her head gravely, as if she's just remembered she's supposed to. "I'm sorry for your loss."

"What are you talking about?"

She goes ashen.

"Then you don't—oh, but I assumed you—well, look." She scoops the newspaper off the welcome mat and shakes it open to the obituary page. There she is: my sister Josephine. Smiling out of a headshot from the forties, when we were in our thirties. My eyes glide over the words, my mind struggling to absorb their meaning:

star of Hollywood's golden age, dead. A heart attack in her Malibu home. I skim down to the list of survivors. My name does not appear.

"I've seen all of her movies," she says. "Everything she was ever in, really. Her talk show, both seasons. And that episode of *What's My Line?* She was my college thesis. I got the tapes."

Me too, I want to say. I've seen it all too. But the words are trapped in my throat. Is it grief I feel? Maybe after all this time it won't be. Maybe I long ago forfeited my right to grief.

When I look up from the paper, she is studying me, her forehead tense. Her cream-colored silk blouse, fussed into a bow at the collar, looks brand-new, her blazer looks borrowed from some older woman's closet—special clothes chosen for an important day. If she'd said she was writing an article for the school paper I would have believed her.

"How did you even find me?" I ask. "How are you here?"

"Oh, I called up your publisher and got your address." She beams, as if she expects a merit badge for resourcefulness. "I read one of your books, you know."

"You did?" I feel an old, sheepish pleasure. She nods brightly.

"For my thesis. I thought it might be relevant. Of course it wasn't, but I'm not sorry I read it. I liked it!"

Of course, of course: my life, my work, just a footnote in some coed's thesis. As far as Miss Delaney is concerned, I'm the family dud, the tragically abandoned second fiddle, a nobody stunned by her sister's magnificence. But as soon as I allow myself that bitter thought, the grief I worried I had no right to feel floods my chest, threatens to spill out my throat in a cry. Josie! But it's always been this way! The desire to be known, to mark my own clear edge, is tethered to the desire to keep her close.

For a wild instant, I think I can make Linda Delaney understand. This girl who wants to make sense of the person I once knew better than anyone in the world, the person who once knew me. Maybe the story I need to tell isn't exactly the story Miss Delaney expects to hear, but I can make her hear it. My life may not have demanded notice the way Josie's did, but it was never a footnote. I was never a footnote. I grab her arm.

"Would you like to come in?"

In the study, she makes a beeline for the photo on the bookshelf: Josie and me in the harness, eleven, or maybe twelve, dressed in ruffles, with Little Bo Peep bonnets and a shepherdess's crook resting against my shoulder.

"Incredible," she says. Her fingers are smudging the glass. "No one talks about the Siamese Sweets. I read six obituaries this morning, and none of them even mentioned you. Everyone's just forgotten your part of the story, which is crazy, because—I mean, what a story! To have performed with Josephine Wilder, and then to have lost her."

My part of the story: to have performed with Josie, and then to have lost her. That's all she can imagine.

"What I want is to paint the complete picture," she's saying. "She's always been flattened out, hasn't she? Into whatever they needed her to be. Ingenue, vixen, mother."

"Trailblazer," I say. "Ball buster. Grand dame."

"Exactly." Now she's growing excited. "Wife. Ex-wife. Camp queen." She holds up the photograph. "Do you have anything else like this?"

I'm beginning to worry I've made a mistake, inviting her in, but I open the big oak trunk opposite the desk. She kneels on the floor beside it and starts pawing through the archive: clippings and photos, ticket stubs, handbills. I sit next to her on a stool. It's been years since I looked at any of it. Josie, a smudge of ink on a yellowing piece of newsprint, cuts a ribbon outside a new home for wounded soldiers. Josie, in pearls, hawks Lustre-Creme shampoo. A bill promotes our appearance at a county fair: "The Siamese Sweets! Born joined together!" Paper flakes beneath my fingertips. The scent of old fibers, of dust and wood and the soft hint of mildew, seems like the scent of memory itself.

"What's this?" she asks, handing me a typewritten manuscript tied with a ribbon. The paper is thin, yellowing. I read:

Maude Foster emerges into the steam and hustle of the platform at Grand Central Station, clinging to her suitcase and
staring, with great purpose, some yards ahead, the surest
way, she has learned, to keep busybodies from asking why
she is traveling alone.

It takes me a moment to recognize the words as my own. I wrote
them twenty-five years ago, right after Mama died. Absurd to think
of oneself as an orphan at fifty-three, but that was how I felt. My
parents were gone. The truth of what had passed between us was
fixed. All I had left were their stories. For a week, I holed up in my
apartment, writing what I knew, or what I thought I knew, or what
I dared to imagine. There should be a word for what I am now: or-
phaned in all directions. Sister-orphaned. And once again, the urge
arises: to tell the story, to make it stick.

"Just something I wrote once," I say, at last. "A long time ago."

"Another book?"

"Not another book."

If she hears the coolness in my answer she makes no sign. With
an absent smile, she pulls a tape recorder and microphone out of her
briefcase and sets them up on the desk. I sit across from her, still
clutching my parents' stories. I'll need them if I'm going to make
her understand. If I'm going to properly tell my own.

I settle into the comfortable groove of my chair. The recorder
starts to whir. She leans forward, legs crossed, notebook propped on
one knee.

"Now," she says. "Where should we begin?"

PART
ONE

A RAINY MORNING, LATE SPRING OF 1918. JOSIE AND I, five years old, sat together at the table in the little, muggy kitchen, pressing craters into our porridge with the backs of our spoons and watching them ooze shut again. Mama, who had warned us twice already not to play with our food, was stirring something in a pot, her hair wrapped in a red flannel cloth, a cigarette clamped between her teeth, her forehead mottled and glistening, when the door swung open and Daddy swept in, waving a pale garment high above his head. I dragged my spoon through my porridge and sighed just loudly enough for Josie to hear. Another costume.

For as long as I could remember, Daddy had been trying to convince Mama to get us into show business—the family business, he called it, when we scrambled up onto his knees and begged him for a story, and instead of a fairy tale he told us about his grandfather, the dancer, or his grandmother, who had been in a traveling show, or his parents' puppet theater, or, best of all, the stories we wanted most but knew better than to ask for, stories that would only come when Daddy was in the mood to offer them, which depended on Mama being in the mood to give him tacit permission: stories about their glory days, when Mama was a star of the *Follies,* and Daddy built the sets on which she performed. (We knew Mama had had an accident, that it was the reason she used a cane, that it had ended her career and inaugurated the poverty into which we had been born, though that didn't figure into Daddy's lore, and I couldn't have said how I learned any of it; the accident was a foundational fact of our lives, part of the history that belonged neither to memory nor to telling. The history that simply was.) When Daddy described relieving Mama of an unwieldy freight of roses as she came offstage, she pretended to scoff. When he told us about how she'd come on as Lady Godiva in a flesh-colored body stocking, her long yellow wig arranged to reinforce the illusion of her nudity, and three young men had actually fainted from excitement, she swatted the back of his head and said, "Oh really." But Josie and I knew it was okay to smile. If Mama had really been angry, she would have gone silent, or retreated into one of the long baths she took to escape the rest of us. Instead, she lingered. She fussed at a potted fern. She sat and mended a blouse, only pretending not to listen.

But whenever Daddy turned the conversation to Josie and me—when he said let's just teach them a number, see what they can do—Mama's eyes would go cold. Absolutely not, she'd say. Over my dead body. Until one morning Mama and Josie and I heard a ruckus outside and went to the window. There was Daddy on the sidewalk beside an upright piano, a crowd at his back.

I don't know what finally persuaded Mama: the sight of our father, sunburned and panting, arm draped over the piano as if it were a prize rhino he'd just shot down; the four men who emerged from the crowd to carry the piano up to the third floor, who laughed as they wiped the sweat from their faces, who insisted on kissing Mama's hand and then toasting her fine specimen of a husband, who'd just moved that piano ten blocks, all by himself; his blistered feet and bloodied ankles, which she cleaned and bandaged. But the next morning, she took Josie and me to a shop on Twenty-Third Street and bought us tap shoes on credit. That afternoon, she sat down at the piano and taught us our first song. Just like that, we were an act: The Magnificent Singing Szász Twins.

Right away, Daddy started making costumes. He sewed skirts of rose tulle. He bent slim wires into the shape of butterfly wings and wrapped them in green net. He constructed denim overalls and red cotton work shirts for us to wear during choreographed trots on broomstick ponies. He dressed Josie in an ivory wedding gown and me in a shiny black tuxedo and a top hat fashioned from a scrap of black silk and some rolled-up pasteboard. Whenever he came home with another bolt of fabric Mama would scowl. She'd ask him if he'd married and murdered an heiress she didn't know about. Sometimes he brushed her aside, sometimes he risked a fight by snapping back that the fabric had been a gift from a friend—they still had friends in the theater. But by the time he sat down at the sewing machine and fed a cotton cuff or a pleated panel of butter yellow organza under the needle, he would be grinning.

As the months wore on without a callback, let alone a job, no one blamed me, not out loud. But I could see as clearly as anyone that Josie's voice was effortlessly sweet and true, while I had to try and try again to match the pitches Mama played on the piano. I knew that when Josie danced, her whole body seemed to float, as if carried by invisible strings, while I got stuck in the sludge of my own thoughts, trying to remember where my feet were to go next, how to hold my hands, how to keep my balance.

A year had passed, and all we had to show for our efforts was a trunk full of useless costumes. That morning, in the kitchen, I was certain nothing would come of Daddy's latest creation, whatever it was, save a quarrel, a fact that struck in my belly with a hot, awful thud. A few nights earlier, I'd listened through the wall as Mama had begged Daddy to ask his friend Bert for some work. By then, from the glimpses I got of the lives of the other children who lived in our building and on our block, I had gleaned that normal fathers worked every day, while my father worked only occasionally. It was Mama who took in mending and laundry, Mama who sold paper fans out of a cart in Union Square, each fan printed with the name and biography of a star, while Josie and I played nearby, tethered to the cart with a length of clothesline. I knew that Josie was like Mama—it was something people always said—but in a way I couldn't explain I sensed that I was like her too, that we worried with the same heat, while Josie and Daddy seemed hardly to worry at all.

I sighed again, a little louder this time, but Josie's eyes were fixed on Daddy, her spoon gripped tightly in her fist. Daddy draped the costume over his arm, delicately, as if he were handling a fine French frock, though this garment, a corset-like contraption with open sides, was obviously improvised. Buckles lined both edges of the back panel, matched on the front by short belts. It took me a moment to recognize that the garment was double wide: its two neck holes were separated by a strip of canvas.

Mama tapped a little ash from her cigarette into a tin can on the narrow counter and looked at him, as if to say, "Well?"

In a single, swift motion, he stepped toward the table and lifted our bowls.

"Stand up, girls," he called.

The bowls crashed into the sink.

"Up up up."

We stood. He pushed my shoulder into Josie's and lowered the harness over our heads, then threaded the buckles with the belts and pulled them tight, crunching our inside arms together. Josie's eyes didn't fall from Daddy's face, not for a second. After he'd yoked us in, he wrapped one hand around our waists—our waist—and lifted.

The enamel tabletop was clammy against the bottoms of my feet. Daddy turned to Mama, raised his fist against his lips, and blew as if it were a trumpet: Ta-ta-ta!

"I present to you, Josephine and Harriet Szász, the Siamese Twins who will also dance and sing!"

The lid rattled softly on the pot. The shadows of raindrops twitched along the foggy window. The harness crushed my arm so tightly against my ribs that I could feel my heartbeat in my armpit. I worried Josie could feel it too, that it was communicating to her the fact of my fear. All year, she had been alert to my fear. In hallways before auditions she would sometimes pinch me from wrist to elbow, to distract me, she said, but she couldn't do that now, any more than Mama could lean over and whisper in my ear, "Big girls don't cry, Harriet."

Daddy's explanation came tumbling out: he'd been to the library, he said, and history proved his case. Chang and Eng. The Two-Headed Nightingale. The Chalkhurst Sisters. Twins were a dime a dozen, Daddy said. We were pretty girls, maybe we could carry a tune, but that didn't make us special.

A long groove formed between Mama's eyebrows. She kneaded her bad hip with her fist, as she often did when she was thinking something through. Josie was smiling wildly, theatrically. I felt the stirring of a powerful desire to perform, and I knew that it had been Josie's desire first, that she had passed it to me. As far back as I could remember, we'd been able to do that—pass things back and forth, thoughts and feelings and dreams. Sometimes—when Mama wasn't listening—instead of telling us stories about our forebears, Daddy would tell us stories about ourselves as babies, which dipped into a period of family history I knew we were not supposed to discuss, but which I loved nevertheless for the proof they offered of our twinnedness: how in the cradle, Josie and I had babbled in a language of our own invention; how our teeth had come in at the same time, all in the same order.

He flicked his wrist at Mama, his cheeks starting to pink. Her silence always flustered him. Of silence, Mama was a virtuoso, every variety of discontent expressed in a quiet of its own key. If rehearsal went poorly or if dinner burned, she stamped around the kitchen, cleaning roughly, her silence an interior stir that drew in any part of herself on which our blame or disappointment might otherwise hitch. If one of us hurt her feelings she signaled her unforgivingness—and she had a great capacity for unforgivingness—with a silence like a block of ice: still and cold and slow to thaw. Even at the best of times there was something brisk and stiff in Mama, as if happiness were palatable only as long as no one suspected you might be feeling it.

"You'll come up with something—a name." He turned to us, his gaze pressing, urgent, as if he were willing us to understand something crucial. "Show your mother, girls."

She nodded. Josie stepped to the left—the opening move from

"Coffee and Cream," a song Mama had written for us. For a split second the harness tugged against my ribs, but then I was moving with Josie, singing with her. At first, my inside arm wanted to stretch, but after a moment her left arm was my left arm, and my right arm belonged as much to her as to me.

"The cat's got his cradle, the fish has the sea, I've got my sister, my sister's got me."

We swung to the left, Josie's hip a hip for both of us, and we swung to the right. Our bare feet pounded the tabletop. I was sure of the choreography as I'd never been at an audition. It was as if the harness had granted me a share of Josie's muscles, as if the breath beneath my voice were pouring from her lungs as well as my own.

"We go together," we sang the last line, our voices billowing in the snug kitchen, "like coffee and cream!"

We stood on our inside toes, lifted our outside feet in perfect unison, and then I pushed off and we began to spin. When we came back around to the front, our inside feet crossed. We pointed our outside feet, beaming at Mama and Daddy, and reached high into the air, our outside hands spreading open like starfish, our rib cages knocking our inside arms together as we caught our breath. Daddy clapped and shouted brava. From the apartment below there came a shout, followed by the sound of a broom handle pounding the ceiling. But I couldn't stop smiling.

Mama studied us, her expression perfectly calm, a shutter against whatever roiled within. After several seconds, she pronounced her verdict:

"Okay, Lenny."

THEY SOLD EVERYTHING THAT wasn't nailed down. Mama bought us tickets to Chicago—"our starting over place," she called it, brightly, now committed in every outward way to Daddy's scheme. In Chicago, we'd find a crop of producers and casting agents who didn't already know us as an ordinary twin act that had failed to get off the ground. We took our first rail journey in the harness; when we disembarked I was too giddy, too charged with excitement, to worry about the fact that I couldn't feel my inside arm, or about the blood I could feel, seeping into the bottom edge of the harness, where it had rubbed the flesh of my stomach. Josie muttered directions: get ready to turn right, I should take the suitcase and she would hold the railing. People crowded and gawked; Mama hurried us along; Josie beamed.

In our rented room, Mama stuffed a towel in the crack beneath the door and a bit of sponge in the keyhole. Daddy bought daintier buckles for the harness. He reworked its necklines so they couldn't gape and lined its bottom edge with a strip of velvet. He ripped up our old costumes and repurposed the fabric for new ones: a pink gingham dress with two Peter Pan collars; a satin gown with a wide sash that traversed both our waists; a forest green leotard with double turtlenecks. We rehearsed every day, Mama choreographing on the fly. Daddy watched with his hands pressed together, index fingers tapping his slightly parted lips, face glazed with pleasure. At night, in our narrow cot, I would come right to the edge of sleep only to feel Josie's finger poking between my shoulder blades, then her warm breath against my neck as she whispered: "Harry. I was just thinking. What if we rode in a limousine?" Or, "Do you think we'll get into the pictures? Someday?" Or she would hum the song we'd learned that afternoon, and I'd hum back, and then next thing I knew it would be morning.

Three weeks after our arrival in Chicago, we were hired as an opening act for a benefit concert at the Studebaker Theater.

A warm evening early in June 1918. The curtain rises for the first time on the Siamese Sweets. Two-girls-in-one stand at center stage wearing pink gingham, two arms extended, fingers loose but energized ("like you're holding an egg," Mama had told us), our smiles wide slices between round, rouged cheeks. For the first time, I hear the hush of an audience, a not-quite silence, electric with anticipation. The footlights heat my chin and, somehow, sharpen the scent of paint and muslin. From the pit comes the plink of the piano.

We were off. One two wink smile shuffle ball change. Every note, every step, every breath unfurled in exquisite synchronization. In the harness, Josie's body pressed warm and solid against mine. The audience faded to nearly nothing. It was just Josie and me, our harmonies shimmering and clear, the perfect unison of our footwork approaching something like flight. But as soon as we finished there they were, all those watching, listening people, clapping and hollering and stomping their feet. The great wave of sound buoyed us into the wings.

Backstage, Mama fixed our hair, but there was an unusual tenderness in her touch that made me want to lean toward her fingers like a petted cat. Daddy walked a tight, elated loop and kissed the stage manager's forehead. I could tell he wanted to pick us up but didn't dare. He was like that sometimes: shy, his affection tinged by woundedness, as if we were a treasure of which he'd been robbed. Josie, panting happily, her cheek a pink blotch in my peripheral vision, raised her free hand toward mine. I pressed my fingers into hers, one by one. It would become our secret sister salute, meaning whatever we needed it to—don't worry, or I'm sorry. But in that moment it meant only that something important was happening, something I didn't have a name for. Later I would name it like so: our real lives had begun.

THAT NIGHT, WE ALL stayed up well past midnight, too giddy to sleep. Already, Mama had spoken to a booking agent: we'd have a weeklong engagement at the McVickers Theater, and then four more jobs on the road. The Road! The words rang in my ear like something unreal, the name of a kingdom in a fairy tale. Finally, Mama insisted on pajamas and lights out. Josie's breath fluttered in my ear, soft and even, but I fought my own exhaustion to listen to Mama and Daddy.

"It's all riding on the illusion," Mama said. "Your harness. If we're ever found out—"

"We'll be ruined."

In my gut, I felt the sickening bloom of worry, a feeling so familiar it was almost a comfort. But the day's exertions overtook it. I
soon fell asleep.

When Josie and I woke the next morning, Mama sat us on the
edge of the cot. Daddy stood in the corner, combing the end of his
beard with his fingertips. Looming over us, hands on her hips, Mama
announced the new cardinal family rule: Josie and I would never go
out unattached.

TWO WEEKS LATER WE left Chicago with work lined up through
the fall. Daddy released us from the harness only behind locked
doors and drawn curtains. If secure conditions could not be achieved,
in the harness we remained, even if we had to sit up all night in the
third-class carriage, even if we were just passing through some little
place where no one knew us. If we needed to buy shoes, if, on a rare
afternoon off, Mama agreed to take Josie and me to the movies, we
were yoked up and buttoned into one of our double-wide dresses.
The whole time we were out, Mama would hover, making sure no
one looked too closely.

Sometimes I cried at night because my left arm, my inside arm,
still felt tingly, hours after being unbound, or because my right flank,
where the harness held tight to my skin, had flared once again in a
bright, bumpy rash that stung at the slightest brush of my nightgown. And I felt a pang when I remembered the games of stickball
or hide-and-seek we'd played in New York, or the comfort, in our
building, of any of a dozen mothers' aprons that might be dragged
roughly over a teary face after a fall, of a dozen kitchens where I felt
entitled to snag molasses cookies or crispy pickles or glasses of cold
milk. But in boardinghouse rooms and dressing rooms and green
rooms, Josie and I now played the games of pretend I had always
preferred. We invented an invisible pet rabbit named Jenny, which
we carried around and cradled and stroked, and which Daddy
obliged us by kissing good night. We held our hands in front of our
bellies as if we were gripping reins and trotted around on imaginary

horses. Late into the night we whispered under the covers. After Mama hushed us a second or third time, her voice taking on a dangerous edge, we communicated through a system of hand taps and kicks.

We were in Wabash, Indiana, when we decided that if we didn't play cat's cradle before a matinée then the theater would catch fire. In Indianapolis, we agreed that when we entered a new dressing room for the first time we had to go in backward or we'd fall onstage. In Vincennes, Josie decreed that after every curtain, one of us had to say "zing zing" before we said anything else, or the next time we took the stage we'd go mute. From Indiana, we traveled west, back into Illinois. We played churches and Elks clubs and library meeting rooms, and stores with folding chairs set out where that afternoon there might have been a display of potatoes or washing powder. But over the course of that first summer, Daddy filled three sketchbooks with designs for new harnesses and trick props and spectacular sets. And every time we stepped onto whatever platform there was, into whatever light there was, I felt a tugging in my chest, a swell of pride, as if I'd entered Daddy's grandest drawing. Whatever separation remained between Josie and me melted away. The rapt attention of the audience, the skill and power of my own dancing legs, the way my voice and Josie's voice slipped into each other and wrapped around each other: it all summed and shimmered, and seemed to prove we were exactly who we said we were. It wasn't that when we stepped onstage I believed our lie. It was that for the duration of a show, it wasn't a lie; it was simply a different sort of truth. I was the Siamese Sweets, I was Josephine and Harriet both. Our false body was irreducible, indivisible. The truest fact in the world.

WE WERE IN WISCONSIN that October, performing a two-week engagement at a proper theater where we shared a proper dressing room with Little Tibby Longfellow, a girl a few years our senior who had begun to make a name for herself on the circuit by delivering comedic monologues as adult personae—washerwomen, fishwives, gold diggers. One afternoon, Daddy finished our makeup and then, instead of staying to watch our act, went straight back to the boardinghouse with a headache. Josie turned and whispered, her breath hot and awful in my ear, that his headache was actually something called a hangover. I didn't answer, not quite knowing what this word meant but recognizing that it must be something vile.

The three of us—Mama, Josie, and I—were alone in the dressing room, Tibby having gone to perform and her mother having followed to watch, when a stagehand knocked on the door. There was something wrong with one of our sets, some question of whether another would be suitable. They needed a decision right away.

Mama put down her mending with a frown. After a moment's hesitation, she crouched down and looked beneath the counter, where Josie and I were hunched over our drawing of a castle.

"You stay put," she said sternly. "No funny business."

"Yes, Mama," we said. She followed the stagehand out.

It seemed impossible we could get into any trouble in just a few minutes alone. But not long after Mama left, Tibby returned, flushed from her outing on the stage. Her own mother wasn't with her. Josie looked up at her, curious, even lifted her hand as if she might wave. I looked down at our drawing, cheeks hot, willing Josie to be good.

A few weeks earlier, a pink-faced old comedian had observed slyly, insinuatingly, that we certainly kept to ourselves. Since then, Mama and Daddy had taken us to a couple of parties, just to make an appearance, and some meals in the restaurants where other troupers gathered. But we were strictly forbidden from speaking to other children. Children had a way of poking at things, Mama said, and asking questions they shouldn't. How lucky we were, she said, to have each other. Who needed friends when you had a sister?

Tibby took a step toward us and bent to get a better look. I felt like an animal in a burrow.

"I heard something," she said, pulling up the front of her dress to wipe her damp face. "I know why you are the way you are."

Josie crawled us forward, out from under the counter, and pulled

us to our feet. If I could have resisted without giving away the falseness of our body I would have. Instead, I clenched my crayon and
scowled.

"Why?" Josie asked. Inside the harness, her muscles seemed to
tauten, as if she were preparing to run.

Tibby looked over her shoulder at the open door and then back
at us.

"Your mother was raped by the devil."

We were staring at her, tongue-tied, when Mama returned.
Tibby gave her a little curtsey and retreated to her side of the dressing room, where she poked at her hair with a comb. Mama looked
sharply from Tibby to Josie and me, but we scrambled back beneath
the counter. Tibby's mother turned up not long after that, com-
plaining of her bad stomach. Mama offered her a tight smile before
turning back to her mending.

That afternoon, Josie and I danced with a ferocity that won us a
standing ovation. I knew that she had been picturing the same thing
as me: Tibby's dumb face on the stage beneath our feet. It was the
fact of the insult we understood, not its substance. But we spent the
next several days plotting revenge. Josie came up with ways to punish Tibby we didn't have the means to pull off: replacing her face
powder with itching powder, bribing the lighting man to plunge her
act into darkness, retrieving the dead rat we had seen in the street
near the boardinghouse and leaving it in her bed.

But before we could take any more revenge than glaring across
the dressing room, everything changed. We were in our room at the
boardinghouse, dressed and ready to go to the theater, when Mama
came in, pale. She whispered in Daddy's ear. Daddy ran his fingers
over his pockets until he found his pipe, which he squeezed in his
palm but didn't light.

"You can take that off," Mama finally said to Josie and me, lightly,
as if it weren't anything to make a fuss about. "You won't be performing today after all."

Every theater in town had been ordered closed on account of
Spanish flu. We were stuck; there was no work to be had within a

hundred miles, and even if she had managed to find something for us, Mama said she didn't trust the trains. Daddy would go out for supplies, or down to the parlor in the evenings to play cards with the other stranded members of the company. But save for a half hour every afternoon when Mama took Josie and me out for a walk, harnessed and masked, wearing camphor stuffed into the toes of old stockings on strings around our necks, we stayed in our room.

Late one night, I was supposed to be asleep when I heard Mama tell Daddy about a family musical act we'd shared a bill with not a month before; the mother and two of the brothers had died in a single afternoon.

I knew what dead was: dead was a cat I'd seen once in an alley, rigid, with little flies in its eyes. Dead was why a girl we'd known in New York only had a father and a grandmother but no mother. Dead was soldiers in Europe. Dead was, even, the row of pine boxes we'd seen lining a street the day before, two girls skipping from one to the next, chanting, "I had a little bird, its name was Enza, I opened the window, and in flu Enza," until a woman came out of a house with black bunting over the front door and screamed for them to come inside. But now a terrible fact surged through me: dead could be any of us. Mama or Daddy or Josie could catch the flu and be dead by the end of the day.

I turned from them, toward the heat of Josie's sleeping body, and pulled the quilt over my head. But the low, grave hum of their voices still reached my ear. I screwed my eyes tightly shut, as if the deep darkness might provide some relief. Instead, an even more horrible understanding crashed over me like a black wave: even if influenza spared us, we'd all die eventually, of something. Everyone died. Mama would die, Daddy would die, Josie and I would die. The fabric of the quilt clung to my face. But I couldn't push it away, I didn't dare.

That night, and the next night, and the one after that, instead of sleeping, I found myself listening to Mama and Daddy's conversation, waiting to hear another name I knew, the story of another death. Usually, all I could make out was a whipping tension, but even that gave me a stomachache. I worried we'd have to stay in that little room forever. That for eternity, I'd have to look at those four walls, those two beds, that brass lamp, the painting on the wall of the boardinghouse itself, which, even before we'd been trapped, had made me feel slightly uneasy. And if someday we did get out, I worried we'd never work again. What if the act failed, as, I remembered now, our first act had? What then? Who would we be? The life we had made as the Siamese Sweets was still new, but already, any alternative seemed like its own sort of death.

I dragged through the days that followed my sleepless nights. Every afternoon, I collapsed into a long, dense nap, from which I woke hot and damp, certain I sensed the beginnings of a fever. I irritated Josie by asking her to feel my forehead, asking if I could feel hers.

But the fever never came. In November, Mama found us a job, and, anxious, masked, we boarded a train for the first time in a month. After that job came another, and another, short stints here and there until January, when, at last, Mama booked us a long engagement, in Moline. We settled into a new boardinghouse room, hanging postcards on the walls and putting bundles of dried flowers in the drawers. In February, we had a new job in Joliet, where Daddy won a ukulele in a card game, and that seemed to mark with certainty the return of our good fortune. We learned to play: Josie made the chords while I strummed.

Sometimes, when I lay awake at night, listening to the soft sounds of the rest of them sleeping, the black wave would come crashing over me. But as winter gave way to spring, as the tense weeks of the fall of 1918 slipped further into memory, the wave came less and less. One afternoon that May, Josie and I picked lilacs from a bush outside our rooming house. After dinner, we begged Mama to let us braid them into her hair. She relented, settling on the floor beside the bed, leaning back on her palms, legs straight forward, skirt smoothed out around her. I maneuvered her thick plait around my little fingers. Beside me, Josie cradled the flowers, trying not to laugh lest she swallow the hairpins poking out from between her lips. Daddy sat across the room, sketching the three of us. In that instant, I could almost believe my fear that any of us would die, that anything about our lives would ever have to change, was just another game of pretend. A nightmare I'd confused for real life.

*

THAT SUMMER, THE SUMMER OF 1919, OUR SECOND ON THE road, Mama started writing us sketches to perform between songs. Daddy had the idea for a Siamese cartwheel, and Mama worked out how we could do it, training us on whatever stage she could get us into early in the morning, or on days we didn't perform. We were in Terra Haute when, one morning, just after sunrise, we arrived at a dance school, where Mama had arranged for us to use a studio. She went in search of the studio key, leaving Josie and me waiting in the hall. I had brought a book of fairy tales I'd found some months back, abandoned in a rooming house parlor, and was idly turning the pages when I realized I wasn't just looking at the pictures: I was reading some of the words.

I slammed the book shut, recognizing danger, though I couldn't have said what exactly that danger was.

"Hey, I was looking at that," Josie said. But Mama returned then.

We were staying in a cheap hotel, lucky to have a bathroom en suite. That night, I dragged the book in with me and turned the flimsy lock. I sat on the toilet lid and opened the book over my knees. Sure enough, there were the words, rising up from the black shapes my eyes had been sliding over for months as Mama read aloud.

After that, whenever I could get a moment alone—when Mama retreated into a bath or a nap, and Daddy went out to look for some company or a drink, and Josie settled in a corner for one of her private spells of daydreaming—I would crawl under a bed or into a closet with the book and run my finger under each row of words, whispering them to myself. From Mama's briefcase, I stole a stubby pencil and a few sheets of paper so I could practice writing the letters, matching what I saw on the pages of that picture book to the alphabet song. All summer, I decoded words in newspaper head-lines and on posters and billboards, every new word like a piece of candy in a secret stash. I scrawled letters and crumpled them up before anyone could see I hadn't just been drawing. That I could read and write stirred in me the same flushed-cheek thrill as being onstage, but better for being private, contained entirely within my-self. And at the same time, for the same reason, a source of shame. As if to possess an experience so wholly were somehow deceitful. Greedy.

We were in Kalamazoo one bright, golden morning that fall, sit-ting at the back of the house, on a bench that had been put there for us special, since the harness made it impossible for us to sit in the seats, waiting for our turn to rehearse, when a suited woman with a clipboard swooped in. The manager of the theater watched with crossed arms as she approached. After a brief argument, the man-ager made an angry sweep of his hands and walked away, and the woman pointed at Little Tibby Longfellow. We'd been annoyed to discover she was also on the bill in Kalamazoo, and were quietly satisfied when the woman, who had an authoritative, punishing aura about her, ordered Tibby to follow her into the hall.

Mama hurried to join the cluster of mothers whispering in the corner. When she came back she spoke urgently: "If she asks your age keep quiet. Be smart." But before she could explain what exactly being smart entailed, the woman returned a tear-stained Tibby to her mother and pointed to Josie and me.

When she saw what we were—what we wanted her to think we were—she turned to look at the wall, as if she couldn't trust herself not to gawk. Josie and I followed her into the hallway and perched together on a folding chair. I tried to keep from slumping too badly over the edge, so the harness wouldn't dig into my latest rash.

The woman took the chair across from ours and lifted her clip-board, shifting her shoulders and blinking rapidly as she forced her-self to look right at us, take us in.

"Age?" she said.

We shrugged, our shoulders rising and falling in perfect unison. The woman peered at us over her glasses and scribbled something on her clipboard. The questions continued: What was the nature of our act? Did we do any juggling, acrobatics, fire work, animal work? We folded our hands together in our lap, and I kept my gaze forward and level, while Josie answered the questions, one after the next. I began to relax. Be smart, Mama had said, and Josie knew just what to do.

"And have you ever been enrolled in school?"

Josie's inside arm went stiff against mine. She opened her mouth and closed it again. The lady pursed her lips, made another mark on her clipboard. Then she handed me a blank piece of paper and Josie a pencil.

"Write your name—your names—your name, please," she said.

My secret rose like an itch to the surface of my skin. If the woman had handed the pencil to me instead of Josie, I might have managed something close to H-A-R-R-I-E-T. But Josie clung to it helplessly. My heart pounded in my throat.

The woman made one last mark on her clipboard and ushered us back into the theater.

"Mrs. Sweet?" she said. Mama followed her into the hall.

The next morning Mama woke us early, but instead of readying us for the dance studio, she had us sit on the edge of our lumpy mattress and declared—cheerfully, matter-of-factly, as if it had been her plan all along—that it was time we learned our ABCs. She set a phonebook on my knees and on top of it, a sheet of paper with the alphabet written out in neat rows. She handed me a pencil and before she could say another word, I was copying out the letters, so excited that I forgot I wasn't supposed to know how yet.

"Why, Harriet!" Mama said. I braced myself for trouble. But she was smiling at me the way she smiled at Josie when she made a joke or mastered a new song. Pleasure swirled in my chest.

Josie grabbed the pencil with her right hand, the hand she always grabbed with when we weren't in the harness. Mama swatted her fingers gently.

"No, no," she said, and moved the pencil to Josie's left hand—her outside hand.

Josie frowned but accepted the phonebook and the paper from me. Tongue pressed between her teeth, eyebrows knitted together, she tried to fill in a row of letters below mine. But no letters emerged, just tangled lines, some thickly scrawled, some trailing off in a barely visible thread. She pressed harder, and the pencil slid the paper off the phonebook. Again, Mama said no. She said let me show you, begin at the beginning, and reached to guide Josie's hand, but Josie yanked her own hand away. She looked at Mama, and then she turned to me, her eyes burning with anger, and snapped the pencil in two.

We didn't perform for a few days—we were waiting for the Gerry lady to clear out of town, Mama explained, to find some other hard-working Americans to harass. But every morning, she sat us down for a reading lesson. Josie snapped another pencil, tore the page with its printed alphabet into confetti. When we were finally able to return to the theater, Mama seemed more relieved than any of us.

On our first day back, during our first matinée, in the middle of our first sketch, a wooden pear fell from a rickety stock set tree, right onto my head. I was startled: there was a lag, a tiny one, during which I felt myself blinking stupidly into the dark house. But I had recovered and was about to say my next line when Josie scooped up the pear.

"Say, why don't you lay off my sister!" she said and mimed a puni-tive bite.

The audience's laughter was electric, quickly out of control. She tossed the pear over her shoulder with a wink, and there was an-other wave of it. People clapped and whistled. For the first time since New York, stage fright crimped my belly. I started my next line but couldn't get it out over the sound of the crowd. Inside the harness, Josie pressed her elbow into mine; I waited until the laugh-ter trailed to a trickle, as we'd been trained, and then, finally, I got out the line, and on we went. We made it to the end of the act with-out another mishap, but the whole time, I felt peculiar. Cold. Sepa-rate from Josie as I had never before felt onstage.

As we took our bows, Josie gave an extra wink and wave and there was a rush of fresh applause and a shrill whistle. Just for her. It was impossible: there was no her on the stage, there was only us, a single being. But as we hurried off I understood: Josie was the star. When we were onstage together and I felt so free, so warm, so alive, so gifted, it wasn't because of some mutual effort, some equal exchange. I was basking in Josie's light.

Backstage, Daddy shook his head and laughed, as if he couldn't decide whether he wanted to slap Josie or give her a dollar. But Mama grabbed her shoulder and dragged us both down the hall toward the dressing rooms. As soon as we were alone, she crouched down and whispered fiercely in Josie's face.

"What were you thinking? What business do you have, improvising? Showboating? Don't think I didn't know that was exactly what you were doing." As she went on I looked down at the floor, as if by refusing to watch the scolding I might make it end. My chest was heaving, my muscles jelly, my undershirt clinging to my sweaty skin. Mama promised her a spanking when we got back to our room. Josie didn't even flinch.

I was certain then that she had done it on purpose. Because I could read, and she couldn't. It had been a message, a warning. Look, sister, she had said. Never forget how things stand.

A FEW WEEKS LATER, Mama attempted another reading lesson, but Josie hummed "Yankee Doodle Dandy" until she threw up her hands. She tried again a few months after that, and a few months after that, and then periodically over the next few years, the lessons usually following a visit from a Gerry agent, or a warning that one was at hand. But Josie refused to listen. She refused to learn.

We outgrew harnesses as quickly as Daddy could stitch them. Our dolls, Susan and Emily, evolved from babies into dancers, whose pink painted mouths we filled with words of the women we eavesdropped on backstage and at parties, words we didn't quite understand but knew better than to say loud enough for Mama to hear—pessary and blotto and cramps. I moved from storybooks and headlines to newspapers and whatever reading material I found discarded on trains and in hotel lobbies, forgotten in backstage nooks: novels and popular histories and magazines and seed catalogs and collections of speeches and volume "M" of an encyclopedia. Still, every time Mama tried to teach her how to read, Josie sighed, she broke pencils, she ripped paper, she split strands of her hair and tore out the hems of her clothes, calmly, as if she was only asserting her right to be left alone, until, at last, Mama closed her eyes and said, "All right. That's enough. We'll try another time." A dancer who had run away from home offered us whatever we wanted from a stack of her old books. I took eleven, of which Mama gave me permission to keep three: I chose *Anne of Green Gables* and *Little Women,* and, for self-improvement, an old exercise book that I worked through, over and over, until the front cover tore from the spine. Josie laughed as if the dancer had offered us her old underthings.

Onstage, I made occasional mistakes: garbled a lyric, missed a note, forgot a line. Josie rescued me when she needed to but never again drew attention to herself as she had in Kalamazoo. Still, I didn't forget what she'd shown me that afternoon, didn't lose track of the distinction she'd drawn. When fans approached us after a show, or when we came off a train and found a crowd waiting for a glimpse of the medical and theatrical miracle, I signed the autographs. Josie mugged and chatted, absorbing their admiration.

1903

Maude Foster emerges into the steam and hustle of the platform at Grand Central Station, clinging to her suitcase and staring, with great purpose, some yards ahead, the surest way, she has learned, to keep busybodies from asking why she is traveling alone. The sanitary belt they gave her in Philadelphia cuts into her abdomen, and she can feel on her thighs a stickiness that makes her grateful for the heaviness of her skirts. But for the first time in months there is also a lightness beneath her breastbone, a sense of possibility both exhilarating and terrifying that propels her through the throng of travelers. In a glove now damp and slightly yellowed, she clutches Vera's address. She scolds herself, gently, for thinking of her so familiarly—"Miss Vance," she ought to say.

When she passes through a revolving door onto the street, the noise and the brightness and the jostling of the crowd pull her up short. A sob collects in her chest, and she cannot keep it from escaping her lips. There, for a moment, is the baby—a mite of a thing, oddly heavy for his size, gauzy blue eyes shocked open as he tries to absorb the impossible newness of the world, of her own face, which she was careful to keep still, ungenerous, as if to say, no, child, I am not for you. Now she presses her lips together, tamps down the sob. What is done is done, she thinks, willing a plaque to form against the soft, throbbing surface of her heart.

"Can I help you, miss?" He is an elegant man, with a smooth, pink forehead, a thin, aristocratic mouth, and she is aware that she must look weak and lost. She considers it. She could hand him Vera Vance's address, she could ask him to take her there. But if she is certain of anything after the last few days, after

Eugene Creggs and his late-in-the-game attention to her honor, it is that she has no interest in saviors. She has made a decision: she has refused to let herself be saved. By now, Eugene will know she has gone, he will hate her for it, but he will do right by that baby, she is sure of that much, so let him have that—let him save the boy, and leave her to her own fate. And let this posh city man find another lost girl to rescue. She shakes her head and begins to walk, uncertain of the way but determined to look certain. It is a warm evening, and the sun is still high in the sky; she has time to figure it out.

If they heard back home that Maude Foster had found herself in a pinch and refused help from a perfectly nice man, they would call her a showoff. Stuck up, they would call her. Arrogant. They have called her these things since she was a little girl, and she can hardly blame them. The truth is there has never been a moment of her conscious life in which she has not understood that she was designed for something better than Hobart, Ohio. When she was younger, she collected stories about city girls from old copies of smart papers a friend of her mother's sometimes brought over in a bundle. She dressed her paper dolls in shoes and hats and gowns cut from *The Delineator,* suitable to the future she imagined for herself: one of fine fashion and fresh flowers in crystal vases and elegant, cultured people. She would be the wife of a city doctor, or a senator. Propel herself as far as she could from dreary, pig-smelling Hobart, Hobart with its church suppers on Saturday nights and high school basketball games on Wednesday nights and the county fair every summer, ad infinitum, the same pudding-cheeked, blond boys in overalls growing up to help their fathers on the farm or at the store, the same virtuous girls with their excruciating conversations about the overalled boys, about what sort of curtains they planned to hang in the houses they would live in up the road from their mothers after they got married. That she was not destined to remain in Hobart was as simple and natural an understanding as the fact of day and night, as the fact of her beauty, her surety of which, after

so many months of feeling like a lumbering stranger, is returning
to her. She glimpses her reflection in a window and is pleased by
the glossy waves spilling over her shoulders. Her color is back,
the complexion Laura Zimmerman's mother once called "English
rose." "She'll break hearts," Mrs. Zimmerman said.

Maude is not without shame. She has felt the full measure of
her shame, in the oppressive silence of her father's house, on the
chattering streets of Hobart, in that dismal room in Philadelphia.
And yet, now, as the policeman blows his whistle and she crosses
the street in a dense stream of city people, walking at a city pace,
shame seems slight, gauzy. Like it might slip off her shoulders in
the breeze. Her breasts ache and there is a flushed, prickly feeling
creeping along the band of her hat, but she is steadier on her feet
than she has been in months. It is as if she is coming back into
herself—as if some part of her had been physically displaced, and
now there is room for it again, for her again. And she is on her way
to find Miss Vance, to start a life in New York City. New York
City—imagine! It's all happening, just as she planned, more than
she planned, sooner than she planned—Hobart is behind her now.

At Forty-Second Street, a delivery boy splits the crowd on his
bicycle, ringing the bell, and someone shouts, "Get off the sidewalk," and the mean surprise of that shout sets her heart racing.
She hurries away and nearly collides with a woman in heavy,
smelly clothes, and when she turns from her, a man with a parakeet on his finger is inches from her face, smiling at her as if he
knows all her secrets. "Excuse me," she murmurs, unable to avoid
letting her sleeve brush his as she pushes past. Then she is moving with the crowd again, back in the flow of it, but the distance
to Fifteenth Street seems suddenly vast. She doesn't dare close
her eyes, but she summons a vision behind her real vision, returns in her mind to last Christmas morning, to the Miller Pond,
where she skated for hours with Marion. She lets the scrape of
the blades against the ice cut against the frenzy of city voices, the
drone of traffic. There's the sharp, coppery flavor of the cold air,
there's its whip against her cheeks.

. . .

That night—Christmas night—was the first time she had
wept over her secret. She pressed her face into her pillow,
but Marion heard her and asked, in a sweet, sleepy voice, what
was wrong. "Mind your own business," Maude snapped, and
after that Marion watched her closely, cagily, like a detective
gathering clues.

Maude was no fool—since she was a little girl she had seen
the boars mount their sows in the south meadow and understood
that the litters farrowed a few months later were a consequence
of their frenzied joining. Over several years, with the help of several sources—a book discovered in a carpetbag at the bottom of
her mother's closet (*What a Bride Must Know*), a bundle of dirty pictures unearthed from beneath a rotting log out behind a neighbor's orchard, a human anatomy manual examined for a
hot-cheeked half hour in the public library—she had filled in the
particulars. She knew she knew more than other girls, and she
had once carried this knowledge like a private treasure, like further evidence of her specialness. It had distinguished her, like her
marbled eyes, like her fifty-yard dash, faster than all the girls and
most of the boys in her class.

In January, Maude thought to ask Bertha Gilbert, an older
girl with a particular reputation, a vague series of questions; Bertha, kindly, asked no questions of her own but gave her Mrs.
Sherlock's name and address. Mrs. Sherlock told her she was too
far along for her to do anything about it and she'd better tell her
mother and father and see if they couldn't get the fellow to
marry her. It was in that moment that Maude understood, crystal
clear, a thought that had been forming for months, since the first
wave of sickness and the first absent blood: she did not want to
be a mother. Not ever.

She had never heard of such a thing, a girl not wanting to be a
mother. And hadn't she played house and dressed baby dolls and
pushed Marion around in a pram until Marion turned five and put

her foot down? When Maude was twelve, Mrs. Creggs, the reverend's wife, had chosen her out of all the Sunday school girls to play
Mary in the nativity play, and when the ladies of the church
clucked and cooed at the sight of her in her blue robe, holding the
swaddled baby Jesus, she had felt a tiny thrill, as if she'd passed for
a moment into her own future. But now, when she thought about
the thing growing inside her, it was not a baby she saw but a weed,
rooting in her, sapping the life from her blood. She worried about
what this made her: a deviant, a monster.

When she found there was no more give in her loosest dress,
she confessed to her mother. For a week, the crisis was local to
the family. Her mother met her with wet, wounded looks and ac-
costed her father in hallways, in the kitchen, demanding that he
take some action. He retreated to the barn, where he had always
gone to escape his house full of women and the errors women
made. Maude lay in bed for hours at a time, a hand pressed
against the hill of her belly, the thing in her shuddering occasionally, as if it were joining the family in its sorrow. Marion watched
all of them, figuring.

Finally, her mother prevailed on her father to visit Mrs.
Creggs. The two of them went together in their Sunday best, and
when they came home Maude's father went straight to the barn,
and her mother shook her head before retreating to her bedroom
to weep.

At first, Maude felt indignant: hadn't she been in that woman's house almost every afternoon that summer, waiting for
James to get home with the new jacks he'd promised her, or with
the cigarettes he'd stolen for her to try, or because they planned
to row across the oxbow in the Sandusky River, to the shaggy
woodland where they'd found the rope swing? Hadn't she helped
Mrs. Creggs peel eggs and sterilize jars, hadn't she listened to her
drone on about modesty and botulism and how to treat tooth-
ache with a piece of onion, hadn't she nodded politely while she
bragged about her older son, Eugene? Maude could only barely
remember Eugene as the baseball hero, Eugene heading off to the

U with a scholarship, winning a championship and a major
league tryout, but Mrs. Creggs must have reminded her a dozen
times that summer about how he had turned down a contract
with the Reds to travel to China as a YMCA secretary, about
how, when his father had gotten sick, he'd come home and taught
natural science at Hobart High, and how, for a year after his father's death, he had hardly left his mother's side. Sometimes Eugene himself, home from his first year of seminary, sat with
Maude at the kitchen table, apparently determined to bore her to
tears by trying out every idea he'd ever had for a sermon, by explaining the etymology of every word either of them uttered, by
listing the different types of rock or identifying whatever species
of bird happened to hop along the backyard fence, as if she were
one of his old students, while she drummed her fingers on the
underside of the table, willing the door to swing open and James
to come through it, hair falling into his eyes, cheeks aflame from
his run up the hill.

But when her parents called at the Creggs house, James was
off with his friends and Eugene had returned to his studies in
Pittsburgh, which meant there was no one to appeal to other
than Mrs. Creggs, and Mrs. Creggs had no compunction about
sacrificing Maude's honor to protect her son's future. Maude's
mother told her Mrs. Creggs had put it like this: Who would believe a slatternly farm girl over the son of a reverend? And even if
the answer, in the quiet of folks' kitchens and sitting rooms,
might have been "who wouldn't?" Maude knew full well she
would find herself friendless in the public square. That folks
would enjoy seeing her taken down a peg. So she would not be
saved by marriage. Her mother spent whole minutes staring at
her, letting tears roll uninterrupted down her cheeks; if her father looked at her at all, it was just long enough to shake his head
and turn.

And then Mr. Dickinson, the principal, called Maude into the
school office, and her mother was already there, and less than a
minute later Maude had been expelled. How Mr. Dickinson had

learned her secret she never knew for sure, but for a long time she blamed Marion: watchful, curious Marion, whose friends were the indiscreet little sisters and daughters of known busy-bodies. When Marion came home from school that afternoon, Maude threw a hairbrush at her and locked her out of the bedroom.

After supper, Maude sat on the landing, eavesdropping as her parents made a plan: Maude would stay home until the baby came, and her mother would claim it as her own. Maude thought of the several times since Marion's birth that her mother had taken to her bed, bleeding away what had failed to form into a child, and felt a pang of something like responsibility. But she thought, too, of her life unfolding in the house she'd grown up in, a cloister of shame she'd made for herself. Caring for a sister who was really a daughter. An Ohio farmwife without the benefit of a husband, shelling peas and rolling crusts alongside her mother, a red-faced child latching to her breast, grabbing at her with dirty fingers, and the only hope of escape a boy dumb enough or ugly enough or shameless enough to transport a whore from her father's house to his, where all the same chores would be waiting.

Many hours later, long after everyone had gone to bed, Maude lay awake in the dark, thinking about Cousin Sara. Seven years Maude's senior, Sara had taught herself French from a book. From the age of eleven, she had played piano in church every Sunday and recitals at the opera house twice a year. Her talent was a point of pride for the whole community; when she left to study at the Oberlin College Conservatory, a delegation of the Sunday school girls had presented her with a bouquet of carnations in crimson and gold. Most of Hobart assumed she would come home and teach piano until she got married, and some of the savvier, younger folks suspected she'd move to Cleveland, fashion herself a New Woman. But Sara had surprised everyone by choosing Philadelphia instead; she and a friend from Oberlin had found teaching jobs at a school there and an apartment to share.

Sara, Maude was certain, would know what she should do. And how to get it done.

And so, just before dawn, Maude kissed Marion's soft, sleeping face and made her flight, carrying nothing but a pasteboard suitcase and a finger-sized roll of bills she'd stolen from the tea tin her mother kept behind the flour, wearing a thick old coat of her father's. She walked a couple of miles up the road and flagged down the first northbound wagon driven by a stranger with a kind face.

In Cleveland she bought a third-class ticket to Philadelphia, a cup of coffee, and an egg and mustard sandwich, and found herself a place on a bench in the terminal. The wooden seat pressed against her spine; a hot pain struck her lower back; her feet took up too much room in her boots. She began to wish, impossibly, that she'd brought Marion with her. Marion had always been an emotional child, involved overlong in a babyish fantasy life (she still swore fairies lived in the cherry orchard, assigned every feral kitten a name and elaborate psychology, wept easily and bitterly at advertising circulars). Maude worried, now, that her little sister was ill-equipped for a life alone in that cold house with those parents and their congenital sense of disappointment, their long sulks, periods of numbing silence that ended in spectacular, crockery-shattering arguments. And she longed for her company, for any company.

Just when she thought she might be sick from loneliness, a tall, thick-shouldered girl of eighteen or twenty sat down on the bench beside her with a little sigh. She wore a long blue coat trimmed in glossy fur and carried a matching muff. Her red hair crowned her head in a hive of twists, and on top of them she wore a crushed velvet hat with a ruched band of violet silk from which three glossy black feathers sprung like flags. The girl turned to Maude and smiled; her eyes were wide and bright as buttons, set in a round, smooth face.

"Where are you headed?" she asked.

For a moment, Maude was startled into silence—so relieved

by the prospect of someone to speak with that she could not actually make herself speak.

"Philadelphia," she finally sputtered.

"Oh, Philly," said the red-haired woman, lighting up, as if Maude had just made a clever joke. "I'm right up the road—New York City." There was a tickled-pink-ness in the way she reported this information that made her glamour less intimidating. It was then that they properly introduced themselves. Vera Vance told Maude she was traveling back east from Pocatello, Idaho. Her mother had been sick, and now she was gone. Maude murmured, "I'm sorry," and Miss Vance thanked her bravely and changed the subject. In New York, Miss Vance said, she lived in an apartment with two other girls. Two of them worked in shops, one as a private secretary, and they were all trying to become actresses. Maude told Miss Vance her cousin in Philadelphia was a pianist, and thought Miss Vance seemed duly impressed by this.

"You a musician too?" Miss Vance asked. Maude considered this for a moment, wishing she could say yes. Cousin Sara had tried to teach her one summer, and she'd shown some promise, but she'd never bothered to practice her scales. The lessons had slowed, and then stopped.

"I sing a bit," Maude said, thinking of her solo verse of "Silent Night" in the nativity play. Miss Vance nodded eagerly, as if this information confirmed some sweet suspicion. She spoke of a musical revue she had seen just before leaving for Idaho, in which her friend danced in the "Lantern Man" number with a jack-o'-lantern fitted over her head, dozens more jack-o'-lanterns floating above the stage on invisible wires, all of them glowing softly, as if lit from within by real candles. When Miss Vance glanced at the clock on the wall, Maude spent a precious dime on doughnuts and coffee, just to keep Miss Vance beside her, talking. Talk Miss Vance did: about the manager at the department store where she worked, who had proposed to her twice; about cafés where she and her friends drank coffee at three in the morning; about Greenwich Village, where you couldn't walk ten steps without bumping into some important poet or painter or political radical. When Maude's train began boarding, she could hardly bear to make herself stand up. From her handbag, Miss Vance removed a notebook with a flowered cover. "Look me up if you make it to New York!" she said, scribbling the address. Maude thanked her, and as soon as she sat down on the train she pressed the scrap of paper into her diary.

The next morning, she presented herself at Cousin Sara's door. Cousin Sara, despite her exotic talent, despite her daring expatriation from Hobart, shook with rage. She threatened to wire Maude's mother, to telephone the police. Maude, with the help of Sara's roommate, languorous, bushy-haired, soft-bodied Claire, persuaded her not to, but in the four days Maude spent sleeping on the sofa in Sara and Claire's tidy flat, Sara remained tense and snappish.

Then early one morning, Maude walked into the kitchen and found Sara and Claire pressed up against the counter, kissing. Maude watched for a moment, stunned, a feathery excitement winding through her body, trailed quickly by shame. Before she could muster the sense to turn and leave, Sara noticed her and grabbed a spoon from the counter and threw it across the room. Maude ran into the parlor and hurried to pack her things. She heard Claire speaking to Sara, her voice low and soothing. She was about to slip out the front door, to run away again, and this time with no plan at all, when Claire came through the kitchen door.

"Poor Miss Maude," she said. "Poor little thing." She pulled a piece of paper out of the roll-top desk in the corner. "I know a girl who went here." She shook her head as she handed her the paper, which was worn to near translucence from folding and refolding. Maude copied the faded address. "There's a woman who will help," she went on, so soothing, so big sisterly. Maude felt ashamed of her earlier shame, even if she couldn't quite shake it away: Claire pressing up against her cousin like a man. She was certain it made her provincial, that Vera Vance would have taken it in stride. She wished, with sudden, childish fervor, that she could stay in that apartment with the two of them, and that when it came time to have her baby Claire could be there, whispering kindly. And she wished she could make Sara understand her secret was safe, and not just because she wanted her own secrets kept. But Sara stayed in the kitchen, and Claire escorted Maude downstairs and into a cab.

The driver delivered her to a large brick house with a dirt yard. It had no sign, no marking of any kind. Every window was blotted out by a blue drape. But the driver smirked as he handed over her suitcase, and Maude hurried away, conscious of the way his gaze traced the edges of her body.

The house, run by Mrs. K and Dr. P, was clean and orderly. It had a cafeteria, a lounge, and designated rooms for examinations, labor, delivery, and recovery. Lined up in profile, its residents would look like a chart in an obstetrics textbook. There was a girl on a semester's leave from Radcliffe. A girl whose father was rumored to own half of Old City. But their common dilemma blurred such distinctions: The Radcliffe girl roomed with a girl who had worked in a beer hall, next door to a girl who had sewn hosiery at a factory. Tall Vivienne wore silk dressing gowns and a heavy emerald necklace and insisted she was there because of a terrible misunderstanding, that her fiancé Milton would retrieve her any day now. Mousy Helen had worked with her widower father in his butcher shop, where she telephoned him from the pay phone outside the lounge every day at closing time. Prostitutes were officially forbidden, but there were a few of them anyway, and there were girls who might as well have been prostitutes. Maude was not sure where she fit. Her dim bedroom sat right above the kitchen and filled each night and morning with cooking smells. She roomed with Birdie, the first Jew she'd ever met (technically, it was a Christian home—a local minister came every Sunday to preach an excoriating sermon—but Mrs. K did not stand on technicalities).

Maude had been at Mrs. K's a few weeks before she realized

that many of the girls stayed long after they gave birth, paying off debts. Mrs. K charged not only for room and board but for the services of Dr. P and her own help with the delivery. You paid if you wanted Mrs. K to find someone to adopt your baby, and you paid if you wanted her to find someone to keep the baby temporarily, while you got things sorted out. For her room and board and delivery, she had already given Mrs. K most of the bills from the roll she had stolen from her mother; the rest of her money she kept sewn into the lining of her suitcase, knowing she would need it when she finally left. When she asked about the adoption fee Mrs. K laughed. "Tired of my hospitality already?" But then she told her: If Maude wanted to work it off, she would have to stay six months at the home after her baby was born. Then she accidentally broke a platter one evening at dinner, and Mrs. K made a note: three more weeks.

On a hot afternoon in June, Maude and Birdie were scrubbing the bathroom when Maude doubled over. "Let's go lie down," Birdie said. Maude knew she ought to get out her notepad and check the clock, as Dr. P had instructed. But even after the hot current stopped rippling through her belly, she felt feverish and uncomfortably physically alert, as if the quaking of her insides had activated all her senses. The scent of boiling cabbage wafted up from the kitchen, seemed to coat the insides of her nostrils and throat. Better, for a moment, to just submit to Birdie's ministrations, to the little breeze she was making with a paper fan, to her gentle shushing.

Mrs. K's shout carried from the foot of the stairs. "Foster! Visitor."

She sat up carefully. "You sure you can make it?" Birdie asked, and Maude considered a moment before nodding. She slid her legs off the bed and slipped her swollen feet into her house shoes. How had they found her? Who had found her? Her father, after all this time? But no—his business with her had ended as soon as she relieved his household of the black mark she made. Her mother wouldn't have dared to make the trip without her father's permission, which her father never would have given. Could it be Marion? Not likely. Marion was barely thirteen, and gentle-hearted and cowardly. Maybe it was Cousin Sara, she thought. Or Claire, having come without Sara's knowledge.

She shuffled out into the hallway and down the stairs, twisting her hip with each step to counterbalance the weight swelling out ahead of her. With one hand she gripped the banister and with the other she pressed her belly protectively (how strange, this instinct to keep the baby safe, when months earlier she had contemplated throwing herself down the stairs to shake it loose). She waddled into the lounge, with its heavy furnishings, well-scrubbed by the inmates, and there, beside the floral-patterned settee, was Eugene Creggs, his clean-shaven cheeks waxen in the dim lamplight.

"Hello, Maude," he said.

She began to cry. He hurried to hand her a handkerchief and then turned as if to study the painting by the door, a portrait of someone's dour, bald ancestor. Her cheeks were already hopelessly slick; fat tears slid off her chin, speckling the purple apron she wished, now, she'd taken off before coming downstairs. She was so happy to see him, that was all. How could it be she was so happy to see dopey old Eugene Creggs? It was the first time she had seen him in a clerical collar; his neck looked too small for it, as if he were a boy dressing out of his father's closet.

When, after a minute or two, she'd stopped whimpering, he placed a hand on her back, his touch so gentle she barely felt it, and ushered her to the sofa, murmuring news from home as if it were a healing spell: The old schoolhouse had been struck by lightning and burned to the ground. Mr. Miskimen had retired from the Post Office and they'd taken up a collection and gotten him a very nice plaque. Marion had won the county poetry prize—fifteen dollars' credit at Freedlander's Department Store.

When she was calm, he tucked his hands thoughtfully behind his back and began to pace. Even through the first few minutes of his monologue, Maude was still not quite able to explain to herself: What was Eugene Creggs doing here? How had he found her? Why had he come? His speech was abstract and incorporated a great many quotations and metaphors. The subjects seemed to be, approximately, honor and family and sin, and how a wilted flower might be made to bloom again. In other words, her condition, and his brother's involvement in it, though she couldn't quite make sense of his position; it lacked the clarity of her father's, or of his mother's. When he stopped speaking and turned to face her, he was, for an instant, his own father, looking down with such authority from the pulpit at Hobart's First Presbyterian Church.

He didn't think there was any arrogance in reporting that there were men in Pittsburgh and beyond who wished to follow where he might lead, he told her. To wit, forward, into the future. The church needed to follow its flock that it might shepherd it better. Take a big tent meeting, he said, growing excited, white flecks collecting at the corners of his mouth. A fine way to reach a few thousand men. But say you film it. Bring in a fellow who knows his way around a camera. Make the crucial pieces into a moving picture, and send it to all the exhibitors across the country to play between the cheap entertainments. "Reach the sinners where they are!" he nearly sang, smiling, his teeth white and large and even. He went on: The other week he attended a presentation by some men who were developing a system of wireless telegraphy to transmit the human voice. It was only a matter of time, he said, before you would be able to broadcast sound practically instantly across vast distances to anyone with a receiver. The church needed to be ready. Say you transmit that revival; you could witness to millions on a single afternoon. Say you put a transmitting device right in a church and broadcast a service every Sunday. "It would become a church without walls! A church of the sky!" He pinched his fingers to his thumb and made a gesture like throwing a paper airplane.

It was the first time she'd seen him like this—lit up with an idea. Later, when people described Reverend Eugene Creggs's "vision," whatever else she might say about him, that word would always strike Maude as accurate. This quality of Eugene's, whatever it was, manifested in his eyes, the milky blue of them sharpening into a clearer, deeper azure, and something channeling through them, pressing out from within. He took a step forward and looked right at her, his purposeful gaze hooking into hers. She felt commanded to sit up straight.

"I can say with confidence that I will be a man who makes a contribution," he said.

And then she understood: Eugene Creggs, preposterous white knight. He had come to fall on his brother's sword. He was making the case for himself. This was a proposal.

With one hand, she gripped the edge of the couch cushion; with the other she softly pressed the hill of her stomach, as if to keep things calm beneath the surface, just a little longer, just until this extraordinary event had reached its conclusion. There was a muffled cry from down the hall. That would be Jane, or Matilda, or maybe Clara—it sounded like Clara's voice, though it was really too soon for it to be Clara. She'd grown used to the cries of girls passing through the pain of labor, but she could see it flustered Eugene, as if the presence of another girl pregnant out of wedlock complicated whatever story he'd told himself about Maude's dented virtue and his brother's wickedness and his own gallantry. She gave him an encouraging smile. He swept around to face the mirror above the mantelpiece. To hate a brother is to murder him, he said, soberly, to his own reflection.

But this was madness. Could Eugene have been in love with her? All this time? She tugged on a loose thread in the cushion, conscious that he could see her in the mirror, that she needed to keep her face neutral until she'd decided what she wanted it to say. Those tedious kitchen table conversations, the way, when James came in at last, Eugene would stand and interrogate him about where he had been, demand to know if he had finished some chore. The thread slipped loose. She brushed it to the floor and felt for another. She remembered one rainy afternoon when

she had asked Eugene if he had a photo of himself in his baseball
uniform (she had sensed he wanted her to ask—it had seemed
the polite thing to do). Paging through the album they'd come
upon a bundle of blond curls tied with a blue silk ribbon. He had
told the story like a joke—imagine a six-year-old boy, running
around town with skinned knees and a dirty face and the golden
locks of a princess because his sentimental mother has refused to
let anyone near them with a pair of scissors! But now she thought
about the way Eugene had said, "My brother's first haircut"—he'd
spat out the words like coffee grounds, and even back then it had
occurred to her that Eugene must wish that somewhere in that
album there were a ribbon-bound bundle of his own curls. Of
course, he didn't have curls—just a thatch of coarse dark hair that
by the end of the day, however thickly pomaded, managed to rise
toward the ceiling. Another cry. Yes, definitely Clara. Maude
folded her hands neatly on her knees, blinked prettily and
blankly.

But no, this wasn't about love. Or, if love was involved, love
was secondary. What Eugene had to offer was more fundamental:
Absolution. A way forward. No seven-month indenture at Mrs.
K's, no scratching like a stray dog at society's door. A genteel step
up, as if into a carriage, the aid of a gentleman's extended hand.
And for him, the pleasure of having given her that. Of having
saved her. It thrilled him, she saw, to imagine himself capable of
that kind of sacrifice. He was leaning against the mantelpiece
now, as he explained how a husband must love his wife as God
loves the church, and his profile—the straight, firm nose, the
shapely chin—was handsome, she had to admit, if a different
handsome than James possessed. His posture at the mantel might
have seemed theatrical except that when he turned to look at her
his face was open, guileless. He meant every word.

Years later, Maude would realize that this was Eugene's great
power: He always believed himself to be utterly sincere. And no
unsavory charge—hypocrisy, or self-righteousness, materialism,
or envy—could stick to a man who knew himself to be very good,

to act only out of pure, honest love, love of God, love of man, love of country.

She allowed herself a quick glance at the clock, but she had no idea when she had come downstairs. Eugene could have been speaking for five minutes or half an hour. Clara had gone quiet, worryingly so. Maude wondered if he would get down on one knee. She hoped he wouldn't.

But that was not the same as wishing away the proposal itself. If James had tried to marry her, if he had been forced, or if he had volunteered, she would have stayed in Hobart, she would have let her life shrink to fit the mold the two of them had cast (even now she had to fight not to smile every time she reviewed the tally: cast on the riverbank, in the root cellar, in the tree house the Lanier boys had built and abandoned in the woods out behind the elementary school, in the vestry of the church that had once been his father's, and in his twin bed, on a sagging mattress, atop a quilt whose pattern of green and blue scrap she could still trace out with her finger). It was the first time she had admitted this to herself, and she was shocked to discover what a weak, stupid girl she had been, not so many months ago!

But marrying Eugene—this Eugene, a Eugene who had left Hobart behind, a Eugene growing quickly into a man of distinction—would not be the same thing as marrying James, or any other Hobart boy. To be married to a man who made a contribution—that had always been the outer limit of her fantasy.

He did kneel, with a dippy smile and one hand pressed against his heart, as if he had learned lovemaking from vaudeville. At exactly that moment, a hammer struck her lower spine; the pain wrapped quickly around her abdomen, twisting into an asterisk behind her belly button.

The question he'd just finished uttering hung between them, like a veil of heat shimmering above a sidewalk. "Please get Birdie," she said, trying to keep her face calm, her voice sweet, even as something like cold fire was cascading through her gut. He returned with her a few minutes later, flustered, and said he had better go. Maude collected herself to say goodbye. The intensity of his smile made clear: he believed she had accepted him.

And why wouldn't he assume as much? What he had offered was so extraordinary that no sane woman could say no. And, in fact, she had not said no. She hadn't said it. But as soon as the third party in the conversation had asserted itself, she had known what her answer must be.

When he came the next day, Maude was in the thick of things; Mrs. K turned him away. The following morning he came again, and Mrs. K cleared the other girls from the room where Maude was recovering so she could receive him. The arrangements were all made, he told her. They could be married tomorrow; a minister would come to the house. He did not ask to see the baby, and she was grateful for that; she had already refused to have him brought to her a second time. But with that same sickening smile, Eugene produced from behind his back a single red rose.

. . .

As she makes her way downtown, heat prickles the nape of her neck, warms up her temples, blazes in her cheeks. She thinks of the scrambled eggs Birdie snuck her before dawn, along with her packed suitcase, and the liquids in her stomach churn. She wonders what she will say when she arrives at Miss Vance's apartment. For the first time, it occurs to her to wonder whether Miss Vance will be pleased to see her. Then she allows her thoughts to return to Eugene. Already she is starting to tamp this part down, which she will do every time she tells the story to herself, until it becomes as dense and tidy as a stone and slips into a deeper layer of memory, one she'd have to choose to excavate if she wanted to know it again: During her second encounter with Eugene at Mrs. K's, when she might have told him the truth—that she did not want to marry him—she dropped her eyes demurely and accepted his rose. And then she allowed him to go, believing something false only because she had decided not to tell him what was true.

The simple fact was, she needed him to return once more to Mrs. K's. She needed him to find her gone and pay what she owed Mrs. K, freeing her to start her life without having to look back over her shoulder. He's probably relieved, she tells herself. Or he will be, when he realizes how cheaply he has been able to discharge his brother's debt. Thirty-Sixth Street.

By the twenties, a pain has hit her, just above the elastic of that sanitary belt and deep inside, tight at first, like a clenched fist, and then rolling in waves to fill her abdomen. The dampness beneath her skirts is spreading. She grips her suitcase and wills herself forward. To her right she glimpses green lawn—a park, which she walks toward now, thinking she will sit for a moment, only a moment, on a bench. She has three nickels left in her purse, and with one of them she buys an ice cream on a stick. She eats it very slowly, pressing her teeth deep into the ice cream and leaving them there until they throb with cold, like she used to do to make Marion shudder. The sweet chill soothes her throat, and as her stomach fills it calms a little. Her face, though, grows hotter, and the whole world starts to bend, as if she is studying it through the bottom of a glass.

"You there," she hears, and she lifts her head, realizing only then that she has fallen asleep. The sun is slinking behind the tall buildings on the other side of the park; the stick from her ice cream is stuck to her skirt. She squints up at the owner of the voice: a police officer with a bristly black mustache and mean, pencil-point eyes.

She stands and backs away from him. "Miss!" he says, sternly, and she turns and hurries up the path, is nearly running when she hears him call again, "Miss!" She hears, in her wake, murmurs of disapproval from upstanding citizens out for their evening strolls, but she does not care. She allows herself a glance over her shoulder and sees the cop is staring after her, holding up her suitcase, looking annoyed, and also looking as it if it is not worth the bother of chasing after her. Now she feels stupid—maybe he only meant to help. But she presses on; here is Twenty-Third Street, which means only eight more blocks, and what if he was trying to trap her? It's a crime, isn't it, abandoning a child? And Eugene tracked her to Philadelphia; maybe he's already discovered her flight to New York. Tied around her waist beneath her jacket is the little coin purse holding its two nickels; it will have to do.

The sun has begun to set in earnest when she arrives, finally, at Fifteenth Street. She turns right, scanning the buildings for addresses. She is hungrier, now, than she was before she ate the ice cream, and it takes her too long to realize the numbers are moving in the wrong direction. She turns around. Her face is still quite sticky but no longer warm—an eerie coolness has settled over her skin. That fist in her gut clenches and stretches its fingers. She feels as if the air around her has grown thick and tacky. The muscles in her legs are like worn strips of elastic.

At last: here is the building whose number matches the one scribbled in Vera Vance's large, looping hand. She holds tight to the railing as she climbs the steps and presses the bell firmly with her thumb. She presses the bell again, and a blue-black corona surrounds her vision. A voice carries from a window high above: "Leave her alone, Ricky!" But she finds she does not have the strength to lift her own voice in return. All at once, she has no choice but to lower herself to the stoop, and there is hardly time for that before the blue-blackness overtakes the bluing-blackening of the sky, and there is only the darkness behind her eyelids and the roughness of brick against her cheek, and that for only a moment.

IN THE SPRING OF 1922, NOT LONG AFTER OUR NINTH BIRTHDAY, the theater where we'd been booked to appear from May through July converted to a movie house and cut its live bill by seventy-five percent. A week before we were to open, and for the first time since the flu, we were out of work.

Mama scrambled, but all she found was Dr. Whimple's Vitameen Spectacular. Instead of settling into a little apartment and spending most of the summer on a decent stage, we would zigzag across Indiana and Kentucky and Ohio in a clattery bus with a man-sized, dancing bottle of Dr. Whimple's Vitameen Tonic painted on the exterior, and perform in a revue while girls in matching outfits passed through the stands, selling bottles of the stuff out of trays strapped to their fronts. Daddy said it was beneath us—no better than a circus. But Mama signed the contract.

We lasted less than a month, Daddy in a pout all the while. Our firing was unceremonious; one minute we were on the bus, and the next we were off it, standing beside our luggage at the depot in French Lick, Indiana. From the tongue-lashing Mama got as we all hurried up the aisle, Josie and I gleaned that the night before Daddy had gotten drunk and offended an important local official. But after a few cryptic words, he and Mama buttoned up their own conversation on the subject. We learned nothing further about what had transpired.

For a few weeks, we stayed in a cheap room in French Lick as Mama tried without success to find us another job. And then one night, she shook Josie and me from a sound sleep, her finger to her lips. Daddy hustled us into the harness and out the door. When we woke again, bleary-eyed and disoriented, on a train, Mama explained brightly, as if this were a grand adventure but also something absolutely ordinary: we were going to Toledo, to stay with Aunt Marion and her family. And when we asked who Aunt Marion was, Mama laughed, as if she'd ever mentioned her sister, as if she'd ever told us anything about her girlhood, as if we'd grown up sharing a Christmas goose with Aunt Marion and Uncle Eugene and Cousin Ruth.

At the station in Toledo, as we waited for Mama to ask for directions, the stares of passersby felt more dangerous than usual. Even Josie bristled and scowled, taking no pleasure in the attention. We walked along a country road, arriving dusty and tired to a sprawling house the color of buttermilk, with lacy trim hanging from every edge and spindle. Mama knocked on the door and then grabbed my hand. I couldn't remember the last time she'd held my hand or Josie's when she wasn't trying to yank us somewhere. Daddy hovered a few steps behind the rest of us, as if he wasn't sure he had really been invited.

The woman who opened the door was slim and trembling, like the trick whippet that had been trained to guzzle Doctor Whimple's on command. It was only when she kissed Mama's cheek that I knew for certain she was Aunt Marion. She let us in, drawing back to where the others were waiting: a girl who must be my cousin Ruth, a man who must be Uncle Eugene. Aunt Marion rested her hands gently on the girl's shoulder; light from a window in the stairwell glanced off the sharp bones of Aunt Marion's face, making shadows in the pits of her cheeks, the deep hollows out of which gazed her wide gray eyes. Our mother had told us Ruth was twelve, but she was hardly bigger than Josie and me. Her blouse hung loose around her frame; her scraggly hair was parted in the middle, each side burdened by a heavy blue bow. Only Uncle Eugene looked robust, strapping; a small smile was pressed like a plum into his pink, clean-shaven face. The sunlight turned his hair into a plume of white flame.

He stepped toward us, the softness of the smile, the filminess of his pale blue irises, dissonant with the flint in his voice.

"First things first. Mrs. Szász—Maude. As you know, it has long been the policy of this family not to expose your deceit. But nor will we endorse it." He looked right at Josie and me; his smile stretched and hardened. A flick of his hand, indicating Aunt Marion. "Mother will show you upstairs. And you will return in the form given you in love by your Heavenly Father."

When we got up to the attic Josie grinned at me and began to turn, so we could walk in backward, as we did whenever we entered a new dressing room. But Mama put a hand firmly on Josie's shoulder, stopping her. As soon as Aunt Marion was gone, Mama crouched down, grabbing each of our outside arms.

"None of that here. No superstitions, no magic business, and watch how you talk. He won't brook any foolishness. Do you understand?"

We nodded, though we didn't, yet.

The harness was locked in a trunk; Josie and I were given old clothes of Cousin Ruth's to wear. We couldn't rehearse, weren't allowed to go to town. Sometimes, at dusk, Mama let us sit for a little while in the backyard, which had a high, tight fence, but mostly we stayed upstairs, where we played hide-and-seek behind old crates and boxes and pulled sheets off the furniture to make tents. When Mama caught us trying on old hats of Aunt Marion's, she gave us both a spanking. "You must never touch their things," she said, face pinched with fury or fear.

It was like that every day—don't touch, don't speak, don't draw attention—as if Aunt Marion's family was contagious. Or we were. Mama and Aunt Marion sat talking for hours in the kitchen or the parlor; they roamed through the garden, doing unhurried work—deadheading, pruning—Mama in a borrowed straw hat. But even though they held each other's hands, even though they erupted into undignified laughter that transformed them, for an instant at a time, into the little girls they must long ago have been, these talks always ended with Mama retreating upstairs, pale, exhausted, professing a need to lie down.

At lunchtime, we sat across from Cousin Ruth at the kitchen table. She stared at us, her dark eyes seeming to bulge from her thin face. We glowered at her over our glasses of milk and shoveled soup or forkfuls of baked potato into our mouths as quickly as we could without eliciting a scolding from Mama. As soon as we were finished, we raced back up to the attic.

At dinner, Ruth and Josie and I sat in a row across from Mama and Daddy. Ruth kept her eyes on her plate or in her lap. Only the grown-ups spoke, but the conversation was strained and strange. No one's expressions quite matched the words they said; it felt, at times, as if they were all speaking in code. Daddy rarely said anything at all. After dinner, we sat in the parlor. Aunt Marion brought coffee for the grown-ups and warm milk for Ruth and Josie and me. A few times, Ruth set up a game of Chinese checkers and sat beside it, looking disconsolately at her folded hands. More often she read or worked on a latch hook rug.

I tried to read but increasingly found myself occupied by the task of keeping Josie out of trouble. Over the course of the evening, a prickly energy would collect in her: I would feel her urge to speak, to do, to be reacted to. Even at the dinner table, she would swing her feet and twiddle her thumbs. In the parlor, she would hum, softly at first and then louder and louder, testing the grown-ups' hearing. I'd glare at her. I'd grab her fingers to stop her from spinning her mug like a top. Finally, when the clock struck eight, Ruth and Josie and I would say good night to the grown-ups and go upstairs, Ruth lagging a few steps behind Josie and me. At Ruth's bedroom door, we'd exchange a stiff good night before Josie and I continued to the attic.

One night, Mama came up, long after we should have been asleep, though she didn't seem surprised to find us with the light on.

"You could try," she said, "being friendly to your cousin."

She told us that Ruth had been ill the previous winter. Scarlet fever. That was why she was so scrawny, why her hair was so short and thin—it had been cut when she was sick, when it had seemed as if she might die and Aunt Marion had insisted on it, even though Uncle Eugene had said the practice wasn't scientific. She had missed a whole year of school. She was quite the little scholar, apparently, Mama told us, as if this were something we ought to respect. It had been difficult for her to stay home.

"Do you hear me, Harriet?" Mama asked. I nodded solemnly while, just out of Mama's line of sight, Josie crossed her eyes and stuck out her tongue.

In the parlor, a few days later, Uncle Eugene was holding forth on some subject when he landed with sudden, unexpected emphasis on the "th" at the end of the word. As he did, spittle arced through the air, a fine spray that caught in the soft, warm lamplight.

There was a moment of held breath, of fevered blinking. Then Josie laughed: a coarse, nasal, unambiguous laugh.

Silence settled over the room, as neatly and firmly as a cap. Aunt Marion put down her sewing. Ruth kept her eyes firmly on her latch hook, a flush spreading over her cheeks. Uncle Eugene smiled, calm in his anger.

As if he'd issued an instruction, Mama crossed the room and yanked on Josie's ear. After those weeks of monitoring her, of keeping her in line, I was shocked to feel a rush of pleasure. As if I were allied with Mama and Uncle Eugene instead of my sister.

"Straight upstairs with you, miss."

Josie stood and went to the door, but there she paused and turned to me with an expectant, puzzled look. I held up my mug, still half full, and shrugged, as if I had no choice but to keep drinking, as if finishing my milk were an imperative to which I must submit as surely as gravity. A shadow passed over her face, but she turned.

As soon as she was gone, I missed her. But I also felt a soft warmth in my belly, a secret pride. A suspicion I'd been nursing since our arrival had crystallized: I had always been good at obeying, at sitting quietly, at blending in, at managing the impulses of my body, which meant that at Uncle Eugene's house, I was the sister who shone.

When the clock struck eight, Ruth folded her latch hook rug and put it away in her workbasket. When I stopped, as usual, to say good night at Ruth's bedroom door, she wrapped her cold, sticklike fingers around my wrist. I let her pull me into a soft, apple blossom of a room, pink and white and pale green, velveteen and lace. Moving quickly, as if she were anxious not to lose my attention, she crossed to a bookcase on the other side of the room. It was one of two—glossy white, packed floor to ceiling. I thought of what Mama had said about Ruth being such a little scholar and missing school so terribly. I'd never really considered our not going to school any deprivation, especially after I'd learned to read. A stagehand had taught us to add and subtract on our fingers on one tour, and our times tables on another. The year before, we'd shared a bill with Carlo Parasini, the Boy with the Silver Flute in His Throat, and we'd eavesdropped on his lessons with a French dialect coach. I'd understood that I wasn't really learning French, just the pronunciation of the lyrics of the one French song Carlo Parasini sang, but I still sometimes said those words to Josie, as if they were conversation, and she responded in her own French, which was just nasal gibberish sprinkled with "chocolat" and "escargot." A few months back, we'd toured with the English actor Dick Figge, who smelled of the patent medicines he took compulsively and that, we overheard someone say, had destroyed his career. At parties, he would pay Josie and me a nickel apiece to perform monologues from Shakespeare; when we were done, for as long as he could hold on to his audience, he would pontificate about their historical and literary contexts, and I would listen, enjoying the rhythm of his speech, his rich, rolling erudition, even when I had no idea what he was talking about.

But now, as I stared at Ruth's packed bookshelves, more books than I'd seen, let alone read, in my entire life, right there in her own bedroom, envy wormed into my heart. The bookshelves flanked a window seat along whose pink tufted cushion sat dolls with gleaming china faces and glossy hair. The curtains were white lace, suffused with the candy colors of the sunset.

Ruth handed me a clipboard. LIBRARY OF RVTH, she had written across the top of a sheet of yellow paper, with a grid marked out below. There were only a handful of entries, all of the books signed out to her mother or Gladys, the housekeeper, who had been sent on vacation before our arrival.

"You can check something out, if you want to."

It was almost enough to overcome my envy—the pleasure of Ruth having recognized me as someone who might want to borrow a book. But Josie was upstairs, alone, and as long as that was true, I knew it was disloyal for me to be anywhere else. I pulled a random volume off the shelf. Ruth dutifully recorded the title—*Black Beauty*. I signed my name and was preparing to leave when she plopped down on the window seat.

"I suppose you know all about me," she said, bitterly. "About my hair."

I shook my head, not meaning to lie, exactly, but worried in a way I didn't quite understand; it didn't seem right, that I knew something private about her she hadn't told me. I sat gingerly beside her. Her hair had once fallen all the way down to her waist, she said. She could still hear the snap of the scissors in her ear. It had been like being stabbed.

She hurried over to the vanity table in the corner and returned with a thick blue glass bottle.

"It's a growth serum," she whispered.

Even though she was three years older than me, even though I'd heard her use a great many large words, even though I suspected she was even more orderly and self-regulated than I was, just then I felt as if she were the younger girl. She opened the bottle, squeezed a little from the dropper into her palm. "Gladys got it for me from a peddler." She rubbed it into her scalp then held the bottle toward me. I let her give me a drop, which I spread politely through my own hair, even though I didn't want it to grow—we'd been begging Mama for bobs for a year, and she'd finally given them to us for Dr. Whimple's. "Please don't tell Father. It's vanity, of course."

"Okay," I said. And before she could snag me again, I mumbled my thanks for the book and hurried from the room. As I left, I felt her gaze pressing against my back.

Josie was sitting on the floor between our cots, one of Aunt Marion's dresses pooling around her, one of Aunt Marion's hats on her head, her feet lost inside a pair of Aunt Marion's boots. She looked at *Black Beauty* with silent disdain. But then she pointed to a long mauve coat with brass buttons hanging alone on a rack.

"I saved you the Queen's Coat," she said.

I hurried to put it on, grateful for her forgiveness, grateful that she'd spared me making the apology I owed.

At lunch the next day, Mama and Aunt Marion told Ruth and Josie and me that the parents would all be going to the fairgrounds that afternoon for Uncle Eugene's big tent revival.

"Even Daddy?" Josie asked.

"Even your father," Mama said coolly, and I knew she was irritated at Josie for having asked a sensitive question in mixed company. "Ruth will be in charge."

A ripple traveled around the kitchen table—a danger of which our mothers were unaware.

An hour later, we watched Uncle Eugene's big, noisy car pull away from the house. Ruth, who had been making lemonade, chipped a large piece of ice and dropped it into her pitcher, which she set on a tray with three glasses. She moved with a stunning authority, confident, perhaps, in the lure of lemonade, but more than that, confident in her own power as the oldest child, the child of the house where we were staying, as if she'd been waiting since we arrived for someone to remind her: this was her turf.

After weeks of avoiding Ruth, Josie and I now followed her meekly across the hall, into a shady and spacious parlor furnished with child-sized versions of adult things: miniature armchairs and a matching tiny sofa; a miniature dining table, where Ruth set her tray; a toy kitchen with a miniature frying pan and a wooden pork chop and a bowl of wooden fruit; three school desks and a little chalkboard on wheels. All of it was pristine, as if it had never been played with. Ruth sat down at the little dining table, her knees practically bumping her chin, and measured out the lemonade to the exact same height in every glass. For a little while, we drank in silence.

"Who would like to play school?" It was a command, not a request. To my surprise, Josie sat at once at one of the school desks. Ruth, beaming, directed me to help her drag the little dining table over—now it was the teacher's desk. She topped it with a stack of books, a cup full of chalk, a hand bell. She commandeered the wooden apple from the little kitchen and gave it to me.

"This is what we'll do," she said. "You come in when you hear the school bell and give your teacher this apple. That's how it begins."

Once we were alone in the hallway, I expected Josie to laugh, to demonstrate her superiority to the game and to Ruth, but instead, she grabbed the wooden apple from me.

"I want to give it," she said, with a strange fierceness; I recognized it in myself then, a hunger for play, for a game of three instead of two.

We went in.

"Why, thank you, Miss Szász," Ruth said in a prim, teacherly warble, accepting the apple. "What a thoughtful gift. Now please take your seat."

Josie and I sat down in two of the little desks while Ruth wrote on the board.

Ruth turned around. "Class has begun," she said. "Miss Szász, please read what I have written," she said to Josie, pointing at the verse with a yardstick.

Josie frowned.

"For the wages of sin is death; but the gift of God is eternal life through Jesus Christ our Lord," I hurried to say.

"Miss Harriet, it was Miss Josephine Szász's turn. Please pay attention."

She erased the board and wrote a new verse. Her mother had

pulled her hair into two meager plaits that morning, and in the wide part between them, her scalp showed pink.

"Now, Miss Szász," she said, turning around and pointing at Josie with her yardstick. "It is your turn."

Josie slid low in her seat, crossing her arms, as I read:

"Thy word is a lamp unto my feet, and a light unto my path."

Ruth gasped.

"Miss Harriet Szász to the corner!" she said. "And Miss Josephine Szász! Please sit properly!"

She was still in character. She seemed even to appreciate the drama my disobedience had added to the game. But her authority felt real. I went to the corner as I was told, and watched miserably as Ruth began to erase the board.

"There is no speaking out of turn," she said, dust rising around her in a cloud.

Josie pulled from her pocket a twist of waxed paper, in which she'd been storing a wad of gum. Ruth busied herself writing a third verse; Josie began to chew.

"Now, Miss Josephine Szász, it is your turn to recite."

When Ruth turned around, Josie stuck a finger into her mouth. Slowly, deliberately, she pulled the gum out of it in a long, pale strand, which she swung between her closed teeth and her index finger, as if it were a jump rope. Ruth flung down her chalk, cracking it.

"Miss Szász, this is unacceptable." Josie returned the gum to her mouth but smacked it noisily. Her expression darkened, as did Ruth's, and it was still part of the game but it was something else too. Josie was punishing Ruth for the night before: for Josie's having been sent upstairs, for my having accepted Ruth's book. Ruth pointed to the verse again.

"Recite," she said.

Josie dipped her finger into her mouth and once again stretched out a glistening string.

It happened in an instant: Ruth lifted her yardstick like a sword and advanced, as if to slash the strand of gum. But before she could, Josie shot out of her desk and tackled her. Something surged in my blood. I ran over, sat on top of Ruth, and pinned her arms at her sides with my knees. The game was over, now; the other thing had taken over. I was as much in its thrall as Josie.

"A little worm for a little worm," she said, dangling the long, wet strand of gum over Ruth's face, and Ruth must have understood what was going to happen a moment before it did because she squirmed a final time. I pressed all my weight against her. I must have understood too, because I was shocked but not surprised when Josie ground the gum into one of Ruth's braids.

Josie and I were playing jacks in the kitchen when Mama and Daddy and Aunt Marion and Uncle Eugene came in, the four of them lively and laughing, as if in town they'd traded themselves in for new versions. "Girls, quick, upstairs," Daddy said brightly, after weeks in which I'd barely heard him speak at all. "Our room."

"And where's Ruthie?" Aunt Marion asked. I pretended not to hear.

Upstairs, Daddy pulled the harness from a trunk and gave it a shake, as if to wake it. He was tightening the buckles when Mama came in. I waited for her to ask what he was doing, to demand he let us out at once, but she crouched down. "Listen, girls," she said, and she sang: "Safe in the arms of Jesus, safe on His gentle breast."

"Repeat," she said, just as she'd done countless times before when she'd taught us a new number.

Daddy finished with the buckles. Mama sang and we repeated. Line by line, we learned the hymn. Daddy fished a dress out of the suitcase and lowered it over our heads.

"Are you paying attention, Harriet?" Mama asked, as Daddy helped me straighten my arm, and I was paying attention, but I was also waiting for Aunt Marion to storm in, to tell Mama and Daddy what Josie and I had done. And as Daddy tied our sash I heard, finally, her soft, swift steps in the hallway, followed by a cry. "Why, Ruth, what on earth!" My heart began to pound. I concentrated and sang: "Hark! 'tis a song of heaven, borne in the sweetest voice."

When we were able to sing through a full verse without making a mistake, Mama nodded at Daddy, and we all went downstairs, into

Uncle Eugene's dim office, which smelled of leather and paper, where we'd never been allowed to go. Before Toledo, putting on the harness had always felt like assuming our truest form. Now, standing in front of Uncle Eugene, I was quietly ashamed, as if the harness were a disguise. A lie.

But he shook hands with Daddy, as if they'd been friendly all along.

"Just like we rehearsed, girls," said Mama. "Show your uncle."

We sang our verse, Uncle Eugene beaming and bobbing his head from left to right.

"Just as you said, Leonard," he said, when we were finished. "Surely an instrument sent by the Lord."

"I think you'll have to build a bigger tent," Daddy said, grabbing Uncle Eugene's hand and giving it a hearty shake. I allowed myself to exchange an excited glance with Josie: whatever was going on, they meant us to perform again. But would Uncle Eugene want us in his show after Ruth told what we had done?

We found her in the parlor with Aunt Marion, who stood when we came in, her forehead puckered, her lip trembling. Ruth's face was tear-streaked, her hair, that precious hair that for a year she had been nurturing with a forbidden serum, had been chopped into a ragged bowl that fell barely to the tops of her ears. Uncle Eugene stopped short.

"Ruth, what on earth—"

"She wanted a bob like her cousins," Aunt Marion said. Her voice was clearer and sharper than I'd ever heard it, and I understood three things: First, that the lie was Ruth's. Second, that Aunt Marion did not believe it. And third, that this reference to our bobs would be as close as Josie and I came to blame.

Uncle Eugene shook his head gravely.

"Charm is deceptive, and beauty is fleeting; but a woman who fears the Lord is to be praised," he said. "To bed without your supper, Ruth."

She marched out of the room, head high, sparing neither Josie nor me a parting glance.

LATER, IN THE ATTIC, when we were getting ready for bed, Mama explained: That afternoon, Uncle Eugene had preached on and on, and the crowd had gotten fidgety and bored—imagine him at dinner but a thousand times worse, she said. A lady had fainted, people had started filtering out of the tent, into the fairgrounds. It was Daddy who'd understood the situation, she told us, smiling shyly. On the way home, he had pitched Uncle Eugene as if he were any old producer: It would draw a crowd, wouldn't it, he'd said, to see a couple of girls with a terrible affliction and good Christians all the same, singing hymns to Jesus. Mama admitted to us that she'd thought he was about to get us turned out onto the street, that she'd been ready to slug him in the jaw, but instead, something miraculous had happened: Uncle Eugene had smiled.

Mama told us that Uncle Eugene had been fired from his last job, that people in his church didn't like some of his ideas, his way of going about things. How funny, that our own Daddy had helped him find a way forward.

After those long, dull waiting weeks, performing in Uncle Eugene's revival felt like coming up for air, even if the hymns we had to sing were boring, the standing-still routine unfamiliar to our legs. It was hot in the tent, but sure enough, the crowds began to come. Daddy helped Uncle Eugene recruit some additional talent: a brass band, a one-legged boy with a dog that jumped through a hoop. Uncle Eugene summoned us onstage, twice, three times an afternoon. Whenever we came out his preaching seemed to grow particularly fevered. He placed his hands on our heads, he dropped to his knees and his voice thickened with emotion as he prayed. He declared to the people that Jesus was a friend, a true friend, to each and every one of them. Sometimes, in friendship, He disguised a gift as an affliction, which made it doubly a blessing. On the drive home, he would explain in simpler terms whatever it was we'd just heard him preach, and I'd feel as if we were in the thick of some transformation, as if by putting us to a new use Uncle Eugene were making us into new people. If I looked over at Josie, she would usually have her eyes shut, asleep or bored.

At lunch, whenever our mothers were out of earshot, Ruth would say things to us. That pretending to be someone you aren't is a lie, and lying is a sin. That not being baptized was like opening the front door to the devil. That unconverted Jews had their own special branch of Hell. In the same unspoken way we had always known about my mother's accident, I knew that Daddy was a Jew; I began to see him in my dreams, but dressed like the Jews we'd seen once on a train. Black suited, with a long beard and a wide-brimmed hat and long ringlets falling past his ears, he tumbled into a pit of fire, of ice, of snarling dogs. I tried praying for him at night, into my pillow so Josie wouldn't hear. But praying felt like nothing but the echo of my own mind. Every time I prayed I ended up feeling embarrassed, as if I'd made a mistake on a stage in front of a thousand people.

I HAD FINISHED READING *Black Beauty,* and one morning, when Ruth was downstairs, practicing the piano, I snuck back into her room to return it. First I put it on the shelf, and then I put it right in the middle of her bed, so she'd know we were square. Her quilt was pink and yellow and green, stitched out of little triangles that made me think of waves. I trailed a finger along it, and then I picked up the stuffed lamb that was resting on her pillow. I could still hear her, hammering through her scales, so I went to have a closer look at her china dolls. Each was set into a wire stand; none of them had a hair out of place. I sat at her vanity table and combed my own hair. Her silly clipboard, with its silly ledger, was sitting there, beside her bottle of growth serum and a little china box full of hair ribbons. I picked it up with a snort and flipped through the pages. Behind the ledger, I found another list. BOOKS READ BY RUTH MIRANDA CREGGS, 1922, she'd written across the top. The titles listed in her even, boxy handwriting must have filled six pages, front and back.

The scales stopped. I hurried over to Ruth's bed, grabbed *Black*

Beauty, and slipped out of her room. As I carried it up to the attic, I thought maybe I felt a soft burning on my forehead in the shape of the cross Uncle Eugene had made in oil when he'd baptized me at the latest revival; it was like a warning, as if God really were the holy peeping Tom he sometimes seemed to be in Uncle Eugene's sermons. Still, it was with more pleasure than remorse that I hid the book in the secret compartment at the bottom of my valise.

ONE NIGHT NOT LONG after, at dinner, Uncle Eugene took a sip of water and pushed his chair back a few inches from the table.

"My apologies to the ladies for talking business at the table," he said, including Josie and Ruth and me in the sweep of his smile before turning to Daddy. "I've a proposition. Friends have sent word about a church in Nebraska that has begun transmitting its weekly services over the radio. This is an approach I've long advocated, and I'm pleased someone's put it into practice. But picture this: a whistle-stop revival tour, culminating on the grounds of the church, where the final meeting would be broadcast live from coast to coast." He turned to Josie and me with a nod. "And of course I hope the girls will join me."

Mama patted her mouth delicately with her napkin.

"I'm afraid they aren't available," she said, taking pleasure in it, I could see—both in being in possession of the answer, when Uncle Eugene had assumed the management of the act was Daddy's business, and also in the answer itself, which was this: That very afternoon, she had booked us a job in Indianapolis. We would be leaving at the end of the week.

Uncle Eugene looked down at his plate; he shifted his jaw back and forth. When he looked up, he was smiling.

"Josephine, Harriet, Ruth. Please leave us."

We abandoned our half-eaten dinners and, without discussion, went straight down the hall to the playroom. We didn't shut the door. I heard Uncle Eugene's voice:

"This summer has offered your family an extraordinary opportunity for redemption, Mrs. Szász. I have even lately had hope of your husband's forming a friendship with Jesus. But it seems you would choose, instead, to return to a path that will surely lead to the further exposure of your yet-innocent girls to a base and immoral backstage life, likely to result in their growing into women of whom no one would be proud. Surely, Maude, surely you of all people—"

"Hypocrite!" The word erupted out of her. "Jesus God, what a hypocrite! Convinced he's the second coming, lording it over us, what you have, and let's look around, how much did this house cost? Is that God's will, that Eugene Creggs should dupe every sucker in three counties into paying his mortgage? Buying him a shiny automobile?"

"Please, Maude," said Aunt Marion.

Uncle Eugene spoke next, his voice more menacing but too quiet for me to pick out individual words. I turned around. Josie was sprawled out on the miniature sofa, eyes closed. Ruth sat on one of the school desks, watching me. Her mother had tried to even out her haircut, but it looked somehow worse: blunt sheaves around the temples, a longer, feathery strip at the base of her skull. Still, I was struck by how much healthier she looked than she had when we'd arrived six weeks before; her cheeks were fuller, her color pinker. Her eyes were brighter and, in that moment, seemed extra vivid with spite.

Aunt Marion cried out. Daddy barked something unintelligible. The dining room door slammed, and a moment later, the front door did. Uncle Eugene started up again, his voice a vicious hum. I waited for Ruth to speak, felt her readiness to speak as a binder against my own speech.

"I know what he's saying," she finally said. "He's telling your mother where you're going. Do you know where that is?"

"Indianapolis?" I whispered, feeling, in that moment, no muddle over our ages. I was nine, she was twelve, I was little, she was big.

Ruth shook her head. "H-E-L-L," she said. "Oh—sorry, Josephine. That spells 'Hell.'"

THE NEXT MORNING, we were on a bus, bouncing along a county road not twenty minutes from their house, when Josie pulled a piece of paper from her pocket and spread it over our lap.

"Show me," she said, in a low, clenched voice.

I glanced a few rows up, to where Mama and Daddy were sitting, Josie having whined until they agreed to let us sit apart from them. Daddy's head pressed hard against his seat. Mama's tipped toward the aisle; her eyes were closed.

I steadied the paper with my own outside hand and murmured the strokes as best I understood them—up, down, cross; down, bump, bump; half a loop—while she traced them out, gripping her stubby pencil. Inside the harness, her arm heaved against mine with the rise and fall of her breath.

After Indianapolis, we crossed Michigan; then it was Wisconsin, and into Minnesota. Josie's letters took shape, shaky when we worked on a bus or a train, surer when she practiced under the covers with a flashlight. As summer faded, we started in on words. I wrote them out and held a finger under them: MAT, CAT, RAT. RAKE, LAKE, BAKE.

Bake not back—silent *e*, I reminded her.

"You need to clean your nails," she snapped. "Honestly, Harriet, it's a wonder we don't get fired more often if you're going on looking like that." I curled my finger into my palm, hiding the sliver of dirt, and pointed with my knuckle. She kept on scowling, but then she tried again, the thing in her that for years had resisted Mama's instruction now applied, just as fiercely, to the task of proving she could learn.

That October, in Duluth, in a little hotel room whose windows glittered with frost, Josie showed Mama and Daddy seven pages she'd copied out of the exercise book I'd taken from the runaway dancer. They cried out in delight. Mama handed her a pencil.

"Show us," she said. When Josie had finished writing out her name, Daddy hefted her up onto his shoulders and spun in a loop, all three of them laughing. That night, before bed, they presented her with a gift: a diary. It had a cover of navy-blue leather embossed with a silver rose, and a shiny lock and a delicate key strung on a silver chain, so it could be worn like a necklace, though Josie wrapped hers around her ankle. After that, every time she took off a sock and I saw it shining there, I felt a spark of irritation: Who did she think she was, wearing a necklace somewhere other than her neck?

*

WE MADE OUR FIRST APPEARANCE ON THE MAYFIELD CIRCUIT the following spring, right around our tenth birthday, and over the next couple of years became circuit fixtures. In 1925, when we were twelve, we signed a contract for our first Mayfield's Modern Bally-hoo Tour.

Mama wouldn't let us forget that Mayfield's was still small-time: regional vaudeville, the farm team. And Josie and I had been at it long enough by then to notice how the whole business was shifting underfoot. Theaters slashing their live bills in favor of moving pictures. Trains hurtling past towns where once they'd have made three stops a day, where once there'd been a reason to stop. Big Baby Bridget, who had done an infant impersonation specialty for thirty years, spoke with bitter pride of two-a-days with lines around the block, of sharing the stage with Maurice Barrymore and Maggie Cline, and Baron Littlefinger and Count Rosebud, and Chauncey Olcott, the Irish balladeer. She said we were living in the End Times. Goldwyn, Mayer, Bow, and Valentino she referred to as the Four Horsemen.

But our new wages kept Mama in stacks of rings and hats adorned with feathers and beads and stuffed birds, and Daddy in natty suits. We went out for steak dinners. Instead of boardinghouses or shabby apartments above theaters, we stayed in decent hotels. In each new room, as soon as Daddy got us out of the harness, Josie and I would investigate, shouting out our discoveries: thick white quilts, spotless bathtubs, flowery soaps, chocolates on the pillows, carpets that held

our footprints long after we'd walked across them. Sometimes we
found treasures other people had left behind: a diamond cuff link, a
bottle of perfume, which we dabbed behind each other's ears. "Your
scent is simply divine, darling," Josie said. "Thank you, darling," I
said. Once we found a correspondence between lovers written into
the margins of a Gideon bible. We cut it out with the little silver
scissors from Daddy's makeup case and sewed it into the lining of
my valise, and then we peeked through the curtains, and picked each
other husbands from the men we saw out on the street. When she
chose me a man with a white beard down to his bellybutton, I swatted her arm.

"He's a hundred years old," I said, laughing.

"Yeah, a hundred years rich," she answered.

Daddy roused from a nap and asked what we were going on
about and we laughed until we could hardly breathe.

That same year something shifted in Josie. She'd always had a
temper, but now it seemed constantly provoked. Once, Mama told
her to finish a glass of milk, and she calmly knocked it over. When
Mama told her to put on one pair of shoes, she deliberately chose
another. She dared me to look at the pictures of naked ladies Daddy
drew in his scrapbook between his designs for the act and laughed
when they made me blush. She made me try on Mama's slips and
face cream, though she knew full well we'd be spanked if we got
caught going through her things.

"The difficult age," I heard Mama say to Daddy, and I burned
with embarrassment, determined she would never say such a thing
about me.

When I started breaking into Josie's diary with a hairpin, I told
myself I was doing it to protect her. To make sure she wasn't getting
into trouble. But even as I paged through three years of sporadic
entries, finding nothing save summaries of ordinary days, descrip-
tions of meals and dreams, and lists of clothes she wished she could
buy, I knew this wasn't quite true. We were never apart, we weren't
allowed to be apart. How could she be in any trouble that I didn't
already know about?

*

WE WERE IN IOWA THAT FALL WHEN A LETTER ARRIVED, SENT care of Mr. Mayfield, from Uncle Eugene. He must have done some digging to figure out how to reach us, and even so the letter made its way to Mama months after its postmark. If she hadn't been in shock, I think she would never have told us what the letter said, let alone left it out on the desk in our hotel room, where I found and read it myself.

Aunt Marion had died some months earlier; Uncle Eugene and Ruth had moved to Chicago, where he had accepted a job as the director of radio ministries at the Institute for Bible Study. Mama knew, of course, of Marion's difficulties, Uncle Eugene wrote. They had been grateful to think the Lord had finally seen fit to bestow upon them the blessing for which they'd long prayed, but alas; he took some comfort in knowing the little soul, and all of the others, had the company of his mother in heaven.

TO MY KNOWLEDGE, MAMA never responded to Uncle Eugene's letter. But in the years that followed, as we gained a reputation in our little sliver of the Midwest, we watched from afar as Uncle Eugene came into real fame. All up and down Illinois highways, he was quoted on billboards. Sometimes we'd come into a greenroom or a hotel lobby and we'd hear his voice on the radio. If anyone objected to Daddy changing the station, we'd leave.

We were fourteen, and had just embarked on our third Mayfield's Modern Ballyhoo tour, this time with second billing, when Josie pointed with her chin to a table in a restaurant lobby: there was Uncle Eugene, on the cover of a magazine. On our way out, she swiped it—she'd grown adept at stealing things, right under Mama and Daddy's noses, while I stared straight forward and later pretended not to know the origins of the deck of cards or the ring or the stick of candy. That night, when Mama and Daddy went out for a drink, she asked me to read the article out loud, still her preference though she could now manage herself.

That article told us more about Mama's hometown than she had ever revealed. And more about Uncle Eugene than we'd ever wondered. His father had been a reverend too, it turned out, and his brother was a pilot. He had been offered a tryout to become a professional baseball player but had chosen the ministry instead. According to the article, since the tragic loss of his wife the light of his life had been his little girl, now nearly grown, who he expected would shortly join the ladies' missionary training school at the Institute for Bible Study.

Josie snorted.

"That'll suit her," she said. "When she runs out of people to boss around close to home, she'll find a new crop halfway around the world."

She rolled over, and a minute later she was asleep, or wanted me to think she was. I finished reading the story, and then I went through and reread the sentences about Aunt Marion and Ruth, over and over, as if on a dare, forcing myself right to the edge of the chasm that still opened up in me if I thought too hard about losing Mama, about losing any of them. It was only when I heard Mama and Daddy's laughter in the hallway, and then the key rattling in the lock, that I tucked the magazine under my pillow and turned off the light.

1889

eonard wakes each morning just after four o'clock to listen to his father come in. He does not mean to. He is not supposed to. His mother will not wake until six, and Leonard will not get out of bed until his brothers wake, sometime after that. But ever since Papa started cleaning office buildings late at night, after the lawyers and bankers and men of business have gone home to their suppers and beds, Leonard's eyes snap open each morning just before his father turns the key in the lock. Papa is a stocky man, not much taller than Leonard's mother, but with his thick hands he can lift Leonard high into the air, even now that he is a big boy of nine, and just as easily tug a string between his index finger and thumb to unfurl the fine paper wing of a butterfly puppet as it emerges from a chrysalis made of wire and felt. This morning, Leonard has been awake for several minutes, long enough to hear his brother Laszlo, who sleeps on the cot to his left, recite his seven times table in his sleep four times. All around Leonard and his three big brothers, puppets slump—lifeless piles of wood and cloth and wire that will become vibrant in his parents' hands, on street corners and in public squares, and every rare while in a theater. "Show business is in your blood, Leonard," Papa says, and it is true: his grandmother, Olga, ran away from home when she was thirteen to join a traveling show, and his grandfather, David, danced in the ballet at Kecskemét until he snapped his ankle, forcing his retirement at seventeen. Olga and David met in Pest, where they married and ran a dry goods store in the Jewish quarter. They dreamed of putting away some money and opening a small theater, but the babies came, and although they worked from dawn to dusk there was never quite enough of anything. To their delight their youngest son, Leonard's own papa, began to construct puppets from scraps he fished out of the trash. At eighteen the boy eloped with Leonard's mother, the daughter of a button manufacturer who promptly disowned her. And now they all live together in two rooms, Mama and Papa, and Leonard and Laszlo and Max and Matyas, hungry boys who outgrow their coats and boots each year before winter has even ended. Papa says Leonard has a talent for puppetry, but what Leonard loves is to spend hours painting and cutting and folding and gluing paper scenes in front of which his parents' puppets will bob and dance.

But there is the gong of the clock in the other room, which means it is not just late, it is four thirty, nearly a whole half hour after Papa usually gets home. Leonard hears his mother rise and stir, which means she is worried too. Around him, his brothers sleep, but Leonard feels a slow pounding in his belly; he is wide awake now, and though he does not know it yet, days will pass before he can sleep again.

It is his mother who finds the body in an alley a few blocks from their apartment. A robbery, the police conclude.

There are too many boys and not enough food, so three months later, his mother pins the name and address of her maternal aunt to her littlest son's collar and puts him on a train, the first leg of a long journey to America.

. . .

He's only been in New York two days when his great-aunt sews a nickel into his pocket, lunch money, and sends him to register at the neighborhood school. He navigates up Allen Street, slipping between barrels of pickles and carts of bread and fish, passing wooden stands that creak under the weight of strange fruits and vegetables, and men pushing carts full of objects for sale: jack-in-the-boxes, wooden spoons, tea kettles. Even the familiar produce, the potatoes and cabbage, are alien to Leonard. They are the wrong size and who ever saw a potato that color? He presses his knuckles against his stomach, trying to settle it; his nostrils are still full of the stench of steerage.

The vendors bark in half a dozen languages, each scramble of vowels and consonants sounding, to Leonard, like a demand for his nickel. Something catches his eye: a pyramid of tough-skinned fruits, each the size of his own head, stacked on a red wooden cart with a bright hand-painted sign. He trades the vendor his nickel for what he doesn't yet know is called a "cantaloupe."

When he pulls it from his pouch at lunch the other children gather around him and laugh. They pelt his ears with rapid-fire English, their words indecipherable but the thrust of the gibberish clear enough. In tears, he flees the schoolyard. He tries to find his way back to his great-aunt's house but loses his way in the tangle of streets and alleys crisscrossing the Lower East Side, and runs west when he means to run south, or south when he means to run east, and soon he is lost. He careens up and over, past black buildings that seem to growl like great stone dragons. Red-faced women cluster at a corner, passing around something to drink, and brawny men toss barrels onto carts easily, as if they are filled with feathers or air, glowering at Leonard as he stumbles past. At the edge of an alley, dark and sluiced by a liquid that smells of rain and manure, he pauses to catch his breath, but a scrawny yellow dog runs up to him and barks, slapping the ground with its paws and baring its teeth. He takes off down the alley, tears burning the corners of his eyes. When he glances back over his shoulder to see if the mutt is chasing him, his head smacks into someone's elbow. Purple stars crowd his vision; a warm, droopy feeling tugs on his skull.

When he opens his eyes again he is on his back, looking up at a woman's heavily rouged face. She snaps her fingers beside his ear, talking at him in English. A cigarette is dangling from her other hand, its tail of ash threatening to break off and powder his nose.

He sits up, still dizzy. The woman takes his hand. He lets her lead him into a building and up a flight of stairs. She pushes open a door, and the hallway brightens with pink light. He follows her into a room both gay and dingy, the flocked paper peeling off the walls in wide strips, feather boas and satin girdles and silk stockings hanging from the pipes in pastel splendor, like the foliage of some ladies' jungle. The air smells like powder and bergamot and lavender and close, warm bodies, and all around him, women lounge and wobble, lean toward mirrors as they tweeze their eyebrows and mustaches and chin hairs, set each other's curls with hot iron rods, dab at their lips and eyelids with horsehair brushes. One of them notices him and squeals, and in an instant they have surrounded him. They pinch his cheeks, they rub his hair, they gush in bright voices.

"The theater is in your blood," Papa said. And now Leonard is in the dressing room of Lippmann's Burlesque, which for the next seven years will be his home.

That very night he starts as a water boy, toting around a glass bottle nearly as tall as he is, pouring water into paper cones and serving it to the dancers as they come offstage. His great-aunt tracks him down. Twice she drags him back home to the apartment she shares with her three grown daughters and tucks him in on the living room couch, where he stays up all night, stalking bedbugs and crushing them between his fingertips. Twice he runs away again, back to Lippmann's. After his second escape his great-aunt comes to the stage door with a small bundle: his spare suit of clothes; a warm, towel-wrapped crock of chicken paprikash; three handkerchiefs.

"I'm not your mother," she says, sadly. "I can't make you stay." He grins, and she spits once, the sharp, wet collision with the cobblestone signaling the end of the conversation.

The Lippmann's girls start sending him on errands. He fetches their stockings and hairpins, cigarettes and face powder and peanuts. Soon he is jabbering in English, and they have him order their dinners from Murray's and schedule their dates. At first, the girls support him with tips, which he spends on wandering feasts of pickles and knishes and saltwater taffy. But after a few months they corner the stage manager in the green room and insist the boy be put on the payroll. If he sleeps on a cot behind the costume rack, if his face gets cleaned only when one dancer or another corners him and smothers it with a rosewater-soaked hanky, what of it? He is home.

He's been running around Lippmann's for a year when Harold Delacroix, the scenic designer, decides to put him to work. Lippmann's Burlesque peddles an unsubtle art; Leonard's nimble fingers prove useful when it comes to affixing feathers or tiny reflective squares of cellulose to an archway or flat. But each night, after their work is done, Harold teaches him techniques he claims to have mastered in the grand opera houses of Paris and Berlin and on London's West End. How to paint a drop to a vanishing point so the stage stretches far beyond its back wall, into a vast battlefield, or a mountainscape replete with pine trees and babbling brook. How to counterbalance a flat so a stagehand can send it soaring neatly into the flies with just a tug. How to light a scrim so a richly detailed scene will evaporate into nothing at the flip of a switch. Lenny, Harold calls him, and he learns to like this nickname: it is a sharp name, an American name.

When Lenny turns sixteen, a dancer named Coco Cohen relieves him of his virginity on the dressing room cot. And maybe someone tells, or maybe it is simply obvious to all who see him—with his new, hard way of laughing, with the patchy stripe of mustache he wears proudly over his upper lip—that Leonard Szász is now a man. Or maybe Coco Cohen and Harold Delacroix have simply simultaneously detected that manliness rolling off Lenny like a musk. Because not too many days after Coco drags him behind the costume rack and presses a finger to his lips, Harold calls him into the shop, puts one hand on his shoulder, smiles fondly, fatherlike, and gives him the boot.

"Time for you to find a job worthy of your talents," he says. "You've outgrown us, Lenny."

It takes him a couple of years to get on his feet, to determine what, exactly, it is he wants to do. He assists a costume maker in his Greenwich Village studio, and he works props for a medium-sized vaudeville house on Prince Street. Finally he is hired as second assistant carpenter at the Star Theatre on Thirteenth Street and Broadway, the heart of the new theater district, for a legitimate play called *A Great White Diamond*.

When Lenny goes to share the news at Lippmann's, Harold disappears to the dank basement and returns with a bottle of champagne, with which he and the girls toast Lenny in the greenroom. Lenny drinks two paper cones full. He floats out to the street, the lipstick shadows of the Lippmann's girls' kisses rosy on his cheeks, eighteen years old and effervescent.

After *A Great White Diamond* closes, he works his way up and around the backstage, gaining a reputation as a fellow who can build or decorate or operate just about anything. He is a second assistant carpenter, and then a first. He is a set painter, a rigger, a stagehand. He works at the Star, the New York Theatre, the Madison Square Theatre. For several years he lives in a boarding-house on Twenty-Third Street. Every room is occupied by a stagehand. A Scottish woman cooks and cleans for them, and mothers them on occasion and chases down their rent, and threatens them with eviction when they keep the neighbors up until dawn, pounding on the old upright in the parlor, singing and emptying pails of beer. She looks the other way when red-faced chorines slink out the front door in the morning. He leaves at twenty-two to shack up with Noble Laureen, a ceramicist and spiritualist eight years his senior, in an apartment in Hell's Kitchen. They are two years into their affair when the stage manager of Arthur Fleischer's *Follies Magnifique* tracks Lenny down at Handrahan's and buys him a whiskey. Fleischer's needs a new head carpenter; the job is his, if he wants it.

As head carpenter at Fleischer's, he oversees the construction of the most lavish sets on Broadway. Three pyramids and a sphinx, painted to look like sunbaked stone; the court of Louis XIV, the edges of a throne sculpted from papier-mâché, painted pearly white with peach marbling, embellished in gold leaf; a tropical scene with real palm trees and a fat red sun that courses an arc along an aluminum track mounted to the backstage wall. When he sits in the back of the house and watches his sets slide and unfurl and loom, he has to pinch himself up and down his forearms, hard enough to leave a little track of bruises, so improbable does it seem that he has made this. He, Leonard Szász, lucky immigrant bastard.

And yet: there is this niggling dissatisfaction, this grit in his pride. At home, at night, while Noble Laureen sleeps, he leans toward a lamp and sketches sets of his own: the luminous, cratered surface of a moon for a cosmic ballet; the labyrinthine innards of a whale, through which the girls, suspended on ropes, would appear to swim; an ice queen's transparent throne room, the whole surface of the stage a frozen sheet to be traversed on skates. Morty, the set designer, has taken a look at some, has whistled and given Lenny a firm squeeze of the shoulder, and said, "Not bad, kid," in a distant, cautious way that made Lenny wary, confirmed his suspicion that his talent might pose a threat. But this much he knows: Someday these drawings will find life onstage, will lift and frame and cradle scores of Fleischer's famous showgirls. Someday, Lenny Szász will build worlds of his own design.

WE WERE IN THE TEAROOM OF THE OSCEOLA STATION, waiting for a connection, when I spotted Herb Fitz, buying cigarettes out of the machine. This was the spring of 1928. Josie and I were nearly fifteen. In our years with Mayfield's, we had often heard Fitz's name whispered reverently backstage. He had discovered Bindi Bruno and transformed her into the first of the famous RKO Dolls. He'd tracked down the Roscoe Family after a Mayfield circuit show; four months later they were starring in *Big Top Blues*. Daddy had cut his picture out of the *Vaudeville Tattler* and taped it to the inside of the costume trunk.

"Good girl, Harriet," Daddy said, softly, after I pointed him out—we were all speaking softly, holding still, trying not to alert any of the other members of the company to Fitz's presence. I flushed with satisfaction. Under the table, Josie kicked me, accidentally on purpose.

When Fitz left, Mama stood, gesturing for Josie and me to follow. We caught him in the hall. Josie and I curtsied (outside hands fanning out our skirt, outside feet tucked prettily behind inside ankles), and offered our best smiles. Mama delivered the pitch, Fitz looking us over with his little, damp, thick-rimmed eyes. At the end of it, he handed her his card.

After that, Fitz was like our shadow producer. Every choice was made in reference to Fitz, every number, every costume, was measured against the likelihood that it would earn his approval. Whenever we were in the same place at the same time, he met up with Mama and counseled her: cut that song, move that other one from the bottom to the top of our act. He alluded to opportunities out west—it was always "out west," never "Hollywood," never even "California," as if to candidly describe our ambition would have been unthinkably vulgar. But he said we weren't ready, not yet, that if we went too soon it would be a waste. When we reupped on the Mayfield's Modern Ballyhoo tour, it was only after Mama wrote to Fitz for his opinion, and Fitz said yes, absolutely, another year with Mayfield's would season us right up.

Josie persuaded Mama that she and I should start joining her meetings with Fitz, that it was time we start playing a more active role in the business side of things. At these meetings, Josie laughed at all of Fitz's jokes, a strange, high-pitched laugh that eventually I realized she had copied from a comedienne we'd performed with twice and met at a few parties. She asked him questions, and then she leaned over her lemonade, hardly blinking, listening to his answers as if her life depended on them.

LATE THAT DECEMBER, we arrived in Sioux City, Iowa, for an engagement that was to last the whole month of January. On New Year's Eve, some local big shot invited the whole company to ring in 1929 at his house, a brick monstrosity that rose out of an empty field a couple of miles from our downtown hotel, with a few shivering saplings flanking a vast circular drive. The next day was a rare day off, and the company descended like locusts upon the buffet and the bar. The party's benefactor, a red-faced man with stiff fronds of sandy hair splayed across his red scalp, roamed the crowd, encouraging people to drink more, to have another bite of something, looking both pleased with himself and vaguely nauseated, as if he liked the idea of his own generous hospitality but only up to the point where he began to contemplate the bill.

Daddy had been mostly on the wagon for months, and he drank

in the spirit of a man who had earned a night off. Mama trailed him closely, leaving Josie and me to drift through the crowd. We eavesdropped on adult conversations, drank from abandoned glasses, maneuvered ourselves into Roger Fey's path, giggling and clutching our outside hands whenever he noticed us watching. Fey was a two-bit juggler, a drunk, but at fifteen, Josie and I thought he was a dead ringer for Douglas Fairbanks, and that his wife, Vicky, was stingy and sexless, their marriage a tragic farce.

We counted down from ten and watched the grown-ups kiss. When the other young people—the Five Fiddling Millers and Carlo Parasini and Little Alice—grabbed pots and spoons and went to run around the house, Josie and I followed, and perhaps it was the moonlight, or the excitement of a party, but none of them seemed to mind when we stampeded over frozen mud under a hard, glittering sky, adding our own voices to the chorus of whoops and cries.

When we came back in again, the others were collected by their mothers. We leaned against a wall under a pink paper lantern and watched Daddy spin a quick draw artist named Maybelle Montgomery around the dance floor. From the other side of the room, Mama was watching too. When the song ended, forcefully, she caught Daddy's eye. He grinned and went over to her. He whispered in her ear, gesturing at the piano. She shook her head firmly and stalked away.

That was when it happened: A boy I had never seen before sidled up to Josie and me, grinning, as if we were well acquainted. Before I could say anything, Josie greeted him with a familiar hello. From behind his back he produced a little frosted glass full of ice cream, out of which a tiny spoon stuck up like a flag. He leaned forward, close enough that he could easily have seen the tiny dent where our dress slipped into the gap between our shoulders that wasn't supposed to exist, and he whispered in Josie's ear as if I weren't there, as if he didn't have every reason to believe we were a single entity, capable of hearing each other's thoughts. She laughed, the comedienne's laugh, until he scraped up a tiny curl of ice cream and popped the spoon right into her mouth. Even as I filled with horror at Josie's glib risk-taking, even as my brain trundled ahead to imagine the punishment Mama would concoct if she caught us, I could almost taste the sweet flavor, feel its coldness against my tongue. But when the boy leaned in again for another round of whispers, I couldn't begin to imagine what he might be saying.

"My mother is coming," Josie said, quietly, and the boy slipped away. Mama had just come back into the room, wearing her own coat, Josie's and my coat slung over her arm.

"Who was that?" I hurried to ask. But before she could answer, Daddy intercepted Mama; he took our coat, and eased her out of hers, and pulled her over to the piano, where he whispered in her ear again. This time she let herself smile. After another brief back-and-forth she kissed Daddy on the cheek, and then went over and talked to the pianist. When she looked back at Daddy, she shook her head playfully. He beamed.

"Josie?"

"I think Mama's going to sing," she said.

The party had thinned by then. The couple dozen people remaining quieted and gathered to watch—interested, not indulgent, as they might have been, had Mama been a different sort of backstage mother. Someone dimmed the lights and someone else rigged a table lamp into a spot. She curtsied at the light man, then saluted the party's red-faced host, who had settled into an armchair as if it were a throne, as if the entertainment had been arranged in his honor.

Already, the transformation was under way: Mama's eyes, unobtrusive on ordinary days, with their irises a mix of hazel and gray and their short tawny lashes, had become beacons. She settled into the piano's curve, rested her hand against it lightly, casually. You'd never guess she had a bum leg, that the piano was subbing for a cane.

The pianist began to play, and a moment later, the smooth stream of Mama's voice spilled into the rich man's house, filled up his rooms. Her face was an instrument now. Every small movement— the turn of a lip, the press of her eyelashes—was expressive, deliberate. With each lyric she told a story. I glanced at Josie. Her eyes glistened as she mouthed the words. I looked back at Mama, thrumming with the pride I always felt when I saw her sing: my mother had once been a star.

When the song was over, our host sprang to his feet, calling for an encore. Mama bowed graciously, but the pianist started in on something hot and dancy—I was certain she'd asked him to—and the small crowd cooperated, closing ranks, filling the dance floor before anyone could prevail upon Mama to sing again. She took our coat from Daddy and crossed to us.

"You ought to have been asleep hours ago," she said briskly, as if the last several minutes hadn't happened, as if she'd come to us straight from the cloakroom. We knew better than to say a word about what we had witnessed.

Back at the hotel, Josie climbed into bed without so much as a good night. It was as if we had fought, as if there were some reason for us to be particularly quiet with each other, instead of the opposite: a boy had spoken to Josie, had fed her ice cream, had put a spoon right into her mouth, and then Mama had performed. Surely there was a great deal to say.

An hour later, when Daddy turned up three sheets, Mama refused to open the door. Josie slept through the hubbub, or pretended to. She didn't get out of bed when the room service breakfast arrived and she didn't wake when Mama agreed to let me have my own cup of coffee, a vanishingly rare allowance. It was only when the company manager telephoned at quarter to noon, asking Mama to please come collect Daddy from the town square before he caused a scandal, that Josie stirred.

Still she didn't speak to me. Eyes closed and arms dangling as if her hands were made of lead, she dragged herself to the bathroom.

I hadn't checked Josie's diary in ages, but as soon as I heard the click of the lock, I retrieved it from her valise and jimmied it open. I flipped to the most recent entries, looking for evidence of the boy, whoever he was.

Instead, I found page after page with names in block letters, as if on a marquee:

JOSEPHINE SWEET & CLARA BOE
JOSEPHINE SWEET & ROD LAROK
JOSEPHINE SWEET & LON CHANEE
JOSEPHINE SWEET & GLORIA SWANSON
JOSEPHINE SWEET & RICHERD ARLIN
JOSEPHINE SWEET & HH CALDWELL
JOSEPHINE SWEET & TOM MIX
JOSEPHINE SWEET & SHELDIN LEWES
JOSEPHINE SWEET & EDMOND LOW
JOSEPHINE SWEET & BEEBEE DANYILS

Then came a full page on which her name appeared alone, the block letters giving way to a shaky script, not a signature but an autograph:

JOSEPHINE SWEET
JOSEPHINE SWEET
JOSEPHINE SWEET
JOSEPHINE SWEET
JOSEPHINE SWEET
JOSEPHINE SWEET
JOSEPHINE SWEET
JOSEPHINE SWEET
JOSEPHINE SWEET
JOSEPHINE SWEET
JOSEPHINE SWEET
JOSEPHINE SWEET

The bathwater stopped running; there was a soft splash, then quiet. I stuffed the diary back into Josie's valise and climbed into bed. One awful fact thumped in my brain, plain and undeniable: nowhere in that list of names was "Harriet."

ON OUR LAST DAY in Sioux City, a telegram arrived from Fitz. He was on his way to our neck of the woods with a big shot from out west who was working on a picture that Fitz thought might have a role for us. They'd be in Peoria when we opened, the day after tomorrow.

All afternoon and evening, Daddy seemed to bounce instead of walk. Mama inventoried our costumes and props, as if business would keep excitement—undignified excitement—at bay. I waited for Josie to acknowledge some excitement of her own. But she dragged through the day, same as she had every day since New Year's, remote and dull, as if with exhaustion. She didn't utter a word about the telegram and avoided my attempts to catch her eye, just as she'd ignored every question I'd asked about the boy who had fed her ice cream on New Year's Eve until finally I'd stopped asking. Since then, silence had accumulated between the two of us. Every time I looked at her, the names I had seen in her diary seemed to tangle around my heart like a net.

That night, the company's final ovation went on for five minutes. To my right, Big Baby Bridget stretched her neck like a swan and blew kisses at the mezzanine. To Josie's left, Voldrick the Great tossed his top hat; a dove shot out of it into the flies. Josie and I bowed and bowed, bathed in golden light so thick I could almost taste it. But back at the hotel, Josie remained aloof. She hurried to pack her things, but it didn't feel like she was hurrying because she couldn't wait for tomorrow to come. It was more like she simply wanted to go to bed.

"Do you think he'll send us to California right away?" I asked as we brushed our teeth. "That's what it sounds like, don't you think?"

She shrugged.

"I think when we're movie stars we should get a roadster we can both drive together. Custom-made. And have a big white house with a swimming pool the color of the ocean."

She spat.

"Do you think pink champagne tastes different than regular champagne?"

In the mirror, she met my eye. After a long moment, and as if she were an adult and I were the child she was treating with great patience, she smiled gently.

"I don't know, Harry," she said.

We got into bed. Silence descended once more, grew thick between us; but I could sense her wakefulness, the urgent flitting of her mind, until my own mind succumbed to sleep.

OUR TRAIN BROKE DOWN twice on the way to Peoria. By the time we arrived it was nearly midnight; my stomach was raw with hunger, and my inside arm felt like a stocking stuffed with sand. A bitter wind blew across the river. Even among the members of the company, there was no friendly talk, no lingering on the platform. Voldrick the Great emerged from the parlor car, his throat wrapped in a ruby scarf, and disappeared into a waiting taxi. Big Baby Bridget barreled up Liberty Street, head pressed into the wind, dragging her own trunk. The wind stole Roger Fey's hat, and he chased after it, calling back to his wife, Vicky—"Wait, baby! Baby! Wait!"—his voice conspicuous against the other passengers' prickly quiet. Vicky stalked ahead.

I thought about nudging Josie and remarking on the Feys' latest drama. But I was cold and sleepy and sore, and Josie had pulled her knit cap down over her eyes, as if she couldn't bear the effort of seeing anything or anyone. Mama hurried through some business with Lou, the company manager, Daddy breathing into his cupped palms. There was some confusion about a cab, and then Mama decided it would be faster to walk, and then we were walking, Daddy trailing behind Josie and me to block the wind that still bit at our ankles. The walk seemed interminable until we were slumped against the mirrored wall of an elevator going up. Finally, the door of our hotel room was locked, and Daddy was unbuckling the harness, and I was taking my first full breath since morning. I lay down beside Josie on the soft mattress, under a thick blanket and a coverlet embroidered with tiny pink rosebuds, and quickly fell asleep.

I woke to the sound of my name, a faint echo of my own voice, deep in my brain, and then it was Josie's voice, Josie's breath against my cheek, Josie's hand shaking my shoulder. I opened my eyes. She was looming over me, a shadow with gleaming teeth. Despite my irritation, I felt a wash of relief—she was speaking to me, voluntarily. But before I could even ask what time it was, she clapped her hand over my mouth and shook her head.

She climbed down from the bed. A moment later, silvery light poured into the room. She had opened the curtain, was standing right in front of the window, where her individual form would be visible to anyone who happened to look up. I rushed over and yanked the curtain in front of us, so we were hidden from our necks to our knees.

"Geez, Josie—"

"Look," she said softly, unruffled. She pointed through the fabric.

Half a block away, Mama was standing under a streetlamp. I turned to the other bed, where Mama was supposed to be, as if the Mama on the street could be an illusion, but no, Daddy was alone, a single, snoring lump. I turned back to the window, tried to make sense of the scene. The street was empty and dark save the streetlamp whose three globes cast Mama in a cone of filmy light; her face looked pale, her hair beneath her tall fur hat redder than it was in ordinary life, under ordinary light. She was wearing the new sable coat Daddy had given her at Christmas, and had one arm folded across her chest, hand clutching the elbow of her other arm, at the end of which her palm pressed against the handle of her cane, cigarette hanging between gloved fingers. There was something about her posture that summoned the memory of New Year's Eve, of her singing in the crook of the piano. Only now, it was alarm, not pride, that quickened in me.

She took a puff of her cigarette and blew out a curl of smoke. A streetcar rumbled past—a swift-moving husk, full only of electric light—blocking the sight of her for a moment.

"What is she doing there?" I managed to say.

"She goes out sometimes. At night." Josie's tone was light, but her words were barbed with a deliberate meanness, as they'd been when we were six and she'd told me that Daddy's headache was called a hangover, when we were nine and she'd made me show her how to write the words "shit," "damn," and "hell" in her beautiful new diary.

"How do you know that?" Mama tossed her cigarette to the sidewalk and ground it out with the tip of her cane, then started up the street. My breath caught—her moving was infinitely more worrying than her standing still had been.

"I followed her once."

I pinched her arm, right above the wrist. "Don't lie."

She jammed her elbow into my ribs, and I lost hold of the curtain. I scrambled to raise it again.

"It's not a lie, dummy."

Daddy snorted in his sleep. For a moment longer, I watched Mama's receding form, and then I pulled Josie into the bathroom, the one place where we had any hope of a private conversation. I stuffed a towel under the crack in the door before turning on the light. Josie climbed into the gleaming white tub, mugging like a ditzy flapper in a moving picture, as if we were in the middle of a gay adventure, as if she hadn't just said something catastrophic. I climbed in after her, and we sat cross-legged, knee to knee. There was, briefly, the still vertiginous feeling of looking into a face so like my own face, though on Josie, our shared features—the dark eyes with their crowded black lashes, the pink bowed mouth, the slight gap between the front teeth—achieved a loveliness I never detected in the mirror. Her face was narrower than it had been a year ago, the lines of her cheeks sharper. She'd braided her hair before bed, and now as she smiled at me, palms resting on her bent knees, she looked polished, assured. I knew there was a nimbus of frizz around my head, that Mama would complain tomorrow, when she tried to fix my hair, that I made everyone else's job harder when I failed to take pride in my own appearance.

Josie leaned against the back of the tub and closed her eyes serenely. "I'm not lying, Harriet," she said. I tried to match her posture, to signal my own superiority to the conversation, but my spine bumped the faucet. I realized only then that it was dripping slightly. That I was sitting at the edge of a small puddle.

"You couldn't have gone out in the middle of the night. I would have noticed." I heard the strain in my own voice, the effort of my insistence. My backside was growing damp, but I didn't dare move and risk throwing Josie off course.

"You sleep like Papa." A French pronunciation. This was new. "I had to practically shake your brain out of your skull just now. You snore like him too, you know."

"What did you do then? Where did you go? If it's true, tell me."

She danced her fingers along the edge of the tub. "It was in Berwyn, last fall. I thought maybe I would go outside and then come right back in, just to see if I could. But when I got out there, I saw Mama, sitting on a bench about a block away. When she started walking, I followed. She didn't do anything interesting, so I came back. She came in the next morning and changed her clothes and got us out of bed, like nothing had happened."

I closed my eyes. She was telling the truth. If she'd wanted to lie, she would have come up with a better story. But it didn't make any sense. Daddy was sensitive, the artist, the one who stayed out all night, the one who occasionally lost a week's pay at craps, or loaned it to a fellow with a sob story and no known address. Mama was the manager, the one who kept the Gerry people at bay, the one who made sure we got our nutrition. A Mama who wandered at night— who left us. I felt the return of something I'd grasped the edge of on New Year's Eve, when I watched her sing. Just beyond my pride there had been something else, the awareness that my mother was as real as I was, that the boundaries of her experience extended somewhere beyond my view. When she performed, at least, that separate self, the non-mother, was a shadow, a briefly summoned figment of the past. But now Josie had revealed her in the present, a figure strolling up Jefferson Avenue.

And the idea that Josie had herself gone out alone, in the middle of the night. I didn't know what I resented the most: that she had done it, that she had done it without me, that she had told me.

"We could go, if you wanted to." Her voice was small. She was looking down at her own hands, folded in her lap, one thumb tapping against the other. "Go out, I mean."

"Ha ha."

"We could, Harriet. No one is around. No one would see."

"Stop it, Josie."

There was another moment of awful silence, a silence laden with the threat of what Josie had suggested, with the possibility that she would persuade me, that I would let her. I thought of her standing in front of the window, blithely, as if breaking the cardinal family rule were as trivial a bit of misbehavior as talking back to Mama or trying to smoke Daddy's pipe.

In the end, though, she just stretched one leg and gave me a gentle kick in the stomach.

"It's a joke, Harriet." She laughed. "You're a funny kid, you know?"

She climbed out of the tub, laughing again, a little too loudly, as if to prove she wasn't afraid of waking Daddy. But she was careful to turn off the light before she opened the door.

I reclined in the spot she'd abandoned, meaning just to think, or to quiet my thoughts, to be apart from her for a minute. But after a fitful sleep I woke to pins and needles in the arm crushed under my body, my nightgown soaked at the hem. Laid over top of me was the rosebud coverlet.

When I came out of the bathroom, Daddy was still alone in bed, sound asleep. I crawled in beside Josie but stayed on top of the blanket, wrapping myself in the coverlet. Tomorrow felt terribly near. Fitz. The big shot. And I'd hardly slept. My body ached. What if I tripped onstage? What if I flubbed a line, as I had a few months back in Des Moines, what if my leg cramped, as it had in Kankakee, what if I cracked on a high note? What if Fitz left laughing, wired everyone he knew to forget about it, we were just a small-time freak act after all?

The channel at the edge of the curtain was beginning to fill with light. Daddy snuffled in his sleep. Josie turned over, and her stomach growled. Joining the tickertape of new worries running around my brain was the familiar list: that I would die before Josie, that Josie would die, leaving me behind, that Mama and Daddy would die, that I would sleepwalk into the hallway and expose the secret of the harness, that my breasts would grow too large to conceal, making undeniable our arrival in those audience-sickening years "twixt twelve and twenty," that I would have some catastrophic menstrual accident on the stage, that Hell was real, that Cousin Ruth had been right when she'd told me we were all headed there, that it had been my particular task to ward off Hell on behalf of the whole family and I'd failed. Every worry was amplified by the worry that worrying was keeping me from sleep, which made it all the likelier that I would make a mistake, that I was dooming myself to a future worth worrying about. But sleep must have won over worry, eventually, because I opened my eyes and there were Daddy and Josie investigating the contents of a room service tray, and Mama repairing a hem. The brightness of Mama's voice rang falsely in my ear: "She stirs! Out of bed, Harry. Today's a special day."

1904

Fleur and Maude and Vera walk up West Forty-Fourth Street, past the new Stuyvesant Theatre, past the Hudson. And then they pause and crane their necks and take it in reverently: Ned Wayburn's Training School for the Stage.

"Shall we?" says Fleur, briskly. She has been brisk ever since Katy Blodgett told the three of them what she'd heard: that Wayburn himself would be there at the last class of the session. They know Wayburn's isn't just a school, it's a pipeline: Wayburn's imprimatur can get a girl a spot in a Broadway chorus or on an Orpheum tour or in Fleischer's *Follies Magnifique*. Fleur has been taking class here for two years, Vera for a year and a half, Maude for only three months.

Maude didn't grow up dreaming of the stage as Vera did, back in Pocatello. She didn't learn ballet from an honest-to-god Frenchwoman, as Fleur claims to have done. But she did grow up knowing she was meant for something better than Hobart, Ohio, and maybe there's something contagious in that apartment.

It had been Bonnie, returning home from a shift at the flower shop, who had found Maude on the steps a year earlier—pale, bleeding, a dusting of dry vomit on her jacket collar. She'd run up and retrieved Vera and Fleur. Vera had gasped, recognizing the girl from the train station; the three of them had dragged her upstairs. Vera had nursed Maude, feeding her rice and ketchup and beans on toast. She had quietly cleaned Maude's stained skirts, and after a few weeks, when Maude was well, everyone behaved as if "well" was the condition in which she arrived. When Bonnie threw over her too-persistent suitor, Ricky, to accept a proposal from her second cousin, a mortician back home in Bettendorf, they all cheered the perfect timing. Maude took over Bonnie's room and, as soon as she found work, her share of the rent.

She started going to acting classes with Vera and took her turn singing in the tiny bathroom down the hall from their flat. It was only a matter of time before she felt as if the object of her ambition had always been the stage. Vera helped her enroll in dance class at a little studio on West Tenth Street, and the teacher said she had nice lines and a great vivacity. She took over Fleur's share of the cooking and, in exchange, Fleur gave her piano lessons that picked up where Cousin Sara's had left off. But when Vera got her off the waiting list at Wayburn's, Fleur's attitude cooled.

"Don't worry," Vera said. "She didn't speak to me for three weeks after my first Wayburn's class."

They ought not be competition for Fleur, with her long neck and golden hair. Vera is nearly six feet tall with heavy features, and Maude, at five one in stocking feet, still looks like a child. But as Maude puts it, Fleur is ambitious. And as Vera puts it, cheerfully, Fleur is a ruthless bitch.

That afternoon, the ordinary dressing room chatter has given way to nervous quiet. Some of the girls are in bathing suits, but Maude has just bought herself a practice romper from the shop in the academy lobby, and as she puts it on she's pleased with the way her waist cuts in, with the proportions of her legs, however stumpy they look beside Vera's or Fleur's. She is conscious of the crackle of paper as she unwraps each tube and brush and pot in her new Wayburn makeup kit, and she wishes she'd thought to open everything at home. Vera joins her beside the mirror, her makeup in a little brown basket with a red plush chicken attached to the handle by a loop of thread, and does her face up breezily, while Maude carefully follows the steps in the instruction pamphlet. Fleur passes, her head high, her arms held at a slight angle from her side, as if to make room for her own billowing loveliness; she meets their eyes in the mirror and gives them a beneficent nod, like a monarch in a procession. As soon as she is out of earshot the two of them laugh. It's the first real noise anyone has made in minutes, and it seems to loosen up the others. Katy asks if she can borrow Maude's powder, and Blanche pulls out a cigarette and says, "No one will tattle, right?" Smoking is strictly prohibited at Wayburn's, where it is often said there is no reason a showgirl can't be a lady. Some of the others ask for a light, and one offers around a bottle of rum, sips for luck, which Maude declines, and another starts a stretching routine in the corner focused on parts of the anatomy that inspire a great deal of laughter, and soon the excitement in the room is a clamor that Maude thrills to be part of, even as she holds herself a bit apart, stretching on her own and scrutinizing her reflection. Her thinking is orderly, clean, focused.

They leave the dressing room in a great cheerful gaggle and burst into the long mirror-lined studio. The few girls already waiting at the barre or in awkward isolation at the floor, Fleur among them, bristle at their presence, or hold their heads a little more erect, marking their superiority to the hoi polloi. The class's start time has always been sacrosanct, but Wayburn sweeps in five minutes late, followed by an assistant with a clipboard. The high chatter collapses into a hum, and when their teacher lifts a hand, absolute silence. Fleur stretches her arms above her head in fifth position, and Maude feels a flicker of embarrassment on her behalf. Vera grabs Maude's hand, panicked. Maude's nerves are just right: a pleasant thrum under her skin. She squeezes back, feeling generous. Sisterly.

As Wayburn speaks with the instructor and the accompanist, Maude begins to doubt. Can this be the famed dance teacher? A man in prim wire spectacles, with thinning hair and a chestnut brown suit, watch chain dangling from vest pocket, he reminds Maude of a librarian, or her old English teacher at Hobart High. He has a bowling-pin body, tall with wide hips, that seems engineered to tip over. But as soon as he starts moving, she is struck by its grace: his shoulders are relaxed but full of power, his hips slice even lines through the air. The floor seems to repel his feet, as if he could, at any moment, take flight.

He claps his hands twice and faces them, smiling. She hardly hears his opening remarks, though she understands he is trying to put them all at ease. He instructs them to line up by height. Vera blows her a kiss and goes left, with the other Amazons. Maude goes right, with the other little girls, "my ponies," Wayburn calls them, and for a moment, they are all elbow and hustle. The clear, orderly stream of Maude's nerves threatens to swell into a flood. But she throws her shoulders back and leads with her chest, as if there is a wire pulling up from her breastbone. She levels out her breath, connecting, once again, to the ready strength of her body. The assistant assigns each girl a number, warning that they mustn't forget—one through forty-six—and then sweeps over to Wayburn just in time to catch the jacket he has already started to remove. In the same motion, he hands Wayburn a handkerchief. Wayburn taps his brow.

Hands folded behind his back, the great teacher moves along the line, scrutinizing. Now and then he issues an instruction: smile please, posture, show me your fingernails. Maude is surprised, when her turn comes, by how clinical Wayburn's assessment feels. Her femaleness is an essential part of the transaction, no doubt, but he does not seem excited by her body as he examines it. She has met enough men who have claimed connections in show business to understand that this is not something to be taken for granted. Before moving on to the next girl, he offers her a courtly nod; she nods back, meeting his eye.

He breaks them into lines, Fleur managing to jockey herself into position right up front. He reviews the eight directions and reminds them to distribute their weight equally between the feet, to keep their gazes strong and forward and level, then teaches them a combination.

"Any questions?" he asks after the third time through. Maude lets her gaze flit around the room. Some of the girls look anxious or confused. Katy looks near tears. But Maude is calm; she knows the steps.

They dance the combination over and over, the girls in the front moving to the back and the lines advancing, until they've all had a chance to appear twice in front of Wayburn, who watches them, hands on hips, occasionally leaning over and whispering to his assistant, who marks on his clipboard. When Maude's line gets to the front for the final time, Wayburn's scrutiny feels like something vibrating against her skin. She is aware of the contraction and expansion of each muscle. She executes every detail of every step: not just the kick but the extension of the toe, not just the turn but the perfect angle of the arm, just as Wayburn asked.

When they've finished, the girls sit together at the back of the room; no one utters a word. After a conference with Wayburn, the assistant calls out some numbers. The girls who weren't called shuffle into the dressing room, some in tears. The others dance some more, and the process repeats, until there are only ten girls remaining. When Wayburn wends along that final row and taps on five shoulders, Maude isn't the least bit surprised that one of them is hers.

The other five are dismissed. The assistant repeats their numbers but Wayburn says he would like to learn their proper names, and their regular teacher, her voice quavering proudly, goes along the row, introducing each: Priscilla, Karen, Fleur, Vera, Maude. Wayburn shakes their hands, smiling in his gentlemanly way. Now, he tells them, the real work begins. In six weeks, they will make their debut in the chorus of Fleischer's *Follies Magnifique*.

Later that night, Fleur cooks hamburgers, sheepish now that it's all over. Vera invites over some boys who bring some beer, and Katy comes by and it's no hard feelings. Priscilla and Karen and Blanche and some of the others show up, and Paulette Skinner, who quit Macy's six months earlier to make moving pictures in France, arrives, alarmingly thin, but thrilled as hell for the five of them, she keeps insisting, and by midnight it's a proper party.

Maude drinks more than she means to, and Lionel turns up with a banjo and they all sing. The downstairs neighbor pounds on the pipes, once, twice, three times, and Fleur makes a great show of going to bed and locking her door, but it is practically daybreak when the apartment finally clears. Vera says she's still too excited to sleep, so Maude climbs into bed with her. She likes the feeling of Vera's warm, wet breath in her hair and her soft, solid arms close around her torso. She watches through the bars of the fire escape as sunlight suffuses the blue-bottomed clouds, and then, in pale shafts, breaks through them. In the cold brick face of the building across the street a window fills with light. She has not thought about the baby in many months, but now he appears to her: a year old, with a swirl of fine reddish hair and mouthful of teeth that he shows when he wails. And her face is wet with tears, but whatever sorrow she feels is overcome by the relief that trumpets in her heart, for the little boy's sake as well as her own, that he has some other mother.

AFTER BREAKFAST, WE WENT DOWN TO THE THEATER TO rehearse, and then we locked ourselves in our dressing room. Daddy trimmed his beard with the little silver scissors from his makeup kit and combed back his hair (for several years, jet black instead of salt-and-pepper; we all pretended not to notice when the dye rubbed off on a pillowcase). Mama sat in the corner between a dressmaker's dummy in a red-and-black paneled bustier and a costume rack, knitting her preshow nerves into one of the scarf-like masses she had taken to making and then unraveling, only to knit and unravel it again and again until the yarn was too kinked and greasy to reuse. Josie and I played with a set of dice we found on the counter among the usual detritus: brushes and pots, paper felt liners, sticks of greasepaint, a rusty tin of peppermints, soiled hankies and fresh ones, a swan's down puff and a rabbit's foot, its toes stained mauve from repeated dips into the rouge box.

But beneath the veneer of business as usual, everything was off. My hip and shoulder ached from my nap in the tub. All day, Josie met my pained attempts at conversations with breezy "hmm"s and "huh"s, with "Oh really?"s that made me feel as charming as a mosquito. That afternoon, as Daddy did my makeup, I knew that beneath the greasepaint my face was puffy and wan, that purple crescents loomed under my eyes.

I watched from my stool as Josie leaned toward the mirror to color in her own brows, her mouth hanging open so that her breath clouded the glass. When she'd asked Daddy to teach her how to do her makeup, a few months back, I'd refused to learn. It hadn't seemed fair to Daddy, somehow, who lately seemed to have so little to do. Now, I wished I were standing at her side, working on my face as she worked on hers.

"Quit slouching, Harriet," Daddy said. I unhunched my shoulders, closed my eyes, and breathed in familiar scents: the thick, clean tang of greasepaint, the perfume of wool and talcum powder, the dusty odor of the electric lights ringing the mirror, the breath of the cinder block walls. But there was no comfort in any of it. I saw myself forgetting my lyrics. Throwing up on stage. Tripping and dragging Josie into the orchestra pit so we had to be carried out of the theater by a couple of stagehands, unconscious and bleeding.

All at once, there was a crash and the clatter of objects rolling across the floor. Daddy's makeup kit had fallen off the counter. In an instant, Josie was crouched down over the mess, shoveling supplies back into the kit. I felt an odd jolt of hope, as if this small disaster might obviate the larger one I'd been anticipating.

"A couple of klutzes, that's what we have here," Daddy said cheerfully—a signal to Mama that she could be cheerful too, that there was no need to let this incident drag her into anything other than cheerfulness. There was a dangerous moment of silence, during which Mama blinked icily at the three of us, but then she turned back to her knitting. Relieved, I slid off my stool and crawled under the counter to retrieve a spool of yellow thread. When I crawled back out, Josie was holding the makeup kit open for me.

Beneath the rouge-drawn Cupid's bow, her mouth was pressed into a thin, serious line. Her face was all done save her eyes; against all that paint they receded into tiny, lifeless dots. I dropped the thread into the kit.

"Hey, Harry?"

My heart accelerated.

"Yeah?"

"Just, break a leg is all."

I nodded. Instead of looking away, she lifted up her hand and held her palm out to me. I drew a sharp breath: our old sister salute. I couldn't remember when exactly we'd stopped doing it; over the last few years, we'd abandoned all of our old backstage rituals, one by one. Now, as I pressed my hand against hers, tapping each of her fingers with each of mine, I felt the heat of tears.

Josie stood and brushed off her knees, and I scrambled back onto the stool. I watched her in the mirror, waiting for her to meet my eye. But she was focused on the cosmétique: unwrapping it from its foil, positioning the stubby candle beneath the dollhouse skillet of the Lockwood stove. Biting her lip in concentration, she struck the match. Daddy cleared his throat softly. I turned toward him and looked up at the ceiling. Daddy brushed a wad of cheesecloth along my lower lids. I smiled, willing him to believe my tears were nothing but a reaction to the acrid scent of the cosmétique.

Josie finished her makeup, and Daddy finished mine. When it was time for the harness, Mama put down her knitting and came over to watch, as if, even after all those years, even though the harness had been Daddy's invention, she didn't quite trust him to buckle us in properly. I took a full breath, claiming all the lung space I'd have until he freed us again at the end of the show. He bound my inside arm to my torso with a long strip of cotton, and then did Josie's inside arm. We stood side by side. Daddy lowered the harness over our heads.

As he tightened the straps, Josie's inside arm felt hard against mine, flexed, when we'd used to nearly melt into each other, save for the points of our elbows. Daddy frowned and shook his head slightly; I knew he was considering the next alteration he'd need to make to the harness to accommodate our changing bodies, and I felt a familiar flicker of embarrassment. We stepped into our petticoat and held up our arms. Daddy lowered our dress. Mama did up the buttons and brushed a few loose hairs from the skirt. When they were satisfied, the two of them stepped aside so Josie and I could look in the mirror. There were the matching doll faces, pink dots for cheeks, the same white Peter Pan collars we'd been wearing for a decade, the familiar wide body. At the same instant, we reached to remove the cheesecloth headbands that held back our hair. I sensed more than saw Josie smile, and calmed a little. At least she still felt a rush of satisfaction when we moved as one.

Cheering and applause ripped through the ceiling: the show had begun. We knew Voldrick the Great's act almost as well as our own, could track it through the ebb and flow of the audience's response. The first eruption came when he appeared onstage in a cloud of violet smoke; the polite rumble was for the parade of birds he extracted from his hat; the bigger whoop was for the audience volunteer who agreed to be hypnotized; the whistles were for Voldrick's assistant as she levitated in a golden throne. Mama fixed our hair. Daddy paced, hammering his palm with the bowl of his unlit pipe. We listened.

After Voldrick came Patty and Timmy Trawler, who did a comedy act called "The Art of Marriage," even though, in real life, they were brother and sister. It was hard to tell for sure, but the laughter seemed muted. Mama caught Daddy's eye in the mirror and shook her head. I knew what she was thinking: to make the best impression on Fitz and the man from out west, we needed a lively house, folks eager to laugh and cheer. Nerves rippled in my stomach and tightened the muscles in my back. Josie dug the thumbnail of her outside hand into the flesh alongside each of her fingernails. I swatted her gently to make her stop. She didn't look at me, but she balled her hand into a fist.

A knock on the door: "You're up, girls."

We faced Mama and Daddy for a final inspection. Small red patches bloomed on Mama's cheeks. Daddy's eyes were wide, as if with shock, and his rough, grayish face seemed open, tender, like something from which a layer had been peeled away. I felt overwhelmed, then, as I often did, by a sense of my parents' need, by my own clumsy longing to meet it. Mama's agitation was especially startling. Maybe that was why she had wandered the night before, I thought. Maybe she'd only been nervous. Maybe Josie was nervous too. She insisted she never got stage fright, but I didn't know what else to call the terse, mean mood she'd fall into before important shows, her determination to pick at her cuticles until they bled. And here we were, about to perform for a couple of men who could transform our futures with a single telegram.

Daddy jammed his hands deep into his pockets.

"You knock them dead, girls," he said. There was that wounded look in his eye.

"Thank you, Daddy," Josie said, quietly.

"Enough, Lenny, you're upsetting them." Mama waved, dismissing him, dismissing the emotion that had colored her own face. I rubbed the toe of my tap shoe against a dried splatter of blue paint on the floor, unable to keep looking at any of them. I hadn't dabbled in prayer since that summer in Toledo, but now something like a prayer passed through my mind: Please, I thought. Please.

Mama handed Josie our ukulele. Up we went.

From the wing, we watched Big Baby Bridget push a hoop across the stage, her pinafore and petticoats fluttering up to reveal flounced bloomers. She sang in a sweet, dimpled voice, purring her r's as w's. I glanced at Josie; light from the stage gilded the edge of her nose and bounced off the coppery spangles in her dark hair. I wanted her to look back, to acknowledge my looking, but she concentrated on Big Baby Bridget, who was taking her bows to thin applause.

"Tough crowd," she murmured as she passed us in the wing. I lost my breath, as if it were a step that had just collapsed beneath my weight. But even if Josie wouldn't look at me, she was beside me in the harness: solid, an anchor. I drew air into my lungs; I held it there; I pushed it out again. The curtain swung shut; we pattered to center stage. Big Baby Bridget's flats swooped up and ours dropped into place.

When the curtain opened again, Josie lifted the uke, and I placed my hand over the strings, ready to strum. A pale glowing crescent crossed my chest—the follow spot operator taking aim. An instant later the spot came up properly, its tight circle illuminating Josie's face. When we first started to play, she would strike her tongue against her teeth when she was ready to begin, but it had been years since we'd needed such a signal. I felt her heart as if it were in my rib cage, her breath as if it were passing through my lungs. She formed the first chord. I brushed my thumb across the strings. She sang:

> A pretty girl's a special thing
> A shiny pearl, a diamond ring
> A most enticing treasure here on view

I allowed myself a glance over the footlights. The house was packed, every seat occupied, extra people dotting the aisles, leaning against the back wall, stirring and coughing and fanning themselves with their programs.

> But wait to see, what I've in store
> I guarantee, you'll like it more
> My word, would you believe—I'm one of two!

The band came in then and the lights came up full and we turned our heads to smile at each other. Very slightly, she winked. At that, the tense muscles in my back seemed to release. My smile stretched, not because I was making it stretch, not because it was supposed to stretch, but because I couldn't help its stretching. Josie had winked: a signal across the transom.

When our shoes hit the floor, the unison snap fed something in me as it always did, confirmed the reality of the four-legged oddity the audience believed us to be. By the end of our first chorus I was sure I felt every person in that theater, leaning very slightly forward, as if Josie and I were tugging them by invisible strings attached to the tips of their noses. The applause began before our last note stopped ringing. We'd cracked them open. No one else had managed to do it that afternoon, but Josie and I had. We galloped off-stage. Josie handed the ukulele to Mama.

"Give 'em teeth, Josie," she said, running her hand over Josie's hair. Mama's face was a smooth blue mask in the backstage light, but there was an uncharacteristic tension in her voice. "Harriet, high feet." But I knew she was wrong: my feet had been plenty high, they'd been spring-loaded, they'd threatened to send us skyward. Mama was anxious, saying the habitual words because to have even tried to discover truer words would have been tempting fate, and I wanted to laugh, because for the first time that I could remember, I was on the outside of the worry, I was the one who recognized the better, happier truth: Josie and I were masters of that still-cheering crowd.

The band played our cue and we charged back on. It was time for our signature cartwheel. It wasn't as fluid as it had been when we were little girls and our centers of gravity were lower, but I led with my right foot and Josie kicked off the ground and I could feel at once the power of our muscles, the mastery of our form. Our legs swept the air in a perfect unified arc. My hand absorbed our full weight for an instant, my wrist as firm as an iron beam, and then we were upside down, our petticoat a perfect fan. We tumbled out of it, landed on Josie's feet, and then my own. The audience erupted. "Brava!" someone shouted.

A stagehand placed a bench and a tree down left, and we crossed over to them to begin our sketch. The audience could hardly wait for Josie's punch lines: their laughter was a simmer, ready to bubble over. Someone whistled; Fitz, I thought, giddy.

Offstage again after the sketch, Mama fitted us each with a fedora for "Little Miss Mobster." Daddy was getting in the way of the stagehands, grabbing shoulders and slapping backs with such genuine cheerfulness that even when the stage manager said, "Watch it, Lenny," he sounded more amused than angry. The first notes of our intro floated out of the pit.

I glanced over, expecting to see my own exhilaration mirrored in Josie's face, hoping rashly for another wink. But her expression was stiff. She was remote from me once more.

There wasn't time to wonder why. The band played our cue. On we went: step, step, step, step, my outside hand on my hip, Josie's extended. The air in the house felt humid with applause, and Josie was beaming, even as her expression remained somehow shuttered. We bent forward, grinned, fluttered our hands at our hips, dragged left feet to right oblique, hopped left then right, every step and every note correct, but something was slipping from me. The correctness of our movements felt superficial. I knew I was smiling, that on my face there was the form of a smile, but from the inside it just felt like a display of teeth. One and two and three and four.

She stopped. The harness caught me, dug into my ribs and thigh, and I lost my footing. As soon as I recovered my balance, she lunged forward, dragging me with her.

"Wahooooo!" she belted, a great, blaring burst of notes. A low murmur traveled through the house. She tossed her hat into the front row.

"Wahooooo!" she sang again, a long chromatic run.

There was no loveliness in it, no vanity. It was a bid for attention, furious and stark. The conductor stuck his head out of the pit. At first, he kept waving his baton at the band, which had come unspooled, half the members having quit playing altogether. Then he stopped. The rest of the instruments trailed off; chatter rose in the house. I was peripherally aware of some heated discussion offstage; Josie had positioned us on the apron, downstage of the curtain line. Was someone going to pull us off? Should I drag her off before they could? And then I felt it—her right arm moving inside the harness.

"Josie?" My voice was tiny, a pinprick. I wasn't sure if I had said her name at all. Time, sound, motion had all become warped, as if the whole theater had plunged underwater. Her elbow was rubbing against mine, and then moving more fluidly—her cotton strips were loose, I realized, there was more room between us than there was supposed to be—and with her outside hand, through our dress, she was fiddling with the buckles on her side of the harness. I could see her inside hand, unbound, writhing against the navy fabric of our dress. She had unhooked our petticoat. It started to slip.

That knowledge drilled through the numbness in my brain. There was something to do, something I could prevent, even if Josie was methodically dismantling life as I understood it: I swiveled my hip to hold up the petticoat. Josie was still howling, banshee-like, as she unbuckled her side of the harness.

She turned to me and for a split second was silent, her mouth drawn. Then she yanked her head down through her neck hole and shimmied out of the harness, down through the bottom of the dress, pulling the petticoat with her to the floor. Daddy's little silver scissors clattered to the stage; she must have swiped them when she knocked over the makeup kit, I realized, and even through my shock I felt a kick of admiration. She crawled out of the petticoat, shook off the cotton strips from which she had cut herself free. Our half-empty dress bagged around my frame. I clutched at it with my outside hand. A follow spot found Josie on her hands and knees, panting, staring into the house.

She stood up, proudly, insistent that they see her: individually torso-ed. A discrete person, a mere twin, not an attached one. A girl with her own right arm, her own lungs and liver, her own undershirt and bloomers. There was a moment of stunned silence followed by halting applause, which was quickly overpowered by a chorus of angry shouts. Objects started flying toward the stage: a shoe, a crumpled program, a sandwich shedding salami as it fell from the mezzanine.

She ran left, and then down the small flight of stairs that led into the house. The gasps and cries of the crowd grew louder, men leaning forward to jeer as she arced around the orchestra pit and raced up the center aisle. But no one actually reached for her. I didn't move. It was as if she had cast some spell that meant we couldn't touch her. The double doors at the back of the house swung open, the lobby lights framing a man whose features I couldn't make out. Just a silhouette, clasping hands with Josie's silhouette, and then their receding backs.

A hand clamped down on my shoulder—the stage manager. It was only as he pulled me offstage that I realized—as if it had taken that long for my brain to make sense of the sound in my ear—that my mother had been frantically calling my name. I didn't know if Josie and I had been singing together seconds ago or minutes ago.

The backstage was in chaos. Someone turned up the work lights, and the brightness made me want to throw up. Daddy was standing against a wall, face contorted with shock, hands tucked into his armpits, as if his whole body would spill open if he let go. I couldn't see Mama anywhere. Voldrick the Great poked his head through the door that led to the dressing rooms, clutching his hat, his mouth popped open in a delighted O. Other members of the company were filing into the hallway behind him, standing on their tiptoes. The noise in the house had become a roar. The stage manager barked a command, and a stagehand moved to bring down the asbestos. The last thing I saw as it fell was the crowd spilling into the aisles and making for the exits, as if they had collectively decided to follow Josie, to chase her down and hold her to account. And it was for that reason alone that I closed my eyes and activated the private telegraph that had been strung between our minds as long as I'd been aware of my own mind, for that reason alone that I sent a message along the wire, even as I felt the telegraph's power beginning to fade: Run, Josie. Run.

Daddy snapped out of his shock long enough to lead me down to the dressing room, where he freed me from my cotton strips and wrapped our sprawling coat around my shoulders. Mama met us at the stage door, flushed and out of breath. She shook her head. Each of them grabbed one of my arms, and, grimacing, Daddy pushed open the door. We stumbled through a gauntlet of jeering audience members and exploding flashbulbs and into a waiting car, and despite everything, there was an odd pleasure in being flanked by my parents. Held within their protective grasp.

AS SOON AS WE got up to our hotel room, Mama ordered me to take a bath; I let the water run and pressed my ear against the door, straining to hear what she and Daddy were saying to each other. I could tell the conversation was angry, but I couldn't make out the words.

A few hours later, I was dressed in my pajamas, sitting at the window, behind the curtain. There was a knock on the door. Daddy

unlocked the bolts with trembling hands, Mama gripping his arm.
But it was only Lou, the company manager. He stepped inside, patting his forehead with a handkerchief, and shot me a nervous glance.

"Say whatever you've come to say," Mama said.

"A kid's missing. A new grip. We picked him up in Sioux City.
Frank Dunn."

I knew Frank Dunn had to be the boy who had slipped Josie the
ice cream at the New Year's Eve party. Had they been whispering
about running away that very night? Had they met in secret in the
weeks since? The night before, when Josie told me about Berwyn,
had that been only a partial confession? Had she meant her words as
a warning? A goodbye? Had she wanted me to extract her plans
from her and talk her out of them? Had she been giving me a chance
to join her? "We could go," she had said. "If you wanted to."

Mama took a sharp breath.

"That's all you know?" she said.

"Mr. Mayfield's not happy, Mrs. Sweet."

"Well, Lou, I'm not surprised to hear that."

Lou said good night, promising he'd let us know if he heard anything, and not long after that the police turned up—three of them,
led by Officer Cleo, special agent for delinquent girls. In a syrupy
voice I didn't trust she asked me about Frank Dunn: if Josie had
been his sweetheart, if they had ever spoken. I shook my head, practically growled "no." And it was partly from a desire to protect her,
but it must also have been partly from a desire to protect the family
secret—she couldn't have been, couldn't have done, because the
rules didn't allow it, and even though Josie had obliterated the rules,
even though no police officer would be asking me these questions if
the rules meant anything, they still felt baked into my bones. Officer
Cleo asked if she could look at Josie's things. I shrugged. I had already hidden her diary in the false bottom of my valise. In the end,
Officer Cleo said she'd be in touch if she had any news, but there
wasn't much she could do about a runaway who didn't want to get
found.

Late into the night, Mama and Daddy paced, each accusing the other of having driven Josie away. What would we do now? Both of them kept asking the question, demanding to know, as if the other were hoarding the answer out of spite. Their fight only ended when Daddy left. At dawn, he knocked softly on the door, and Mama let him in without a word.

A few hours later, a delivery boy turned up with a letter. Mr. Mayfield was suing us for breach of contract. Mama spent the day at the desk, chain-smoking, drafting letters of her own, going over the family accounts. When Daddy finally crawled out of bed he went out with his coat collar turned up and returned with coffee and rolls and newspapers. My picture appeared on the front page of the local daily: SIAMESE DOUBLE-DEALERS, the headline read. FRAUD EXPOSED. The photo had been taken by the stage door. Mama and Daddy were headless forms on either side of a me I hardly recognized: hunched over, my double-wide coat pooling around my shoulders, my face mostly washed out by the flash, my mouth a black smear, my eyes frantic dots.

Mama had always kept our clippings in a hatbox none of the rest of us were allowed to touch, along with contracts and receipts and other important documents, but when Daddy offered her the picture of me in the alley and the short mentions he'd found in the *Trib* and the *Times,* she blinked at him, uncomprehending.

I closed my eyes against a rush of tears, remembering the night of our debut in Chicago, how I had lain beside Josie in our cot, fighting sleep to listen as Mama and Daddy discussed our future. And the next morning: the solemnity with which they had impressed upon Josie and me the importance of our secret. Now, Josie was gone. Josie had exposed our secret so she could go. Nothing would ever be the same.

The rolls tided us until supper.

"The last room service supper of our lives," Mama declared it, grandly, as if from a stage. But we only picked at the rich food. Afterward, Daddy and I sat side by side at the foot of the bed, and Mama stood before us. Even though she was wearing a dressing gown and slippers, both of us sat up straight and folded our hands

in our laps. Josie had left us no choice, she said. We had debts and
no prospects. We were a laughingstock. Finished. It was time to in-
voke the emergency protocol, to repeat the desperate measures we'd
taken the last time we found ourselves in need of rescue, though
without Josie, without the act, I couldn't begin to imagine what
"rescue" might entail. Nevertheless, she had decided: we would go
to Chicago. We would throw ourselves on the mercy of my uncle
Eugene.

1905

On a Tuesday afternoon, Lenny stands in the back of the house with Ralph O'Connor, the technical director. Clarice Newhouse is out of the cast—"a personal matter," the stage manager said, winking. So they are working a new girl into the moon number on a trial basis, some kid in the chorus who hasn't even been around a year, and Lenny and Ralph are on hand in case the routine requires any technical adjustments. Technical adjustments: nothing more. Mr. Fleischer promised to look at some of his sketches for the Christmas Fantasia but took them and never said a word. Lenny saw red, went around to some other theaters, talked to friends, called in favors, and arranged conversations with two directors of note, with an ambitious young playwright who wants to put the legend of Orpheus and Eurydice on a giant revolving stage and claims Charles Frohman will finance it. All of them looked politely at his drawings and said the same thing: terrific, but we already have a design man. What we need is someone who can build it, are you interested? He leans against the wall, enjoying the weight of his own furrowed brow. He lights a cigarette for himself and one for Ralph. The lights go down and the rehearsal pianist begins to play.

The girl drops from the flies on a crescent moon, the squeak of the winches just perceptible in the nearly empty theater. She lounges in the spotlight, her face serene and haughty. She appears aware of her own loveliness and fearless of the chasm of dust-laced air between her perch and the boards. A headdress of ostrich plumes reaches up from the coil of her braids, three feet toward the sky, and high-heeled silver shoes dangle from her crossed ankles, their laces twining her calves. At the end of her number, Lenny looks down and is startled to find his cigarette in his hand, burned halfway to ash.

. . .

Maude feels as if something has become luminous in her: a fluorescent tube has threaded her veins and is lighting her up from within. After only six months in the *Follies,* she is the new featured performer, not Fleur, who makes no secret of her indignation; not Vera, who is mostly just relieved it isn't Fleur; not any of thirty other chorus girls, most of them with longer tenures and longer legs; not some outsider, some leading lady. But Maude Foster, all of seventeen and new to the stage. Two years ago she was running from Hobart, Ohio, and then from Philadelphia and the promise of a comfortable and respectable future. Now she is riding a moon in Fleischer's *Follies Magnifique,* and though the goodness of life is suddenly abundant, she feels greedier for it than ever, anxious to gobble it up.

A few days after her debut, she discovers a gift on her dressing room table: a tiny parakeet, carved from soap, its feathers so fully formed and perfectly proportioned that it looks as if it could flutter out of her hand. The next day: a tiger, poised to pounce. Over the course of six evening performances and two matinées, Maude finds a dog, pressing its paws against its nose, as if embarrassed; a galloping horse; a centaur with an extravagantly muscled chest; a lady's daintily arched foot; a dragonfly, its wings formed from pennants of rice paper, water-colored pale green; a tandem bicycle; an ice-cream sundae; and a monkey in a fez, holding a bottle-cap cymbal from a crooked finger no thicker than a sewing needle.

The evening after Maude finds the monkey, Vera bursts into the dressing room, beaming. "What do you think?" she asks, grabbing Maude's arm. "Lenny Szász was caught in the Royal Hotel men's room this afternoon, stealing soap." When Maude

returns to the dressing room after the first act, she finds on her
table a mother rabbit carved from an apple; the apple is already
softening, but the rabbit's etched face still shows her perfect re-
pose; her browning body, curled around her kit, appears warmed
and furred. After the final curtain drops, Maude finds Lenny
backstage and says hello. He stares at her, stunned, as if she has
stepped out of a painting, out of a dream.

"I'm awfully hungry," she finally says.

He takes her to a small tilting room on MacDougal Street
with sawdust on the floor and a dozen wobbly tables covered in
white cloths. The waiter juggles the napkins. The busboy plays
the harmonica. They eat spaghetti with tomato sauce and share a
jug of red wine, which she feels tugging her brain like a balloon,
and which he hardly feels at all. It is half past one when they
press their fingertips into the melting remnants of their spumoni
and empty their glasses a final time.

The streets are still lively. Young people move in swarms. A
man passes on stilts, a little dog in a sling against his chest, and a
woman bustles past, swathed in white fabric, her jewels surely
glass. These are their people. Nighttime people, theater people,
poets and dancers and exiles: they have all come from someplace
else—Tampa, or Toledo, or London, or Istanbul—and now, together, they share the narrow streets of this village-in-a-city.
Four men spill out of a lounge singing an Irish ballad in uncertain harmony. Long after the streetlamps have dimmed, a girl
leans over a glass in the window of a Bleecker Street café. Maude
has never felt so deeply and securely rooted in a place, and Lenny
not since he was a boy of nine. In the course of the evening, each
has heard the other speak a watchword. Already, they are kin.
Holding Lenny's hand, Maude climbs up onto a low brick wall
and walks along it, sketching the whole of her ambition: She will
become a star of the *Follies,* and then a leading lady, a proper actress, a Sarah Bernhardt. She will play Juliet and Ophelia, Hedda
Gabler and Hecuba and Lady Macbeth, names she has only recently learned but which she dashes off with brio. Lenny tells

Maude about his designs, the illusions he'll render with wood
and plaster and light when he's given a chance not only to build
but to invent. Maude tells Lenny about Marion, a little sister
growing into a woman she doesn't know in a farmhouse in Ohio
that is deathly still except when her parents' rage bubbles over.
Lenny tells Maude about the puppets he grew up with, the spare
siblings slumped along the walls, waiting for his parents' hands to
give them breath. He tells her about the night his father did not
return from work. At daybreak, they find themselves sitting on a
bench, watching the sky lighten and pink over the backs of the
factories across the East River, their mouths dry and sour, their
heads throbbing for want of sleep, each willing the sun to slow in
its ascent.

A month later, Maude moves into Lenny's apartment in
Hell's Kitchen, after, she insists, a trip to City Hall. In the closet
she finds a lady's scarf and garter belt, and beneath the sink a jar
of cold cream. Trembling, she presents these objects to her husband. He admits to Noble Laureen, his erstwhile ceramicist. She
wants to believe this is thrilling—she has defeated a romantic
rival she didn't even know existed—but cannot help but feel that
something in their young marriage has been spoiled. She allows
herself an afternoon of weeping. But only an afternoon, because
if she thinks about his secrets, it becomes difficult to forget her
own.

By the end of the following year, Maude is a star. With his
nimble hands, her handsome husband builds an enormous revolving seashell, from which she emerges dressed as a mermaid as
bubbles of light transform a curtain into a blue velvet sea. He
sketches at the kitchen table, and she brings him coffee, flushing
with pleasure at her wifeliness. They laugh about the time he fell
asleep on top of the flower wagon. He builds her six shop fronts
on flats that descend from the flies to form a Wild West; she
dances with a lasso, her oversized silver spurs whirring as she
kicks. They do not speak about the time she retrieved him from
the Eighteenth Precinct, where he had spent the night in lockup

after slugging a man in a bar (she does not know that earlier that afternoon he had received a bundle of his own sketches in the mail with a note from a director—wild stuff, but not what he had in mind). For the Lady Godiva number, Lenny builds her a fairy-tale forest—real pine trees harvested from Mr. Fleischer's estate in New Jersey, wound with foil ribbons that reflect the lights as Maude rides across the stage on a live horse, wig strategically parted and placed. "A golden couple," Mr. Fleischer calls them, urging a glass of champagne on each of them at the New Year's party. And Maude glances at her husband's glass, but then she raises hers toward Mr. Fleischer, and the smooth light beneath her skin burns and burns and burns.

PART
TWO

AS THE TRAIN RUMBLED THROUGH A LITTLE TOWN—
a strip of slumping houses I would have guessed were abandoned if
not for the smoke rising from their chimneys—I wondered how
quickly the gap between Josie and me was growing, if I was hurtling
away from a fixed point or if she was also on a train or on a bus or in
an automobile, hurtling at the same time, in some other direction.
The last time we'd crossed paths with the stagehand who had taught
us arithmetic, he'd set us problems involving trains leaving from
points A and B, John on one train and Mary on another, a mosquito
flying toward the caboose. Josie had made jokes—can't he just check
the timetable, someone get the fellow a fly swatter—and even
though I'd shot her warning looks and kicked her ankle, in truth, I'd
been grateful for her interruptions, the excuse to abandon the lesson before I had to admit how little I understood. Now I was helpless against the notion that if only I'd stuck it out, if only I'd listened
more carefully, if only I'd had proper schooling, I would be able to
get to her. Or at least locate her on a map.

The night before, Daddy and Mama had fought again, but this
time they'd shut themselves in the bathroom and kept their voices
low. All I'd gleaned was that Daddy objected to the plan—that he
didn't want to ask Uncle Eugene for help. Once again, the argument
had ended with Daddy storming out. I had waited a little while,
pretending I'd slept through his going, before I got up to help Mama

finish packing. He had returned at dawn, just starting to sober up; now, he slumped at my side, newspaper draped over his face. Mama, across from me, was knitting. Every couple of rows she set her needles down in her lap and turned to gaze out the window. Milky sunlight bathed her face, flickering with shadow as we passed a silo, a copse of pines; her expression was impenetrable, a china mask.

I felt painfully conspicuous, my body possessed by the old rules even though my brain knew they no longer applied. As we pulled into Union Station, I wished that there could be a perpetual journey instead of the terrible business of arriving, of getting up, of walking exposed into the next public place.

The train groaned to a stop. We gathered our things and climbed down to the platform (how many times had Josie taken a porter's hand and smiled as we swished down the steps, right then left, the synchronization second nature?). Mama made arrangements for the delivery of our trunks. We ate sandwiches, hastily, at a stand, and after a strained conversation about the expense, we piled into a cab, in which we were silent all the way to Mrs. Broom's, our unvoiced irritation filling the air like a stench.

Vera Broom was Mama's oldest friend, the only friend she and Daddy had held on to from New York, the only person outside the family who had been allowed to know the secret of the harness. I could find her in my earliest fragments of memory: Miss Vance back then, in our apartment in New York, standing on a stepladder to hang a curtain; Miss Vance, wiping Josie's face with a rag; Miss Vance and Mama, passing a turkey leg back and forth, laughing between bites. A few years back, she'd married a Chicagoan, the president of a factory that manufactured galoshes, and we'd started seeing her whenever we passed through the city. Once she picked us up in a large chauffeured car and took us for tea. Another time, she came back to our room where she poured Josie and me a glass of champagne to share and asked us questions that shocked me into silence: Did we think she'd been a fool to marry for money? Had our monthlies started and were they giving us much trouble?

The last time we saw her, Mrs. Broom had been in a sorry

condition—weeping over whiskey while Mama held her hand and Daddy paced, muttering about what he'd do if he ever saw the guy. Eavesdropping diligently from our bed, Josie and I had managed to cobble together some understanding of the crisis: Mr. Broom had been indicted for embezzlement—a word we didn't know, and that night, under the covers, we speculated that it must be very serious, that maybe it had something to do with bootlegging. First chance I had, I looked it up in a dictionary, and I didn't have the heart to tell Josie what I'd found. She made the mistake of asking Mama, who slapped her and told her to mind her own business.

The taxi delivered us to a sooty brick house with worn limestone trim. A broad bay window ran up all three stories; in the first-floor window, a sign advertised furnished rooms. The house was packed closely with its neighbors: to the left, another house with a sagging porch and boarded windows, and to the right, a leaning clapboard cigar shop. In a former, more refined iteration of the neighborhood, this had been Mr. Broom's boyhood home. When his financial affairs were settled, it had been the only asset remaining in his wife's possession. Against his objections, pencil-scrawled on prison stationery, Mrs. Broom would tell me later, she had converted it into a boardinghouse.

We were climbing a steep flight of stairs up to the narrow porch when Mrs. Broom burst through the door. She wore a blue silk kimono and a white turban pinned with a jeweled brooch. Mama and Daddy hurried up the last couple of steps. Mrs. Broom pulled Mama close and at the same time leaned over and kissed Daddy, right on the mouth. She was taller than he was, even in her slippers (pale blue, with clusters of feathers on the toes). She stepped back and fanned her eyes.

"Oh, Vera, you sentimental old bat!" she said.

I stayed behind Mama and Daddy, struck dumb by shyness, until Mrs. Broom took my hand and pulled me forward. She leaned down so her face was inches from mine. Her body emanated a soft warmth, and her scent surrounded me—lilies and silk, and beneath that, faintly, not unpleasantly, housekeeping smells: onions, bleach. I saw that her kimono had a patch on the shoulder, that it was faded in spots. On a belt around her waist, she wore a heavy ring of keys. She took my chin between her thumb and finger. Her brows tipped together as she examined me, as if she were trying to extract from my face the full story of Peoria and its aftermath. Her eyes were wide and bright, her mouth full, chin sharp. Finally, she stamped a kiss onto each of my cheeks and straightened, rubbing her arms together so their sheaths of bangles softly clicked.

"Well," she said. "Let's not stand out here until we freeze to death."

We followed her through the vestibule and into a parlor, where a man sitting on a horsehair sofa gave us a nod, then turned back to his paper. There was a spinet piano in front of the bay window, a potted ivy hanging above it. (It was only later that I'd notice the watery discolorations in the wallpaper's pattern of peacocks and ferns, the patches of carpet worn to strings, the cigarette burns stippling the arms of the powder blue chairs.) At a desk near the staircase, Mrs. Broom listed us on the guest register under a false name—for our protection, she said.

She led us upstairs. The second-floor hallway smelled of paint and new wood; the doors were hung with brass numbers. There was a paper notice tacked to the bathroom door: ONE HOT BATH A WEEK; STRICTLY ENFORCED.—THE MANAGEMENT.

"Don't mind that," Mrs. Broom said, taking my arm and leaning down confidentially. "You'll have your own."

It hadn't occurred to me that we might not. We climbed to the top of the attic stairs. When, after several tries, Mrs. Broom produced the correct key, she had to duck to fit her turban under the door. We followed her into a long, narrow, low-ceilinged room with walls of pale yellow plaster. The floor was painted gray and shingled with faded rugs. There was one small window facing the backyard. Mrs. Broom fluttered about, switching on lamps, gathering up an abandoned coffee cup, scattered hairpins, a pile of crumpled stockings—evidence of the three schoolteachers she'd evicted when Mama telephoned, lovely girls, she said defensively, very respect-

able, she was sure they'd find another place easily enough. One corner of the main room had been fitted into a kitchen: there was a
cupboard, a table, a white porcelain sink, and a gas burner, the sheet
of newspaper tacked to the wall behind it spackled with the evicted
schoolteachers' grease. The apartment smelled of ammonia and
mingling varieties of perfume.

A thin green curtain separated the main room from an alcove at
the front of the house, where I was to sleep. The alcove walls were
covered with cheerful wallpaper, pale brown with yellow flowers;
soft light poured in through the three panels of the bay window.
There was a painted chest of drawers with a mirror, a narrow frame
bed, and, between them, a pink and green rag rug.

I left my valise in the alcove, and Mrs. Broom showed us the rest
of the apartment's features and quirks: a bathroom skylight that
could be opened with a hook mounted to the end of a pole, a splintering floorboard that should never be stepped on, the wardrobe
door with the broken hinge that had to be opened with care. She
showed us how to work the bed in the main room, which folded
down from a cabinet in the wall. When she'd finished, she turned to
Mama.

"You'll come down as soon as you can and tell me absolutely everything? You promise?"

"I promise," Mama said. Something passed between the two of
them, a silent exchange of memory and affection. Mrs. Broom
turned to Daddy.

"And Leonard. I expect you to behave yourself."

"Don't I always?" he said.

Mrs. Broom laughed and patted his cheek.

As the door shut behind her, I felt a swift sadness, like a sudden
loss of breath. Mama sent me into the alcove to unpack. On the
other side of the curtain, she and Daddy started discussing which of
our things we could pawn to get through the week. I pulled Josie's
diary from the false bottom of my valise, and, leaning against the
bed on the floor, thumbed through the familiar entries. Something
tightened in my chest: already, the record the diary offered of my

sister's life was out of date. I knew her less well than I had two days earlier. Josie had run off with a man. Had she gone to bed with him? Once she'd wondered out loud what it would be like to go to bed with Roger Fey and I'd thrown a potato chip at her, told her, laughing, to stop, that she was being disgusting. We'd been thirteen then; in the months that followed, as my mind had filled with my own speculations and curiosities—who did what to whom, exactly, and could it really be as awful or as splendid as the women we eavesdropped on at parties made it sound?—I had regretted having so forcefully refused that conversation. Now maybe she had gone to bed with Frank Dunn, and even if she did come home, that fact would separate the two of us, utterly.

Embarrassed by my own thinking, I hid the diary under my pillow and set to work emptying my valise. My pajamas, underwear, and socks I folded neatly and put away on my side of the chest of drawers—the side that would have been mine in the harness. Those were all the clothes I had meant for one. On the bed, I made a pile of clothes Josie and I had worn together, which Daddy was to alter for me to wear alone. Eventually, he went out with a first batch of things to pawn, and there was only the sound of Mama's movement through the apartment, a constant flurry, as if she didn't dare stop and rest, until she appeared at the alcove curtain and told me she had better see to that visit she owed Vera. The door clicked shut behind her, and just like that, I was alone. The silence in the apartment made me horribly conscious of my heartbeat, of the patter of my own eyelashes, of the rush of breath, in and out my nose. I lay at the foot of my bed and napped fitfully. When I heard Mama return, I rushed to the curtain but there I stopped: her eyes were pink, her face puffy. I'd never known my mother to cry.

Daddy got home just in time for supper. We ate at the long table in the dining room with the boarders, five of them, three men and two women. Mama insisted I sit at her side. She rebuffed all the boarders' attempts at conversation with a cold smile, as if they were somehow a more disreputable lot than the company we'd kept in vaudeville. Daddy made a few overtures, but talk around the table remained formal and strained. Minnie, an Irish girl who came every day to help Mrs. Broom with the housework, did most of the serving. Mama whispered that I should pay attention, that starting the next day I'd be helping too.

After dinner, I went down to the cellar, where our trunks had been stashed, and retrieved my little pile of books, the five-at-a-time Mama had allowed me to keep on the road. As I trudged back up to the attic, I wondered if maybe Mrs. Broom had an old shelf somewhere that I might use. It would be nice, to look at my little collection, properly displayed, in some reasonable order.

In the alcove, as I stacked my books on my dresser, my hand stopped on the copy of *Black Beauty* I had stolen from my cousin Ruth. I carried it to bed and flipped through the pages. I'd forgotten Aunt Marion's inscription: "For darling Ruth, my brilliant bookworm. Love, Mommy." I tapped my hand against her lacy handwriting, feeling a belated spasm of pity for Ruth. Where was she now? I calculated that she must be nineteen years old. Maybe she was off at college, or maybe she was married, or maybe she was a missionary in the Congo.

For the first time since Mama announced the plan to appeal to Uncle Eugene, I thought to wonder what made her confident he would help us. I closed my eyes and pictured him as he had been in Toledo: broad shouldered, sitting so erect at the supper table. I remembered the change in his expression that last day, when Mama told him our plans: a flash of rage, all the more frightening for how ably he controlled it. At nine, I hadn't wondered too deeply why we hadn't heard about Mama's relations before that summer. Now, at nearly sixteen, I wanted to know. What had happened between Mama and her sister's family? Had it just been their disapproval of the Siamese Sweets? Had it been Daddy? Or had the rift come sooner? Had it happened during the unspoken period, when she fled Ohio and went to New York? Had it been the reason she'd gone?

"Knock knock."

Mama, in her bathrobe and nightgown, came in through the alcove curtain and sat stiffly at the edge of my bed near my feet. I could smell her cold cream and the special soap, flecked with real rose petals, that she carried in a net bag, and which Josie and I were forbidden to use. Her mouth grew taut, as if she were struggling to draw words to the surface.

"It wasn't fair of me," she said at last. "To put you on the stage. You weren't cut out for it. It was your father's dream. I should have stopped it, given you a more typical childhood. But I let him persuade me. And you know how Josie took to it."

The room seemed to dissolve out from under me. Until she'd said the last part, I hadn't realized that her "you" had been singular. Not the collective "you," the standard "you" that had always meant Josie and me both, but a "you" that meant me alone. I breathed sharply through my nose, determined not to cry. Mama patted my ankle and glanced up at the ceiling. Daddy had climbed out through the skylight, and we could hear the creak of his footsteps on the roof. "Your father isn't a practical man. You understand that, right, Harriet? And your uncle Eugene—well, he's become someone quite powerful. A leader. You know he never cared for your father. And the last time we saw him—he and I didn't part on the best of terms."

"I remember," I made myself say, though I was still caught on those words—not cut out for the stage. She smiled grimly, as if she had been hoping I didn't.

"Eugene Creggs has always had a penchant for rescuing damsels in distress. He fancies himself some sort of white knight." She stood and went to look out the window. "He'll like you, Harriet. He always did like you. You're the sort of girl he approves of. Sweet. Cooperative. I need you to show him that. Can you do that?"

"I think so."

"You need to know so," she said, sharply, turning back toward me. "I'm counting on you. Your father isn't ready to admit this yet, but we don't have a future without Eugene's help. And you are the one who can make him want to give us that help. And if you do your job, he'll keep on helping you, lift you right up into a fine class of people, a life where you don't have to worry about things. Do you understand what I'm saying?"

I nodded, though I was struggling to make my mind form any thought, to know for certain that I understood anything.

"Good girl, Harriet," Mama said. And then it was as if I had exhausted her—my presence, my situation, the possibility that I would need something more from her. With a swish of fabric—nightgown, curtain—she was gone. I heard the groan of the hinge as she pulled her bed down from its cabinet. For a little while her lamp glowed, a bright bead against the alcove curtain. And then it went dark.

The alcove was still awash in soft light from a streetlamp, a low-slung moon, and the neon sign that shone in the window of a music hall that operated out of an old house across the street. I looked up at the ceiling and traced the shapes in the cracks. Mama had said it without qualification, without making the case, as if it were simply the obvious premise of our lives, something everyone had understood all along: I hadn't been cut out for the stage.

It wasn't as if I had considered myself Josie's equal. Ever since Kalamazoo, when Josie picked up that wooden pear, I had understood that hers was a special talent. But for nearly eleven years our life on the stage had been not just what I'd done but who I was. Eleven years, practically the entirety of what I could remember. When Josie cut herself out of the harness, when she left me alone, she inexorably altered my future. But now it was as if Mama had altered the past as well, erased everything I had always understood to be true about myself. And as casually as she might have suggested I comb my hair.

After what felt like hours, I heard the clatter of Daddy coming back down through the skylight. I crawled out of bed and crouched against the hard, cool floorboards to spy around the edge of the curtain. When he came out of the bathroom, Mama didn't turn on a light, but she rose from bed and started toward him, without her cane, her steps faltering, her nightgown appearing blue in the dim light. I felt as if a thread in my chest had been drawn taut and might snap. But when she reached him, she simply stood for a moment, the two of them arrested in each other's gazes. And then she collapsed against him, pressing her cheek against his chest. He whispered and stroked her hair.

It was worse, somehow, than another argument would have been, their paired-ness a reminder that I was no longer paired. I climbed back into bed, horribly conscious of the empty space beside me, of the fact that save for the stack of books on the dresser, the room looked no different than it had when we'd arrived that morning. Without Josie, I was meager. I exerted no force.

I cast my mind through the contents of the big trunks in the cellar—a velvet opera cloak for two, a rabbit's fur muff for two, tap shoes, greasepaint—but it was the stuff of a life that Josie had ended, a life Mama had now declared a mistake. All of it junk now, mere junk, because of a choice Josie had made in which I'd had no say. I closed my eyes. Exhaustion and grief were the same weight. I let it roll over me, press me into the lumpy, dust-smelling mattress, as I waited for the relief of sleep.

THAT SUNDAY MORNING, MAMA AND DADDY AND I WALKED half a mile to the Institute under a bright sky. Clumps of melting snow slipped off branches and the tops of automobiles; cold streams trickled across the sidewalks. The air smelled of thawing earth. By the time we turned onto Chicago Avenue, Mrs. Broom's old mink was heating me up like a furnace. Beneath it, I wore an old gray dress of Mama's that, even belted, hung around me like a sack. Daddy had started altering one of Josie's and my dresses but hadn't finished; it had pained him, he'd told Mama, to undo his own hand-iwork.

Since our arrival on Monday, he'd left every morning before I'd even had my breakfast—to look for work, he said, though when he came home in the evening, Mama never asked if he had made any progress, and he volunteered no report. Every night, he'd ended up on the roof with his sketchbook and bottle. Mama had spent her days digging through our drawers and trunks, finding things to pawn: her furs went first, then Daddy's watch and emerald tie pin. She wrote letters to Mr. Mayfield and various creditors. I knew I was in her way, that she wanted me out of the apartment, and I obliged, though it felt wrong to go out by myself. Her suspicion had made me shy of boarders. If there weren't any in the parlor I might sit there and play solitaire, or fiddle around on the piano. If there were, I would go to the kitchen to see if Minnie or Mrs. Broom would talk to me, or give me something to do. But inevitably, I would find myself underfoot in the kitchen too, and when it couldn't be avoided any longer, I would put on Mrs. Broom's old fur coat and go outside. At first, it had been difficult even to walk down the porch steps. I gave myself assignments: walk a block, walk another, nod hello to the newspaper agent. Wherever I went I thought I saw Josie—looking out through the window of a passing cab, staring down at me from a fire escape.

After a couple of days, wandering came a little easier. To the south I found block after block of rooming houses. To the west was the slum, where Mrs. Broom had warned me not to go, but I went anyway, right to the edge of it, as if I could lure Josie home by imitating her recklessness. North of Mrs. Broom's house I discovered mansions behind wrought iron, hotels with doormen who looked at me coldly, cars idling outside of galleries and shops, awaiting fur-wrapped ladies trailed by clerks carrying stacks of parcels. On Friday morning, I hiked over to Lincoln Park, where I stood on a stone wall beside the lake and threw things—rocks, bottles, a stained negligée I'd retrieved from a bush with a stick—into the dark, ragged water.

But I had no spending money, and unlike the men and women who pressed against the wind, who trod decisively through slush, confident in their galoshes, determined to get to wherever they were headed, I had no place in particular to go. After a couple of hours in the cold, my feet would go numb, frozen tears would score my cheeks, the tip of my nose would smart where I'd blotted it repeatedly with my mitten. When I couldn't bear it any longer, I retreated to the boardinghouse, where Mrs. Broom might give me cocoa, and Minnie would let me taste whatever she was cooking for dinner. By afternoon there was usually some task I could perform for Minnie, and otherwise it was back to the solitaire or a book, or maybe to sitting very quietly in the corner of the parlor while some boarders listened to the radio, until it was time to set the table.

Each day of our first week in Chicago had passed slowly, as if time had dilated to contain both new experiences and the lack of responsibility and, more than anything, Josie's absence, a thing impossibly vast. But Sunday morning had still seemed to arrive in a rush. As we walked up to the Institute, a five-story building that filled the middle third of the block, I felt as if I hadn't yet had a chance to catch my breath, as if the nerves I felt were continuous with the nerves I'd felt before we took the stage in Peoria.

The building's east and west wings flanked a small courtyard, a patchwork of mud and melting snow. Two tall antennae stood on the roof, wires threaded between them. A banner hung from the west wing: RADIO WIBS, A MISSION IN THE AIR. A sign directed us around the corner to the chapel, which was housed in a separate building, a red brick box that would have looked more like an office than a church if it weren't for the cross towering over the flat roof. We joined the crowd filing into a deep, windowless sanctuary and claimed an empty pew near the back.

In some ways, a church wasn't so different from a theater—an audience, gathered into rows, a stage set for what was to follow—though a solemn hush took the place of the anticipatory chatter. A microphone the size of a plate was mounted on the pulpit, and additional, smaller microphones dangled from the rafters. Purple curtains covered the walls; the floor was thickly carpeted. On the back of the pew in front of ours, hymnals and prayer books filled a rack mounted beside a placard: YOUR VOICE MAY REACH LIVING ROOMS ACROSS AMERICA; BE ALERT, LISTEN WELL, AND SING PRAYERFULLY, FOR SOULS ARE ON THE LINE. Mama selected a prayer book and read it, or at least pointed her face at it and made her expression contemplative. Daddy watched the men in robes who milled about the front of the room. I was too anxious to ask Daddy whether he had spotted Uncle Eugene. I wondered if Ruth was in the chapel, if she would try to talk to us before the service, and what we do then, when the plan was to speak to Uncle Eugene after. I had heard Mama and Daddy discuss Uncle Eugene exactly once since our arrival in Chicago. Mama had said: "You'll let me do the talking." And Daddy had said, "You're the one who knows the man," then climbed up to the roof. And though their exchange had taken the form of agreement, my stomach had clenched as if it were a fight.

A bell sounded, and at the front of the sanctuary, a sign lit up: READY, it said. The hush deepened into a pin-drop silence. The READY sign went off and a sign that read ON-AIR came on. As the organ blared, a black-robed figure stood and walked toward the front. With a shiver, I recognized Uncle Eugene's broad back, his shock of white hair. As he stepped into place behind the pulpit, I wished I were close enough to properly see his face. I thought, maybe, I could see how he looked older—his forehead higher, his chin a looser pouch. But the brightness of his smile dazzled all the way to the back of the room.

"Good morning, Christian soldiers, from the Institute for Bible Study, broadcasting straight to your home from Chicago, Illinois, on WIBS, a mission in the air." He enunciated crisply; his voice through the speaker was slightly tinny, collared in static, a fraction of a second divorced from the movement of his mouth. "WIBS transmits by authority of the Federal Radio Commission on a frequency of ten hundred eighty kilocycles. I am Reverend Eugene Creggs, and this is your Sunday service."

A few minutes later, on some cue Mama and Daddy and I had missed, the congregation was on its feet, hymnals open. It was like that throughout the service—we tried to stand when the others stood, kneel when they knelt, but it was like playing from a script we'd never seen before. The service moved swiftly, the organ filling any gap in speech. A man came up from the front pew and read from the Bible. Another, this one with gold-rimmed spectacles and thin pale hair that blurred into his face, offered a report on the mission to evangelize the Jews of Chicago. "A message for Mrs. Sparrow of Wheaton, Illinois," he said. "We have received your generous gift of $5. Reverend P. J. Purvis has asked me to convey his personal gratitude. And to all our friends in the chapel this morning and listening at home, remember to think of how many more Jews might make it to Heaven because of your generosity!"

I glanced at Daddy; the muscle at his jaw knotted slightly.

Uncle Eugene watched the proceedings with a kind of benevo-
lent patience, as if he knew he was the main event and that meant he
was in no hurry—every other man could have his chance to shine.
At last, he took the pulpit.

"O come, let us worship and bow down," he said, and offered a
prayer. He took a long moment to put on his spectacles and this
time the organ did not play, as if only Reverend Eugene Creggs had
the power to hold the radio audience's interest through such a silence. He looked at his notes and then he looked back over the
house—the congregation. Before he spoke he offered a small, wry
smile, as if to signal to all of us on this side of the radio signal that
we were no less part of the program than he was, though of course
that wasn't true, and that was part of the gift of the smile—that in
order to assure us of our importance he was humbling himself.

He began with a story about four brothers he had ministered to
at juvenile hall. They were good boys, deep down, he said, whose
father was dead and whose mother had to leave them to work. By
the end of their conversation, all four of them had accepted the
friendship of Jesus. The youngest asked Uncle Eugene to find their
mother. To tell her what he'd told them.

"My friends, there is not a single influence in a formation of a
child's character more crucial than Mother," he said. "Mother in-
stills in boys and girls the values we hold dear, Mother attends to
them with that infinite gentleness, that love that 'suffereth long and
is kind,' that love that 'seeketh not her own,' that 'never faileth.'
Father is the captain of the home, but Mother is the compass that
keeps the ship true north. But would you believe me if I told you
that I found the mother of those four boys in a saloon, mug of beer
in hand? And that when I counted up the occupants of that establishment, eleven of the seventeen were women?"

As he continued on the theme of Mother's special moral sensitivity, I listened, but only vaguely, the way I listened to a familiar act
from the wings as I waited to perform my own. My mind was fixed

on the afterward, on the possibility that Ruth was among us, on the question of how Josie was spending her Sunday morning. She wouldn't guess in a million years how I was spending mine.

"And now I'd like to lay a special message on the hearts of our girls, our future mothers."

I sat up in my seat. My heart was pounding, as if he'd caught me not paying attention.

"Friends, our girls are in trouble. Reverend, you might say, our modern society places a great many pressures on our young people. Yes, Mother and Father managed under the keen eye of the chaperone, but what harm is there if a girl takes a quick ride in an automobile? Of course Grandmother knew her beauty required no enhancement save soap and water, but what harm in a bit of paint? And what harm, save perhaps an epidemic of frostbite among female patients aged sixteen and twenty-five, of the apparent national fabric shortage afflicting hems from coast to coast?"

Soft laughter rustled through the pews. Uncle Eugene absorbed it with pleasure. I recognized the pleasure, I knew it exactly, having felt it from the stage. And then he made his face serious; he leaned slightly forward, gripping the sides of the pulpit, and continued in a hushed, grave voice. "Friends, the slope is slippery, and greased by Lucifer himself. Our girls cannot prepare to be mothers, to guide their families toward what we know to be true, if their character has been debauched through sin."

Sin. The word landed in my heart with a startling force, plucked at the thing in me that had always relished instructions and rules. As Uncle Eugene went on, his forehead grew slick and gleamed under the electric lights. But his voice remained measured, and his pale eyes were less excoriating than pained, as if he personally paid the price for female sin with his own broken heart.

"Paul asked the Galatians, 'Who hath bewitched you, that ye should not obey the truth?' I see that question echoed every day in the letters I receive from Christian mothers across this nation. Who hath bewitched my little girl?

"Mothers of America, this is what we know: The spell is a simple one, and Satan has many helpers who are glad to cast it. There's the so-called friend who offers a girl a cigarette or a drink. The vice-peddlers in Hollywood, who tempt our girls away from their studies, their duties at home, and fill their minds with vile thoughts.

"But daughters, the choice is yours. A Wise Daughter makes friends with other Christians, who support her pursuit of an upright life. A Foolish Daughter makes friends with loose thinkers, with girls who are sloppy, idle, and vain, and endangers her own character by keeping company in which she might be enticed to sin. A Wise Daughter honors her parents, trusts her mother with her confidences, obeys her father. A Foolish Daughter substitutes her judgment for theirs. A Wise Daughter keeps her mind clean with right-thinking books and poetry and music of the highest quality; a Foolish Daughter pursues what is popular and tawdry, allowing her mind to be cultivated for the flourishing of sinful ideas."

By then an energy was coursing the chapel, like the energy of an audience at the height of a vaudeville spectacle—the seventeen synchronized somersaults, the hoop on fire, the swell to fortissimo. Uncle Eugene's voice rose and trembled. Here was the grand finale.

"Daughters, if sinners entice thee, consent thou not! If you have been enticed, if you have woken from the spell long enough to see it, remember this: Our Lord and Savior Jesus Christ forgives as fiercely as he condemns. He loves the sinner as well as He hates the sin. Consent to His enticement, little sisters. Consent to Christ, and be a Wise Daughter, that someday you might mother well!"

The energy in the chapel wanted to be applause, but Uncle Eugene said, "Pray with me, friends," and we bowed our heads. His voice in prayer returned me to Toledo, to the revival: I saw the crowds waiting for the preaching to begin, I smelled the roasted corn, I felt my terrible longing for a souvenir wooden nickel. I saw people filing up the aisles to get saved, while Josie and I sang endless choruses of "Safe in the Arms of Jesus." I felt Uncle Eugene's thumb marking a cross on my own forehead, felt Josie with me in the harness, felt his hand on her head, felt the heat of the sun on our faces, saw its pink glow on the backs of our eyelids.

When I'd tried to pray in Toledo, I'd felt as if I were talking to myself. But in the Institute Chapel that Sunday, Uncle Eugene's prayer seemed to move through me like a living substance. He concluded with a booming amen, and the organ shuddered in response. Once more, Mama and Daddy and I flipped frantically through the hymnal, a step behind the rest of the congregation, but then we found the page, we sang too, and if at the beginning of the service our singing had been wrong—showy—now Mama and I sang in the right sort of voice, sober and inconspicuous, and though Daddy did not sing, he stood with his hands folded respectfully in front of him. I felt riveted, as if Uncle Eugene had won the attention not just of my brain but of all of my senses, all of my cells.

The ON-AIR sign went dark. Chatter kicked up over the lingering strains of the organ. A line was forming at the front of the chapel, and at the end of it, Uncle Eugene received his congregants. We hung back until the room had nearly cleared.

He didn't seem surprised to see us approach, nor did he move in our direction. He remained in position in front of the pulpit, waiting to receive us.

"Maude Szász." His smile was stiff, unchanging, as if he'd drawn it on with ink. I took a nervous breath. In a matter of seconds he might turn us away. Before I'd even had a chance to fulfill the task Mama had charged me with, to make him want to help, he could refuse. "And family. I wondered if I might be hearing from you."

"You've learned, then, about our troubles." Mama's voice bounced along lightly, cordially, but in their back-and-forth was a quality I remembered from Toledo—the feeling they might be speaking in code.

"I read something, in one paper or another." He turned to the other robed men, asked them to excuse him, and then ushered us past a group of bustling women who were removing the flowers that had decorated the altar, out the back of the chapel and through a covered walkway to the U-shaped building we'd passed earlier. A hallway was lined with oil portraits of the Institute leaders: ministers, missionaries, trustees, each name and position inscribed on a

brass plaque tacked to the frame. Uncle Eugene smiled humbly at
his own portrait: REVEREND EUGENE P. CREGGS, DIRECTOR OF
RADIO MINISTRY. He didn't speak except to identify features of the
building: meeting rooms and classrooms, the radio studios, the library, the hallway outside of which was painted with a mural of Jesus
on a rocky seashore, lifting a hand toward two fellows in a boat.
Above the painting, cursive script read, FOLLOW ME, AND I WILL
MAKE YOU FISHERS OF MEN. I pictured a sewing needle threaded
with fishing line, Uncle Eugene driving it through a row of identical
men in brown suits and brown hats and brown mustaches, stringing
them like popcorn.

In his office on the fifth floor, he gestured at the two leather
chairs facing the large desk—a slab of dark wood, topped with a
blotter, a pen, a lamp with a green shade, and a cut-glass bowl full of
lemon drops. Daddy took one of the chairs, his limbs seeming to
jangle within the cavity of his suit, and Mama took the other, sitting
very upright, her hands resting, one on top of the other, on her lap.
I stood between them, trying to project modesty, good sense, a cooperative spirit. Uncle Eugene removed his robe unhurriedly and
hung it on a rack in the corner. He put on his suit jacket and took his
place behind the desk.

"Candy?" he said to me, gesturing at the bowl. In the past, when
a producer or a director or a booking agent had asked us a question,
Josie had always been the one to answer. Now I had to force myself
to speak.

"No thank you, sir."

He folded his hands and tapped his fingertips against the tip of
his nose and shut his eyes. We were silent—without saying a word,
he had commanded our silence.

"We spoke about you often, my beloved wife and I," he said finally, his voice soft and faraway. "Poor Maude, she would say, poor
Maude and the peculiar life she's chosen for her girls. I can still see
the"—he waved his fingers like a child miming rain—"flutter of confusion that would pass over her face as we talked it through. She was
a purely feminine creature, my wife." My skin felt tight. Aunt Mar-

ion had been one way—feminine—which implied, somehow, that Mama was another. Which meant unfeminine. And her life—our life—was peculiar, which was a way of saying bad.

The righteous clarity that had come from hearing him speak of sin grew muddled. Don't frown, I commanded myself. He went on with a clipped assurance.

"It brought me no joy, Mrs. Szász, to learn of your predicament. But I fell to my knees and prayed. And while I believe there's a lesson here, a reminder that we sow as we reap, I hear my gentle wife in my ear. And I know this is the Lord's way of calling me toward mercy rather than reproach."

Daddy sprang up and leaned over the desk.

"Mercy," he said. "That's the ticket, Reverend Creggs. Why, if I'm not mistaken it was a theme you took up back in Toledo, the last time we had the privilege to hear you preach. And I have thought often of that whistle-stop tour you proposed then, after the girls were so instrumental in your work. I've regretted that we chose to pursue another opportunity. Maude has. But look at the opportunity before us, Harriet right here with the voice of a nightingale and—"

Daddy's suggestion could hardly gain purchase in my mind, so alarming was his misbehavior, his deviation from plan. Mama had stood and placed a hand on his shoulder. He shook her off, eyes narrowing with determination, but then Uncle Eugene stood and gave Daddy a cold, firm look. That ended it. As Daddy sank back into his seat I was relieved but also pained by what I'd witnessed: my father scolded by my mother, put in his place by my uncle, now drained of hope.

Uncle Eugene came around to the front of his desk, leaned where Daddy had stood, and folded his hands in his lap. He shut his eyes again, and when he opened them, he went on in a soft, friendly voice, as if Daddy hadn't spoken at all.

A member of his congregation owned a furniture factory, he said. He was quite certain he would give Daddy a job there, operating a machine, if Uncle Eugene asked. He could arrange a position for

Mama too, in the Institute mailroom, where she would help to sort the thousands of letters that came in each month from congregants and listeners all across the country. He suspected I was not yet enrolled in school—was that correct? Mama nodded. His secretary would make arrangements as soon as possible.

"Would you like that, Harriet? To attend school with other boys and girls?"

"Yes, sir." As soon as I said the words, I found they'd given form to a longing that seemed to stretch back to my earliest childhood. "I'd like it very much."

"Mr. and Mrs. Szász?" he said.

"You've been very generous," Mama said. I wondered what she would have done if he hadn't offered to help. What our plan would have been then.

"And we shan't mention Harriet's troubled past in this building. There are impressionable young ladies in our congregation, Maude. You understand."

"Of course," she said, shaking her head vigorously, disavowing the whole act, the whole of show business, as if it had been something she'd been dragged into against her better judgment.

"Now, Len, what do you say?" Uncle Eugene went on, his manner now avuncular, generous. "Would you like a tour of the station?"

"I'm sure we'd all enjoy that," said Mama.

This time I understood the gap between the spoken words and the impulse behind them: Uncle Eugene was showing Daddy what he couldn't have, what we were never to ask for again. I wasn't sure if I regretted or welcomed this fact. That Daddy thought I should continue performing alone had come as a shock, especially after Mama's speech in the alcove. I wondered if that was what they'd fought about in Peoria.

But it didn't matter: the plan was the plan, my responsibility plain. Mama had said I was the type of girl Uncle Eugene approved of, and now his sermon had made concrete what type of girl that was. I was to be a Wise Daughter, which meant the tour of the radio station was purely academic. I paid attention with what I hoped was appropriate, polite, Wise Daughterly interest. Uncle Eugene opened up a cupboard and showed us all the objects they used to make sound effects on the dramatic programs: a panel of doorbells, a washboard and stick, a sack of seeds. He named every state-of-the-art piece of equipment and told us its price, which he had memorized down to the cent. Mama laughed obligingly at his jokes.

Daddy trailed along without speaking. When we left the Institute, he took off in the direction opposite home. It was only as Mama and I walked back together, in a silence I knew better than to disrupt, that I thought of Ruth. Uncle Eugene's sermon had been full of daughters; but in all the time we'd been with him, no one had so much as spoken her name.

BY THE TIME DADDY got home, I was in bed. I went to the alcove curtain when I heard him, heavy-footed but not stumbling. His cheeks were red, but his speech was clear enough as he began to rail. Mama rested her fingers lightly on the back of the couch. She was already in her nightgown, hair braided. She watched him, unmoved, as he paced, waving his arms as if trying to land a blow on some invisible enemy.

"Now you expect me to submit to this charlatan, this so-called man of God, as he tries to humiliate me and trap my family? My wife? I won't do it, Maude."

"You will."

In the face of her calm, he only grew more agitated.

"She has a right to decide for herself."

"I'm not going to carry you this time, Lenny."

He swept across the room; my breath caught when he reached her, but he kept going, into the bathroom. The skylight creaked open.

"You have your sulk, Lenny," Mama said, her voice rising, as it so rarely did, toward a shout. "But you'd better not fall off. You'd better not make me a widow, or I'll call up that old girlfriend and have you séanced straight back to Chicago."

"Nice talk, you'll have to wash the showgirl out of your mouth if you want to hold on to that man."

"If you'd ever bothered to provide for your family I wouldn't even have to, would I?"

"Go to Hell."

"You go to Hell."

She pulled down her bed and turned out the lights. I waited for sleep, which wouldn't come. From the roof, I heard a long, low creak followed by a few shuffling steps; I pictured Daddy tripping, tumbling off and down into the bushes.

These hours later, I could admit to myself that part of me had thrilled to Daddy's proposal in Uncle Eugene's office. Part of me wanted to know how it would feel to perform by myself on a stage. Part of me wondered—if I'd been the one who had run and Josie had been left behind, would Mama have resisted putting her in a solo act? Would she have been charged with becoming a Wise Daughter and keeping the family in Uncle Eugene's good stead?

But that was exactly it, wasn't it? She had run because she was Josie, and I had stayed because I was me. We'd already had our categories. I'd been given my charge, by Mama and then by Uncle Eugene. I understood what was expected of me. What I was capable of.

I needed to pray. If I were really to become a Wise Daughter, prayer seemed part of the equation, however much trouble it had given me in the past.

I tried saying the words of a prayer in my mind, but it was like trying to draw water from a dry well. And then I remembered Josie's diary. My diary, I thought, as I pulled it out from under my pillow, not anticipating the shift before my mind had renamed the still-lovely object. I ran my finger over the soft leather of the cover, traced the silver rose. Wishing she'd left the key behind, I took out a hairpin and expertly jimmied the lock. I tore out every page she'd written on, careful not to leave any ragged edges. I cut a hole in the edge of my mattress, rolled the pages into a scroll, and pushed them inside.

"Dear God," I wrote. And that was a little easier. But as soon as my pencil hit the page I knew I was also writing to Josie, praying—whatever that meant—to Josie. I told God/Josie about Mama and Daddy's fight. I told God/Josie about Daddy's idea that I should perform alone. I told God/Josie that I hoped Daddy would alter a few dresses, or that at least Mama could fix me up something a little less ugly to wear before my first day of school. I confided in God/Josie that I thought maybe I would shine at school. I'd taught myself to read—did He know that? I told God/Josie I hoped Daddy would take the job Uncle Eugene had found him so we could pay our debts. I asked God if He would please make Daddy do it. I told Josie that I missed her. That I thought she should come home.

I was going to write that it was okay, that I understood, but then the word "sin" flashed in my mind and stayed my hand. Sin meant not just that Josie was gone and that I hurt, but that I hurt because Josie had done wrong. Josie had disobeyed, Josie had broken our family, Josie had done God knew what with Frank Dunn. Josie had sinned. We were all paying the price.

It was satisfying to think that way, but in the way dipping a finger over a flame is satisfying—only for a moment before I felt the burn. Still, sin gave me something to decide against, a way to decide to make myself, in contrast to Josie. She had sinned. I would show Uncle Eugene that I was a Wise Daughter. I would become one so I had something to show.

I put the diary back under my pillow, and then, on second thought, widened the hole I had made in my mattress and slipped the whole diary inside. After a week of wakefulness and anxious dreams, I fell at once into a calm, hard sleep.

I couldn't say whether the victory was Mama's or God's, but when I woke the next morning, Daddy had already left for the factory. Not long after, Mama headed out to the Institute, bare-faced, wearing an old hat she'd denuded of a cluster of feathers and net. When she arrived home that evening, she was the dangerous kind of tired in which the slightest provocation could send her into a rage.

She went into the bathroom; I heard the tub start to fill. A moment later, she appeared at the alcove curtain in her robe. In a low voice, eyes closed, as if speaking would cost her what remained of her strength, she told me that the arrangements had been made: in the morning, I would join the tenth grade at Robert A. Waller High.

O UTSIDE, SNOW FELL AT A STEADY CLIP. IN MISS TANGUS'S classroom, the radiator hissed and clanked; my feet sweated in my boots. Miss Tangus strolled to the chalkboard, hands folded at her waist. Her purple scarf had slipped and was trailing along the linoleum, but she didn't seem to notice. I watched intently, pencil poised above tablet.

For a month, I'd been getting lost in Waller's crowded hallways and stumbling into class late and out of breath, every day exposing my ignorance of some basic fact: that you had to dribble a basketball or that humans were mammals or that Spain was part of Europe. I'd watched the other girls as they moved through the hallways in packs and primped together in the girls' lounge. I'd cataloged their gestures and outfits and turns of phrase. But I hadn't managed to make myself noticed or heard, let alone liked. I took my lunches to the library, where I ate adjacent to the other misfits: a freckled sophomore with a brace on her leg, a pasty girl who wore her hair in a heavy black braid and ate Bremner wafers with butter she carried in a little aluminum cup, a boy who spent the hour building mazes out of pencil shavings. I had thought that maybe the library crowd could be my crowd, that I might find among them a Wise Daughter who would not only keep me company but help me to live uprightly. But whenever I tried to speak to one of them, all the language in my brain dissolved.

Several times Miss Cavour, the dean of girls, had called me into her office, a bright white cell with a roll-top desk and, on every surface, dogs: brass paperweights shaped like Great Danes and Irish wolfhounds, water-colored spaniels in frames, a pen stand shaped like a bull terrier, a whittled sheltie, a pair of brightly painted ceramic cocker spaniels. She reminded me that my uncle was a distinguished man. She suggested I join the remedial study clubs. She eyed Mrs. Broom's old fur coat and remarked that the most popular girls didn't make themselves stand out too much. After that, I went to school in shirtsleeves until Mama brought me home a plain gray wool coat from the Institute charity shop. But a new coat did nothing to improve my lot. I failed an algebra quiz, and then another. I stunned my civics teacher when I could not name the capital city of Illinois. I didn't manage to have a single conversation with another student.

Miss Tangus had returned my first theme lashed in purple ink. But in the thicket of misspelled words and split infinitives and subject-verb disagreements, she'd underlined a sentence and written a note in the margin: "An astute observation!" The subject was *Hamlet,* the observation was Dick Figge's, one I'd retained from one of the parties where he'd paid Josie and me to recite. But that encouragement had given me something to grip. That night, I'd stayed up until after midnight with the quilt over my head and my flashlight on, copying the words I'd misspelled, rewriting sentences, making a list in my diary of the rules I'd broken so I wouldn't break them again.

Miss Tangus finished writing on the board: "Hamlet, Act 3, Scene 1."

"We come to the famous soliloquy," she said, turning, dusting chalky handprints onto her skirt. "Scholars, before we journey deeper, let us hear it read aloud. Let us enjoy the poetry of it. Do I have a volunteer?"

Before I could stop myself, I'd thrust my hand into the air.

"Why thank you, Miss Szász," she said. And for an instant I was thrilled to have beaten the girls and boys who aspired in every class to demonstrate they knew first and most and best, and most of all delighted that I'd made Miss Tangus smile.

But as soon as I stood, I became uneasy. Reading a monologue smacked dangerously of vaudeville. For weeks, Mama had been bringing tracts home from the Institute and leaving them on my pillow. She'd borrowed Mrs. Broom's Emily Post, which we traded back and forth. It had been my idea that I should start memorizing a Bible verse and reciting it for Uncle Eugene each week after church. The first time, Mama had tapped my shoulder and I had curtsied, but I saw this displeased my uncle—reminded him of show business. So after that, I recited my verses accurately and humbly, and refused to add anything that might resemble staging. As Miss Tangus blinked at me expectantly, I imagined Uncle Eugene watching from the corner, shaking his head. But being helpful when your teacher asks—surely that fell within the mandate of a Wise Daughter. Maybe that outweighed the danger of using my old skills. And maybe if I read well enough, someone would compliment me afterward. Maybe that could be the first step to making a friend. I swallowed and pressed my knuckles against my sternum. Miss Tangus nodded. With a final, deep breath, I began: "To be, or not to be."

The classroom fell away. I was Hamlet, or, at least, I was Harriet-and-Josephine-Sweet, doing Hamlet at a party. I wasn't reading, I was performing. I thrust my hand—my outside hand—in front of my chest, feeling the weight of the real human skull Dick Figge had insisted on using, which the props man had once let Josie and me hold backstage. As the words tumbled out of me, I felt as I did sometimes on Sunday morning when Uncle Eugene prayed, as if I were channeling a force from outside myself.

"Nymph, in thy orisons be all my sins remembered." I stood with my face tipped toward the ceiling, suspended between the dream of the performance and the classroom, which was returning just as the house used to return in the instant before an ovation.

Only my classmates weren't clapping. Above me the lights buzzed. Outside, snow shook soundlessly from the sky. My chest rose and fell. They were tittering behind their hands, widening their eyes in mock sympathy.

Oh, of course they were. Of course! It was like this every day: the realization of some social error an instant after I made it, never before, never in time to stop it, but inevitably afterward. I wished I were oblivious, like the boy from the library with the pencil shavings. No one bothered him because he was impervious to bothering— content to be exactly who he was. No one had bothered me either, so far, not because I lived comfortably within my own oddness, but because no one had even noticed me. I'd been beneath notice.

I lowered my arms. Miss Tangus clasped her hands. "Brava! Oh, Harriet, how marvelous!" A girl in the next row offered me a little pink smirk that made me think of Tibby Longfellow. I remembered scheming with Josie to punish her, and for the thousandth time, I wished Josie were with me at Waller, that we could scheme together to punish the snickering boys and girls. Though if Josie were here, we probably wouldn't even need to punish them. We wouldn't even be thinking about them. I wouldn't have made such a mistake.

Swaddled in my own embarrassment, I could hardly follow the rest of the lesson. When a page from the front office came in and handed Miss Tangus a note, she had to say my name twice before I answered.

"It's for you, Miss Szász," she said, with a chipper bob of her head. "Miss Cavour wants you after class."

I went, wretched. It was my lunch period, and my stomach felt emptier and rawer for the humiliation of my impassioned performance and the trouble heralded by yet another summons from Miss Cavour.

"Miss Szász." Miss Cavour greeted me with a curt nod. "Give this to your mother."

I felt as if all the dogs' eyes were fixed on me, glowering at me with a disapproval that echoed Miss Cavour's. She held my gaze, as if waiting for some response. When I didn't say anything, she turned back to her work.

"That will do, Miss Szász. You can go."

"Thank you," I mumbled, and rushed out of her office.

In the girls' lounge, I barricaded myself in a stall and opened the envelope, my first crime, but I had to know. Inside I found a pale green card. DEFICIENCY NOTICE, read the header, the particulars of my deficiency filled in by the algebra teacher, Mr. Van Lan.

YOUR CHILD IS DEFICIENT IN Algebra.
HIS/(HER) GRADE IS 32 out of 100.

Mr. Van Lan and Miss Cavour had both signed the card; below their signatures was the awful instruction: PLEASE SIGN AND RE-TURN, followed by a long blank line.

Some girls came in, laughing. Happy girls, girls who knew how to attract the right kind of attention, girls whose educations had prepared them for algebra. They spoke excitedly about a boy who had shown one of the girls his thing in the hallway behind the au-ditorium, which they spelled out, "t-h-i-n-g," every time, which I thought was very stupid—if you weren't going to call it by a dirty word, what was the point of spelling? I watched through a crack in the stall door as a lipstick was passed around, and then a cigarette. Foolish Daughters, I branded them, hating them, will-ing them to go. When they finally left, I hurried to the lunchroom and bought my sandwich and bottle of milk, though the lunch pe-riod was already half over and the thought of eating made my stomach turn.

In the back of the library, I found an empty table below a sign that said SILENCE and a small leaded window through which the winter light seeped in, watery and gray. I rested my deficiency no-tice on my knees and read it over again. In Miss Cavour's office, I'd felt hot and breathless; now a chill spread across my skin. I was fail-ing algebra; Mama would know that I wasn't living up to my respon-sibility, that her faith in my ability had been terribly misplaced. And maybe Uncle Eugene would decide we weren't worth helping. Maybe Mama and Daddy would both lose their jobs and we wouldn't be able to pay our rent. I sniffled, letting tears flow unimpeded down my cheeks.

"What's wrong?"

It was a boy, sitting on the floor beside a low shelf of reference books topped with four globes. He had a volume of the encyclopedia open in his lap and a pen in his hand. He'd been drawing something, but before I could see what he snapped the volume shut and put it back on the shelf. When he stood and came toward me, I saw that his pants were a bit too short. His fawn-colored hair hung in girlish curls around his ears, too-long hair somehow part and parcel with too-short pants. But rather than making him seem improper or unkempt, they made him more interesting, as if he knew something about pants and hair that I was not sophisticated enough to have gleaned. Through round glasses, he fixed on me a steady, curious gaze. Beside one eyebrow he had a small, even scar, a perfect triangle, as if someone had gone in with a penknife and tidily excised the skin.

I'd stopped crying. He was waiting for me to say something. Without quite meaning to, I handed him the deficiency notice.

"Aha. What's her name?"

"Whose name?" I glanced at the librarian's desk on the other side of the room. She continued checking in books from a large stack.

"Your mother's."

"But how can you just—"

"Do you want to tell your mother you're failing?"

"No but I—"

"So don't. What's her name?"

"Maude Szász."

"Spell it?"

I did. He wrote it on the line, in a neat cursive that no one would mistake for mine, and blew to dry the ink.

"Voilà," he said. As he handed the notice back to me, the smell of cigarettes wafted off his sweater.

"Thank you."

"Don't mention it." One corner of his mouth tipped up. "I'm

Garth Mosher." I let him take my hand, which was damp with sweat, and, horribly, because I'd used it to wipe my nose, and which seemed all of a sudden to have twice the number of fingers a hand was supposed to have. His hand was stained with ink.

I knew what the script required. My girlhood may have been direly socially stunted, I may not have managed to befriend any of my classmates, but I'd met people, I'd met plenty of people, and in the last month I'd read all sorts of introductions in Emily Post, though this boy, who had just casually committed forgery on my behalf, seemed unlikely to be moved by the protocols of the Titherington Smiths and the Worldlys. But I couldn't say, "I'm Harriet," I couldn't say, "How do you do?"

Finally, he let go of my hand, and with a shrug and a wink at the SILENCE sign, he started whistling and headed toward the door. The librarian looked up and shot him a fierce look. On his way out, he touched his forehead in salute.

When the librarian had returned to her stack of books, I went to the shelf and pulled out the volume of the encyclopedia he'd had in his lap—WXYZ. I flipped through the pages until I found his drawing. It covered the whole entry on Yugoslavia: a pack of dogs with bug eyes and exclamation points in their pupils and lasciviously dangling tongues, circling Miss Cavour and her counterpart, the dean of boys, Mr. Gow. Miss Cavour and Mr. Gow were stark nude, engaged in an act of coitus.

I slammed the volume shut, hot-cheeked, trembling with exactly the indignation I was meant to feel as a Wise Daughter, a Good Girl, a Follower of Rules and Respecter of Authority. I jammed it forcefully back onto the shelf. But I had to hold my breath. I had to slap my hand over my mouth. And then I had to get up and gather my things and go, and I barely made it to the hallway before I doubled over, laughter spilling through my fingers.

THAT SUNDAY, MAMA PARADED me down the center aisle of the Institute Chapel, just as she did every week, playing the role of good

Christian mother with an enthusiasm I might have mistaken for sincerity if I didn't see the mask fall off as soon as we were out of sight of the Institute, when she reached for a cigarette with a trembling hand, or found an occasion to mutter "damn," as if the word had been stuck in her throat like a seed. We slid into the pew near the front that I had come to think of as ours. I knelt, hands clasped together, and silently prayed my apologies to God. I had been enticed by a charismatic forger, a drawer of filthy cartoons. But only briefly. And I'd woken from the spell. After the service, we waited to greet Uncle Eugene, who asked after Daddy, as he always did. Daddy reported dutifully to the factory but had drawn the line at church. If he was awake on a Sunday morning, he'd watch us go with wounded eyes.

"I'm praying hard, Gene," Mama said. I felt heat in my cheeks and hoped Uncle Eugene didn't notice. "I have reason to hope he will join us soon."

Of course, it wasn't true—she didn't pray, as far as I knew, and Daddy came home late and spent his evenings on the roof with his sketchbook and his whiskey. The dresses he was to alter for me still sat in a pile, untouched. Every now and then he got home very late and very drunk, and in the morning Mama would have to pour a glass of water on his face to wake him for work. That night he would bring her a peace offering—a paper bag full of rock sugar candy or doughnuts, a scrap of cheap jewelry. She would remind him that I needed schoolbooks, that there was rent to pay, and then she would slam around at the sink before escaping into the bath. I'd put on the jewelry myself, trying to make Daddy smile. I'd knock on the bathroom door and offer Mama a cup of tea knowing full well that she wouldn't answer, that there was nothing to do but wait. Their fights had become like a fog that spread to fill the space between the three of us. I couldn't make it clear.

"And Harriet," said Uncle Eugene, turning to me. "How is everything at school?"

"Oh, I had the nicest note home from one of her teachers," Mama said, putting her hands on my shoulders. "So studious and diligent."

My blush deepened, and I launched into my Bible verse, conscious that I was failing to enunciate, failing to make eye contact, but I needed to get to the end and out from under Uncle Eugene's self-satisfied smile. For weeks she'd been doing this, inventing accomplishments no more rooted in reality than her promise of Daddy's impending salvation. Both were beginning to feel like debts we could never repay.

I SUBMITTED THE NOTICE Garth had signed to Miss Cavour— what else was I to do?—but after that I threw myself into Wise Daughtering with new resolve. I studied in the library after school, at night under the covers, in the kitchen, textbook pages blistering where I turned them with wet fingertips. I memorized two Bible verses a week instead of one, and paid the same attention to Uncle Eugene's sermons that I paid to my teachers at school, listening for instructions, for guidance, for any answer to the question of how, as a Wise Daughter, I should live and be. Every Sunday, as Mama and I waited in line to greet him, I prepared two intelligent and deferential questions to demonstrate my interest in the material he'd covered in his sermon. At night, I secured loose buttons and tacked up errant hems and brushed my hair a hundred strokes, mindful of the instructions I had read in an Institute tract, "Modesty and Morals: A Guide for Girls." ("Dress each day as if you are His representative, for you are!")

And I made myself pray. Every single night, without fail. If I couldn't make my brain think a prayer I wrote one in my diary, and even if it devolved into a report to Josie about my life and a plea for her to return, as it did more often than not, prayer was, at least, a firmly established part of my routine.

I decided that when I saw Garth again I would explain: I wasn't the sort of girl who forged. I was a girl who lived uprightly. Maybe I'd even tell him I'd been praying for him. It was true that when I wrote to Josie in my diary, Garth's name often flowed from my pencil, and if that wasn't quite the same thing as praying for him, what of it? The important thing was to make it clear: I was a Wise Daughter. No more funny business.

And then, one afternoon, a couple of weeks after our encounter in the library, there he was: being dragged into the principal's office by Mr. Gow. I stood with my spine pressed against the wall, books clutched in front of me, hoping he would meet my eye but relieved when he didn't. He smiled faintly, as if amused by Mr. Gow's exertions. Mr. Gow, gripping his shoulder and frowning angrily, Mr. Gow whom I had seen—but, no, I refused to remember Garth's drawing. I had purified my mind with prayer. I had removed the offending image from my memory.

A few days later, in the library, Garth's name floated up from the quiet conversation the Bremner wafer girl was having with the leg brace girl. I moved, as casually as I could, to the table next to theirs and strained to hear: According to the Bremner wafer girl, he'd been banished from the lunchroom for smoking—that was why he had been in the library on the day he'd forged Mama's signature. The leg brace girl said she'd heard he ran a bootlegging operation out of the boys' bathroom, where he kept bottles of rum in a toilet tank. The Bremner wafer girl said someone had told her he'd been kicked out of his last school for having an affair with the drawing teacher. She looked right at me for an instant, then leaned toward the leg brace girl, shielded her mouth with her hand, and started whispering. I buried my face in my book, uncertain whether my heart was racing because they'd caught me eavesdropping or because maybe they were gossiping about me too. Maybe they'd linked my name with his.

AS MARCH GAVE WAY to April, an unseasonable heat descended over the city. Dense and swampy, it summoned ripe scents from the earth and drew sheets of mud across the sidewalk. It steamed up the windows of the streetcar and spawned flies that burst in swarms from the barrels of fruit that seemingly overnight had started appearing outside of groceries. Mrs. Broom and I stood together at the kitchen sink and held ice against our pressure points, while Minnie read aloud from the paper: three boys had drowned that week, one in Hickory Creek out in Joliet and two in the lake. Mosquito larvae had been discovered in a puddle on Twenty-Second Street and at the Indiana Harbor railroad tracks. I slept in my undershirt, hair pulled up into a stubby fountain to keep it off my neck. At Waller, boys fought in the hallways. Girls neglected their lessons to fold each other paper fans. Couples were caught necking in the catwalk above the auditorium, on the roof above the gymnasium, in a car behind the school. We were dissecting cats when the biology teacher started snoring at his desk. For the first time since receiving my deficiency notice, I failed an algebra quiz, but so did half my classmates; Mr. Van Lan berated us for twenty minutes, sweat streaming down his neck until his collar went limp.

On the morning of April 6, my sixteenth birthday, I woke to a sky tinged green. I breathed deeply at the open window. The air was still warm and heavy but shot through with the scent of rain. Fragile new leaves snapped in the wind. The previous year, Josie and I had turned fifteen with room service steaks and potatoes lyonnaise. Daddy had allowed us each a sip of his martini. That morning, by the time I emerged from the alcove, Daddy had already left for the factory. Mama wished me a happy birthday in a bright, sharp voice, her smile forceful, as if to refuse any possibility of my unhappiness. I escaped as soon as I could, claiming I had a meeting of the Sophomore Volunteers.

But when I reached Waller I found I couldn't bear to go in. I kept walking, not quite admitting to myself what I had decided until I heard a church bell chime nine o'clock: I was officially truant.

I whiled away the morning, sitting on park benches, luxuriating in the sheer, sullen waste of it. Wind stirred the trash in the gutters and dragged dark scraps of cloud across the sky. It gave me a childish pleasure to think that I was making it happen, that the weather somehow answered to the tumult in my heart. I daydreamed that Josie had come home, that she was at my side, that I was giving her a tour of the places I had come to know. I longed to ask her whether sixteen felt different from fifteen. It did for me, though I couldn't say what, exactly, had changed. I wondered if she also felt crampy and cross, if our periods were still the same, or if, in that way, too, she'd unraveled her body from mine.

At noon, I went into a white tile restaurant and bought a ham sandwich. As I claimed a table beside the window, I felt an unexpected stirring of pleasure—it was the first time I'd ever eaten in a restaurant alone. I took out *Mrs. Dalloway,* Miss Tangus's copy, which she had insisted I borrow. I found the book difficult, but I didn't mind that, exactly. Outside, the wind plastered a newspaper against a parked car; it drummed the restaurant's awning and, somewhere nearby, knocked a chain against a flagpole. Silver needles of rain began to tap against the windows. Black umbrellas bloomed and bobbed along the sidewalk. The busboy emerged from the kitchen with a mop, but he left a wide border around my seat, and I stayed put, reading and listening to the rain.

I'd just crammed the last crust of my sandwich into my mouth when I heard a knock. I turned to look. It was Garth Mosher, standing on the other side of the window.

Before I could finish swallowing he had sat down across from me, carrying with him the scent of wool and rain and cigarettes.

"Hi," he said.

I nodded and chewed. Under the table, I pinched my arms. I chewed and chewed until finally, finally, the bite was gone, and then I took a gulp of water.

It was time to make the speech I'd planned. But a girl who was truant couldn't claim not to be the sort of girl who forged, could she? I felt as if I'd stumbled bodily against the standard I had been violating all day, as if it had knocked the wind out of me. "Friends, I saw a girl from our own congregation, shirking her studies to meet unchaperoned with a boy of low character in a seedy restaurant not a mile from this very chapel!" Garth was taking off his cap and shaking away the water that had beaded on the bill. He grinned right at me, as if we had colluded on a joke. I rummaged through my brain for something, anything, to say.

"It's not really raining anymore," Garth said. "Do you want to go for a walk?"

I managed to nod.

The storm had stripped the heat from the air and left a residue of mist. When I shivered, Garth handed me his jacket, which smelled of cigarettes. Its weight against my shoulders reminded me of the harness; I felt a pang of longing for Josie, but only for an instant. My overwhelming impression was of Garth: The few inches taller he was than me. The way he circumnavigated puddles: precisely, neither wasting a step nor risking his shoes. He kept his hands in his pockets except when he took one out to point, revealing the ink that trailed along the thumb and forefinger of his right hand like a tattoo of a vine. He led me to Seward Park, where he pointed to the pool, still locked up for winter, and to the basketball courts.

"Are you a freshman?"

"Sophomore." I grasped for something, anything more to say.

"Me too," he said at last.

"Oh!" Once again, I felt myself choking on my own silence.

He wiped a bench with a handkerchief and sat down. I sat beside him. In the waterlogged field across from us, little brown sparrows hopped along the edges of puddles and nibbled at their own feathers.

"I beg your pardon," Garth said, and just like that he was pulling on the lapel of his jacket, the jacket I was wearing. He reached inside. My heartbeat drummed in my ears. I prayed that he couldn't detect how hard I was trying not to breathe on him.

It was over a second later: He'd removed something from his breast pocket and turned back to face the sparrows. As I tried to steady my heart, he spread a handkerchief on his lap and laid out a pouch of tobacco and sheath of rolling papers. His fingers moved fleetly to fold a paper into quarters, to pinch tobacco and spread it. He tucked one edge of the paper into the fold, making a little tube, which he rolled tightly with his thumbs. With a pink flash of tongue, he licked the edge of the paper and pressed it shut. He lit the cigarette, inhaled sharply, exhaled. And then he offered it to me.

I heard Uncle Eugene's voice in my ear, chiming with my own: no, stop, you mustn't. But the cigarette was in my hand. I was tasting paper and a bead of flavor, dark and boggy.

"Breathe in," said Garth.

Uncle Eugene's voice faded to nothing as the bog flavor filled my mouth. Smoke scraped my lungs. I coughed, terrible, sputtering coughs that made me worry both that my lungs would tear and that Garth would think me ugly and childish. But he reached over and patted my back; I felt the distinct pressure of his palm, all the way through his jacket and my dress. My head reeled. I tried a second puff. Smoke licked down my throat and my eyes watered, but this time, I managed to hold in my cough. Garth brushed the spilled tobacco off the handkerchief and back into the pouch. I braced myself for another lean, another tug on his lapel, but he just handed his smoking things back to me. I put them away in his jacket, face burning.

Every time he handed me the cigarette, I experimented with a different way to hold it. Between my thumb and index finger, like Mama. Scissored between my index finger and middle finger, like Garth. He blew smoke rings at a couple of squirrels who were slaloming through the branches above. I watched them dissipate until I grew too dizzy to keep my head tipped back. I was conscious, each time my lips touched the paper, that his lips had, a moment earlier, pressed the exact same spot. But with each inhalation, it became a little easier to speak, to respond to Garth's observations about the squirrels and the birds and people passing through the park.

When the cigarette was burned down to a stub, Garth smashed it beneath his shoe. As we stood and started walking again, the world seemed extra-visible to me, its colors unusually saturated: a clean blue automobile, a green-and-white awning above a shop full of enormous rainbow-striped lollipops, a woman's rose-colored skirt. The clouds had thinned to a smooth sheet, softly lit by a hidden sun.

"You know, you still haven't told me your name," he said, pressing his thumb against his lip to peel away a fleck of tobacco.

"Haven't I? It's Harriet."

"Harriet Szász."

"How did you know that?"

"Well, that's your mother's name, isn't it? I assumed."

"Oh. Right."

"I must say, Harriet Szász, a girl who got so torn up about one measly single deficiency notice is the last person I'd expect to find playing hooky."

"It's my birthday."

"Aha. That explains it."

"I have a sister. A twin."

"Where's she?"

"I don't know. She ran away. We were in show business."

"Ha ha."

"It's true."

He looked at me with eyes narrowed, smiling indulgently, as if I were attempting a joke that hadn't quite come off. In a rush of indignation, I danced an eight-count combination right there on the sidewalk. Then I hurried forward, embarrassed, conscious that this was exactly how I was not supposed to behave, now that we were in Chicago, now that I was a Wise Daughter.

He caught up with me.

"Okay," he said, fingertips brushing my arm. "Tell me more."

I told him: about the harness and the rise of the Siamese Sweets. I told him about Herb Fitz and Peoria. Speech flowed out of me freely, easily, as if I'd always been in the habit of talking to friends, as if I hadn't grown up hemmed in by secrets. I could see that he found me far more interesting than he'd assumed I would be back in the library.

He asked me about my parents, and I told him about the *Follies,* about Mama's leg, about watching her sing. I told him about Daddy, how he'd built Mama's sets and made Josie's and my costumes. I told him about the skylight, the roof, Daddy climbing up with a bottle tucked into the back of his pants. And then my throat tightened. Maybe it had been too much, to mention the whiskey, when I might have painted a sufficient picture if I'd just mentioned the roof, or maybe it would have been best not to paint a picture at all. Maybe I'd talked too much, revealed too much, not because of any rule but because there was a balance to these things, an order, I saw that now. You couldn't make a stranger know you all at once.

Garth had picked up a stick and was dragging it along a chain-link fence.

"What about you?" I hurried to say, picking up a stick of my own. "Your parents?"

"My dad's a physicist. He teaches." He ran, banging his stick against the fence. At the end of the block, he tossed the stick over the fence, into a lot that had been cleared for building, where lumber was piled under tarps pooling with water. I threw my stick after his and brushed off my hands. We'd reached Division Street. He turned and I followed him, wondering about his mother, though I didn't know how to say so.

He stopped. I followed his gaze to a movie theater, the blinking lights of its marquee garish against the gray afternoon.

"This way," he said, and crossed the street with calculated nonchalance. But instead of going into the theater, he passed it. He went left on Dearborn, then turned down the alley that ran parallel to Division, along the back of the theater. He glanced quickly left and right, then crouched down beneath the fire escape and hooked his hands together like a stirrup. I stepped in. He boosted me up, and I grabbed hold of the bottom of the ladder. It heaved loose and clattered to the ground, showering us with cold droplets.

I went up after him, once nearly losing my footing on a slippery rung. By the time we reached the third-floor fire escape, my whole front was wet and I was gasping for breath. He pulled a ruler out of his schoolbag and wedged it under a window, expertly jimmying it open. I climbed after him into a room full of film canisters and projectors and rolled-up posters. He led me out the door and along a hallway. As we climbed down a dark, cobwebbed staircase, I could hear the piano and the dull chatter of the audience, then a bright peal of laughter. He lifted a finger to his lips. At the bottom of the stairs, slowly, carefully, he opened a door. We stepped onto a stage. Between us and the audience hung the movie screen, bright with a backward cartoon, bordered at either end by a velvet curtain. We slipped around the curtain's edge and down a short flight of stairs into the dark auditorium, where we found a place to sit near the back. He felt around the floor and found a discarded ticket stub.

"Stay here," he whispered.

It was only when I was alone that I allowed myself to name my latest transgressions: I had broken into a movie theater! I had smoked half a cigarette! Garth returned just as the newsreel began and handed me a box of Jujubes. I wondered if he'd stolen those too.

The feature began with a scene in real color: Clara Bow in a pink bathing suit, a wild red cloud of hair bobbing around her head. I only half-absorbed the story. Clara Bow bopped around, she flirted, she kissed her boyfriend. Old men gave her beautiful clothes to wear. And then her boyfriend got jealous, and she stripped off her gifts, one by one, and leaped, naked, into a pool. I heard Uncle Eugene: Hollywood sex mania! Salacious images tailor-made to corrupt young minds! But his voice was remote, minor. My teeth ached from sugar. Light spilled from the screen onto our laps. The pianist's fingers moved nimbly over the keys. I felt, somehow, as if it had all been arranged for my personal pleasure.

Too soon, the words "THE END!" filled the screen. Real life pressed against me with a sudden heaviness. I wondered what time it was. Maybe Mama had gotten home already, maybe she was annoyed to find I was late to help Mrs. Broom and Minnie with supper. I stood. Garth looked up at me expectantly, the light from the screen flickering against his glasses. I wanted to thank him, but that was impossible: I had to go, should have gone already. My skirt caught on his knees as I slid past.

Outside, the sky was hard and clear, the sun a pale button. I folded myself into the end-of-the-day crowd, people making their way home from work or school. Those who had dressed for the morning's heat scowled and crossed their arms. I realized I was still wearing Garth's jacket.

When I came inside, Mrs. Broom was waiting in the parlor, chewing on the end of an unlit cigar. She grabbed me by the wrist.

"Come," she said.

"I'm sorry I'm late. I was just—"

"That's not it, Harriet."

She pulled me past the kitchen, through her office, and into her cluttered private sitting room, which was attached to her bedroom at the back of the house. Mama and Daddy were there already. For an instant, I wondered if I was going to be given a birthday party. But Mama, sitting on a Turkish couch the color of goldenrod, was ashen, and Daddy, pacing beside her, turned when Mrs. Broom and I came in, his expression tense. Mrs. Broom hung back, as if to grant the three of us our privacy.

"She's here now," Mama said. She stood and snatched an envelope from Daddy's hands. "Satisfied?"

He raked a thumbnail through his beard as Mama tore the letter open. Daddy read over her shoulder. He laughed once, sharply, and went to the cart in the corner and poured a glass of whiskey.

Mama put the letter back in the envelope and calmly held it out to me.

Mrs. Broom stood beside me, as if we shared a rank—together, we were next in line to read. The envelope was addressed to Leonard, Maude, and Harriet Sweet. The postmark was California. Inside was a single page, typed, from a man named Raymond Fish, who claimed to be Josie's new manager. We would soon hear of her professional success, he wrote, but we mustn't attempt to contact her. If we gave any interviews to the press, or made any further claim of association with her, he would pursue legal action.

"She made her choice, Maude." Mrs. Broom spoke softly, as if she and Mama were the only two people in the room. "You know as well as anyone how a girl can get it into her head to go somewhere."

Mama's face colored. Her gaze snapped to me and I held it, hoping, in a rush of spite, that she thought I knew exactly what Mrs. Broom was alluding to. Daddy, having emptied his glass, poured himself another, then spun around to face Mama, finger stabbing the air.

"If you'd ever been a mother to those girls." The words spilled as if from a wound. "If you'd ever been a proper mother—"

She slapped his face and told me to go upstairs.

Their argument echoed as I ran down the hall. None of them had even noticed that I was wearing Garth's jacket. None had wondered where I'd been, or who I'd been with. None of them seemed to remember that it was my birthday, the first I'd ever spent without Josie. I clung to the letter as if it were something precious, even though it wasn't even from Josie herself but from some man, some manager, brushing us all aside as if success hadn't always been shared between us. Anger thickened in my heart like a clot. But at the same time and with sudden intensity, I longed for her: to hear the story of her flight in her own voice, punctuated by her husky laugh, to breathe in the salt scent of her neck, to feel myself crammed against her in the harness, our bones a neatly matching set of points.

Upstairs, in the alcove, I wrote her a letter, care of the office of Raymond Fish. Not in my diary, but on proper writing paper. I told her that I would keep any secret she wanted me to keep. That I understood why she'd had to go. That I loved her. That I would always love her. That I missed her, and that whatever she was planning, surely she could write from time to time. To me, if not to Mama and Daddy. That there oughtn't be secrets between us. That out of all the people in the world, I was the one most deserving of her trust.

I put down my pen. My face felt hot, my throat tight. I went to the window and took in a deep breath. Along with the sharp night air, I caught the wool-and-smoke scent of Garth's jacket. When I closed my eyes, I could almost taste my first cigarette at the back of my teeth. I could very nearly feel it, resting between my fingers.

CHAPTER

8

ON A WARM SUNDAY MORNING THAT JUNE, MAMA BROUGHT my final grade report to the Institute Chapel to show Uncle Eugene.

"We have you to thank, of course," Mama said, as he looked it over. I had passed all my classes, even algebra by a hair, and would be promoted to the junior class. This despite the hours I'd spent with Garth after school—sitting by the lake, sharing cigarettes, pretending to be shocked when we left a candy shop and he showed me his pockets, full of nicked peppermints and bullseyes and chocolate ice cubes.

"Very good," Uncle Eugene said, folding my grade report in two with a self-satisfied smile. "Very good."

He invited us up to his office, where he gave me a fountain pen engraved with my initials. As I thanked him, I wondered what he would have done if I had failed. Would I still have gotten a gift? Would he have held on to the pen, hoping I would earn it eventually?

"You're a fine girl, Harriet." He looked down at his own fingertips, splayed against his desk. "Positive. Prayerful. A problem solver. There are many girls your age who could learn something from you."

"Thank you, sir," I said. And then I concentrated on putting the pen away in its slim velvet case, not quite trusting my expression, his praise feeling, as it so often did, like an admonition.

———

GARTH LEFT NOT LONG after that to visit his grandparents out east, and for the rest of the summer I was an exemplary Wise Daughter. I turned up early to meetings of the Junior Altar Guild. I memorized Bible verses and studied and practiced my Emily Post. Josie hadn't responded to the letter I'd written her on our birthday, but every few days, when I checked the mail slot, I found something from Garth, usually a cartoon with a caption: his grandmother chastising him for the way he held a soup spoon, his grandfather doing calisthenics in the garden at dawn, his cousin shrieking at her mother. In the alcove, at night, when the house was silent, I thought of him and pressed the soft flesh of my upper arm into a pair of lips and practiced kissing, wanting so badly to really kiss I felt I might split my own skin. Sometimes, I pulled a blanket over my head and turned on my flashlight and spent a feverish half hour scribbling in my diary: a contemplation of the Sex Act, or a romantic story, Garth cast as pirate, as cowboy, as sheikh. When I finished one of these stories, I was often almost pleased. I half-wanted to show them to somebody. But they were dangerous, written proof of something that would make Uncle Eugene hate me if he knew about it. So every time I finished writing anything that even hinted of sex, I burned it in a coffee can I kept on the windowsill.

ON THE LAST NIGHT of summer vacation, I patted lettuce leaves dry in the boardinghouse kitchen, contemplating the outfit I would wear in the morning: a dress from the Institute charity shop, bird's-egg brown, with a dropped-waist skirt of tiered ruffles, a hand-me-down jacket of Mama's, with black velvet trim and nut brown glass buttons, and the new silk stockings Mrs. Broom had given me. I pictured Garth coming up the steps of Waller High, where we had agreed to meet before the first bell, and catching his breath at the sight of me. Maybe I'd bring a book to read. The collection of Keats one of the boarders had given me over the summer on his way out of town, maybe. How elegant I appeared in my own imagination: leaning against a column, hair glossy in the sun, expression serene as I turned the pages.

There was a ruckus in the hallway: heavy footfalls and laughter. A moment later, Daddy stumbled in, his arm wrapped around the shoulders of a short man with a bushy red beard. Mrs. Broom cried out and bounded over. She threw her arms around them both, leaning down so the red-bearded man could kiss her cheeks.

"Bert Koster!"

"In the flesh," he said.

"But what on earth?"

Daddy saw me. His cheeks were deeply flushed, his eyes glassy.

"Bert," he said. "This is our daughter. This is Harriet."

Bert took both my hands in his, his little brown eyes bright with feeling. "Harriet Szász. An honor."

In overlapping voices, Daddy and Bert Koster and Mrs. Broom explained. This was their old friend from New York City, did I remember? I thought I did, maybe. I was to call him Bert, or Uncle Bert, if I wanted. He had been the stage manager of Fleischer's *Follies Magnifique,* where Daddy had been a carpenter, Mama a star, Mrs. Broom in the chorus.

"Where is Maude?" asked Bert.

Mrs. Broom clasped her hands together.

"Upstairs. Minnie, Harriet, you can manage, can't you?" Without waiting for an answer, she threaded her arms through Daddy's and Bert's and started singing. Daddy and Bert joined in. I recognized the song—an ode to the wit and beauty of a Fleischer's girl. Daddy had sung a few lines once, many years ago, before Mama told him to knock it off. The door swung shut behind them.

Minnie thrust a bowl of bananas into my arms.

"All of her work to do, but do you think she'll be paying us a penny extra?" I shook my head, though she'd said it more to herself than to me, and already she'd huffed back to the stove, mumbling a stream of complaints about Mrs. Broom, God love the woman, she said, but she has no notion of how to run a business. I peeled and sliced the bananas, laid them out on the lettuce leaves, and topped each with a spoonful of mayonnaise. I was sprinkling them with crushed peanuts when I heard voices on the stairs. I rushed into the dining room just in time to see them pass, laughing. They hardly even looked at me. Mama moved lightly, nimbly, clinging to Bert's arm.

A few minutes later, Minnie rang the supper bell, and the boarders filed in. For the first half of the meal, as I went back and forth between the kitchen and the dining room, carrying pitchers of water and baskets of bread, filling bowls with soup, there was no sign of the group in the back of the house save the occasional eruption of laughter. And then, as Minnie and I plated the pie, Daddy appeared at the kitchen door.

"Harriet," he said, damp-faced and unsteady, but beaming. "We need you."

I called over my shoulder to Minnie that she'd have to finish on her own, and followed Daddy to Mrs. Broom's sitting room. Mama was sitting beside Bert on the goldenrod couch, shoeless feet curled up underneath her. Mrs. Broom was across from them, draped over a blue chaise longue, ankles crossed on its arm.

"She's here!" Mama cried. She had never sounded happier to see me. "Our daughter is here."

Daddy sat down beside her, and she leaned into him, a girlish flush in her cheeks. He sat upright and laid his hands flat on his thighs. I knelt beside Mama on a sheepskin rug and took a cookie from a plate on the coffee table, trying to make sense of them all: Mama and Daddy, acting like twenty-years-younger versions of themselves; Mrs. Broom, cackling uncontrollably at some joke I'd missed; and their old friend watching them with a satisfied expression, as if he were the host. He set about topping off everyone's glasses and then poured a fresh glass, which he tried to hand to me.

"Now, Bertie!" Mama said, grabbing it before I could. She wagged a finger at him and poured all but a drop of the whiskey into her own glass, and then filled my glass the rest of the way with water. As she handed it to me, a little sloshed on my dress.

"Oopsie daisy!" she said, and laughed. I realized then that she was drunk. I'd never seen my mother drunk. I took a sip. I couldn't taste the whiskey at all.

"All right, Lenny," Mama said, settling back on the couch and smoothing her skirt over her knees. "She's here now. Tell us everything!"

Daddy nestled closer to Mama, grinning, though the cords in his neck tightened. He nodded at Bert, almost gravely. Bert stood and tucked a hand into his vest.

"Congratulate me, Harriet," he said. "I'm going to be working with your old man."

Daddy put a hand on Mama's knee.

"I pass him on the L platform this morning. And I think, that man looks awfully like Bert Koster, and then I turn around—"

"I'm thinking I'll be damned if that isn't Lenny Szász."

"So we go to a nearby establishment for a chat," but chat meant drink, and while Mrs. Broom and Bert laughed, Mama's smile contracted.

"Who could say no to an old friend? After all these years!" The first note of defensiveness had slid into Daddy's voice.

"Say, Vee Vee, do you remember the clamshell hair trap?" Bert asked, looking at Mrs. Broom.

She sat up, smiling, though I could tell she was also keeping an eye on Mama, that she had also noted the shift in Mama's mood. Mama's worry was the same as mine: Daddy hadn't gone to work. What did that mean? Would he lose his job? What would Uncle Eugene say? Bert was telling the story, oblivious, or pretending to be, to the new stiffness in Mama's posture: In rehearsal, Mama's braid had gotten stuck in the hinge of a giant clamshell from which she was supposed to emerge, dressed as a pearl. Bert, as the stage manager, had said they were going to have to cut it off, and Mrs. Broom, who had been Vera Vance then, had stormed onto the stage and insisted they would do no such thing. Daddy, Bert explained, had ended up unscrewing the hinge of the clamshell and disentangling Mama's hair strand by strand.

Daddy gripped Mama's knee, looking at her hopefully, as if wanting her to affirm the memory of his gallantry. She studied the bottom of her glass.

"But what do you mean?" I asked. "Working with Daddy?"

"Yes." Mama nodded at me appreciatively, which made me bristle—I hated being put to use in that way when she fought with my father, treated as her ally, when all I ever wanted was for them not to fight, when their fights made me feel so frightened and ill. But in that moment, more than that, I wanted to know. I needed to know.

"Tell us what this is all about," she went on. "Lenny has a good job now. Or had one."

Bert ignored her smile's razor edge.

"You're familiar with the Civic Opera?"

"My no-good husband and I used to go," Mrs. Broom said, lightly. "The new building is supposed to open in November, isn't it?"

"That's right. And I'm production manager. I worked it out with the union this afternoon. Lenny is coming on as an assistant carpenter."

"And who knows, down the line, what it might amount to?" Daddy went around to the back of the couch and put his hands on Bert's shoulders. "Bertie's going to pass along some of my designs."

"Now, no promises, Lenny," he said, patting Daddy's hand with his own.

"Of course, of course," Daddy said, and kissed the top of Bert's head. "But Maude, this is a real opportunity."

"So you are fired from the factory?"

He raked his fingers through his hair and released a booming laugh.

"Christ, Maude. You sure know how to see the silver lining and find the cloud."

"But you are fired. That's what you're saying?"

"I've signed a contract with the Civic Opera. What don't you understand?"

Mama lit a cigarette with a shaky hand, her lashes clumping wetly around her eyes, and smiled at Bert. "Tell us about the season, then, Bertie. What's on at the opera?"

He spoke brightly and smoothly, as if filling the silence were the same sort of service to the party as filling our glasses had been. Thirteen weeks of grand opera, thirty-two operas in the repertoire, starting with *Aída,* Rosa Raisa in the title role. Live radio broadcasts at least once a week. A season of operetta would follow, and a national tour. Negotiations were under way for a European tour in the summer.

"Marvelous." Mama interrupted him, raising her glass. "To Lenny Szász, back in the theater where he belongs!"

Bert clinked his glass against hers, laughing as if Mama's congratulations had been sincere, and then he went back to reminiscing. I was struck by the awareness that he'd known my parents longer than I had, that he knew them, perhaps, more deeply than I did: Did they remember the stage door Johnny who kept turning up with flowers for Maude, and then one night tried to push into her dressing room, and she smashed him clean across the head with the vase? Did they remember the popcorn vendor? Harriet, you should have seen it. The fellow called Lenny a name, never mind what, and Lenny socked him and stole his cart. Before the fellow came to, Lenny had given free popcorn to every child and beggar in Union Square. Did they remember when Maude emptied that whole bottle of champagne and stood up in front of a crowded restaurant—

"Oh, I don't remember it quite like that," said Mama, flicking away a bit of ash.

And she'd done half a striptease before Vera—

"Harriet," Mama said sharply. "Aren't you supposed to be helping Minnie?"

"But Daddy said I—"

"Go."

Back in the kitchen, Minnie kept trying to catch my eye, and I knew she wanted me to gossip or explain or at least to allow her to complain about my having left her before. But I concentrated on scrubbing the counters and the stove. What would Uncle Eugene do when he heard Daddy had returned to the theater? Had all my effort, my diligent Wise Daughtering, been for naught?

Minnie and I were gathering up the table linens when Daddy and Bert came into the dining room.

"Harriet," said Bert. "It was a great pleasure to meet you."

Daddy watched us shake hands.

"You're proud of your old dad, aren't you?" he said, his smile tight and awful. I nodded, swallowing against a painful lump in my throat.

The two of them left. Minnie carried the bundled linens into the kitchen. I slipped down the hall, back into Mrs. Broom's office, where I pressed my ear against her sitting room door.

"—needs to feel like his work means something, Maude."

"What about Harriet? What am I going to do with her if Eugene decides to cut ties?"

"Maybe he'll make a go of it. Wouldn't that be better? Than wasting his talents at a factory?"

"His talents, his talents. Everyone has always been so concerned about wasting Lenny's talents. Oh what's that, Lenny is late for rehearsal because he woke up at half past three in a puddle of his own piss? Sorry, can't fire him, don't want to waste his talents. You can't pay the grocery bill? Mustn't ask Lenny to get a proper job, don't want to waste his talents. What about my talents? I could still sing, you know. I had a name. I could have gotten a cabaret. I had offers."

"I know, Maudey."

"But there were the girls to think about. We had to be realistic. And when he swept them into his little fantasy, what did I do? I made it work. And when Josephine decided to hell with the rest of us, I went to goddamn Eugene Creggs and made sure we didn't starve. But no, not grand enough, not fine enough, for thwarted genius Leonard Szász. Isn't the Civic Opera always going belly up? How does Lenny get paid after the season ends? Does he expect to go on tour? Am I supposed to keep up some lie for Eugene for what, months? Years? And that monstrosity that Sam Insull is building by the river. Is he in his right mind? What do I tell Eugene if it all goes to pot?"

"You'll figure something out. You've always known how to handle that man."

"And what kind of wife does that make me?"

"Hush. Every girl needs an insurance policy."

"I could kill Bert Koster with my bare hands."

"Oh, poor Bert. Lenny was the one who decided not to go to work today."

"That's right. You were always sweet on Bert, weren't you?"

"I was not."

"You were. I remember now. That weekend at Mr. Fleischer's estate? Oh, Vera, I remember! You disappeared for an hour."

"You're thinking of Karen. At Wilma's parents' place in Connecticut, on the Fourth of July."

"No, I'm thinking of you. At Mr. Fleischer's. That weekend he and Melva had everyone out to celebrate their divorce. I remember feeling so badly for you, because you were missing the cake. I looked for you everywhere."

"Fine. If a million years ago I exchanged pleasantries with Bert Koster on a summer afternoon, that doesn't change the fact that doing an old friend a favor is hardly grounds for murder."

Mama snorted. "Bert feels guilty. All these years later. He could have given Lenny something when it counted, instead of turning up and interfering now."

"What would you have done if he had? I seem to remember your telling Lenny he ought to hire himself out as a handyman."

"Bert didn't know that. And he never came to see the girls. None of that crowd did except you. Karen a few times."

"He did once, early on," Mrs. Broom said. There was a long silence. "I didn't mean—"

There was another pause, and then I heard Mama's jagged step. I barely had time to crawl behind Mrs. Broom's desk before the door flew open and Mama slammed through the office. I stayed behind the desk, heart racing, until I was certain Mrs. Broom wasn't going to come chasing after her.

When I finally crept out of the office and down the hall, I found the kitchen dark, Minnie's irritation seeming to linger alongside the scent of dish soap and onions. I ran a rag over a spotless countertop, wondering what Mrs. Broom had said to drive Mama away. I worried that when I got upstairs, Mama would try to draw me into some awful conversation about Daddy's recklessness, and I worried about what his recklessness would cost us with Uncle Eugene. But underneath all that was a feeling I didn't quite understand, a needling sense of loss. I kept coming back to that first afternoon in Chicago, Mama telling me I wasn't cut out for the stage, and then to Daddy in Uncle Eugene's office, wild-eyed, begging him to let me sing. Had he ever really been serious about my performing on my own?

Even as the question formed and grew urgent, I knew where I could find the answer. I threw down my rag and hurried upstairs. The apartment was dim and silent, Mama barricaded in the tub. As quietly as I could, I retrieved Daddy's sketchbook from his sock drawer and flipped past a year's worth of drawings: the yellow-and-black checkered dress with all the gathers at the waist, a gauzy pink tutu, the green-and-red tartan we'd worn in our final Christmas show, the blue satin party dress with dozens of glass beads sewn onto the net overskirt, which we'd been wearing on New Year's when Frank Dunn had slipped Josie that spoonful of ice cream. And there it was. The thing I had hoped to find, but still, at the sight of it, my breath caught. A drawing of me, dated the day after Josie's flight. The drawing was rough, my features vague, just a few marks. But maybe Daddy had captured something of my posture, or the way I held out a hand, or the cast of my eyes: There was no question it was me, me and not Josie. I turned the page. There I was again, three times, modeling another dress from three different angles.

He'd drawn me the rest of the winter and into the spring. On page after page, my skirt fell dramatically to the floor. My sleeves swept from shoulder to wrist in graceful lines. Smaller drawings revealed details of the designs: the pleats at the top of a sleeve, the lace adorning a collar, the bow on the toe of a high-heeled boot. And there was the birthmark on my cheek, there was a tentative smile I felt forming on my own face the instant after I saw it on the page. In Daddy's drawings, I was lovely in a way that I'd never consciously been aware of being in real life, but that nevertheless struck me as familiar—something he had discerned, not invented.

The last drawing was from April, a few days before my birthday. After that, the sketchbook was blank. For all those months, when he'd taken it up to the roof it had been nothing but a prop. I was struck by a sickening grief, which was quickly overtaken by bitterness: He'd have something to draw now, I thought, and I understood that I was jealous. Not of Daddy, but of the opera company itself. Of the claim it would make on his attention.

I tore the drawings of me out of the sketchbook and hid them in the slit in my mattress, alongside Josie's old diary entries, the cartoons Garth had sent me over the summer vacation, and my diary, full of letters to Josie and God, all of my earnest wishes and apologies for my sins, and the tattered edges of the pages I had filled with smutty daydreams and then ripped out to burn. Mama emerged from the tub, eventually, but I had long since turned off the light; I willed her to believe I was asleep. By the time Daddy got home, I actually was.

THE NEXT MORNING, I got to Waller early and stood in the shadow of the second column from the left. Though it wasn't yet eight o'clock, streams of sweat had already pasted my new stockings to my legs. My dress clung to my skin like a licked stamp. My stomach felt sour as I remembered how Mama had slammed around the apartment while Daddy lay on the couch, sleeping off his night out with Bert. I was more desperate than ever to see Garth, not to talk to him about the business of the night before, necessarily, but because his company meant I could talk about, think about, anything else. I squinted out over the dazzling lawn, where my schoolmates were greeting each other, linking arms and heading inside. His name looped in my brain: Garth, Garth, Garth, hurry up, Garth.

The first bell rang. A teacher came out to round up stragglers.

"Are you lost, miss?" He glared at me from under wild white eyebrows. Without waiting for an answer he huffed down the steps to confront some boys who were smoking under the oak tree. I willed Garth to appear. The teacher came past again, the boys slinking behind him, abashed. He gave me another warning look, and I followed them all inside, feeling as if my schoolbag had filled with rocks.

Every time a classroom door opened that morning, my breath caught. But it was never him. I dawdled in the hallways, just in case. But he never appeared. At lunchtime, I bought a roll stuffed with a piece of pale ham and sat alone in the clattery, humid corner of the lunchroom where students in white aprons and caps scraped dishes and carted them back to the kitchen to be washed. I picked at the bread I couldn't bring myself to eat, rolling the pieces into little white pills.

When I emerged after the last bell, there he was: slouched against a column, turning an unlit cigarette around in his fingers. He straightened as I passed, grinning as if he expected me to be pleased to see him, as if he hadn't humiliated me and doomed me to a day of misery by not showing up that morning. I stalked down the steps.

"Hey!" He ran out in front of me, and when I kept walking, he jogged backward to keep up. He took off his cap to fan his face. He'd had his hair cut short. A painful-looking scab split his bottom lip. "Hey. Don't you want to know what happened? I wanted to be there this morning, you know."

"You weren't though, were you?"

He spread his arms to show off his clothes: trim gray jacket and trousers, plain black tie, shoes that looked as if they pinched. I shrugged and kept walking.

"I'm not going to Waller anymore. I would have written, but there wasn't time. It all happened right at the end."

I slowed down.

"It was these bastards," he went on, tugging his tie loose. "These brothers across the way my grandmother tries to get me to pal around with every summer. All they ever want to talk about is sailing. I found them drowning a kitten in a birdbath." I gave him a look. "I swear to God. I beat them both bloody before the gardener pulled me off. They had it coming, but Granny is in DAR with their mother. She took to her bed. Everyone else gathered up to decide what to do with me. Long story short, I'm done at Waller. Hey."

We were walking past a vendor selling vegetables from a cart. Before I could stop him, he'd slipped a tomato into my hand. I flushed and shoved it into my schoolbag.

"I don't steal, you know," I said, through gritted teeth.

"Oh, don't you?" He smirked. I looked away from him, concentrated on keeping my expression cool, steeled by the summer I had spent apart from him. But when I looked back, his smirk had faded. He'd shoved his hands into his pockets.

"So where are you going now?" I hurried to ask, sorry to think I'd actually hurt his feelings.

"Latin." He sounded relieved. "I was there before. You remember."

I did. He'd told me he'd been expelled for filling the lock of the headmaster's office door with glue. I tried to remember where exactly Latin was, to picture the route from there to Waller. He must have skipped his last class to have intercepted me.

"My grandfather made the arrangements. He would have preferred to ship me off to military school then and there. Dad stopped that. But it's a last-chance situation. If I mess up again, off I go."

I took a sharp breath, embarrassed by the tears I felt pricking my sinuses. We were passing the playing field Waller's teams shared with the boys of the nearby manual training school. Both football teams were running drills, two separate clusters of boys in their respective school colors. A chorus of trilling whistles and barking coaches was punctuated by the thud of boys' bodies colliding with dummy defenders. Garth touched my forearm.

"Hey," he said, gently. I scowled, annoyed that he'd noticed my need for gentleness. It was just that it was an awful thing to think about: Chicago without Garth. "Follow me."

He led me to the far end of the playing field, around to the back of the field house, where he pushed through a stand of goldenrod and cattails into a small clearing. At its center was a shed made of bare, weather-beaten wood. The air was still and humid and smelled of dead plants and something like sodden fur.

"I found this place, last winter," he said, wiping his sleeve against the shed's window. He pressed his hand against his forehead as he peered through the spot he'd cleared. "I used to come here after school, just to be alone. To think." He pulled his ruler from his schoolbag, jimmied it under the window, and levered it up until he had enough room to work a few fingers in. When he'd gotten the window open he climbed through, disappearing for an instant before popping back up and extending a hand to me.

I pulled my dress from my sticky chest to waft some air against my skin. I wasn't even an hour into my reunion with Garth and already we were breaking into a building. And right after he'd told me he had one more chance before his grandfather would send him away. I leaned through the window. The shed was dim and smelled of wool and leather and ancient sweat, and the wooden planks that made up the walls and floor. Garth grabbed my arms, and I felt a rush of excitement, as if one of the stories I'd written and burned were coming to life. He pulled; I tugged one leg and then another over the sill, managing to pull the muscle in my calf as I tumbled in.

"Steady?" Garth said, and I nodded.

He let go of me and began emptying crates of their contents—gloves and baseballs and clipboards and basketball jerseys. I brushed thick brown dust off the front of my dress. The ceiling was low—a few inches above his head at its peak. In the small square of open floorspace, he arranged the crates as table and chairs.

"Ta-da," he said.

I was warming to the idea now. What trouble were we causing, really, by being here? We would straighten up again, when we were finished. I shouldn't be alone with a boy, not like this, I knew that, but Uncle Eugene's warnings were nothing but a mosquito-like hum in the back of my brain. I laid a handkerchief over the table. Garth pulled snacks from his schoolbag: a couple of apples, a box of Cracker Jack, two Hershey's bars. I added my tomato to the spread and sat down across from him. He pulled out a pack of cigarettes—he'd switched to tailor-mades—and lit one for himself and one for me.

The first nicotine I'd consumed since June rushed through my veins and made my mind crackle. We were quiet for a while, as if we couldn't quite remember how to talk to each other. Then Garth squinted up at the ceiling.

"What?" I asked. He stood and took a step. "What is it?"

He reached into the rafters and pulled down a pint bottle. For an instant, I wondered if he'd left it there the last time he was in the shed. If he'd brought me here on purpose, in a scheme to make me drink it. I stood to get a better look. The bottle was only half full, coated thickly with dust. No, it must have been sitting there for ages. Forgotten.

He unscrewed the cap and held it out for me to sniff. And then the bottle was in my hands. I'd taken it from him, the decision frictionless, like movement in a dream. The liquid carved a sharp line along my tongue and throat and filled my sinuses with heat before I'd even registered its flavor—sharp, chemical. My stomach heaved, but I took a deep breath through my nose, and then another small sip. Garth watched me admiringly. Heat striped my chest. I handed him the bottle. He drank and wiped his mouth with the back of his hand.

We ate Cracker Jack. My fingers grew sticky. My teeth grew sticky. I drank more to rinse them. Things began to blur around the edges. Garth tossed a piece of Cracker Jack into the air, mouth open beneath it, but it bounced off his chin and to the floor. Laughter trickled past my lips in a way that felt foreign to my body—as if I were listening to myself laugh rather than laughing, which only made me laugh harder. Garth laughed too. I wondered if Josie had done this, felt these things. If her body had ever seemed to soften, as if she were being done over in watercolors. If her fingers had ever grown thick and clumsy, if she'd ever had to concentrate with all her might to make them cut a tomato in half with a penknife.

When the bottle was nearly empty, I stood to offer the last sip to Garth. The shed rolled forward like a Ferris wheel. He laughed and drank. I hadn't sung a note in six months save a hymn on Sunday, but I started to hum. Garth drummed the table. As soon as a bead of self-consciousness formed, the soft, smooth heat of my body melted it away again. I slid my shoe against the dirty floor and lifted the ball of my foot just enough to bring it down again with a solid tap: brush, step. Then my left foot, brush, step. Touch, scuff, touch, scuff, my hum turning to syllables: baa dee baa.

His eyes were bright and fixed on me. At first, my left arm felt extraneous, but then I made it do things: I slid it like a sunburst from my body, I waved it, I cupped it under my chin. He buzzed his lips against the mouth of the empty bottle as if it were a trumpet. I spun, the ball of my foot inscribing a disc in the dust on the floor. I tried to focus my eyes on a knot in the wall over his head, my spotting knot, but the knot started spinning too, and then the whole shed did. I stumbled forward, and all at once he was underneath me. I'd knocked him off his crate. The press of our bodies, the tangle of our limbs was excusable, an accident, but I forced myself to scramble off of him, to crawl away, to lean against the wall. The shed was so small, Garth's body still so close to mine, Garth's body that a moment earlier had been right against mine. Uncle Eugene's voice came blaring back to life, preaching of the preciousness of virtue, a girl's special responsibilities. My face grew hot.

"It's a little—I'm feeling a little—" I rushed for the open window, hoisted myself through. But I moved too quickly, not quite sure of my limbs, and the windowsill scraped hard against my shin. I spilled out onto the ground, landing on my hands, my dress slipping down to my hips until I managed to drag my feet down after the rest of me. The scent of the weeds was thicker than before; it coated the back of my throat. I tried to stand but the ground tipped beneath my feet. I bent over, pressing my temples with my fingertips, and saw the blood streaming down my shin, soaking into my sock. As soon as I looked at it, the scrape began to throb. I lowered myself to the solid, sun-warmed ground and let my head fall into my hands, retreating into the pinkish dark behind my eyelids.

Garth clambered out after me.

"Christ, Harriet, your leg," he said. I nodded miserably. The afternoon had become a knot I didn't know how to untangle. In the distance, I could still hear the thumps and grunts of the football practice. I tried to concentrate on closer, gentler sounds: wind rustling through the goldenrod and cattails, the buzz of insects.

"Come over," Garth said, his voice so soft I wasn't sure I'd heard it. "Dad's teaching. You could get cleaned up."

I opened my eyes. He was standing over me, a shadow with a glowing outline. I let him help me to my feet. His new clothes were rumpled. A velvet sheen of sweat filmed his upper lip. He was waiting for my answer, something pulsing in his expression—a fear or a need that made my breath catch. I nodded, not quite trusting myself to speak.

But as soon as we started toward his house, I worried I'd made a mistake. Had the invitation not been sincere? Or had I responded in the wrong way? "Dad's teaching," he had said. I remembered that his father was some sort of scientist, that he taught at a college. Who would be home, then? The mother he never mentioned? A maid? I thought about everything he'd said about his grandparents—DAR, soup spoons, his grandfather's club. Latin was a private school. Oh, God, he was rich. I was dumb for not having realized it before. In books, rich children always had nannies. Did Garth have a nanny? I wouldn't have put myself in Mrs. Broom's path just then, let alone Mama's. Was a nanny more like a mother, or like a mother's friend?

We turned onto Dearborn and passed honest-to-god mansions, and I grew more certain: there would be a nanny, maybe a nanny and a maid. I was tempted to tell him never mind, not on my account, but blood was pooling in my shoe, and I was desperate to tend to the squelching as much as the pain. Besides which, his jaw was set, he was pressing forward with a grim determination I couldn't quite make sense of. I blew up into my own nostrils, trying to gauge the potency of the liquor on my breath.

He turned down a street of greystones, not as elegant as the Dearborn Street houses but still imposing. A brick wall topped by a wrought-iron fence ran the length of the block, the black bars gleaming as if someone had been paid to polish them. The lawns were a vibrant green, the elms that lined them evenly spaced, their branches arching over the street to form a canopy that rustled quietly and admitted sunlight in glittering streams. I imagined his nanny shaking her head at the uneven haircut Mrs. Broom had given me the week before and the bright strip of fabric at the bottom of my skirt where two nights earlier, in anticipation of the first day of school, I had let down the hem.

"Well, here we are."

He'd stopped in front of the one house on the block with chipping paint and a shaggy lawn. Yellow weeds reached through the fence. I concentrated on keeping my face neutral. We squeezed sideways through a gate rusted partway open. The porch was strewn with leaves, the mailbox overflowing with waterlogged letters.

He pulled a key out of his jacket pocket, and there was the answer, blaring in my brain like a siren: no nanny, no anyone. The siren became Uncle Eugene's voice: a Wise Daughter does not enter an empty house with a boy unchaperoned.

The vestibule was crowded with suitcases, from their trip, I assumed, half of them open, clothes and shoes and books spilling out in all directions. We climbed over the mess, toward a staircase that curved gently to the second story, boxes and stacks of paper littering the steps. To our right, in a parlor, dust swam in the weak light, furred a mantelpiece and bookshelves and an armoire missing two drawers. We went left, through a wide archway into a dining room, where the table was crowded with books and graph paper and index cards.

"We had to let the housekeeper go," Garth said, his voice hard and wary, as if he were daring me to disbelieve him. "She moved some of Dad's papers when he was onto an important discovery. It was a disaster." He cleared a chair of two books and a slide rule. "You can stay here. I'll be right back."

He stepped boldly on a dried splat of ink, the capsized bottle still lying beside it, and disappeared through a swinging door.

On the floor near my chair, a small mountain of spent tea bags, mold foaming up one side, rose from a pink china plate. Tacked to the wall across from me was a strip of butcher paper, chalked with diagrams and figures. Beside it was a large framed photograph of Garth as a small boy. He wore a white gown and stood beside a wooden horse with wheels, smiling shyly at someone off to the side of the camera. A chip of glass was missing from the corner of the frame.

A few minutes later he returned, arms full of towels and bandages and iodine, and directed me to a powder room up the hall. My face swam in the tarnished mirror. The faucets were stiff with lime. I propped my leg up on the sink and, ignoring a grimy chip of soap, cleaned myself up as best I could. The scrape was as wide as my finger and three inches long, but not deep. After a few attempts, I managed to get a bandage to stay wrapped around my leg. I rinsed my mouth and spat into the sink, then cupped my hand over my mouth and tested my breath again.

When I returned to the dining room, Garth offered me a pop, his voice bright but tense, as if he were afraid I would say no and leave, now that my immediate need had been addressed.

"Yes. Thank you."

In the kitchen, there were crumbs on the floor, and, along the baseboards what looked like cat hair, though I hadn't seen a cat. But otherwise, things were more orderly than in the front of the house, if only because there were so few of them: two sets of dishes—plate, cup, fork, knife, and spoon—sat on a crusty towel beside the sink, along with a single frying pan. In an open cupboard, a canister labeled FLOUR sat between one labeled LARD and a small tower of tinned sardines. He pulled two bottles of Coke out of an electric refrigerator and hurried to shut it again. I tried to picture Garth eating dinner. Did he clear the dining room table? Or did he eat standing up at the empty counter? Who cooked for him? Where was his mother?

A twisting back staircase carried us up into close, warm air, the ruddy dimness brightening as we neared a porthole window. My shin stung; the Coke bottle sweated in my hand. I was conscious that we were moving away from the public parts of the house. This seemed a deeper transgression than being alone with Garth in the shed, with the busy field right there, the window open to the park.

At the top of the stairs we stepped into a large room, but it felt more like stepping into a different house: The air smelled of lemons and vinegar. Light poured in through two large skylights and tall windows that lined the front and back walls. The woodwork gleamed. Mrs. Broom would have approved of the trampoline tautness of Garth's sheets, though the pillowcases didn't match, and the quilt folded at the foot of the bed was faded and threadbare. Propped along every wall were canvases, some empty, some draped in cloths, others painted: bright stripes and boxes of color stacked into forms that made me think of people or buildings or birds. Tacked between the canvases and to the window frames and the bookcases were Garth's cartoons. A huge sheet of butcher paper like the one I'd seen downstairs was filled edge to edge with a crowd scene, detailed heads affixed to vaguely sketched bodies. I recognized Calvin Coolidge and Charles Lindbergh and assorted teachers from Waller. He'd drawn dinosaurs and leggy girls, a line of wiener dogs dressed as pilots, a gleaming glass city on a cloud. There was an enormous caveman perched on a seaside cliff, swinging a club into a round moon with a scowling face.

At the desk—a board on sawhorses—Garth took off his watch and methodically emptied his pockets into containers. I pictured him coming home at the end of the day to an empty house, dragging a bucket up the stairs, scrubbing the dust from every surface in his room, his sanctuary. Maybe he ate dinners he made himself at the tidy desk where he also sat to draw. Beside the desk was a bookshelf. The top two shelves were crowded with paints and brushes and bottles, and the rest with books: *Robinson Crusoe; Ralph 124C 41+;* a dozen issues each of *Youth's Companion, Amazing Stories,* and *Weird Tales;* Every Boy's Library editions of *Treasure Island* and *The Last of the Mohicans; The Time Machine; Knots, Splices, and Rope Work; The Hound of the Baskervilles; Naval Heroes of the American Revolution.* On the bottom shelf an assortment of objects was arranged as if in a museum display: enamel mugs, a large gold medallion engraved with an image of an old man's face, a small stuffed horse with a leather saddle. When I bent down to study them, I saw the nameplate from Mr. Gow's office. A thump of shame as I recognized what I was looking at: a display of stolen goods.

I stood too quickly and the room began to spin. I steadied myself against the bookshelf. Once more, I had slammed against the problematic fact: I was alone with a boy, a thief, in an empty house, woozy with drink. I felt the want of my reliable good sense, everything I had practiced over the summer. I wished I could press a button and shed the lingering effects of the liquor, think clearly, properly.

"You ever seen one of these?" Garth asked, hurrying, as if he sensed my unease, to a telescope on a tripod beside the window. I shook my head. "My grandparents gave it to me."

He removed the lens cap and gestured for me to look.

"Tell me when it's clear," he said, reaching for a knob on the side. My lashes brushed against the eyepiece. If I stepped three inches to the right, I would feel his sleeve against my cheek.

"There." In a circle of light I saw the gray edge of a rooftop where a pigeon perched.

He bent down, his sleeve brushing mine for an instant as I stepped out of the way so he could look.

"Ah, Marcel."

"The pigeon?"

"That's him all right."

"How can you tell?"

"His French accent."

I laughed.

"This used to be my mother's studio. She was an artist. Is an artist. A painter."

He pulled a yellow cloth from his pocket and started polishing the telescope's lens. I was conscious of the thump of my heart.

"Where is she?" I said, and cringed: I'd meant to sound gentle, inviting, but the words had come out like a demand.

He folded the yellow cloth and put it down on the windowsill. "Mexico. She lives there."

"Oh."

"Dad's family never liked her," he said after a pause. He looked out the window. "After I fought those boys, everyone had this conversation in the library—Aunt Cookie and Uncle Stacy and my grandfather, and my cousin Marjorie was hanging around, enjoying every minute. Dad was there but didn't say much. And they talked about her—about my mother—like she had some disease. Like I'd caught it from her and could spread it to Marjorie.

"It wasn't like this before, you know. The house. Mother kept things in order. There was help. But she was unhappy. She'd left before. For a few weeks. The first time she told me about Mexico, she was crying, but she promised she wouldn't be gone long. And then one day she came into my bedroom very excited, with a new suitcase for me, and said we were going together, that it would be a grand adventure. All hushed, like it was a secret. But that's not what happened. I was nine. No one told me anything. Gigi and Grandfather turned up. I think they assumed they'd be in charge, and for a while, they were. They wanted to take me, and Dad said no to that, but he went along with everything else—lawyers, servants, schools. But he is—particular. He likes things a certain way. He needs quiet. And privacy. He fired the housekeeper after a few weeks. The nanny not long after. The first time things really came apart, Gigi and Grandfather let it go on a while. I think they were trying to teach him a lesson, to prove he couldn't manage so he would send me to them. But they swooped in eventually, got things in order, as much as he'd let them. They'll swoop in again."

"Do you see her? Your mother."

His mouth twitched. He fingered the edge of the curtain.

"She came three Christmases ago. I'm supposed to go to her in the summers, but no one ever gets around to arranging it."

He pulled the curtain shut. And then he hurried around to the other windows, closing all the curtains. He stood on his desk chair and dragged shades down over the skylights, plunging the room into darkness. The mattress springs squeaked. I heard a drawer open and close, and a moment later, he was lying on his back on the bed, shining a flashlight at the ceiling, illuminating a galaxy of iridescent silver stars.

"I painted these," he said. "When I was a kid." He wound the circle of light in slow figure eights, naming the constellations it touched: Andromeda, Perseus, Taurus. I saw him as a little boy, consulting a map of the sky, climbing a ladder, his brow furrowing as he applied the silver paint with one of the paintbrushes his mother had left behind. Had she been the one to teach him their names?

"And here are Harriet and Josephine Szász." It was the one constellation I knew: Gemini, the twins. Daddy had pointed to it through a train window when we were small, and after that I'd looked for it any time I was out at night beneath a clear sky. I'd even cut the relevant entry from an encyclopedia in a Des Moines hotel. For years I had carried it in my valise.

He'd said it to please me. But as my eyes fleshed out the stick figures plotted by daubs of silver paint, I felt a stab of irritation. Go away, I prayed to Josie. And then I was bounding across the room, I was climbing into the bed beside Garth and pushing the flashlight to a new cluster of stars.

"What's that one?"

On the handle of the flashlight, our fingers were just touching. I could feel the warmth of his body, I could detect its weight through the mattress, I could smell the liquor we'd drunk in the shed, and the soap he'd washed with that morning. And I felt something in my stomach, like a silk ribbon puckering. I snatched my hand away. But it was as if all the practice kissing I'd done that summer, all the sordid, late-night imagining, had rushed into my body at once. My every particle trembled in concert, willing him to kiss me.

"Orion," he said softly. He turned off the flashlight. The mattress squeaked as he turned onto his side to face me. He took off his glasses; when my eyes adjusted to the darkness, his eyes seemed larger than they usually did behind the lenses. Even though I could see a wanting in them that matched mine, there was also a heaviness—melancholy, perhaps, or maybe just a soberness, the weighty understanding that something had shifted between us that afternoon, that things would be different now than they'd been before.

I kissed him. Quickly, on the cheek. Even in the dark I could see the flush that crept up his neck. He shifted, closing the space between us, and just like that, his hands were pressing against my ears, his fingers sliding into my hair like combs, as his lips flicked against my forehead, my nose. Then at last: his mouth was meeting mine. Pressing mine.

The practice I'd done with my arm hadn't prepared me for the wetness of it or the warmth, or for the tumbling feeling inside me, a desire that somehow only grew, now that the thing I so badly wanted was actually, really, honestly happening. Our teeth clicked together, and we jerked apart. He rubbed his knuckle against his eyebrow and looked sheepishly away. For all his self-assured bad behavior, maybe Garth had never kissed anyone either. Then all at once I felt as unkissed as ever, as if now that the kissing had stopped I would never recall the precise physical sensation. The panic lasted only a few seconds before we were kissing again.

I don't know how long we kissed. For ages, and nowhere near long enough. We kissed until a man's voice carried up the stairs.

"Garth?"

He fumbled for the lamp, pressing a finger to his lips, trying not to laugh. I was as far from laughter as I'd ever been. Caught, I kept thinking, the word slicing through me, we were caught, and Mama would be told, and maybe Uncle Eugene.

"Be right there, Dad," he called.

He gestured for me to follow him—to a window at the back of
the house.

"Don't worry," he said softly, smiling. He opened the window
and unbuckled a rope ladder that was attached beneath the windowsill. "He doesn't come up here. But you'll have to go out this
way. Just give me ten seconds to get down there and make sure he
isn't near the window. Go out the back gate. There's an alley. Can
you find your way?"

I nodded, astounded at his calm. He threw the rope ladder out
the window. It bounced against the back of the house with a thud
that made me cringe. My head was spinning. My knees felt like wet
cardboard.

"What if I slip?" I managed to say.

"You won't."

I climbed out backward, foot swiping the air for a horrible
moment before I found a rung, which rotated under my foot, then
leveled. He was holding my arm, and, briefly, the pleasure of it overwhelmed my panic. I didn't want to move. I wanted in perpetuity to
be dangling out Garth Mosher's window, for Garth Mosher to be
holding me fast, both of us sliding down the thin back edge of in-
toxication. Kiss me, I thought, and he did, but quickly, shyly.

"Garth?" his father called again.

"See you later," he said, and dashed across the room.

I counted ten seconds and started climbing. The ladder twisted
beneath my weight. When I passed the window, I closed my eyes. A
few feet from the bottom, I jumped. My bandage slipped and my
shin stung. But I stood and steadied myself and jogged through a
thicket of yellow-green ferns. A grapevine had tangled itself around
the back gate, but I ripped it away from the latch and pushed into
the alley.

When I came back around to Garth's street, I crossed to the
other side and walked calmly, innocently, as if I were in no way
drunk or wounded, as if I had in no way just been surprised by the
father of a boy while I lay beside him in his actual bed. I allowed
myself one quick look at the attic window, hoping he'd be there,

waving, but all I could see was a smear of sunlight in the glass. A warm sensation filled my body, as if a lamp had been lit inside me, and there was a wetness between my legs that I was dimly afraid was blood, but which I quickly deduced was something else, something relevant to the Sex Act, which made me feel solemn and adult. Pleased to be rooted in my own body. Responsible for it.

On my way home, I stopped in at the Stop and Shop and scraped thirty cents from the bottom of my schoolbag to buy a dozen of the doughnuts Minnie liked. When I came out again, the sun was an orange glaze on the rooftops. As I walked, I ate three of Minnie's doughnuts and smiled at everyone I passed, every shopkeeper and traffic cop and mother walking with her child, wishing I could tell them what I, Harriet Szász, had done.

*

THAT SUNDAY, UNCLE EUGENE CAUGHT MY EYE AFTER CHURCH and beckoned for Mama and me to join him. My eye, not Mama's, and even though I felt embarrassed on Mama's behalf, I also thrilled to think I was gaining some larger role in our dealings with him. My pleasure was tempered by the slightest flicker of unease about Garth. Every afternoon that week, I'd found him waiting beneath the oak tree out in front of Waller after school.

Uncle Eugene introduced us to a member of the board of trustees, referring to me as his niece and Mama as my mother rather than his sister-in-law. When the man had gone, Uncle Eugene turned to Mama and, in a voice like brown sugar, said he had spoken to his friend, the owner of the furniture factory. He had been surprised to learn that Daddy was no longer in his employ.

Without missing a beat, she pressed a hand against his robed arm. "Oh, Eugene, I've been wanting to tell you—he's just moved to a new position, very promising. Foreman. This operation makes galoshes. They'd heard of his good reputation in the position you arranged for him and tempted him away. But Lenny didn't give proper notice. I was ashamed of that." I recognized the architecture of her lie: she was using Mrs. Broom's husband's factory to make the story seem truer, and apologizing for something false so she could blunt his anger without admitting to a more dangerous truth.

But I saw this too: She was protecting Daddy from Uncle Eugene's judgment. Propping him up, as if however angry she was, part of her wished she could tell Uncle Eugene all about the fine new position my father had found himself at the opera. Some of Mama's lies to Uncle Eugene were meant to be visible, to be received as a kind of payment, while others were meant to be secret. But I couldn't tell which were which. Maybe I was becoming a little more responsible for our relationship with Uncle Eugene, Mama a little less. But their shared past was still a mystery.

When she let her gaze drop down to the carpet, I thought, as I often did, that she was laying it on a little thick. But Uncle Eugene folded her hands together between his.

"We can only pray for him, Maude. That's all we can do."

"Thank you, Eugene," she said. When she looked back up at him, her eyes gleamed with tears. I couldn't say whether or not they were real.

A COUPLE OF WEEKS LATER, I CAME HOME FROM THE MOVIES, where Garth and I had kissed more than we watched, and found a postcard in the mail slot addressed to me in a hand I couldn't quite identify. There was no message. On the front was a photograph of a woman performing at a club, a comedienne, she seemed to be, dressed in an apron with frizzed-out hair, waving a fish in one hand, a rolling pin in the other. A banner over her head read TABITHA LONG, ONE NIGHT ONLY! After a moment, I realized the picture was defaced: dark eyebrows and devil horns and pointy teeth, scrawled over the comedienne's face. And then I recognized her: Tabitha Long. Tibby Longfellow, our old vaudeville nemesis. The postcard was from Josie.

Relief rolled over me in a wave. She hadn't forgotten me. But why now, when she'd never responded to the letter I'd sent care of Raymond Fish back in April? Well, maybe my letter had gotten lost in the mail. Or maybe she'd simply been too scared that if she wrote back, Mama and Daddy would have intercepted the letter and discovered all her private business. And then, as if she had transmitted it to me directly, I felt the heat of the anger in which she'd drawn over Tibby Longfellow's face. And I knew, somehow, that she hadn't actually been trying to send me a message about Tibby. She'd been trying to tell me something else, something she couldn't write down.

But what her anger was really about I couldn't say. Perhaps I was even its target.

"Harriet, is that you?" Mrs. Broom called from the kitchen. I stuffed the postcard into my pocket and wiped away a few tears with the heel of my hand, hoping my nose hadn't turned too red, that Mrs. Broom wouldn't ask what was wrong.

All through dinner, I worked on a response in my head. I would make her see that I still loved her, that I needed her to write back, a real letter, to tell me all about her life. When I got back up to the alcove, my pen flew across the page. I asked about her travels and Raymond Fish. I asked whether she'd seen Tibby perform, or if they'd spoken. I told her that whatever she needed she could tell me, and not to worry: She could write me at Garth's address. I was sure he wouldn't mind. We could keep her secrets safe.

That was the whole of the message I'd composed in the kitchen, but when I got to the end of it, I found I wasn't ready to stop writing. In no time at all, I'd filled three pages, front and back, telling her about everything that had happened to me since we'd come to Chicago, and especially about Garth: the time we'd spent together in the spring, the afternoons we'd shared since the start of school. My first kiss, and those that had followed. I signed the letter and folded it into thirds, my cheeks hot, the callus on my third finger tender. It was only then that it struck me as strange that when I'd written her in April, it had seemed enough to ask her to let me back into her life. That I'd felt no great urge to tell her about my own.

*

ON THE FIRST TUESDAY IN NOVEMBER, THE MORNING OF THE opera's opening night, Daddy hefted a rented tuxedo over his shoulder and shot Mama a final, mournful look as he asked us to wish him broken legs. A few weeks earlier, he'd brought home three tickets for the opening night gala, which Mama had pinched between her thumb and forefinger as if they were something filthy he had tracked in by mistake and handed back to him without a word. Daddy had set them in the middle of the table, where they'd sat ever since, getting spilled on, getting buried under mail and surfacing again. Mama still hadn't said a word about them. A few minutes after he left, she told me she was sick, that she wouldn't be able to go to work, and would I please hurry along because she needed desperately to rest. She lay down on the couch with her eyes screwed shut. I had the odd feeling that as soon as I left she would cry.

After school, Garth and I spent an hour hiding behind a boulder on an empty beach, his big coat tented over us to keep out the drizzle. I took my time walking home, in no hurry to get back to the apartment and Mama's mood. Besides, I was enjoying the way the mist beaded on my coat and curled the ends of my hair. A block from Mrs. Broom's I took off my hat. The porch railing was wet and cold beneath my fingers and I thought of the wet metal of the fire escape ladder on the afternoon of my birthday, when Garth and I had broken into the movies.

I stepped into the parlor and stifled a scream—Mrs. Broom was standing there like a ghost in her glossy pink dressing gown. She grabbed my arm and pulled me toward the back of the house.

"Your mother is awfully curious about what's kept you so late after school," she said, but even as I flushed I felt sand in my shoe and wanted to laugh. "And Christ almighty, what have you let happen to your hair?"

She ushered me into her sitting room, where Mama was standing, arms crossed, surveying a profusion of gowns: gowns piled on couches, hanging from curtain rods and lamps, draped over the backs of chairs.

"What's going on?" I asked.

Mama looked at me as if I'd said something stupid, and with a great rush of excitement, I realized that I had.

"It's an opening night, Harriet. Do you plan to go dressed like that?"

———

THE TAXI CARRIED US as far as the Madison Street Bridge, but the driver refused to continue into the chaos on the other side. Mrs. Broom opened up her big black umbrella, and Mama and I huddled beneath it. Across the river, the new Civic Opera Building loomed, freshly stripped of its scaffoldings, crisscrossed by searchlights.

"Well I'll be damned," Mrs. Broom said at last, breaking the spell, and we started over the bridge. Far below, the river heaved, smelling of gasoline. I held my dress gingerly off the sidewalk. Police officers patrolled the bridge in pairs, and there were more of them on the other side, where Wacker Drive was packed with honking automobiles and their shouting drivers, where gawkers and souvenir sellers mingled with the fur-clad and top-hatted. We passed the ruins of an old elevated railroad spur, which marked a stark boundary between Sam Insull's territory and the desolate neighborhood in which he had decided to build.

A wooden ramp carried us out of the street and into the shelter of the opera house's portico, which blocked the rain but channeled the wind. Ladies clutched anxiously at their skirts and their hair. Photographers shouted for us to get out of the way of their subjects. Mama cleared a path with her cane. When she handed our tickets to an usher, he kindly pretended not to notice the jam thumbprint on one or the coffee ring on another.

The lobby was just as Daddy had described it: the thick carpets, the gilt sconces like nested tulips, mounted on magnificent columns with pleated façades. Mrs. Broom kept a protective hand on my elbow. I moved gingerly against the pins with which we had hastily altered her gown—black silk, backless, with strings of black beads. Mrs. Broom and I had pinned Mama into a sheath of silver spangles, which caught the light in shimmering waves. Mrs. Broom's dress was covered in black ostrich feathers, her wrap arranged to conceal the spots where they had frayed or fallen out or been nibbled by moths. Ushers and maids coursed through the crowd. Fireguards stood proudly at their posts, flanked by bronze urns holding massive arrangements of hydrangeas—Rosa Raisa's signature bloom, Mrs. Broom told us, which, according to the paper, had been delivered that morning on a special express train from Florida.

It was only after we checked our furs that I noticed that the most elegant ladies were all in pale smooth dresses—ecru and lavender and pearl—and I could see that the gowns we'd chosen from Mrs. Broom's stash were distinctly out of fashion. My hair bounced around my head like a cloud of cotton candy, an inelegant, in-between length, dried to frizz. Still, in Mrs. Broom's black silk, with her pearl ring on my finger, her perfume dabbed at my wrists and ears, I felt glamorous. I wasn't sure in what spirit Mama had de-cided that we would attend opening night. In the cab on the way over, she hadn't tried to stop me from powdering my face or putting on lipstick. We'd drunk champagne as we'd dressed—Mama hadn't tried to stop that either—and as we moved through the lobby, she seemed to receive with pleasure the gossip Mrs. Broom shared in a voice veering dangerously close to Too Loud. That pinched-faced woman spent twenty thousand a year on wigs, that man in the starched collar was a Field cousin, who kept a boyfriend as well as a wife. That was Mrs. McCormick, and that was Mrs. McCormick's million-dollar necklace. The stock market had crashed a week be-fore, and Mama and Mrs. Broom took guesses as to who had lost what. The room must have been full of gutted fortunes, but every-one had put on a brave—and well-groomed—face.

An old man with a drooping white mustache and round glasses appeared before us, beaming and expectant.

"Congratulations," Mrs. Broom said, shaking his hand. "It's mar-velous."

Overcome with emotion, he did not speak. He took my hand in both his and he kissed Mama on the cheek before drifting to another group. Mrs. Broom laughed and told us we'd just met Sam Insull.

In the auditorium, the seats spread before us like a sea. There were no columns. Daddy had explained that to me—clever archi-tects had eliminated them, so no one would have an obstructed view. The ceiling was pitched and dimpled. Daddy had explained

that too, something to do with acoustics. Gilt woodwork bordered
the ceilings and the rosy wall panels. The theater scents rushed
me—muslin and sawdust and glue, paint, the snappy odor of electric
lights—and I couldn't help looking to my left, as if I might find Josie
there, bound to me in the harness. She had always been telling me
why theaters and people I thought were elegant were actually
dumpy and small-time. But this I was sure she would have considered on her level.

We followed an usher to the front of the orchestra section, where
I sank into a thick, soft seat. A frail man with feathery eyebrows and
a white silk cravat took the seat to my right, grinning as if we were
children together at the fair. "I saw Mary Garden sing it in '22," he
said, a distant look in his milky eyes. I nodded and opened my program.

At last, the lights dimmed. The crowd quickly hushed. The mae-
stro stepped into the pit, and there was a rustle of excited whispers
and a round of applause. As we sang the national anthem, the new
opera house felt like a civic achievement, a rightful source of pride.

The audience was a single organism now—together we sat and
settled into silence. The conductor lifted his arms, and a violin
curled through a snakelike phrase. Mama gripped the corner of her
shawl. Other instruments joined, strings first, and then woodwinds,
brass, and timpani, in thick waves of sound by turns sweet and
strange. The great velvet curtains parted, and we saw what Daddy
had helped to build: tall columns carved with hieroglyphs framed a
backdrop of pyramids and yellow sky. A man clad in a golden neck
plate and white robes filled his broad body with breath and opened
his mouth; a low, rich voice rolled from him like a thunderclap.

At first, I tried to follow the story in the program, but the singers
kept drawing my attention. Even though I didn't understand the
language, they conveyed—with a sudden diminuendo, with the lift
of an eyebrow, with a broadening of the sound, a lean into its full-
ness, like belting but grander—all I needed to know. A soldier's
pride; the pain of unrequited love; the fear of a slave held captive in
the land of her enemy.

The company sang of a coming war and then left Rosa Raisa alone onstage. Her black brows lifted and trembled. Her heavy lips seemed to draw her voice up from her throat in silken sheets. She knelt, reaching her braceleted arms toward the edge of a circle of light, and I felt her anguish pass through my own chest. Her eyes were wide and glistening as she made her plea to terrible love: break my heart and let me die.

A row of columns fell in from the flies. In a swift, silent ballet, black-clad stagehands rolled out massive statues—snakes and dogs with human feet and faces. An altar appeared, upstage right. As soon as the scene was set, troops of priests and priestesses processed onstage, praying in an otherworldly chorus. Dancing princesses wrapped Radames in a silver veil. As the high priest prayed, two others carried a sword and shield from the altar and placed them in Radames's hands. The company formed a tableau, with Radames kneeling beside the altar, the high priest standing over him, arms lifted to the heavens, the other priests and priestesses filling the width of the stage, some standing on platforms, others kneeling, their bodies forming a shape like an arrow, pointing toward the soldier.

The curtain fell, and the lights came up: first intermission. My cheeks were wet. My whole body felt as if it had been flooded with light. It took me several seconds to come back into the world, to realize my mother was holding my hand, that her own eyes glistened with tears.

BACKSTAGE, WHERE WE'D GONE to offer Daddy our congratulations, Mrs. Broom tucked an arm around me. I leaned against her, dizzy with sleepiness. It was late, later than I'd been out in a very long time. As soon as they saw each other, Daddy and Mama became wrapped in each other's gazes. Mama broke away just long enough to whisper with Mrs. Broom.

"Say good night now, Harriet," Mrs. Broom said. Mama would accompany Daddy to a party. Mrs. Broom would take me home.

We made our way back through the house, out into the lobby, where the crowds were lingering, lapping up every last bit of the glorious night. I noticed a girl, standing at the foot of the staircase that led up to the balcony. I knew her. But how could I know such a girl? I blinked away my sleepiness. A few years older than me, she wore her hair cropped, shiny waves curtaining one side of her forehead. Black liner reached like a thick apostrophe from the corner of her eye toward her temple. She had her head tipped back and was laughing, hand on a man's arm. He was handsome, with a gray-streaked beard. Her broad shoulders sat uncomfortably in her dress, as if she weren't used to wearing such a thing, and it had an almost-but-not-quite quality—pastel, like the fashionable ladies', but lime sherbet instead of pearl or rose. As she finished laughing, our eyes met. Her face froze, and I knew. She was my cousin Ruth.

She reached self-consciously for a heavy black stone she wore at her throat. Her escort hadn't noticed her looking at me, and Mrs. Broom hadn't noticed me looking at her. Did she even know we had been in Chicago for nine months? Did she know we were in her father's care? Was she supposed to be here, with that man? I nodded slightly, not wanting Mrs. Broom to see but wanting to acknowledge her, wanting her to understand that she mustn't let her father know the Family Szász was dabbling in the theater again. That I wouldn't tell my mother I'd seen her. She didn't nod, she didn't blink. The man she was with wrapped a fur around her shoulders. The crowd folded around them, and they were gone.

WHEN WE GOT HOME, I was nearly delirious with exhaustion, but I needed to write to Josie. She hadn't responded to my letter, but I'd written again anyhow, a few times, always taking care to use Garth's address, to assure her she had nothing to fear. I fought my drooping eyelids as I described every detail of the evening and told her how much I wished she had seen it all with me. I woke briefly when my parents stumbled in, and then I had to pull my pillow over my head to block the sound of their lovemaking.

When I opened my eyes again it was almost noon. I came out of the alcove and found Mama at the table in her robe, hair falling loose down her back. Daddy was still asleep in their bed.

"Don't worry about school. I telephoned. We're both out sick today." She brought me a cup of coffee, and a plate of eggs and bread, and then she broke an egg into a glass of tomato juice, stirred, and drank it down in one long motion. Gazing into her empty glass she began to speak—to brag—about the magnificence of the opera house and the grandeur of the sets, as if I hadn't been there to see them. She asked if I'd noticed that Daddy had given one of the statues in the altar scene her face—no, she said, she guessed I wouldn't have noticed, but after the house had cleared, he had taken her to the empty back stage and shown her everything up close. He'd persuaded the set decorator to let him do it. How like him that was, she said, to make a friend so quickly, to win people's trust. She smiled absently, scratched at something stuck to the table, and went on in a hushed voice, dipping into the history from before Josie and I were born that she had always left Daddy to tell. She told new stories I'd never heard, of which Daddy was the star. She told me about a wheeled horse he had built that moved across the stage as if by magic. A giant Christmas tree onto which she had been lowered, dressed as an angel. A dragonfly carved from soap, with translucent paper wings.

1912

As soon as the assistant stage manager says, "There's a fellow here to see you—seems sort of uptight," she knows it is Eugene. For seven years she has been a star. She is photographed, she is feted. Her professional name—plastered on posters in the subway, painted on a wall near Union Square—is the same name she had on the day he proposed. And she's seen him in the papers: the photogenic young preacher with the radical ideas about addressing his flock through moving pictures and popular magazines. Sometimes, reading an article describing one of his big tent meetings, she feels a certain kinship with him—Hobart may not take credit for her the way it does him, but there is no question they are the town's two biggest successes.

"Send him in," she says, giving her face a final pat of powder. It is a Wednesday afternoon, just after the matinée. She is wearing a silk kimono over her slip, and she considers leaving it untied. But at the last moment, for reasons she can't quite figure, she not only pulls it tightly shut but wipes off her lipstick.

"Maude Foster." His voice is warm but measured. She turns from the mirror. He is taller than her Lenny, his dark hair combed high, white bristles fanning along his temples. His shoulders are still broad, his years at the pulpit having done nothing to diminish his baseball player's frame.

"Offstage I'm Mrs. Leonard Szász," she says, standing to shake his hand. "It's good to see you, Gene. I suppose I ought to say Reverend Creggs now. You've come a long way, haven't you?"

"I'm not the only one." He gestures at the room, and beneath the praise she can detect his disapproval, carefully masked by his tolerance, as always. "Love the sinner, hate the sin," he writes in his newspaper column so often it is as if he believes he originated the line.

She offers him a drink, which he declines. He explains that he is in New York to speak at the YMCA student volunteer conference, and she says that sounds very interesting. She does not ask about James, but he shares, kindly, she thinks, that his brother has become an aviator and moved west.

"With his bride," he adds.

"I hope you'll congratulate him for me," she says, and is pleased with this response, which feels clever and steady, like something from a play. She is handling the situation. She is in control. Save for a half second in Philadelphia, she has always been in control with Eugene.

"I suppose you've wondered—"

"I haven't," she says and for an instant she fears that control might slip. Because in the seven years of their marriage, Maude has never told Lenny about the son she gave away. Eugene regards her gravely, but then he says, "As you wish," and sits down in the chair she has offered him. She leans back, comforted by the thought of her mirror behind her, and all of her makeup and getting ready things, and a bouquet, a little wilted but still colorful, that Lenny gave her last week, an apology, but Eugene doesn't know that. He lets his eyes pass over the room before settling them firmly on hers.

"There's something you should know," he says, stiffly. "Your mother was called home by the Lord. Three years ago."

She is only able to nod. It has occurred to her, over the years, that she might never see her mother again. But now that Eugene has told her the thing she once imagined has come to pass, the loss is unfathomable—she cannot make her mind hold fast to the idea, mark it as truth. Eugene is describing the funeral—what people wore, the flowers, the sorts of details that always interested her mother's friends, and she remembers one of them, long ago, describing young Eugene Creggs as "such a thoughtful conversationalist." She considers her father for the first time in years (easier, this, than to picture the empty space in his bed, in the pew at church, at the table, the absence that must have forced endless housework into her sister's small hands, all while Maude ate oysters and gave interviews and bought hats). The result is less damning than she might have expected: a man who kept his daughters in decent shoes and paid their school fees on time, but one whose early difficulty—losing two sisters to tuberculosis, leaving school at fourteen to save the farm—convinced him he alone was savvy to the world's cruelty. But no sooner has her sense of her father expanded than Eugene is telling her he died three months after her mother. "A broken heart, everyone said," and Maude peers at him through narrowed eyes, looking for the joke.

Now Eugene arrives at the climactic chapter. He cocks his head and softens his expression, as if anticipating Maude's need for sympathy, and maybe she has inherited something of her father's cynicism because the softness seems to her a mask over a smirk, and she hears the silent echo—poor Maude, how sorry you must be to have missed your chance—trailing his words: He was honored to minister to Marion during her bereavement, he says. More honored still, that when they discovered between them a mutual affection, she agreed to be his wife.

She wants to laugh. So Eugene Creggs went out and found himself another lost girl to save. And how fortunate for his career that the fallen woman was wise when the white knight was reckless, so he was free to rescue someone more suitable: a sweet-tempered, golden-haired orphan. But that the orphan is Marion, little Marion! In Maude's mind Marion is still twelve years old, sweeping out of the barn with a kitten in the crook of each arm, or lying on her stomach beside the pond, narrating the love stories of the dragonflies. Baby Marion, saddled for all eternity to Eugene Creggs. Making love with Eugene Creggs! They must not, she thinks, and then he tells her they have a little girl, Ruth, not quite two years old.

What a natural little mother Marion is, he says. She hears herself congratulating him. They wished so much they could have invited her to the wedding, he says, and trails off.

He smiles briskly, the difficult business over and done with. On to the inconsequential chat, the news from home. Eustace Beall has moved to Oregon where he has cousins. A new family has taken over the old Chewning farm, Canadians if you can believe it. Everyone has gone crazy for the new chop suey restaurant on Main Street. After a reasonable interval, he stands, and sweetly, spontaneously, she thinks, contrary to some earlier decision, he says he is free the following evening and would very much like to see her show.

"I'll have two tickets waiting at the box office," she says, warming toward him. Maybe he won't make such an awful brother.

"I'll only need one," he says.

. . .

heard you had a visitor this afternoon," Lenny says. It is that night, after the evening show. They are at Shanley's, eating clams.

"My, news travels," she says, breezily. But he is already halfway through a third glass of wine, and his eyelids are heavy, his face tinged that dangerous purple. He says nothing more about Eugene at dinner, but his anger lingers like a ringing in the ear. The fight flares later, in their pretty apartment on West Fourteenth Street, the one she has just finished decorating, the one they can't quite afford, but Mr. Fleischer has promised her a raise after Christmas so she called it an early Christmas treat, and since the management of ordinary life has always overwhelmed Lenny, the decision was hers to make: he signed where she told him to sign, with the old joke about at least getting to be the husband on paper, which used to feel playful, which used to make her laugh, but which feels, now, like something twisting between her ribs.

They fight because he is drunk, they fight because her little sister
is married to Eugene Creggs, they fight because even if she can't
say it to herself, let alone out loud, her parents are dead, her
mother is dead. Lenny says she has stopped loving him. Which
fills her with grief because she worries it's true. She insists it isn't.
How many times must she tell him that Eugene is not her lover,
that he never has been, that he is married, now, to her sister. And
he laughs, as if this fact only strengthens his case, and says, "He
comes all the way to New York, after all these years, to see his
wife's long-lost sister in a show?" And because she has already
told him about the YMCA conference, because she can see he is
determined to be jealous, because she suspects this wild, rootless
jealousy is really a manifestation of the other jealousy, the one
neither of them has ever named, the one that somewhere deep
beneath his conscious mind he must believe will only dissipate if
he can design his own sets, create something that shines on a
stage as brightly as his wife, because she is tired, because her head
aches, because she doesn't want to perform tomorrow with a
puffy face, she goes into the bedroom, slamming the door to
make it clear he is not welcome to follow. A minute later, she
hears him leave the apartment. After seven years of marriage, she
knows better than to expect him to return before morning.

. . .

The next night, in her dressing room, her thoughts are of
men and their love. James, with a boy's meager love; Eugene, who offered his love as a favor she couldn't accept; Lenny,
whom she loved violently until quite recently, maybe loves still,
though he seems hell-bent on making a mess of things. Bert
Koster spoke to her again when she arrived: Get him dried out
or we'll have no choice but to let him go, Maude. And she
knows if Bert were any other stage manager, and not Lenny's
friend, it would have happened already. But hasn't she tried?
That afternoon, he slammed into the apartment, changed his

clothes, and slammed right back out again without saying a word. She found him backstage, lifting sandbags, making sure the counterweights were set properly on the big set pieces that would, in the course of the show, fall in from the flies: the castle, the tepee, the red and white barn, the Liberty Bell. She meant to be cool, to allude, primly, to Bert's warning, but then he turned to look at her: his face damp and gray, his breath like an old penny, his eyes the deep wells of grief that belong still to the boy sent from his home at nine. And in that moment, she wanted only to wrap him in a quilt, to bind his hands so they couldn't pick up another bottle, to make him good so he can work properly, alongside her. Because when he is working properly it is impossible not to admire him, and with Lenny, her love has always flowed from admiration. She let him kiss her, even though he tasted like his long night, even though his body was dense and heavy against hers in that way she hated, his drunken slump. On her way to her dressing room, she avoided Vera's eye.

Every time she goes on that night, there is an instant in which she thinks of them—Eugene in the house and Lenny backstage. But then she begins to glow for the audience—not its individual members but the mass of it—and the audience returns her warmth in the frantic energy of its applause, and the men disappear, and Maude Szász disappears, leaving behind a beam of light in stockings and feathers, a beam of light in a green silk gown that weighs eight pounds and rustles like a cornfield with every step, a beam of light cheekily subverting her glamorous image by filling the front half of a cow suit while her very best friend in all the world makes a great joke of the rear, a beam of light dressed in a sequined leotard, red, white, and blue.

It is in that leotard that she spreads her arms to either side, as if to say, "Here she is, gentlemen!" Here she is, and they lean toward her, two thousand watching people. Eugene Creggs only matters because he is one among them, and Lenny Szász because he built the world in which she shines. She begins to sing, and light pours from her throat to fill the theater. It glazes every gilt lily on the proscenium arch, glides under the catwalk and brightens the cheap seats, heats the carpeted back wall. The conductor winks at her, and the strings begin to mark out their pizzicato path beneath her voice:

> I've conversed with gentlemen from Maine to
> Mozambique
> *(Hands on hips, sashay down center.)*
> Men of state, aristocrats, and now and then a
> sheikh
> *(Sashay stage left, toe point, wink.)*
> Something they agree on, men from all around the
> world
> *(Sashay stage right, toe point, wink.)*
> No specimen, does impress a man, quite like an
> American Girl.

The music swells, she twirls to stage right, and twenty showgirls pour down the silver staircase behind her, the stars and stripes waving from the soft, creamy flagpoles of their outstretched arms. Attached to their shoes are sparklers, eighty of them, shedding thin ribbons of fire. "God bless the U.S.A.!" they chant, and their voices lift her up as surely as winches or wings. Billy Bernhard marches on from stage left, dressed as Uncle Sam, six boys with snare drums circling him. Maude salutes. He enumerates the virtues of the American Girl while she gazes up at him, one hand pressing her chin, the other bent at her side like a wing. Adorable, electric, "A SPITFIRE!" the papers have called her, but in that moment she is thinking of none of this, she isn't thinking at all, she is only doing, experiencing the pure joy of

doing. The orchestra plays in a shuffling rhythm as the girls reach
the bottom of the steps and line up for one of Ned Wayburn's
new-style dances. Maude backs into formation at the center as
they sing about the achievements of American men (dams and
locks, bonds and stocks). Bounce, bounce, leg in the air, bounce,
bounce, leg in the air, aligning, with perfect precision, the sizzling
asterisks at their toes.

Maude sings:

> But he needs a lassie from Tallahassee to darn
>   his socks!

The music builds, all brass and drums. A map of the United
States the width of the stage falls into place behind them, the
drummer boys circle, two bald eagle puppets course the air on invisible wires, gobo-ed fireworks splash the proscenium, red, blue,
and green, Uncle Sam tours the kick line on a unicycle, and the
Liberty Bell begins its descent. There is a ripple of approval from
the audience; the bright blur of girls' voices masks the groan of
the ropes:

> When you encounter a patriotic beauty
> You must perform your patriotic duty—

There is a crack. Girls cry out and scatter, but Maude, at center, under her own spell, takes a moment too long to react to the
sight of the bell: swinging loose, free of a snapped guide rope—it
looks as if it ought to be sounding, a great ding-dong to match
the roll of its vast black shape—and then tumbling, tumbling,
until: a terrible sensation in her leg, which she will remember,
later, not as pain but as weight, like concrete packed over her
thigh. The curtain closes. She sees the pale, shocked faces of the
other girls as they cluster around her. Bert rushes over, trailed by

half a dozen grips. He is speaking to her, but she does not hear him, she does not hear the rising panic of the audience on the other side of the curtain, she only hears a voice in her head, a flat, clenched voice, an Ohio voice, her mother's voice, maybe, stating plainly what is plainly true: she will never dance again.

ONE AFTERNOON EARLY IN DECEMBER, I CAME OUT OF school and found Garth underneath the oak tree, hopping from foot to foot to keep warm. By then, I knew his father's teaching schedule by heart; without a word, we started walking toward his house. Already the daylight was beginning to thin. Curlicues of old snow blew across the sidewalk. The cold seemed to sharpen the clang of the streetcar's bell.

A month had passed since the opera's opening night. Uncle Eugene had made no sign he knew that Daddy was back in the theater or that Mama had been lying to him for months, or that I had been lying too, by omission. Eventually, I'd stopped worrying that Ruth would tattle. But I worried about Mama. On unrelated errands, she sometimes dragged me to the opera house, just to take a look around. One night I came upstairs from the kitchen after dinner and found she wasn't yet home. At ten, panicked, I fetched Mrs. Broom. We had very nearly decided to call the police when Mama came in. She stood in the doorway, coat half-unbuttoned, hat in hand, blinking. She'd meant only to stop long enough to see the sets for *Falstaff,* she murmured, but had ended up watching the first half from backstage.

As we walked up to Garth's house, I saw a parcel on his front porch: a bundle of letters, tied in twine, the mailbox stuffed full as usual. Garth scooped them up and peered at them through half-fogged glasses. As soon as he frowned I knew what they were. He handed them to me—my letters to Josie. I'd kept writing them after the opera: a couple a week, no longer really expecting a response. Across every envelope, a message was scrawled in Josie's handwriting: Return to Sender.

"Harriet?" he said.

I couldn't answer. He took a step toward me, reaching for my arm. I snapped back, as if he'd meant to hit me, then turned and hurried down the steps. He called after me, but I didn't stop.

The sun was already setting, lavender shadows lengthening across the snow. Streetlights flickered on as I ran, smudgy ovals of light against a sky like blue smoke. Small, sharp flakes of snow stung my cheeks and eyes. I clutched the bundle of letters against my chest and concocted explanations: She had been in a terrible accident, she had amnesia and didn't remember me. She thought Mama and Daddy were behind the letters somehow, that they were trying to finagle a share of her new success.

When I got to the boardinghouse, I went straight upstairs. Mama would be home any minute, but as soon as I'd stashed the letters in my room I took her forbidden hatbox down from its shelf, convinced I would find some clue: more correspondence from Raymond Fish, some evidence that Mama and Daddy had tried to track Josie down, had written to her themselves. I found receipts, recipes, old contracts, pages of yellow paper on which Mama had scrawled budgets. I found notes she'd taken on Uncle Eugene's sermons and points of etiquette. I found a folded sketch of a naked young woman in a rumpled bed. I turned it over and read "M, Oct 1908, New York," and realized the woman was my mother, the sketch done by Daddy. Red-cheeked, I shoved it back into the bottom of the hatbox and put the hatbox away.

I pulled open drawers and looked in cupboards. In Mama's dresser, I found a Bible with gleaming black covers and gilt edges and an inscription on the inside cover: "With great thanks to our Heavenly Father, who has led your precious family home to the church, and with fondest friendship always, EUGENE P. CREGGS, March 20, 1929." Something slipped out from between the tissue-fine pages: a printed program from the revival in Toledo, wrapped around a photograph. Josie, I thought, for a frantic instant, but when I looked properly I saw a young man in profile. There was a round photographer's stamp on the lower right-hand corner of the print, "Segal's" forming the top half of the circle, "Scranton" closing it. On the back, in spidery handwriting I didn't recognize, someone had written "Robert Lodge, 1920." There was something familiar about the face, but as I reviewed the mental album of monologists and magicians and jugglers and baritones and comedians and dog trainers and fire eaters who constituted the men I had known when Josie and I were seven, I couldn't find it there. Robert Lodge— I was certain I'd never heard the name.

Could this Robert Lodge have been Mama's boyfriend? Maybe she had gone to him on her night wanderings. Maybe she'd confessed the affair to Uncle Eugene, and he'd made her keep the photo in the Bible as a reminder of her transgression. But this was foolish: He looked too young to be a boyfriend, and besides, she wasn't wandering to see this man in Peoria and Berwyn. And whoever he was, he had nothing to do with Josie or Raymond Fish or the bundle of letters, too many to fit in the slit in my mattress, evidence of what exactly I couldn't say, but of something humiliating. Something catastrophic.

Mama's footsteps sounded on the stairs. I stared at the photograph just long enough to memorize the man's features. And then I put him back in the Bible, and the Bible back beneath Mama's slips. By the time she came in, I was sitting calmly on the couch, book open in my lap.

THE NEXT DAY, GARTH was once again waiting when I came out of school. He took me to a fusty confectionary on Michigan Avenue where he'd often gone as a little boy, and bought a hot chocolate for us to share. I explained everything: Raymond Fish's letter. The postcard. My one-sided correspondence with Josie.

"What do you think it means?" he asked. I shook my head, staring down at the ring of chocolate at the bottom of our cup.

"Something's wrong. I don't know what."

"It seems like we only have one choice," he said in a voice so sure and steady, I knew I would agree with whatever he proposed.

"What's that?"

"We need to speak to Raymond Fish."

THAT THURSDAY, WHEN GARTH'S father was teaching, I slipped away from school at the lunch hour. The plan was this: Garth and I would telephone Fish's office. I would pretend to be a secretary, and Garth an attorney, trying to reach Josie to discuss an inheritance. We had spent hours composing and refining a script, hours I should have been using to study for my end-of-semester exams.

The sky was cold and pale; a thin gauze of cloud stretched along the horizon. Ridges of ice banded the sidewalk. By the time I rang Garth's bell my fingers were frozen lumps inside my mitten.

The door opened. A woman with a high forehead and shiny, butter-yellow hair stared down at me over her slim nose. With a jolt, I recognized her from one of the cartoons Garth had sent me that summer: his aunt Cookie.

"Can I help you?" Her blouse was thin, but she did not so much as cross her arms against the cold.

"I'm Harriet? I'm here to see Garth?"

She took a deep breath, her eyelids fluttering slightly, and I knew I should have invented some story. "Well, good afternoon." She almost smiled. Not in a friendly way—more as if my presence were the latest in a long list of other people's messes she'd been charged with tidying up.

She glanced pointedly at my boots, which I wiped on a mat that hadn't been there before. Inside, the vestibule was clear, the stairs emptied of rubbish. The parlor furniture had been pushed to the edges of the rug, which was damp in patches. Windows were open, ice-cold air cutting the heady, wafting scent of ammonia and bleach.

"Some early spring cleaning," Garth's aunt said lightly, as she led me through the dining room. Two maids in uniform flattened themselves against the hallway so we could pass. A third was in the bathroom where I'd cleaned up my scrape, scrubbing on her hands and knees.

Garth's aunt delivered me to a small back parlor. The cleaning hadn't yet reached this corner of the house; there was something comforting about the stacks of file folders and newspapers, and the cobwebs and dust, and the fingerprints on the glass of the framed maps that hung askew on the rust-colored walls.

"You wait here," she said, pressing her thin mouth into a disapproving line. "I'll send him in."

After she'd gone, I looked out through a window, into the backyard. A man in a long camel coat and white whiskers, Garth's grandfather, I guessed, stood at the center of a network of paths that had been dug through the snow, supervising the workmen who were bustling in and out of the house, carrying trash to the alley. I wondered if he'd seen my own boot prints from the house to the gate. If he'd formed any suspicion.

"Who are you?"

I turned. Leaning against the doorframe was a girl with the same blond hair as Garth's aunt. Her eyes were closer together, her nose stretched to a more ratlike point, but her cheeks were babyish and round, making her other features seem too sharp by comparison, as if she were a child wearing a mask of an adult face. Garth's cousin Marjorie.

"Harriet." My heart hammered, as if she'd caught me stealing. She emitted a sound halfway between a grunt and a chuckle. "Who are you?"

"Marjorie Butler. I'm here with Mother and Gigi and Gampa, to see about Uncle Albert's mess. And for Christmas, poor me." She glanced over her shoulder and then slowly, slyly, slid into an armchair, disturbing an arrangement of doilies. "This place was a pit when we got here. Bad as it's ever been. Uncle Albert got rid of the help again. Oh boy, was Gigi cheesed. She and Mother call Uncle Albert the Mad Scientist."

She giggled and waited for my response. I wanted to say something in Garth's father's defense, but her confident meanness had rendered me dumb. She finally went on: "I'm supposed to be a good influence on Garth. Gampa says his mother came from weak stock. They're d-i-v-o-r-c-e-d, you know." She wrapped her feet beneath her, tipping her cheek into her upturned palm.

The door opened and Garth rushed in, cheeks blazing, something clumsy and childish in his gait.

"Scram, Margarine," he said through clenched teeth. She slithered out of the chair and skipped away, pinching his arm as she passed.

He rubbed his arm. "Sorry. They were here when I got home last night. Dad didn't tell me they were coming. Maybe he didn't know."

"Why did they come?"

He scowled at the rug. Nothing was as we'd planned, but I still felt the pull of his body, the desire to throw my arms around his neck.

"I'm in trouble. At school."

"What sort of trouble?"

He regarded me coolly, as if my asking were an accusation.

"I missed some class."

"We only skipped a couple of times. Surely that's not—"

"It wasn't just with you, Harriet. There were other times." He hesitated, his lips twitching, as if he couldn't decide whether he was proud or sorry. "They also think I drew an unflattering picture of the headmaster. On his office door."

"Oh." I turned back to the window. Garth's grandfather was rubbing his hands together, sliding his even gaze over the workers. I felt tears collecting, my nose—my awful, indiscreet nose—turning red. But it wasn't just from sadness at the prospect of his being sent away. I was angry at him. What a stupid thing to have done, when so much was at stake. Why had he done something so stupid? What had he gained from it? All autumn, whatever Garth and I had done, I'd played my part at the Institute, shown I could follow the rules. Had it really been so hard for Garth to do the same? He pulled me from the window and glanced at the door, and then we kissed, quickly, and I could tell he felt as I did—uncomfortable kissing in a house crawling with people, but like something would be wrong if we didn't kiss. My anger softened. "So are you going to—is your grandfather—"

"No," he snapped. "Dad won't let him. Do you have the script?"

I handed him the pages, which he unfolded calmly, as if this were any other day, as if we were safe in his empty house.

"But Garth, should I go? I don't want to—"

"What about Josie?" he said. "Don't you want to know what's going on with Josie?" My cheeks warmed. I was ashamed that Garth had had to remind me to think of my sister.

The telephone sat on a round table, dark wood with a scalloped edge. My palm was sticky against the receiver. My heart beat furiously as I placed the call. A few minutes later, my voice traveled along a crackly line all the way to California.

"Herman Chance for Mr. Fish, please?"

"What is this about?" asked his secretary.

"Some sensitive business regarding one of his clients, a Josephine Sweet," I said. "There's the matter of an inheritance to settle." Raymond Fish's secretary was quiet for several seconds.

"Just a moment, please," she said. I flushed head to toe, certain I'd heard laughter in her voice, but I handed the receiver to Garth. He tapped his tongue against the back of his front teeth. I rested my ear beside his so I could listen in.

"Who is this?" Fish bellowed. The receiver slipped in Garth's hands.

"Um, hello," he managed to say, and cleared his throat. "Herman Chance, here, Ch-Chance, Brewter, and Simmons at law."

"What is this? Sheila, you put me on with a goddamn kid! What do you mean calling me up and prying into my clients' affairs?"

"We want to talk to Josie," said Garth, in his natural voice. "You let us talk to Josie right now."

I grabbed the phone from him.

"Let me talk to her," I said, convinced in my own panic that the best thing would be to come clean. "This is Harriet. I have a right to talk to my sister."

"I don't know what you're talking about," he said, but he didn't hang up. His tone had become cool and taunting.

"I'm talking about Josie. I'm her sister. I am Harriet Szász. Harriet Sweet."

The line crackled with his raspy breath.

"Don't call here again," he finally said. A click, and the line went dead.

I clung to the receiver, burning with humiliation. Nothing had changed. In trying to take some action, to discover what had happened to Josie, I had only demonstrated my little-girlish incapacity. Garth took the receiver from my hand and set it down gently. I pressed my face into his narrow chest. And then I looked up and kissed him, unembarrassed now, desperate for something to blot out the frantic worry swirling in my brain.

From the doorway I heard a squeal. "MOTHER!" Marjorie's voice bounced down the hall. Garth's aunt burst in a minute later, her fine, frail skin pink, as if with sunburn, and told me I was to go home at once.

THE FOLLOWING WEDNESDAY, when I arrived home from school, I found a letter waiting from Garth. I opened it quickly. Inside the envelope I discovered a second envelope, addressed to me at Garth's address. Wrapped around it was Garth's note: "I read it, Harriet. I'm sorry. They are watching my every move, but I have a plan. Meet me on Thursday at four behind the Stop and Shop."

Josie's stationery was thin and doused in perfume. She'd written in green ink. Her writing slipped between the familiar, childish scrawl and a more practiced hand.

Oh, Harriet, it's happening, it's all finally rilee happening. raymond
seys i have terifick prospeckts. i will have a skreen test soon. The thing

is Harriet, Raymond seys if anyone found out about us and what a laffingstock we were and how we lide to everyone, everything Raymond is lining up for me will be ruind. Raymond seys its best just to start over now, and Im sure he's rite. He is very experyenced and has a lot of conexsions. He was going to give me your leters after my screen test because he didn't want a destracshun but you kept sending them so you can see why he got anoyed and neded you to stop. And here is a sekrit that you CANT tell Mama and Daddy: he is not just my manajer but my husbind. I am a marreed woman if you can beleev it! But Harriet, he is very angry that you telefoned. Please don't do that again, Harriet. Ill rite when I can but it might not be for a wile because Im very bizy.

I had to read it through three times before I could hang on to the sense of Josie's words. A year earlier, she and I had shared a life. Now I was an unremarkable junior at Waller High, dressing salads in a boardinghouse kitchen, necking with a high school boy, arranging flowers as a member of the Junior Altar Guild, going to Bible Study and doing my best to prove to my uncle I was nothing like the girl I'd been brought up to be, while my sister, my twin, was a married woman preparing for her first screen test.

Years later, I would return to those words—he is very angry you telephoned, the tender "please" tucked into all that bluster. I would think, with guilt, of Raymond Fish's cold, taunting voice on the phone, and of the postcard Josie had sent in September. Her cryptic anger. I would wonder if I could have spared her some suffering, if only I'd been able to read those words with an understanding of what it all must have cost her—a girl of sixteen, making her way alone in a world controlled by men like that. But for now, my mind caught on the fact that a stranger had a claim on Josie while I had none; that he would obtain for her the things we'd once imagined we'd share. And how casually she'd tossed off the news—not just her manager but her husband, as if it were a bit of fun, a punch line, anything other than a shutter slamming between her heart and mine.

———

I WAS SUPPOSED TO be at the Institute by five o'clock on Thursday, to help decorate the altar for an advent service. But at four, I was waiting for Garth in the alley, holding Josie's letter inside my coat pocket. The sun was quickly sinking. Snow blew off the loading dock and the roof of the store. If I stopped pacing for a second, the cold cut to the bone.

I told myself I would count to ten and if he didn't turn up, I'd leave.

I told myself I'd count to one hundred.

I'd hit six hundred forty-six, dark had finished falling, and my feet and the tip of my nose were numb, when a big black car turned in to the alley. I scrambled over to the loading dock and crouched to avoid the sweep of its headlights. But when it came to a stop, the driver's-side window rolled down, and Garth stuck his head out.

"Get in," he shouted.

I hurried over and bent down beside the window. On the dashboard were four packets of crackers, three Hershey's bars, and a thermos.

"Whose car is this?"

"Get in. We're going."

"Where?"

"Los Angeles. You have a right to see your own sister, don't you? So let's go."

Cold stung the backs of my legs. He looked up at me, breath escaping in jagged puffs of steam. I knew I needed to say something, to make some answer.

"What about school?" I blurted, conscious that I sounded pathetic, that school was beside the point.

"Would you get in, Harriet? My face is freezing."

I leaned a little closer to the window to block the wind.

"What about school, Garth?"

He looked at the steering wheel.

"They're sending me away. Military school. Massachusetts." I couldn't speak. He wiped his eyes roughly with the heel of his hand. "Dad didn't even put up a fight this time. He didn't even try."

"But how would we get to Los Angeles?" I finally said. "What would we do for money?"

"I have a map. I have some money. But will you please get in now?"

Inside the car, the heater spat out dry, warmish air. Garth's gaze was pressing, awful. I closed my eyes and tried to be inside Josie's mind. I pictured her in Los Angeles: installed as wife in the home of an important man. Splashing in a shimmering pool. Touring a studio lot. Getting fitted for a costume. Smiling into a camera. When I opened my eyes, Garth was dancing his fingers across the steering wheel, still gazing at me, waiting. I thought of his chaotic house, his absent mother, and a pit opened in my chest so swiftly I almost gasped. The snow had thickened; it splatted the windshield, drawing a wet curtain around the interior of the car, closing me in with Garth, with the merging threads of our breath.

I kissed him. I kissed him because I didn't know what to say, but then our bodies were doing the saying for us. I crawled into the backseat and he followed, clumsily. We struggled with our clothes. I cursed the winter, cursed the hideous wool union suit Mama had bought for me to wear, but then I had wriggled out of it, I was lying against my coat, clothes piled under my head for a pillow, and Garth's shirt was scratching against my skin as he leaned over to kiss me. His belt bumped my ankle. Rules had once been the hard edges that defined the world; all fall they had been bending, and now they bent a final time. I bent them. My body bent them. I was the want between my legs, and then I was his body and mine both, I was the place where they came together. I felt a dull pain, but I wanted the pain, I wanted what followed, a gathering feeling in the space where the pain had been. Garth moved with his eyes screwed shut until he made a small sound and all at once I felt a burst of wet warmth. He stilled. I clung to him, mind ticking with revelation. We both eased onto our sides, Garth behind me so his breath warmed my hair. Be-

fore I could say anything, quietly, diligently, as if according to instructions he'd read in a book, he'd slid his hand down my front and
was touching me the way he'd touched me a few times before, in his
bedroom. This time, though, my thinking collapsed into a thin,
warm static; the gathering feeling rose toward Garth's hand. He cultivated it, coaxed it along, until, at last, it spilled over its own edge.

I lay there, astonished, outside of time, until my teeth began to
chatter.

"You're cold," he said. We sat up. His cheeks were red. Mine
burned. When I met his eye, we both smiled. But when we began to
dress, it was a relief to look away. I was tying my boot when he spoke
again.

"You never said." His voice was soft, but I could feel him bracing
for my response. "Are you coming?"

My bow had gone lopsided. I pulled it out and started over, allowing myself to concentrate on the task, to keep my eyes fixed on
my bootlaces. I loved him, maybe. But there was something about
that word that seemed like a pair of hands around my throat.

I wasn't a Wise Daughter. I had suspected as much for a while,
but now I knew for sure. Maybe I could be more effective than
Mama when it came to operating in Uncle Eugene's world. But I
was no less a hypocrite.

But I wasn't Josie, either. Maybe I had learned that rules could
be changed, but rules still pricked something in me, they still marked
clear, useful edges. I had lived through the pain of my sister's going,
my parents' suffering as well as mine. And they still needed me.
Maybe more than ever. Leaving had been Josie's choice. I had to
make my own.

I sat up and pressed my hand against Garth's cheek. He frowned
and tipped his head away from my touch.

"I'm sorry," I said. But he was already climbing out of the car. I
went after him.

"Garth, I—" But he'd gotten into the driver's seat. He slammed
the door and turned the key. The tires shrieked. I stumbled back.

For a moment, I was too stunned to move. And then I felt as if something in me was stretching, stretching, stretching, until the taillights disappeared around the corner and it snapped.

The cold reached my ears. I had left my hat in the car. The sky was black lacquer, the stars sharp as the tips of knives. I breathed deeply, the icy air burning in my face, my chest. I would be late, but not too late. I turned up the collar of my coat, pulled my scarf up over my bare head, and set off for my uncle's church.

I WATCHED THROUGH A CLASSROOM WINDOW AS THE SKY PILED
with gray clouds and the branches of the oak tree out in front of the
school whipped back and forth. Thick dashed lines of snow bent
horizontal in the wind. Three months had passed since Garth left
me in the alley; spring had technically begun. But there was a ruckus
in the hall, and then a page rushed in to speak to the teacher: they
were dismissing us half an hour early to get ahead of another bliz-
zard.

Outside, my schoolmates streamed around me in a holiday mood
even as they hurried to escape the lash of the wind, but my chest felt
tight, my shoulders heavy. I blamed my melancholy on the weather.
Old drifts, sooty and piss-streaked, studded with wrappers and cigarette butts, were beginning to disappear under a new blanket of
white. I waded across the street, slush up to my ankles, wary of skid-
ding cars.

But instead of turning left, toward home, I turned right, toward
the nearest movie theater. With Garth gone, sitting among strangers at the movies searching for Josie was as close as I came to social-
izing, save the occasional hour I spent drinking tea and playing
euchre with Mrs. Broom after I finished my weekend chores, and
the pleasantries I exchanged with a couple of girls in the Junior
Altar Guild. When I didn't have any money to spend on a ticket, I
went to the theater on Division and pulled down the fire escape

ladder with a broken rake I kept hidden behind a trash can. But with the opera season having been roundly declared a triumph, and Bert having immediately signed Daddy up to build sets for the operetta season and the company's national tour, my father was, for the first time in my life, flush with cash he'd earned himself. Mama still managed the family finances, and Daddy handed over most of what he earned, but he kept a stack of bills in his pocket from which he liked to make me gifts. That afternoon, with a dollar from Daddy in my purse, I went to the theater closest to the high school, where I paid for my ticket and bought a coffee to cut the chill. The ticket taker, who was wearing a red wool scarf over his uniform, kept glancing anxiously over my shoulder at the blowing snow. The auditorium was mostly empty, a short playing with an all-dog cast. I slumped in my seat, anxious for the feature to begin, or for another short, one with humans.

I thought I'd seen her, once, in February, in a western: a girl who fainted in the background during a shootout. I'd run home and blurted it out. Mama and Daddy and Mrs. Broom had all scrambled to the next show. But they came back in shaking their heads. I'd been mistaken, they said. I went again the next day, and watched with ferocious concentration, and in the end, I accepted that they were right. It hadn't been Josie at all. I recorded the fact in my diary with a prickly relief.

The feature began. Jack Mulhall played twin brothers, one a cop, the other a gangster. During long scenes of dialogue between men, with no girls to raise hope or dread, no crowds to scrutinize, my mind wandered. The melancholy I'd felt as I'd left school deepened and hardened, as if a metal box had lodged itself against my heart. The picture ended: once again, I'd been spared the humiliation of my sister's success.

I stepped out of the theater into an odd, brown brightness, the light of the city trapped between clouds and the smooth blanket of white on the ground. Several inches had accumulated. The traffic lights had little white caps, and fat white flakes were dropping as heavily as rain. Some shopkeepers were trying to keep up with shovels and brooms, while others just looked at the sky, shaking their heads.

It took me forty-five minutes to get back to Mrs. Broom's, where the porch light was burning feebly, the first-floor window dark. A month earlier she had fired Minnie, canceled her dinner service, and, with the help of two boarders behind on their rent, divided the parlor and dining room into several small rooms apiece, transforming her boardinghouse at last into one of the anonymous rooming houses she'd long held in disdain. As I walked down a narrow hallway that still smelled of plaster and paint, I could sense the boarders on the other side of the wall, like animals who had burrowed into their dens to wait out the storm.

Mrs. Broom was at the desk beside the stairs, marking something on the guest register. She smiled when she saw me.

"It's coming down, isn't it?" she said. I nodded. She reached into the pocket of her robe.

"This came for you," she said lightly, handing me a letter. "I thought you might want it kept aside. In case your mother checked the mail first."

It was from G. Mosher, in New Hampshire. Mrs. Broom studied me intently. In her sitting room, on the weekends, in between hands of euchre, she'd sometimes fished for details of my private life; I'd been grateful for her interest but was determined to keep Garth to myself. Now I stuffed the letter into my coat pocket, cheeks burning. I made myself thank her and say, "Good night, then." I made myself walk at a dignified pace up the stairs.

For three months, I'd imagined him in California, negotiating with Josie under an orange tree, or in Mexico, sketching with his mother on a beach. I'd written poems in my diary in which I'd imagined myself pregnant, even after my body proved to me once, twice, three times that I wasn't. It was as if part of me wanted to be, as if pregnancy were the one fitting punishment for what I'd done, shame having caught up to me at last around the time I learned I'd failed half my December exams. One night in January, Mama had come into the alcove and sat stiffly on the edge of the bed. I had always been a very sensitive girl, she said with a sigh, as if my sensitivity had been her burden to bear. But I had to stop moping around. I couldn't worry about Josie anymore. We had our own fish to fry. I'd pressed my face into my pillow, furious that she didn't understand the true nature of my sadness, even though I'd done everything in my power to conceal it from her, and furious, too, that she was telling me something I already knew. Already I had scrambled back onto the honor roll. I was embroidering John 3:16 on a cushion to give Uncle Eugene for his birthday.

I let myself into the apartment and hung my coat on the rack, as conscious of Garth's letter in the pocket as I would be of a hot coal.

"There you are," Mama said. She shoved two withered turnips into my hands.

When Mrs. Broom stopped serving dinner, Mama had said it would be good for me to practice making a proper meal for a family; I should cook for Uncle Eugene sometime, when I was ready. It was only when she set about teaching me that I realized what little experience she had in that arena. For a month, she'd been rushing home from work to whip up dry discs of pork, oversalted sauces, potatoes that crunched in the middle. Whenever I demonstrated some skill I'd learned from Minnie or Mrs. Broom, Mama seemed annoyed, as if I were trying to embarrass her, though she was the one who'd said it would be useful for me to learn.

I set about chopping the turnips, while Mama dumped the beginnings of a vegetable soup into a pot on our little gas range. The soup had just come to a simmer when Daddy came in, epaulets of snow on his shoulders, a web of drops clinging to his eyebrows and beard.

"Put on your coats," he said. "Come. Come!"

"The soup," Mama said. But Daddy took her hands and grinned and promised it would be worth it, and I could see a loosening in her shoulders, a softening around her eyes—the lingering effects of the fever the opera had lit in her.

She turned down the flame and we all bundled up. Outside, we found the avenue clogged with abandoned cars and the streetcar out of service. Daddy kicked a path open ahead of Mama, but she still struggled with her cane. Snow tipped over the edges of my boots. My breath collected damply in my scarf. I squinted against the lash of the wind.

"Where are we going, Lenny?"

"You'll see, you'll see," he said.

We walked a few blocks, and then he stopped and pointed triumphantly at a small house: two stories of white clapboard, a few snow-piled steps leading to a bright blue door. He tromped into the yard, brushed snow from the front window so we could see a sign propped inside. The house was for rent.

"You know Vera can't let us stay forever," he said as he came back toward us, ready to make his case before Mama could object. He draped an arm around her shoulders. "Bert has work for me this summer. There's to be a residency at Ravinia, and next season to prepare for. I have a place here, Maude. Yesterday, I got onto the elevator, and guess who was there?"

"Al Capone."

"Mary Garden. With her little shit of a dog, who's bitten half the men in the company. But he let me pet him and licked my hand, and she said I must be an angel in disguise. Truth is I'd just finished eating a roast beef sandwich." He laughed, but then became serious: "But with Miss Garden in my corner? Maude—sky's the limit."

Mama crossed her arms against the cold; he clenched her more tightly. There was no one else on the street, no sound save the patter of snow landing on snow.

"Every time Vera comes up, she looks like a lion eyeing a gazelle," Mama said softly, studying the house. "She gets out that measuring tape of hers."

"It would be nice for Harriet to have a real room. A real home."

Mama looked over at me, as if she'd just remembered I was with them. She beckoned for me to come closer and when I did, she looped her arm through mine. For another minute, we stood knotted together, firm against the wind.

On the way home, at Mama's urging, I made a snowball and

threw it at Daddy. He swung around, prepared to act cross, but then he looked at Mama's face. The wind swallowed his laughter. He formed his own snowball, quickly, sloppily; it disintegrated before it could reach me. But I squealed. I ran behind Mama.

When we got home, the soup was scorched. We sopped up mushy vegetables with bread and Mama made coffee. Daddy took out a bottle of whiskey.

"We can't have her catching pneumonia, Maude," he said, as he poured some in my cup. She waved her hand, absolving herself.

The two of them made rapid-fire plans: Daddy would go tomorrow to inquire about the house. April 1 was only a few days away; there was no way the snow would be cleared by then, which meant we'd have a little extra time to get our affairs in order. Mama thought there was money for a deposit; she just had to juggle some things, think about which bills could wait. It was more respectable, she murmured, to have an address of one's own instead of a room in a house. She didn't say Uncle Eugene's name, and if Daddy suspected she was thinking of him, he made no sign of it. They hadn't planned together so fervently since the arrival of Herb Fitz's telegram in Sioux City, Iowa, over a year ago. Daddy said maybe next month we could buy a radio. Mama said she'd never forgotten the blue kitchen in the first apartment she'd shared with Vera in New York, that there was something about a blue kitchen, that maybe we could paint the kitchen blue. Mama poured Daddy another cup of coffee. She brought out a sack of the ginger cookies he liked.

"I'll take a bath, I think," I said. They nodded absently.

I poured myself another cup of coffee. They didn't notice when I added a splash of whiskey, or when I slipped over to the coatrack and took Garth's letter from my pocket.

I made a ceremony of it: filled the tub first, and stirred in some of the lavender bath salts Mrs. Broom had given Mama for her birthday, which I was not supposed to use without asking. The water was so hot I winced getting in. Coffee, for courage. And then I slipped my finger under the seal.

He'd been caught. Thirty miles out of the city, his stolen car had run out of gas. A Good Samaritan had gone to a service station to get him some help and had been overheard by a cop who had received the APB. That was the end of it. He didn't say it in so many words, but it seemed the military school he now attended had been, in the end, a welcome alternative to reform school, the judge's mercy purchased, somehow, by his grandfather. It was everything he had anticipated: cold showers, beatings from older boys, food in meager portions. He'd have written sooner, but he'd only just been granted letter-writing privileges.

I was stung by the letter's brevity, its sterility. I wondered whether some official at Garth's school censored the students' mail. Or maybe that was just the way Garth wrote. He'd never really written me proper letters before, just notes, and captions on cartoons. I wished that this time he'd drawn me a cartoon. Then I understood, with a pang: I'd forfeited my right to one. He ended by saying I could write back if I wanted, but if I didn't he understood. He just hadn't wanted to disappear without an explanation.

The melancholy I'd felt that afternoon returned; the metal box pressed against my heart. I knew I was lonely: I felt as remote from myself as I did from Josie or Garth. I also knew I wouldn't write him, not a letter to send. I couldn't. But maybe I would write to him in my diary, as I'd used to write to Josie and God.

I couldn't remember the last time I'd prayed and meant it. I uttered a prayer then and there, quickly, lightly. A prayer that God would keep Garth safe, and Josie. And let us get our house, and be happy there. I promised God I would get back in the habit of prayer. We were moving up in the world. Never mind the house from Uncle Eugene's sermon, the one that sank into the sand. Never mind the article I had read in the *Tribune* that said the rate of subscriptions for the upcoming opera season was falling short of expectations. Never mind. Mama had asked Daddy about that, and he had pinched her chin between his thumb and forefinger and laughed. Business conditions would turn around by fall. The financial wizards all said so. Just you wait and see: Chicago's glamour set will want nothing more than to get to the opera and show off all the automobiles and diamonds they waited, in an overabundance of caution, to buy. And now he had charmed Mary Garden's mean little dog, and enticed Mama into a snowball-throwing, plan-making mood. And at the same time, we were succeeding with Uncle Eugene, who regarded me with affection, treated me almost like a daughter. In a week and a half I'd be seventeen. In a week and a half plus a year I'd be eighteen, and two months after that, I'd graduate from high school. And then, eventually, I would marry. And with my husband, I could again do the thing I had done, so recklessly, with Garth, the thing that distinguished me from the other girls in Junior Altar Guild, the thing that made me like my runaway sister. "I just didn't want to disappear without explanation," Garth had written. As he knew Josie had.

I folded his letter and let it drop to the floor beside the tub. The air was humid and smelled of lavender. My face and the ends of my hair were damp. Above me, the skylight was packed with snow, a soft blue rectangle. Wind whistled along the roof. I pulled my head under the surface, so I couldn't hear the storm, I couldn't hear my parents' conversation. I couldn't hear anything but the roar of my own blood.

1912

When Mr. Fleischer stops visiting her at the hospital, Maude knows the doctor must have told him her prognosis. At least he continues to pay her bills. Vera and Fleur and some of the other girls come by, but she knows it frightens them to see her like this, living proof of the fragility of their bodies and the precariousness of their careers. Lenny comes twice a day, holds her hands and subjects her to apologies, awful apologies—relentless and battering and so full of words.

She has an operation, and another. She applies her still considerable strength to tasks that make a mockery of it: scrape the boot along the floor, stand up straight, do not piss yourself. She is a star pupil with a cane. When she finally goes home to the bright, airy apartment she and Lenny can no longer afford, the girls bring her a little money every month, her pension, they call it, but only Vera still treats her like a person, only Vera complains about her own problems and tells her to buck up. The others give her tender looks and make excuses to retreat to the kitchen, where they cry a little as they scrub pots that are already clean and reheat coffee and arrange sliced apples and graham crackers on a tray so artfully that Maude can only think about how much they must have touched everything, which makes her not want to eat any of it, which makes them murmur gravely to each other about her appetite. At least when they leave she has quiet. Until Lenny returns.

He tries, sometimes, to meet her silence with his own, but soon he overflows with speech: more apologies, more pleas for her forgiveness. Part of her wishes she could sit up with him until

dawn, tell him all the secrets she's already told him and the handful she hasn't, return to those early days when every conversation
was a revelation, every touch a discovery. She grasps at forgiveness, wills herself toward love, feels love, for an instant, when he
strokes her wrist, feels it when she presses her face into the tuft
of hair on his shoulder, feels it as she folds one of his shirts. But
then she starts awake at three in the morning, damp all over and
gasping, and remembers the dream from which she has woken:
the bell falling, pinning her leg to the stage. She wishes he had
never told her that he must have failed to check the counter-
weight. Because in unburdening himself he has burdened her,
and how can she forgive him, knowing what she knows? And will
he ever stop apologizing if she won't forgive? Because she cannot
live with these apologies. They swarm like horseflies, they crowd
her lungs.

It is the morning after another night of talk. She hasn't slept
but she rises before the sun and packs a suitcase and walks right
past Lenny, who is passed out on the couch in a room steadily
emptying of furniture and knickknacks and paintings. By the
time she reaches Penn Station, her stiff new boots have rubbed
blisters into her heels, and her cane has filled her palm with pins
and needles. She buys a ticket and boards a train, and, easy as
that, she reverses the journey that a decade earlier gave her freedom and her career. She runs home to Ohio.

. . .

t feels, at first, like a trick her body is playing on her. A bit of
mischief, a strange nostalgic turn. We're back here? it says.
Then let's be ourself here. Let's be an Ohio body. Her stomach
souring at the scent of eggs. The tingling soreness in her
breasts. The softening and thickening of her waist. Swifter,
this time, though, more urgent. She can't be, she thinks, but
she knows she is.

Eugene presides over the breakfast table, pleased, it seems, to

have doubled the audience for his little daily homily. Marion,
who has grown into a woman with a high, fair hairdo and calm
gray eyes big around as nickels, projects interest and admiration,
but Maude can detect a ripple of discomfort, the slightest embarrassment that this man is her husband, that this is how her husband behaves. At quarter to nine each morning, he walks up the
hill to the church, leaving the two of them alone with Ruth, who
is dark-eyed and oddly somber for a child of two and a half. The
girl makes Maude feel skittish, especially now. But she observes
her closely and finds things that fascinate: the way she listens and
watches, as if she is determined to figure out as quickly as possible how the world works. The stinginess of her affection—three
weeks passed before she would let Maude take her hand, and
there is something interesting in this, Maude thinks. A discern-
ment that makes Ruth's affection more satisfying than the affection of a sunnier child. Even the intensity of her sudden
squalls—the little face twisting and turning red—impresses
Maude. But then, it is Marion who is responsible for scooping
the child up, for kissing away her tears.

   One morning, Maude and Marion linger at the breakfast
table long after Eugene goes. Their coffee cools, the oatmeal goes
stiff. On a blanket in the corner, Ruth builds and topples towers
of blocks. The kitten pads into the room on velvet paws. Clouds
shuttle past the sun, plunging the room into shadow a half second at a time. Maude, staring at the greenish reflection of her
cheek in her orange juice, decides to speak.

   "I'm knocked up." Marion cringes and Maude tries again:
"I'm going to have a baby."

   "Oh, Maude," she says, the words so quiet they seem to settle
on her lips instead of passing all the way through. Ruth crashes
her tower and laughs. Marion scoops up the kitten and hands it
to Maude, as if holding a kitten might remedy the situation, and
then lifts her chin—very proud, very brave.

   "You can stay here, if you'd like. We'll help with everything.
I'm sure Eugene will agree."

Another cloud passes. Maude clutches the kitten to her chest and doesn't say a word.

Late that night, she lies awake in the pretty yellow bedroom with the pretty Audubon prints on the walls, frowning up at the pretty yellow canopy of her bed. Marion spent the day delivering advice out of books, asking intimate questions, preparing plates of food and advising Maude about the nutritive properties of each ingredient, proposing and then withdrawing plans for when and how Eugene would be informed, as if she had already assumed responsibility, appointed herself guardian and benefactress. All day, irritation collected beneath Maude's breastbone, and now it sets her body on edge so she cannot sleep. The girl who ran away to Philadelphia, who escaped to New York, who for seven years was the star of Fleischer's *Follies Magnifique,* did not come home to Hobart, Ohio, to be reduced to a charity case by a younger sister and a supercilious brother-in-law determined to do their Christian duty by her fatherless child.

And hasn't she unfathered that child through her own bullheadedness? Lenny, having wheedled the address out of Vera, has written every week. For three months, she has refused to answer. Now she pulls the letters out from under her pillow and reads them over. In each, he has enclosed a drawing: the rooftops through the window of their bedroom, a portrait of her, finer than a sketch. She goes to her desk. She writes a letter of her own. She tells him to come.

A week later, she is sitting in her bedroom when she sees him through the window, walking up the winding stone pathway to the front door. His long arms cradle a bouquet of hothouse roses. He is wearing a new suit of clothes. And all at once it seems possible. The rest of her life. Not a life she ever wanted but a life, she thinks, she could learn to want, one she could apply her formidable strength and capableness to wanting. Mama, papa, baby. Lenny—whom she loves freshly, with a force that makes her chest ache—will get a job, something respectable, something reliable. She will learn to keep house. The theater is behind them, but ahead of them is this child, a child they can love together, a child who is perfect so far. Untouched by their mistakes. And that's something. Maybe that's enough. She will make it enough.

She wishes she could run down to him and leap into his arms. Instead she swallows her heart and watches through the window until he disappears onto the porch. Quickly, she unwraps her braid so her hair tumbles down her back. She pinches the color back into her cheeks. She is twenty-five years old. She has grown wan during her months of rest and recovery, and the dark rings around her eyes are nearly like bruises. But there isn't a single line on her face, and her mouth is still rosy, and her hair—she knows it is magnificent. For as long as she is beautiful her beauty will cost her some grief, because she knows she will never again stand in front of a crowd and feel its admiration beating in her like a pulse. But she is certain Lenny will not be disappointed when he sees her. There are the housekeeper's brisk footsteps. She rests a hand on her belly, tentatively—an audition—and closes her eyes. She waits.

PART
THREE

ON THE THIRD OF APRIL, BERT KOSTER SHOWED UP WITH A truck and helped us pack our things. Mrs. Broom flitted around, patting tears from her eyes and sighing, but before the last of our suitcases were cleared from the attic, three boarders were lugging plywood and two-by-fours up the stairs, and she'd hung a VACAN-CIES sign in the window.

In the living room of our new house, we installed the radio from the boardinghouse parlor, which Mrs. Broom had insisted we take as a housewarming gift. Daddy built me a bed with scrap from the opera scene shop and a bookcase he painted glossy white. We celebrated my seventeenth birthday with a cake in the kitchen, which smelled of glue from the wallpaper we'd put up that afternoon: a blue field smattered with daisies.

I finished the school year on the honor roll and was awarded the prize for the best essay in history by a junior girl. When Mama shared the news, Uncle Eugene gave me a copy of *Streams in the Desert* inscribed, TO MY BELOVED NIECE. Wild strawberries sprouted in one corner of our backyard, otherwise a small square of gravel and crabgrass. I brought a basket of them to the Institute Youth Picnic, where I sat on a blanket with a couple of girls from the Junior Altar Guild, Polly and Ula, who spoke of their plans for summer travel: a trip to Mackinac Island, a car tour of national parks. My parents had been talking about finding somewhere to go for a vacation when

Daddy returned from a monthlong national tour with the opera company, and I was pleased to have something to contribute to the conversation. As I passed quiet days, reading and studying and doing chores and practicing cross-stitch, I told myself how much nicer this was than all the fretting I'd done over Garth the previous summer. How much more mature.

On the weekends, I went to Mrs. Broom's to make beds and scrub bathrooms. One Saturday, she mentioned that she'd heard the opera was carrying a deficit from last season, and advance ticket sales still hadn't gotten on pace. But the money Daddy sent home was more than enough. Mama and I had just repainted all the window frames and sewn new curtains for both bedrooms.

When Daddy returned home in July, he and Mama abandoned the idea of a vacation for reasons that were never explained to me. But he picked right back up with the opera, leaving every morning to work on the company's residency at Ravinia. He spoke with excitement about *Camille,* a new American opera championed by Mary Garden, which was to have its premiere in Chicago that fall. He claimed he and Miss Garden were thick as thieves; since the elevator and the dog, they had spoken twice, though when he asked Bert to give her some of his designs, or to arrange a meeting so he could give her the designs himself, Bert had cautioned him to wait.

We were eating dinner on the second of August when the landlady turned up, demanding our rent.

"Tomorrow," Mama said, firmly, the door open only a crack. "Good night, then."

She locked the door and sent me to my room. I stopped on the landing.

"You still don't have it?" she said. Daddy didn't answer.

"I don't understand," she went on. "When will you get paid for Ravinia? When does the new season begin?"

"It's just a quirk of the calendar, Maude. A little gap between contracts. You know how these things are. I'm working it out with Bert."

The landlady turned up the next night, and the night after that, increasingly irate. Mama made excuses and, once the door was closed, she and Daddy fought. One night, for the first time in ages, Daddy came home drunk. But he had the money we owed.

After that, there was never a Friday when Daddy didn't hand over some cash to Mama, but it was rarely more than half what he'd been paid by the opera a year before. All he would say was that Mama should be patient, that she should trust him. Mrs. Broom told me she'd heard that the upcoming opera season might be curtailed for budgetary reasons and that Mary Garden put in her resignation every other week, making Sam Insull beg her to stay on. I didn't repeat this gossip at home. When I started my senior year at Waller, there was no money for new clothes, but that hardly distinguished me: my classmates, those who hadn't had to drop out, were many of them worse off than we were. Our teachers clustered in the hallways, speaking tensely about whether they could expect to be paid anytime soon.

And then one morning that September, I was eating breakfast, conjugating French verbs, when Mama stalked into the kitchen with the newspaper in hand. She read aloud: of seventeen legitimate theaters in Chicago, only five had opened their seasons as scheduled. The Civic Opera hadn't yet announced the date of its opening.

"They'll do it when the time is right," Daddy scoffed. "It's a strategy. You have to build anticipation."

"I see. And not finding tenants for all that office space in that idiotic building. Is that a strategy too? Sam Insull just trying to inspire local philanthropists?"

"Christ, Maude. You don't build up a major operation overnight."

"Have you been fired, Lenny?"

"I told you, it's just the calendar, just a gap."

"That's what you said last month, Lenny, and the gap doesn't seem to have closed."

"Bert is taking care of it."

"If I don't know your position, Lenny, that makes it difficult to know how to handle Eugene."

Before he could respond, she folded the paper into thirds and dumped her coffee in the sink.

"Don't be late for school," she said, not bothering to look at me. She stalked out of the room.

As I finished my breakfast, Daddy gripped the edge of the sink, staring out the window into the backyard, where he sat now in the evenings, as he'd used to sit on Mrs. Broom's roof.

"The sets for *Camille*," he said, finally, clapping his hands as he turned to me. "Miss Garden says spare no expense. They've put in forty thousand dollars. Forty thousand. What do you think about that, Harriet?"

He waited for my response, deep tracks between his brows. In his recent fights with Mama, he often presented extravagant figures like these as a coup de grâce—the company's spending as proof of its solvency. At this Mama always waved her hands dismissively, rolled her eyes. Seeing he wanted me to affirm the validity of his argument, I forced myself to nod and grin. But that was all I could bear. I gathered up my things and hurried out the door.

A year earlier, on the walk to school I'd have heard the bright clink of hammers, the rumble of big trucks, and the scrape of steel, but that morning the streets were silent save the flap of a tarp that had come loose and the holler of some boys making a clubhouse out of an abandoned construction site, whose carefree tramping along a rusty girder made me cringe and think of lockjaw. Men milled at bus stops, on corners, under any scrap of roof, smoking, laughing with each other, something menacing about their idleness, especially as it contrasted to the day, which seemed still to glitter with summer— the trees were holding on to their color, the clouds formed high white stacks. Maybe the menace came from the way these men reminded me of my father; he hadn't been in any hurry to get to the opera house that morning.

I passed a hardware store with a forlorn-looking pile of lawn-mowers spilling out from under the awning, marked sixty percent off. Beyond it, the vacant shell of what had once been a children's shoe store had plywood over its window. Next came the shop that

sold newspapers, cigars, and canaries. I braced myself for the usual
wave of nostalgia: inside were big barrels of peanuts, conveniently
out of the line of sight from the counter, to which Garth and I had
helped ourselves with impunity. And then I saw her.

A man bumped into me.

"Watch where you're going," he snapped.

Josie. She stared out of a poster hanging beside the shop door.
Her soft pink cheek was pressed against the smooth-shaven face of
Vincent Romero. James Conlon loomed over the two of them, brim
of his hat casting an ominous triangle of shadow. Josie's eyes were
wide and shining. Her hair, a gleaming shade between honey and
amber, was parted just above the ear and curled under at the nape.
Her forehead was painted to perfect smoothness, her eyebrows two
precisely penciled arcs. The freckle on her nose was gone, but she
had a new beauty mark, just above her deep-dipped, orange-red lip.
Romero had a gleaming dark cap of hair and a deep cleft in his chin.
At the bottom of the poster, in slanting black letters with yellow
shadows, was the title of the picture—SISTER'S KEEPER—and two
declarations in curling script:

STARRING JAMES CONLON AND VINCENT ROMERO
INTRODUCING JOSEPHINE WILDER

I pushed my way inside. The canaries chirped and fluttered in
their cages; a boy about my age glared at me from behind the cash
register, as if I'd agitated them on purpose. I scanned a rack of magazines, woozy from the close, warm air and the dense, sweet smell of
birdseed. There was nothing in *Hollywood Spy* or *Movie Magic,* but there,
in *Picture-Play,* the third item in the table of contents: "Rising Star!
An Interview with Miss Josephine Wilder."

The boy tapped a finger against the counter. Flushing, I fished a
few coins out of my schoolbag. Then I was relieved to escape back
into the fresh air, even though the sun was beating heavily and a
truck was idling nearby, spewing exhaust. I sat at a bus stop and
shook the magazine open with trembling hands.

"What does a pretty newcomer do a month before the opening of
her first big picture? Speak to this intrepid reporter, for one thing!"

The intrepid reporter described a nineteen-year-old orphan who had been raised by an aunt and uncle, now deceased, on a farm in Ohio. In her description of the nearest town, I recognized the details about Mama's hometown that I'd read to Josie from that magazine profile of Uncle Eugene all those years earlier: the ice-cream parlor with stools painted pink; the theater that hosted third-rate traveling entertainments; the whitewashed Methodist church with the stained-glass windows; the seven saloons.

"Was it lonely, I ask Miss Wilder, growing up without any brothers and sisters? She smiles a little wistfully. 'Not so lonely. I had my books, my dreams. My imagination.'"

Saliva pooled at the back of my throat. I leaned over the curb, stomach buckling. I didn't quite manage to throw up, but I coughed and spat. A bus whizzed past. I stumbled back, eyes wet, and dropped the magazine, then I scrambled to pick it up and dusted it off frantically, as if it were Josie herself I'd dropped, Josie I'd allowed to come to harm. When I sat again, my breath was ragged; my throat burned. I made myself read on. More nonsense: Josie lifting a cigarette in a long holder, taking birdlike bites from a cantaloupe salad, gazing through silver streams of smoke. She shows the reporter a photograph of her pet poodle Joey, a gift from Ann Harding. Joey has just been invited to a birthday party for Rin Tin Tin.

"'My most exclusive Hollywood invitation to date,' says Miss Wilder, whose friends say she is too serious to go in for the party-throwing and party-going that spells trouble for many pretty young things in the colony."

Miss Wilder describes her costars as "Like brothers," but the reporter wonders if she's hiding "a more romantic story" behind "her mysterious smile." Raymond Fish didn't seem to figure in Josie's new reality. The reporter observes, beside Josie on the table, a volume of French poetry. "I never feel quite myself if I'm not in the middle of a book—or four," this Josie claims, her cheeks coloring.

I laughed out loud and turned the page to a photo spread. In one shot Josie wore a pair of high-waisted silk pants and a white blouse with dark polka dots. She was mugging over her shoulder, as if the camera had caught her tossing off a joke. Another had her in a flowered apron, carrying a platter of what was captioned AUNT AMY'S FAMOUS CHICKEN FRICASSEE. In a third, she sat at a desk in a dark woolen suit embroidered with silver crescent moons, holding a pen and gazing pensively. She looked more herself in the photographs than she had on the poster, but still: that light hair, that face, so milky smooth it might as well have been carved from marble. And her figure. I realized I was touching my own waist, searching for the shape I saw in the magazine, but the body on the page—trim in the middle and round above and below—was utterly unlike my own, when eighteen months earlier we had been the same body, its two halves.

At school, I slipped the magazine between the pages of my textbooks. By the end of the day I had the interview memorized. Instead of going home, I went into a shop and stole cigarettes. I walked to the lake and smoked two of them. Smoking a third, I walked to Garth's house, where an unfamiliar man was cutting the grass. I walked to Mrs. Broom's. Finding her office door locked, seeing no sign of her, I searched the registration desk and found the bottle of peach schnapps from which she used to pour modest shares for the boarders when she hosted one of her socials in the parlor. I sat on the stairs and drank. The house was dead. No one bothered me.

I left Mrs. Broom's with warm cheeks; the peach schnapps smeared the edges of the red-and-white buses that huffed along the streets, the end-of-day crowd with their weary faces, the pink-bellied clouds that hung low in the sky.

Before I opened the door I steadied my breath, I smiled a Wise Daughter's smile. Mama and Daddy were sitting together in the living room, their own copy of *Picture-Play* open on the coffee table. They looked up, and I faced them, squaring my shoulders. For a moment, they just stared. Then Mama scooped up the magazine. She started reading the interview aloud, hamming it up, giving the unctuous reporter a nasal accent, playing Josie as a vapid starlet. It was a cruel impression, one that had nothing to do with Josie really.

And I could see that it pained her to do it, and it pained Daddy to hear it. But at the same time, it stirred in me the memory of Mama's cool hand against my forehead, drawing out a fever. Oh, how as a girl I had longed for a fever! Daddy laughed. I laughed too. Laughter that tasted like peach schnapps, laughter that bubbled out of my throat like thick, black bile. We all laughed as if we'd never heard a better joke.

CHAPTER

13

IN THE DAYS THAT FOLLOWED, I SAW HER FACE EVERYWHERE: smiling out of newspaper advertisements, tacked to the side of a grocery store, wheat-pasted to the plywood in the window of a burned-out shop. Which meant others must be seeing her face too. Our face. On the kitchen calendar, Mama marked October 4—opening night of *Sister's Keeper*—with a star. At church that Sunday, Uncle Eugene greeted Mama and me with a dark look.

"You've seen?" Mama murmured. He nodded, glancing around to make sure no one else was in earshot.

"Disgraceful. But nothing has changed. That world is behind you, Harriet. Do you understand?"

I nodded fiercely, and then I was struck by guilt. Grasping after some kindness, some way of making it up to Josie, I asked if he would pray for her.

"Of course, child," he said, softening. I felt Mama's pleasure in what she regarded as my performance, but that only made asking him to pray feel like a further betrayal, a betrayal of Josie and of Uncle Eugene, a betrayal of myself.

At school, I waited for curious whispers, for long probing looks. When there were none, I figured it was because I kept to myself, because my hair was still dark, because she had only just entered the public eye. One afternoon, I was sitting in an Institute classroom, the first to arrive for Bible Study, when Polly and Ula came in together. At the sight of me, they stopped short. I sat up straight, braced myself against the swirl of nerves in my stomach.

"Harriet," Ula said, breathless, reaching for my hand. "There's something we wanted to ask you."

"Okay," I said.

Polly sat down beside me.

"Miss Muldoon is getting married," she said. Miss Muldoon, a student in the women's missionary training program, led the Girls' Bible Study each week. "We thought we should make her a gift. Before she leaves us. A quilt. We can each sew a square."

"Oh. What a nice idea. Of course."

"We thought we could take up a collection for fabric. Do you think you could talk to the others? It would mean something, coming from Reverend Creggs's niece, I think," said Ula.

I ought to have been grateful for the way she had reflected back to me the close association with Uncle Eugene on which we'd come to depend. I made chipper conversation about the quilt's design until Miss Muldoon invited us into the studio. But every word I spoke tasted of ash.

DADDY STARTED BRINGING HOME stacks of newspapers and magazines, which we pored through, passing around the scissors, cutting out articles and photographs that proved it was all really happening. Josie's triumph was a matter of public record. We pasted the clippings into an album with a red cover emblazoned with the word "Memories" in foil. I learned all about Josephine Wilder: what she liked to do on a date, the pattern from which she had sewn her kitchen curtains, her favorite hit song, her favorite shade of lipstick. In "candids," she splashed in a pool, rode a golf cart, bicycled through a studio lot. Her legs appeared in a lineup under the headline CAN YOU MATCH THE GAMS TO THE GIRL? She beamed out of a cartoon scoop of ice cream, stacked on a cone between scoops of Ruby Keeler and Carole Lombard, the text to the right reporting each actress's favorite flavor. "'Chocolate is divine, and vanilla is just fine,' says Miss Wilder. 'But I can't resist strawberry, best with marshmallow sauce!'" I laughed out loud when I read that. Josie hated strawberry ice cream. She hated any ice cream with lumps of fruit or candy.

On those nights with the scrapbook, Mama and Daddy would sometimes have a drink, and maybe Mama would look away as Daddy poured me a little, and we would work each other up: Who does she think she is? What makes her think she can cut us out? But eventually, the two of them would go soft-eyed. Do you remember, Daddy would say, before, in New York, when you would hide behind your mother's skirt, but Josie would invite strangers to come over to play or to look at her doll or her hat? Do you remember the time she asked the police officer if he had a belly button? Do you remember how she learned your choreography as well as hers, how she'd whistle your part when you got stuck? And I'd listen, nodding, my smile growing tighter and tighter, until finally I had to escape up to my room, where I would lie in the dark and imagine myself doing something magnificent, something important, something that would make someone want to publish my picture in a magazine. And though I couldn't quite imagine what that achievement might be, I could picture every detail of my parents' faces as they gazed at my photograph, shaking their heads, stunned by love.

WE PAID OUR OCTOBER rent on October third, the landlady's fury ringing in our ears, our radio in hock. That night, before we went to bed, Mama made an X through the final box on the calendar before the one she'd marked with a star.

The following evening, I was sitting at the kitchen table, reading the showtimes at the local theaters out of the newspaper, and Mama was at the stove, stirring a pot of baked beans, when Daddy arrived home. He kissed Mama's cheek, glanced into the pot, and tugged on her apron with a playful frown.

"What's this?" he said. "We've raised a star, Maude. We're going out to eat. I got tickets for the Chicago."

She stared at him.

"Lenny, we can't possibly afford—"

"How could we afford not to celebrate? After everything?"

They were still arguing when Mrs. Broom called from the front door.

"I invited her," Daddy said. Mama slammed the lid on the pot. But she went upstairs to change, and I followed. When we came back down, Daddy was shaking cocktails. Mrs. Broom chattered, trying to ease the mood. I watched my parents warily. Mama leaned against the wall in the space where the radio had been, wearing a blue silk dress I'd last seen her wear to an opera party the previous spring. She kept her lips pressed together, shutting her eyes and grimacing any time anyone laughed, as if anyone else's good cheer were an affront to her mood.

Outside, a horn sounded.

"That's us," Daddy said. Mama's scowl tightened, but she put on her coat.

When the cab dropped us off at a seafood restaurant I'd read about in a society column, Daddy paid from a thick wad of cash in a clip. I heard in my head all the questions I saw behind Mama's glare. Where had it come from? Where had it been on the first?

In a deep banquette with red velvet drapes, he told a tuxedo-clad waiter we would all have the lobster bordelaise.

"I'd prefer a cup of chowder," Mama said, sharply. Mrs. Broom glanced rapidly between Mama and Daddy.

"The same for me," she said, closing her menu. Mama's gaze burned my cheek as the waiter hovered. But I pretended not to pick up on her silent command, I pretended not to notice that a single serving of lobster bordelaise cost $2.25. On the night my humiliation was to play out on movie screens across the country, I wanted to have what I wanted. I handed the waiter my menu with a smile.

Our food arrived, Mama and Mrs. Broom's cups of soup dwarfed by the large plates the waiter laid before Daddy and me. I gobbled my lobster, as if the waiter might notice Mama's hostility and snatch it away again. When he hurried over to clear my empty plate, I was embarrassed by his air of slight surprise. I couldn't even say whether or not I liked lobster bordelaise. I hadn't paid close enough attention.

Daddy was still eating noisily, a napkin tucked into his collar. Mrs. Broom kept up strained attempts at conversations with him, shooting occasional anxious glances at my silent mother. When the check came, Daddy laid the bills on the table grandly. Mama powdered her nose, glowering into her compact. My lobster formed a hard lump in my stomach.

As we walked the three blocks to the theater, Mrs. Broom threaded her arm through mine. Her hips swished, and she swung a shimmery gold purse. Above us, neon signs and marquee bulbs cast a film of light over the sky, reducing the stars to dust. From a block away, we could see the tall black letters on the marquee: "SISTER'S KEEPER STARRING VINCENT ROMERO JAMES CONLON JOSEPHINE WILDER OPENS TONIGHT." My stomach lump pulsed. We joined a line that snaked out the theater doors, halfway to Lake Street. The air was sharp with the promise of an early frost; people huddled close together and made noisy conversation. Daddy lit his pipe and said hello, hello, hello to everyone who passed, as if he were some dignitary, mayor of the Rialto. I knew exactly what he felt: a brimming self-consciousness, the pressure of our secret, which, it seemed, could be relieved only by confessing our connection to the leading lady. I willed him to calm down. Mama refused to look at any of us.

I slipped into a daydream: Josie and I step onto a stage together, each of us claiming her own spotlight. The orchestra begins to play. We open our mouths to sing. But I couldn't hear her. I had forgotten the sound of my sister's voice.

The line advanced a few feet.

"Oh, what a night!" said Mrs. Broom, to no one in particular.

At last, through the revolving door we went, out of the cold night into a red-and-gold lobby that smelled of velvet and popcorn. A poster was propped on an easel, Josie smiling at us as if she were a hostess, welcoming us as her guests. We hustled past her. An usher directed us to our seats. Two women in the row in front of ours were arguing about whether Josephine Wilder was from Ontario or Ohio. It didn't feel real: two strangers, arguing about a lie my sister had spread about herself. I wanted to lean in and answer with authority: *She was born in New York. Six minutes after me.* Daddy went out and returned with a box of popcorn for each of us, and an extra box he presented to the arguing ladies. Mama pursed her lips.

"Aren't you a charmer," one of the ladies said, and they laughed.

Mrs. Broom offered her flask down the row. Mama drank, and passed it over my lap to Daddy. He handed it back to me. Mrs. Broom snapped her fingers and I relinquished it. She fished a chocolate bar out of her purse and gave it to me, a trade. The lights dimmed.

"Pass the popcorn, would you, Marlene?" said one of the arguing women.

"I finished it," said her friend.

"You finished it?" cried the other. "Already?"

"Madam, would you please quiet?" said a gaunt bespectacled man sitting on the other side of the first woman.

"Sir," she said. "Would you please mind your own business?"

He lit a cigarette and crabbed himself up in his seat, shooting a last disapproving glance at his neighbors.

A rectangle of light appeared on the screen. A moment later, the newsreel began. Men in a breadline outside St. Vincent's Hospital in New York City looked vacantly at the camera as it passed. President Hoover spoke in South Carolina. "Government in business, except in emergency, is also a destruction of equal opportunity and the incarnation of tyranny through bureaucracy." I closed my eyes, shut my ears to the familiar difficulty, and returned to my daydream: Josie and me, two individuals, sharing a stage. I hummed as quietly as I could, trying to discover some remnant of Josie's voice in my own.

The news ended, and a cartoon began. A lady cow sang scales in a slinky dress, her décolletage slipping and erupting like a rogue balloon animal. Daddy smiled knowingly, as if his experience at the opera had deepened his appreciation of the gag. In front of us, Marlene laughed so hard she choked on a piece of candy.

"Honestly, Marlene, must it always be such a production?"

"Do the two of you plan to talk through the entire picture?" the man in glasses asked, uncrossing his legs and dusting off his knees.

"What are you, a prosecuting attorney?" said Marlene.

"I am simply an ordinary citizen who hopes to enjoy this moving picture."

"Be quiet!" It was Mama's first utterance since ordering her chowder. At the sheer force of her authority, I felt a flicker of pride. The women frowned indignantly at each other. One of them glanced over at Daddy, as if to suggest he'd better get control of his wife. But through the rest of the cartoon, they were quiet. Mama sat perfectly upright, her purse poised on her knees, her fingers wrapped tightly around the strap. Daddy kneaded his belly with the heel of his hand and focused on the screen as if the doings of Oswald the Lucky Rabbit bore directly on Josie's success, on his own. Mrs. Broom reached over and gave Mama's arm a pat.

The cartoon ended; the screen filled with white light. Lobster bordelaise inched up my esophagus. There was a sputtering sound, and then the Warner Bros./Vitaphone logo appeared. Through the speakers came a flourish of strings. The music continued, lush and foreboding, as the logo gave way to the credits. There was her name, sandwiched between James Conlon's and Vincent Romero's. I felt a pang in my chest, the simultaneous desire to laugh and cry. Across America, audiences would see, had seen, that name. The person in the world who knew me best, the person best known to me, had been named on a movie screen. Josie Josie Josie.

I hardly breathed until she appeared ten minutes in, in a scene set in a department store dressing room: her feet first, in low heels with bows on the toes. One of the feet slips out of its shoe, scratches the other ankle, conveying a shopgirl's exhaustion and boredom after a long day's work. The camera traveled up her legs, past her skirt, a belted waist, a pair of arms burdened by a stack of dresses, a dark bow tie, and then there was her face, filling the screen.

I'd known it was going to happen, that it had to happen, but still I felt as if I'd been knocked in the sternum. Josie's hair formed a halo of curls around her face, which I felt myself relearning through the camera's lingering gaze: There was the deep valley of the upper lip, the gentle roundness of the chin and the sharper cut of the cheeks. There were her eyes, which looked larger than I remembered, larger than mine, lively and playful through their fringe of dark lashes, even as they plainly expressed all of her character Lil's boredom, her physical weariness, her longing for home. A thrum of admiration traveled through the auditorium, and for half an instant I felt like its target, as if just outside the frame must be my face, my body, pinned to Josie's. But at the same time, I was wholly part of that thrum. I admired her as if I were a stranger, seeing her for the first time.

For long stretches, the picture absorbed me as deeply as *Aída* had back in November. And then Mama would shift or Daddy would cough or Mrs. Broom would whisper, and I'd slip out of the picture's spell long enough to feel a surge of admiration: When had Josie learned to do that? To act like that? For a few minutes after each interruption, I saw them both: Josie and Lil, two women moving across the screen in tandem, Josie's posture, every small movement of her hands, the slightest shift of her expression, communicating something. And then Lil would resume control of my imagination, pull me back into the story until I no longer noticed my sister's skill, only felt its effects. At one point she sang a song, and as her voice bloomed in my ear and my brain, richer than it had once been, darker, but undeniably familiar, the voice with which I'd sung thousands of duets, I couldn't believe I'd ever forgotten it, even for an instant.

When it ended, the applause was instantaneous, bountiful, punctuated by whistles. I couldn't move. In front of us, Marlene grabbed her friend's arm.

"Wasn't she divine?" she said.

"Just marvelous. Those eyes!"

The man sitting beside them leaned over.

"She was terrific," he said, bobbing his head eagerly as if they'd been friends all along. "The rest of it—silly stuff, don't you think? But she was something."

Mama was still looking up at the screen. Daddy clutched his armrests, tears spilling into his beard. Mrs. Broom met my eye, something labored about her tenderness, as if she knew I needed it, felt duty-bound to offer it, but wished she could linger instead in her own wonderment. I didn't try to speak. I couldn't have. There was only one thing I could have said anyhow, and I knew they were already thinking it, same as every other person in that theater: Josephine Wilder was a star.

WENT TO *SISTER'S KEEPER* THE FOLLOWING AFTERNOON and again on Sunday after church. By Monday I was out of money, but I went to the Division Street theater after school and took the old route up the fire escape. On Tuesday, I skipped out during lunch and snuck into a matinée. Hours I ought to have spent studying I spent instead skimming papers and magazines for reviews and pasting them into the scrapbook. There was still no sign, in any of her press, of Raymond Fish; she was a gal-about-town, spotted on dates. I fantasized about ratting her out. I'd write to Terry Peat of *Hollywood Spy,* who had called her "the neatest sweet tomato on Hollywood and Vine." Did you know Josephine Wilder has a husband? Did you know she was a disgraced vaudevillian, a fraud? Did you know she is only seventeen years old? But instead, I went to her movie and stared until I felt as if my gaze were fire, as if it might scorch the screen.

On a cold, misty afternoon in November, a month after the opening of *Sister's Keeper,* I slipped away from Waller before ninth-period history. By then, I'd seen it sixteen times, and had begun to feel a proprietary comfort at the theater. I rarely thought about the fact that it was Garth who had taught me how to break in. Some of the ushers recognized me, but they greeted me as a valued patron, not suspecting that I never paid for a ticket.

That afternoon, I found an empty row near the back, where I spread my coat and scarf across a few seats to dry. I took out my history book, and for the first hour or so I read, looking up now and then, occasionally mouthing one of Josie's lines. And then I saw him, a few rows down from me: Daddy.

Light from the screen scoured out the deep hollows that cupped his eyes, filled the furrows in his brow. It caught on a thick stripe of gray in his hair, and white hairs in his beard that sparked like tinsel. I hadn't noticed he'd stopped dyeing it. What could he be doing at the movies, in the middle of the afternoon? The opera season had started at last; every morning, he left for work whistling. The previous week, he'd shown me a portfolio of designs he meant to give to Mary Garden. Still, we'd had to borrow from Mrs. Broom to pay the November rent. And now, here he was. I was struck by a strange, helpless grief: My father was old. He was a failure.

I put on my coat and scarf. As quietly as I could, I slipped out to the aisle and hurried down it. As I passed his row, I couldn't help looking a final time in his direction. He was leaning forward, watching Josie onscreen the way he'd used to watch our rehearsals—with that pained affection, the lost treasure look.

As if he had sensed me looking, he turned. I swore under my breath as he scrambled to his feet.

"Harriet!" His hoarse whisper carried across the auditorium. Several people hushed him.

For a moment, our eyes locked. His gaze was still marked by a pained, loving interest. I couldn't tell whether he really meant to look that way at me, or if it was just the residue of the way he had been looking at Josie. Before I could come to any conclusion, he started toward me. As he stumbled over the obstructing knees of the half dozen people between the two of us, I ran.

I WENT TO THE LAKE, where I threw rocks and trash as far as I could into the dark chop. Mist rose up to meet a mass of low-slung, brownish cloud blurring the horizon. I stayed there until the sun began to set, and the emptiness of the beach seemed suddenly frightening. When I got home, Mama was in the living room, changed already into a house dress, dusting the furniture that remained after a recent trip to the pawn shop. There was no sign of Daddy. From the kitchen came the smell of stew cooking; I realized, then, how hungry I was, and how cold.

"What's wrong?" she said, sharply. It wasn't a question about how I felt or what I might need, but an attempt to manage what she immediately recognized as a situation.

I didn't mean to tell. I'd thought about it, at the lake—how neither of us had been where we were supposed to be, which meant we could be in each other's confidence. But the words came tumbling out, Mama's clear, hard gaze, her tone, and, more than anything, my sense of my family's precarious position, a vision of the house built on sand tumbling into the sea, making it impossible to hold them in.

"I saw Daddy. This afternoon. He wasn't at work."

She stood very still, eyes flashing with anger.

"No one likes a tattletale, Harriet," she said in a steady voice. Then she turned and went into the kitchen.

I went up to my room. The hour for dinner came and went but Mama didn't call me down. When I heard a slam and a clatter, I slipped out to the landing and I crouched in the shadows. Daddy had knocked over the coatrack on his way into the house, and now he was trying to rehang Mama's coat. He kept missing the hook, clumsy with drink.

It was my fault he was drunk: I'd seen him, borne witness to his failure. And he hadn't yet learned how I'd betrayed him to my mother. She came in from the living room, wiping her hands on a dish towel.

"No performance tonight?" she said.

Lifting with both arms, nearly embracing the coatrack, he finally managed to get her coat to stay on the hook. He turned to face her, taking off his own hat.

"Bert thought I could use the night off."

She smiled coolly.

"That's funny. Vera saw Bert the other day. She said he asked after you. Wanted to know how you were holding up."

Was she bluffing? Making up a story about Bert so she wouldn't have to tell Daddy that his own daughter was a lousy tattletale? Or maybe it was true. Maybe she'd already known and I hadn't needed to betray him in the first place.

"That so?" Daddy finally said.

She threw her head back, as if she were about to laugh, but she merely rolled her eyes.

"Christ, Lenny, enough. You haven't brought home a proper pay-check all season. You're not at the opera house now, when anyone with a newspaper knows full well your precious *Camille* is on tonight. The papers are full of the company's financial woes. Enough bullshit. What the hell is going on?"

He took a step toward her.

"You aren't going without, are you? There's food on the table?"

"And how? Gambling? That's not a job, Lenny. How do you ex-pect me to convince Eugene—"

"There's no need to convince that man of—"

"If you won't take responsibility—"

"If you'd give me half a chance," he said, grabbing her hands. "I've worked things out so far, haven't I? Okay, it was hard times at the opera same as everywhere else, and I drew the short straw. I sup-pose Bert told Vera how he would have kept me on if he could? How I was appreciated."

She yanked her hands away.

"Bert turned white as a sheet and tried to play it off like a misun-derstanding. The two of you, like little boys in a club, closing ranks. How long have you been out of work? Has it been all season? A gap between contracts, Jesus Christ. You haven't brought home a full week's pay since the summer tour. Eugene arranged a perfectly good job for you, at a place where he has some influence, but you threw that away. It wasn't good enough for you, wasn't worthy of your genius, was it? And now I have to go to him again, I have to humble myself—"

"I'm not asking you—"

"Asking me? Who are you to ask? A man who gambled his fami-ly's security, his daughter's security, on a tired old dream?"

"You didn't seem to think it was such a tired dream last fall. You seemed plenty impressed, seeing your face in a statue on that stage. Shaking Sam Insull's hand at that party."

"Oh, Lenny, grow up." She threw the dish towel at him and turned. He followed her into the living room. I crept down a few steps, unable to see them now, only to hear.

"I have prospects, you know. Irons in the fire. God damn it, Maude, let me be a man. For once in our goddamn lives, let me be a man."

There was a long stretch of silence.

"Okay, Lenny," she finally said. The steel in her voice was gone. "All right." And then, more firmly: "Two weeks. Take two weeks to work something out on your own. And then I go to Eugene. With or without you, Lenny. I go to Eugene."

The back door whined and slammed. I went back up to my room, where I flipped through my textbooks, unable to concentrate well enough to study. The nausea I'd felt as I'd spied on my parents gave way to the ache of hunger. But Mama was banging around the kitchen, cleaning, and Daddy could come in from the yard at any minute. Eventually, Mama went out through the front. On her way to Vera's, I assumed. Maybe she'd be there until morning.

What did she mean, with or without Daddy she would go to Uncle Eugene? If he refused to accept Uncle Eugene's help, what would become of us? Of the two of them?

My eyes skimmed over the same few sentences until I couldn't keep them open at all. The house was still, the street quiet, when I heard my bedroom door creak. I sat up. Moonlight poured through the window, spilled across the floor, and rolled like a carpet toward Daddy's bare feet. I sat up and reached for the lamp, but he shook his head. He stepped in, closing the door after him. He thrust something toward me: a bowl, hot to the touch—he'd heated me up some stew. I ate quickly, every bite a reminder that I had betrayed him to my mother.

"I was looking for something. Earlier." His speech was halting and odd, as if what he needed to say, or the fact of needing to say it to me, had broken the thing in him that generated speech. "Some drawings I made last year. I think—I think you might have taken them."

I pulled my valise out from under my bed and retrieved the rolled pages I'd taken from his sketchbook. I handed them over. He thumbed through them, smiling shyly at his own work.

"It wasn't fair, Harriet. What your mother and uncle did to you. Not giving you a chance to say what you wanted. It's my job to take care of you and your mother. My job I ought to be allowed to do. The right way. How we're supposed to do it. Show business is in your blood, Harriet. Do you understand that?"

He looked up from the drawings, needing me to agree. I nodded again. He took a deep breath through his nose. But he looked back at his drawings, as if by directing his words at the girl he had drawn he could will her into life. He could see me in a blue gown, he said, a few songs—simple, just to start. A fellow he knew managed a theater, a cabaret called the Pirate's Den. This fellow knew Daddy had gotten into a tough spot. They'd worked together once, on some unrelated business, and Daddy had done this man a favor. No guarantees, but he would at least give me an audition. One night on his stage, to show what I could do.

"Will you, Harriet? Try a solo act?"

A car passed on the street below, its headlights casting a wide stripe along the wall, over Daddy's pleading expression. For a moment I was back in the movie theater, watching Josie. And all at once, envy was like a needle piercing my sternum, trailed by a long green thread. I had never really understood why envy was supposed to be green, but the longer I blinked back at Daddy, waiting for my mind to formulate an answer, the greener I felt. Envy ran green in my veins, it crimped my gut, it tinted my skin. Hadn't I been responsible for fifty percent of our success in vaudeville? If she had taken me with her, couldn't we have been Neat Sweet Tomatoes, two on a vine? That I'd flirted with other math in the past, that we couldn't have played Lil together, that Mama had given me a task suited to what she believed were my particular gifts—none of that mattered. There was only the fundamental injustice I'd been work-ing up to for weeks as I sat in movie theaters, watching, burning: Josie was a film star, while I was nobody at all.

A familiar need was massing behind Daddy's dark eyes and craggy cheeks and newly spangled beard. I felt a deep throb of re-gret. It wasn't only that I'd tattled that afternoon. Since our arrival in Chicago, I'd allied with my mother. Whenever I went to services at the Institute, or Junior Altar Guild or Girls' Bible Study, I re-minded my father that we'd set store by Uncle Eugene, the person he hated most.

And now he'd come to me, humbled, in trouble, out of work. Needing to prove to Mama that he could keep the family solvent. He'd asked for my help, same as Mama had when we'd arrived in Chicago. It seemed possible: I could earn the money we needed, protecting Daddy from another humiliation at the hands of my uncle and whatever Mama had meant when she'd said, "With or without you." Maybe if I was good enough I could even untangle us from our dealings with Uncle Eugene altogether. Maybe in six months we'd be back on track, ready to go to Hollywood, to claim for the family everything Josie had hoarded for herself.

And in the meantime, my various responsibilities didn't need to be in conflict. The previous fall, through all that business with Garth, I'd only gained in my uncle's esteem. Surely I could split my-self again, show everyone the portion they needed to see, honor fa-ther and mother both. And when I took the stage at Daddy's friend's cabaret, I would prove once and for all that Josie wasn't anything I couldn't be. Didn't have anything I couldn't have won for myself, if I'd been selfish enough to try.

"Okay, Daddy," I said. And a look of relief and pleasure passed over his face that I'd only seen once before: on that morning, so many years earlier, when Mama had agreed to turn Josie and me into the Siamese Sweets.

THE NEXT DAY, I MADE MY WAY, TRUANT, TO THE OPERA HOUSE. The factories beside the river coughed smoke into the clouds, forming a low, gloomy cap over the neighborhood. My knees buckled every time I caught a glimpse of the black water through the slats of the bridge. I sang scales and tried to keep my eyes forward. A long barge full of coal slid beneath me, spitting out exhaust.

Daddy was waiting outside the stage door, his collar turned up against the wind.

"When we get in, keep your head down," he said, in a quick, low voice, tapping his pipe against the railing. "Not a word to any of them. Bert's doing us a favor, letting us in here. We don't need to draw any attention."

I followed him down a dark hallway and up a few flights of stairs. At the end of a dim, silent corridor, he ushered me into a dance studio, where a man was sitting at the piano, head propped on his elbow, asleep. I froze, but Daddy cleared his throat. The man roused and came over to greet us.

"This is Eddie Previs," Daddy said. "He's your accompanist."

"Hello, Mr. Previs," I said through a rush of nerves. I had known I'd have to sing in front of strangers eventually, but I hadn't expected to do so that afternoon. He rubbed his nose with the back of his hand, blinking away his nap. He looked closer to my age than

Daddy's. His chin came to a sharp point, and his hair trailed down to the middle of his pink-mottled forehead.

"Eddie's fine," he said, smiling indolently, his cheeks slack, as if his face were weary of the effort of holding itself together. He returned to the piano. There was a mash of notes as he slouched once more against the keys.

Daddy opened up a notebook. Minutes passed as he scowled at the pages, as if waiting for some clear instruction to float up from his notes.

"Daddy, should we—"

He held up a hand. After a few minutes more, he shut the notebook, thrust some sheet music at Eddie, and called me over. I looked at the music over Eddie's shoulder. The scent of his cologne and the shellac subduing the pale coils of his hair rushed my nostrils; my stomach felt weak. He began to play. Despite the scales I'd sung on the way over, my voice stuck in my throat. Eddie fed me my note. I managed to begin, but my pitch wavered. I stopped.

"Could we start over?" I asked, cheeks blazing.

Eddie pounded out my part, and at last, I got through the song. I got through another. Daddy sent me to stand at the back of the studio, against the barre, and he paced in front of the mirrored wall opposite, calling out suggestions: move to the left, try it sitting down, try swaying a little, try your hands on your hips. Eventually, he settled on a stool and watched with that focus I remembered from the old days: elbows on his knees, hands pressed together as if in prayer. He bobbed his head in time. Whenever I let myself look at him for too long I made a mistake, so I started watching my own reflection in the mirrored wall instead. I felt oddly unmoored from the image I saw in the glass, as if my reflection were another girl entirely, a stranger over whom I had no control. But that made it easier: it wasn't me singing, it was the girl in the mirror.

The girl in the mirror felt her way into the songs. She began to move with a little more ease. And watching her, I filled with hope. Maybe this girl could manage it; maybe she was someone who could command a stage alone.

After a couple of hours, my voice was shot. Daddy's clothes and hair were mussed, as if he'd been the one dancing. But he grinned as he handed Eddie some cash. I shook Eddie's hand good night, feeling capable, professional: I was a cabaret singer with a hired accompanist. I'd just finished my first rehearsal.

The air on the streetcar home was warm and smelled of sweating bodies and wet wool. Riders coughed and snapped at their children, buried their faces in papers, struggled to hold on to packages, and yanked purses impatiently over the bulky sleeves of coats. But Daddy clung to a strap, and I held on to his arm, and for the whole ride home we didn't stop talking. Making plans. Two weeks, Mama had said. So in two weeks, we would have an act.

AT FIRST, I RELISHED our secret. At dinner, when Mama asked Daddy if he'd made any progress toward finding work, he would respond cheerfully but vaguely. As soon as she turned her back, he would wink at me, and I would have to hold back a laugh. But after a few rehearsals, I began to dread the sound of his knock on my door at night and his whisper: tomorrow at eight, tomorrow at two. His choreography was imprecise and ever-changing, but he grew angry when I couldn't manifest whatever it was he wanted. He kept saying I was "flat," but I quickly realized his "flat" was a catchall that rarely meant I was off pitch: he didn't have the words to describe in what way my performance was really disappointing him. As my truancies stacked up, I worried about missing class, especially when it was physics or trig or French, where it was so easy to fall behind. I wished I could skip past the tedium of rehearsal to the good part— the demonstration of my talent and competence, a wild ovation, Eddie shaking my hand backstage, congratulating me as a peer.

On the morning of our last rehearsal, the day before Daddy planned to lure Mama down to the opera house so we could reveal what we had been up to, I received a deficiency notice in trig. My nerves were raw when I arrived at the opera house that afternoon. A song I'd sung perfectly three days earlier now seemed impossible:

the notes were nonsensical, the words had disintegrated in my memory. Daddy paced, clinging to a yardstick, sometimes tapping it against the ground or his palm, sometimes swinging it like a truncheon. He quickly worked himself into a sweat.

"Do something with your hands," he snapped. "Eddie, give her two measures." In the mirror, I watched myself lift my hands like fans beside my face.

"No, no, not that," said Daddy. "Again." Eddie played. The mirror showed a girl with eyes as lifeless as gravel, a body as ungainly as a scarecrow's. Daddy smacked the floor with his yardstick, marking out the beats, but I couldn't make my feet move in time with them. I stepped left left, right right, extended my arms out to my side, made my hands do . . . something.

"No, no!" Daddy cried. "You're flat."

My voice slammed against a wall of tears. I wouldn't cry—in nearly two weeks of rehearsal I hadn't cried. I wanted to tell him he didn't know what flat meant, that he didn't know what he was doing, that I'd always performed just fine when Mama was in charge, that he was wasting our chance. But I just let my arms drop to my sides, my fingernails digging into my palms. Daddy put on his coat. He felt in his pocket for his pipe.

"We'll take ten," he mumbled, and was gone.

Eddie went to the window and lit a cigarette. I retreated to the opposite corner and took out my math homework. But I couldn't concentrate. I filled the edges of the page with drawings of little houses with smoking chimneys and pointy-eared cats. When Eddie glanced at me, I stared harder at my paper, half-willing him not to say anything comforting and half-hoping he would.

"Any thoughts about how you might like to proceed here?" He had finished his cigarette and was now studying himself in the mirror, twisting the tufted corners of his eyebrows between his index fingers and thumbs to train them upward. "The boss said ten minutes. He's been gone half an hour."

"Oh." I stood, tugging at my skirt, which felt too tight at the waist. "Well, he must have gotten held up."

"Do you think that we should consider the possibility that he's not coming back?"

I stuffed my homework into my schoolbag, unable to answer. Eddie shrugged and packed up his things, then he lingered at the door, looking at me expectantly. I felt my face color.

"I don't have your—pay," I managed to say. "I'm sure my father—"

"Let's not spoil the mood. I'll see you out, Harriet."

The building was lively with preparations for that evening's performance. We'd have had to stop rehearsing soon anyway, even if Daddy hadn't walked out. Maybe what he'd really said was that we were finished for the night. Maybe Eddie and I had simply misunderstood.

"He drives you pretty hard, huh?" Eddie said, as we passed through the scene shop.

I looked around, wishing he hadn't chosen this moment to start talking.

"I'm just a little rusty. That's all."

"Oh, you mean you've done this before?"

A white cloud of humiliation filled my brain, displacing every possible response. He laughed.

"Look, a voice like yours may not be to everyone's taste. But that's exactly what I like about it."

I hurried out the stage door, uncertain whether I'd been insulted or praised. Eddie skipped down the steps ahead of me, and then turned, grabbing on to both of the railings to block my path. There was a spray of blond whiskers and a single, sore-looking pimple on his chin. A spring of hair had loosened from the pomade and was resting against his temple. Something stirred in me—a nervous energy, the awareness of a potential I couldn't quite name.

"It's bad luck not to go out after a lousy rehearsal, you know."

It seemed possible he was making a joke, but I couldn't see where the setup ended, where the punch line began. At whose expense it was being told. I made myself smile.

"Are you hungry?" he went on, a little sharply, as if I'd tested his patience. "I know a place near here."

I felt my cheeks go red. For two weeks, Eddie Previs had been an element in Daddy's scheme. Now he was a man, older than me, worldly and talented, asking me to dinner. Despite my crummy performance that afternoon and Daddy's anger, Eddie Previs wanted to take me out.

Mama would be expecting me home. But I could explain: I'd been at the library, studying with a friend. I'd lost track of time.

"I'm hungry," I said. "Yes."

He scratched a tooth with his thumbnail, and I was worried that in the time I'd taken to answer he'd changed his mind. But then he turned and started down the alley, whistling. I scrambled to follow.

He took me to a chili parlor, where we passed a flask back and forth under the table as he told me all about himself. After that, we went to a penny arcade, and then to a club fitted into what had once been a dry goods store. The siding was weather-worn, the windows boarded; the place would have appeared abandoned if not for the music that spilled out into the alley every time the door swung open. Inside, the rough-hewn walls were hung with strings of white lights and paintings of cats wearing people clothes. Eddie introduced me as "vaudeville sensation Harriet Smith," and laughed every time someone said, "Never heard of her."

We passed into a second room, which had a small stage. The air was thick with smoke; a band was playing. Eddie took my hand and we wound through a crowd: women wearing dresses with low backs, or Oriental trousers whose inseams hung around their ankles, men in pinstripes blowing smoke rings. A man with a long white beard whispered to a man with a gold tooth and a gold ring on his pinky. A woman with a shiny black bob toured the floor in trousers and a tuxedo shirt, smoking a pipe. I tugged at my too-tight skirt, mortified that I was still dressed in my school clothes.

We joined his friends at a table near the stage. One of the women threw her arms tight around his neck and whispered, pressing her sticky-looking melon-colored lips to his ear. But Eddie shook her off and rolled his eyes at me apologetically.

A friend of his delivered us cocktails, ginger ale and something, and by the time I'd gotten to the bottom of mine, I wasn't so worried about what I was wearing. As someone bused my glass, I retrieved the little curl of lemon rind from the rim and wove it into my hair like a barrette. The melon-lipped woman laughed and called me a pet, then tried unsuccessfully to wind her own rind into her slick bob. Eddie's friends kept introducing themselves to me, but the names slid right off the faces they were meant to stick to— Bill, Johnny, Vernon—and we all laughed at how I couldn't tell them apart. One of them brought over a round of French 75s, another a tray of turkey sandwiches. When we'd finished our sandwiches we all got up to dance. When we sat again, Bill-Johnny-Vernon was ready with another drink for me. When I said, "Thank you," my tongue clung for a moment to my teeth. Bill-Johnny-Vernon laughed, which made me laugh too.

I danced with Bill-Johnny-Vernon, and I danced with men I didn't know, which Eddie seemed to enjoy watching until he didn't, until his face darkened and he came over to claim me, and it was thrilling, how forcefully, how fleetly he swept me across the floor, away from the interlopers. He grabbed at the lowest part of my back, he levered my arm shut at the elbow so I pressed right up against him as we spun. I could feel, through my blouse, through his shirt, the fact of a male body: skin and muscle and hair. I decided: I would let him kiss me, if he tried.

"Your heart is beating," I said. He laughed against my ear.

He delivered me to the table and told me he'd be back in a minute. I leaned back in my chair, damp and exhilarated, and rubbed the beginnings of a stitch in my side. The shade had slipped from a sconce above the table, and the light hurt my eyes. Eddie returned with another cocktail.

"I don't think—"

"Oh, be a good girl," he said, and pressed it into my hand.

Time fragmented. Some slivers of it were gay, bright chips from a mirror: I was swirling, showing off my knees. Bill-Johnny-Vernon was a laughing face, a flash of teeth in a black mouth.

And then, in a corner, in shadow: Eddie was kissing me. The

room spun like a top. There was the sweet relief of a wall, solid behind my back, then Eddie's face pressed once more so close to mine,
making me feel crowded, and he was saying, very soothingly: It's
time to go, don't you think? Let's be alone, let's get to know each
other better. I couldn't keep my head above the surface; my body
wanted to sleep or cry. My feet were walking a path I hadn't chosen
and couldn't unchoose. There was starlight, there was the refresh-
ing clarity of cold; we were going. But it wasn't Eddie I was going
with. It was a girl, with cropped hair and broad shoulders. My cousin
Ruth. And then I remembered: She had shouted at Eddie, moments
before. Slugged him, maybe, or threatened to? I laughed. She smiled,
though she was trying to be stern. We were in the back of a cab. My
blouse was lopsided; the buttons were wrong. Then we were out of
the cab and the cold stung—I had forgotten my coat. But I couldn't
stop laughing.

"Oopsie daisy," said Ruth, helping me up over the curb. I watched
my hand trail along a cold curving stone banister as we climbed a
flight of stairs. And then I remembered, just in time, the waffle shop
we passed on our way in.

"Don't you want a waffle?" I said.

"I suppose it wouldn't hurt to put something in your stomach,"
she said, grimly. Down and up again, this time with waffles warming
our hands through brown paper sleeves. The couch sagged in some
places and poked in others. The wool blanket scratched my cheek.
But what a relief to lie down flat, to let my head fall onto a cushion.
My eyes closed themselves.

RUTH BENT OVER ME, the morning light cool at her back, holding
out a cup of coffee. The smell of it hit me, a sharp, bitter wave.

"I think I'm going to be—"

"Through there," she said, stepping back and pointing.

I sponged myself clean and rinsed my mouth, but when I came
out of the bathroom, I still tasted my own sourness. My skull felt
scrubbed by fire. The night before was returning out of order, in

fragments. Ruth's apartment comprised a single large room. Her bed was behind a curtain in the corner, facing a small sink and a narrow counter with a Sterno stove. Her books filled a shelf that spanned one wall. At the sight of them, I felt a flicker of the jealousy I had first felt as a girl, in Toledo, surveying the Library of RVTH. She'd been sitting on a wide windowsill, knees bent, reading, but had stood when I came in. She wore green lounge pants and a fisherman's sweater, and had a scarf banded around her hair.

"Hi," I said.

"Hi yourself," she said. She smiled tightly, clutching her book to her chest like armor.

"How exactly did I—"

"We ran into each other. Last night. You seemed to be having a bit of trouble."

I sat down on the couch, beside the wool blanket, which Ruth had folded into a compact rectangle. The cup of coffee she'd woken me with was sitting on the edge of the table.

"Thank you for helping me."

"Don't mention it."

"I don't usually—"

"I won't tell," she said quickly. "My father, I mean."

I pulled the blanket into my lap.

"Thank you." I traced a black check with my finger. "It is true, though. That I haven't—done anything—quite like that before."

She put her book down on the windowsill and approached, slowly, as if I were a wild animal that might spook.

"I believe you," she said, sitting very lightly on the arm of the couch. "But don't worry. I'm not—scandalized. I was there too, you know. Do you want some eggs or something?" I couldn't keep myself from making a face. "No eggs then." She smiled. "It's strange, seeing you, Harriet. But it is nice."

"Yes," I said. I took a small sip of coffee. "I've hoped I would see you. Again. Since—well, since the opera. That was you, wasn't it?"

She nodded as she slid the rest of the way onto the couch.

"That was me. And—a friend I don't see much anymore. I

wanted to see you too, but I wasn't sure whether—well, Father has told me a great deal about your family, since you came to Chicago. So when I saw you there, I had this feeling. I found your father's name in the program. Old Eugene thinks Uncle Lenny works at some factory. So I thought best not to say anything. However much I would have liked to have arranged things so we could have—caught up."

"Thank you," I said yet again, feeling myself blush. "It was kind of your father to get Daddy that job, I wouldn't want him to think—"

"There's no need—I won't—he and I aren't—" She tugged on one end of the green scarf she wore in her hair, looking as if she wished she could find the words that would not only make me trust her but understand a truth about who she had become—the reason I should trust her.

"You aren't close?" I said clumsily.

"We write," she said, pulling her knees up under her and facing me, eagerly, as if relieved to have the chance to explain. "I see him very rarely. It's better for both of us this way. But there's no need to get into all that. It's just that I rely on him for certain—resources. So I have to ask—whatever you tell your mother about last night, would you leave me out of it? The less he's reminded about my social life, the easier things go between us."

"Of course." I put the mug of coffee down on the table. "Oh god. My mother. They'll murder me. Where are we, anyway?"

"South Side. I'll walk you to the L?"

Our boots crunched against a thin layer of snow. Puffs of pale vapor rose from dark roofs where the sun was burning away the frost. In a sweater of Ruth's, I felt the cold reach my bones, and I deeply regretted the loss of my coat. But the clean, sharp, metallic flavor of the air seemed to clear the fog from my brain. I thought of all sorts of questions I wanted to ask Ruth: Was she still in school, and what did she study, and how had she come to live alone in that apartment, and what did Uncle Eugene have to say about that? I wished I could talk to her about Josie, about what had happened and about the new trouble the family was in—Daddy's loss of work,

Mama's ultimatum, my mess of a solo act. But I wasn't sure whether we were strangers or friends or something in between—what the rules of communication might be between us.

There was one thing that needed saying, one thing that beat in my throat until, as we came up to the L stop, I finally gave it voice.

"Your mother—Ruth, I'm so sorry."

She kept her face very still.

"Thank you," she said at last, quietly. After another long silence, she smiled. "I'm not sure what to say about your sister. Is that sorry? Or congratulations?"

"Both, I guess? Although there's nothing to congratulate me for, really. No one even knows she has a family."

"Well, I do," said Ruth.

A train clattered into the station along the northbound track.

"I'd better go," I said. All at once, she threw her arms around my shoulders. Her wind-chapped cheek was smooth and cold against my own. When she stepped back, she waved and nodded, as if to offer me the option of a more dignified farewell. Halfway up the platform, I turned and watched as she walked back the way we had come, hands in pockets, shoulders back, pace brisk. Anyone who looked at her would see that she belonged here, on this street, on her own.

WHEN I CAME IN, Mama and Daddy were both waiting in the living room, an overflowing ashtray on the table. Mama staggered over to me. She grabbed a handful of my hair and pulled, pressing her face close to mine.

"Do you realize we nearly called the police?"

Daddy stood.

"Enough, Maude, enough. I told you, I upset her. It was my fault."

She turned to him.

"Oh, you'll get no argument there. The smell of liquor on this girl! Her father's daughter, no doubt. After everything I've done. Yes Eugene, no Eugene, I'll pray on it, Eugene. Now you're out of work, and your daughter has turned overnight into a tramp." She whipped around to face me. "Do you think this has all been a game?"

"No, Mama," I said, voice cracking with tears.

She narrowed her eyes, as if there were something unbelievable, something absurd, about my weakness. Daddy touched Mama's shoulders. She flinched.

"I upset the girl, that's all," he said. "She probably went to stay with a friend. Isn't that right, Harriet?" I nodded, though Mama had closed her eyes; her mouth formed a stiff line, and her chest rose and fell emphatically with her breath. "But listen, Maude. I told you I'd work things out, and I have. Harriet and I have." He turned to me with a soft smile. "Harriet, you get cleaned up."

Before I'd even made it upstairs, I heard her laughter, trumpeting and angry, and I knew he had told her about the solo act. As I scrubbed off the previous night's misadventures, their fight rose through the floorboards in snatches I couldn't decipher. I thought maybe she'd put her foot down—she'd refuse to even consider it. When I came back downstairs, she was gone.

"Telephoning Vera," Daddy said. "We won't wait. We'll go over there now. Vera will play for you, we'll show her what we have. Don't worry. Your mother will come around."

I swallowed some aspirin. He tried to make me drink a little whiskey—hair of the dog, he whispered—but instead I had a tomato juice with an egg, as I'd seen Mama do the morning after the opera. I was relieved not to have to think about seeing Eddie that afternoon, but I was too nervous to absorb Daddy's last-minute advice.

When Mama came in, she gave Daddy a quick, tight nod, but she didn't speak to either of us until we were on our way out the door.

"And where is your coat?" she asked. I shook my head. Her jaw knotted with fresh anger. Daddy gave me his, and we went.

Mrs. Broom opened the door wearing a silk bathrobe with a tattered hem, her cheeks shining with face cream. She gave me a worried glance even as she took Mama's arm and patted her hand. In her sitting room, she and Daddy conferred beside the piano, which had been salvaged from the old parlor. The air was warm and smelled heavily of perfume. Clutter pressed from all sides. I was starting to feel woozy when Mrs. Broom sat at the keys, and Daddy gestured for me to stand at the piano's edge. Daddy offered Mama a chair, but she shook her head.

Mrs. Broom began to play. My headache overpowered the aspirin. But I came in with my part. When I lifted my arms, my hands felt heavy as catcher's mitts. I took a few steps, my feet unmoored, I knew, from the rhythm. But I had the words. The notes seemed close enough to true. Near the end of the song I let myself look right at Mama. I faltered, startled to find her looking at me with a concentration I remembered from early childhood. Not Peoria, not the Mayfield Circuit, or even our first years on the road: this was New York, this was the first dance in the harness, and before that—a way of looking that belonged to the most distant edge of my girlhood, when the boundary between us must have been at its most porous, when she must have known me in a way that I could hardly conceive of now. The muscles in my shoulders knotted. I rushed through the last phrase, wanting only to get it over with. Mrs. Broom kept up, and maybe my speed seemed on purpose. I spread my arms wide and delivered my final note on an optimistic surge of breath.

Mrs. Broom stood. She and Daddy looked to Mama. Mama was looking past me, at the wall. She hushed Daddy with a single lifted finger. But I'd heard what he had started to say: "You saw Josie up there."

My tomato juice and egg rose back up my esophagus. I ran to the bathroom, where I clutched the toilet and cried, vowing that I would never drink liquor again. When I returned, the three of them were huddled at the piano. Mama looked over at me. I was expecting rage, and I saw it: the rage of a trapped animal, and I knew Daddy had trapped her, backed the family into a corner and refused any way out that wasn't an act. But it wasn't just rage. I saw something else too—a tenderness—that startled me. She looked as if she wished, for everyone's sake, that she'd found a way to tell him no.

———

A FEW DAYS LATER, I went to Mrs. Broom's house to rehearse. It had been decided that Mrs. Broom would stay on as my accompanist. I hadn't even had to suggest it; Daddy hadn't dared ask Mama to spend the money on Eddie. We were in debt to the grocer, the butcher. We hadn't reimbursed Mrs. Broom for our November rent. When we passed the landlady in the street, she warned us: We'd better not be late again. December first loomed like the end of days.

"Are you sure this is something you want to do?" Mrs. Broom asked in a low voice as I helped her roll up the rug. We'd already pushed all the furniture against the walls.

"Of course I'm sure," I said. She glanced over her shoulder. Mama and Daddy were due any minute.

"If you're sure," she said, looking at me with a trembling sympathy. "I just wouldn't want—"

I opened up my schoolbag and dug through it as if I were looking for something. She sighed and went to the piano, where she played bright scales until Mama arrived.

MAMA DISCARDED ALL OF Daddy's choreography. He'd been a fool to even try it, she said. Your father never had the first idea about performance, she said, about anything that live human bodies did on a stage. Daddy still came to every rehearsal. She wouldn't let him give me his notes himself, but the two stayed up long after I'd gone to bed, their voices drifting up the stairs to my room. And it pleased me to think they were down there, making plans on my behalf. It seemed to prove Daddy and I had done the right thing for our family after all. I tried not to think about the deficiency notices I'd received when I'd skipped school to rehearse with Daddy, or how, yet again, I was failing to study for my end-of-term exams.

———

ON THE LAST DAY of November, Daddy came home at three in the morning with a busted lip. But he had the money for our December rent. Late the next afternoon, when he climbed out of bed, he told Mama he'd arranged a date for my audition at the Pirate's Den—the Tuesday after next.

"If she just had a little more time," Mama murmured.

"It's now or never, Maude," he said, quietly. She gave him a long pained look, and then she nodded.

Daddy wanted to call the show "A Little Wilder," to market me as the younger sister of the rising Hollywood star, but on this Mama held firm.

"We'll honor Josephine's wishes," she said.

After school a few days later, I tromped a mile and a half through an inch of slush to the Pirate's Den. It was a small place, well out of the way, on a street no one from my Institute life was likely to frequent. Night fell around me as I studied the card in the window that spelled out the family's future. The name was new—Harriet Shore. But it meant me alone, and there it was, printed beneath the words "Coming Attractions."

I N MY DRESSING ROOM IN THE BASEMENT OF THE PIRATE'S Den, I leaned toward the mirror and tugged on my cheeks. The night before, when Mama had called me down to try on my gown a final time, I had panicked. It had seemed as if nothing could happen on that stage save my humiliation. I had sputtered as much at my mother and locked myself in my room. Through the door, she had offered a stream of reassurances. When I'd finally come out, she'd taken my arm and led me down the stairs. I'd put on the dress, and Daddy had folded and pinned a couple of darts. Mama had made me a cup of warm milk, a comfort she hadn't offered since before Josie and I learned how to tie our shoes. Her gentleness had unnerved me; I'd been awake to hear the hall clock chime all the hours and half hours between midnight and three.

Now, my face was pale, and my vocal cords felt gluey, my lungs as if they'd been coated in plaster. Mama and Daddy drifted in and out of the background of my reflection, dodging the bare bulb that dangled from a fraying cord in the middle of the ceiling, attending to tasks. Mama wore the same blue silk dress she'd worn to the opening night of *Sister's Keeper,* Daddy the same sharp suit. Everything in my surroundings cued my body and brain to expect Josie beside me, Josie, preparing to step into the harness with me and take the stage.

"Mee mee mee mee mee mee mee mee," I sang.

"Hadn't you better get dressed, Harriet?" Mama said, unwrapping the tissue from the new foundation and slip she'd bought me on credit.

"Okay," I said. But neither of them moved until Mama caught my eye in the mirror, and, embarrassed, led Daddy into the hall. The improvised walls, plywood tacked to two-by-fours, shook when she shut the door.

I undressed slowly, savoring my privacy, though their conversation—clipped, superficial—was perfectly audible through the walls. The mirror propped in the corner warped my reflection, turning me green. My brassiere gaped at the top, and the straps slipped down my arms. I tugged them up, drew back my shoulders, and stuck out my chest. On each of my hips was a row of scars like thin white moons, a new moon for each harness I had outgrown. I had a large freckle beside my belly button and a mole on my wrist. But otherwise, my skin was unmarked. For the imaginary photographer in the mirror, I shimmied and pretended to laugh.

Mama rapped lightly on the door.

"Are you ready, Harriet?"

"Just a minute," I snapped.

I finished undressing and tugged the girdle part of the foundation up over my stomach. After several tries, I managed to hook the strapless, armor-like brassiere. I put runs in two pairs of stockings, but the third I managed to keep intact as I clipped them to the foundation. I put on my slip and, at last, stepped into my dress. Daddy had been working on it for weeks: It had a bodice with a single strap, studded with emerald sequins, and an overskirt of grass-hued organza, which trailed at the back. The materials, I knew, he had mostly pilfered from the opera house costume shop. I sucked in my breath and did up the hooks and eyes along the side.

When I turned back to the mirror, for an instant I saw a woman, a performer. Hair freshly marcelled, brows tweezed into two fine arches. The foundation had lifted my bust and cut in my waist, giving me a figure. As I twisted my hips to make the green gauze swish around my legs, I felt a rush of hope.

Mama knocked again, more softly this time, but her voice was insistent.

"Harriet? Are you ready?"

The figure in the mirror became a child in costume, her forehead greasy, her expression stiff and unnatural, her gaze unsettled and shy. I sank back into my chair and called my parents in.

Daddy had just finished my makeup when Mrs. Broom arrived, rosy from the cold and full of cheerful conversation. We all relaxed a little, then. She made me stretch and led me through a warm-up. Mama fixed my hair, and Daddy patted me with powder, and all at once it was time. I teetered up the stairs, willing my back not to sweat into my dress, my foot not to snag the hem with one of my new towering shoes.

Mama and Daddy left through the stage door to watch from out front. Mrs. Broom and I waited in the small, cramped back stage. The running order, scrawled on a yellow sheet of paper on which the previous night's running order had been scratched out, was clipped to a music stand beside a lamp covered in a blue scarf, beside which the stage manager sat on a stool with his eyes closed. There was a steady buzz of conversation from the house.

The pianist onstage finished his set and stood to a smattering of polite applause. The stage manager shot to his feet and dimmed the lights. Mrs. Broom gave my hair a final fluff. The whole left half of my body felt superfluous and strange, as if it belonged to someone else. I began to shake.

"I can't." I grabbed Mrs. Broom's arm. The pianist came off, and the stage manager carried the stool out to the stage.

"Bullshit." She looked into my eyes as hard as anyone ever had. "You're her daughter too. No less than Josephine. You hear me?"

At the sound of my sister's name, I felt as if I were receding back from the edges of my own body, shriveling into a speck.

"Get out there, kid." The stage manager's impatient voice sounded miles away. Mrs. Broom wrenched her arm from my fingers.

I was on the stage, perched on the edge of the stool, not sure how

I'd gotten there. The crowd was clustered around tables, drinking and chatting. A few people clapped as the lights came up; I squinted into the brightness and found Mama and Daddy at a tall table at the back. Mama coughed. I nodded, overly conscious of my face: the stillness of my lips, and then their strained lift into a smile, the stiffness of my nostrils as they struggled to draw in breath. Mrs. Broom was playing my intro—of course she was, my nod had been the signal for exactly that—but I couldn't hear my part. I couldn't hear it. It was as if I'd never sung the song before, never sung any song before. Mrs. Broom vamped. The thin, looping chords sounded obviously preparatory—the audience must know, by now, that my silence was a mistake. But my lungs pumped shallowly. I searched for the words. My consciousness of Josie's absence intensified; I felt as if I were standing beside a void, a gap in space that had her shape.

Plink plink plink plink. My note. Mrs. Broom was playing my note.

I grabbed ahold of it, began to sing because I had no choice but to sing. And even though my brain could not anticipate the lyrics before I sang them, somehow my mouth formed them. The conversations in the house continued as if I weren't singing at all. I came down from the stool, per Mama's direction, and grabbed the microphone. There was a squawk of feedback. A dropped glass shattered. I felt the burn of tears.

Mrs. Broom played straight through the meager applause at the end of my first number. But as I began my second, I realized that my voice was no longer shaking. I leaned toward the microphone and ground a fist into my hip—I had filled my own body again, regained control of it. I wiggled my shoulders. When I hit a big note, clear and ruby-hued, someone whistled. People began talking less, watching more closely. Even the clink of glasses became more delicate, less obtrusive. I tapped out a combination, lifting my skirt to show off my feet.

I was doing it, now: the work I'd practiced from the age of four. I was entertaining. And by myself: the void was gone, or at least had been, until I realized it was, and then there was only a flash of Josie's shape, a shimmering outline, before I was alone again. At the end of my second number, applause came in a generous rush. It seemed to stop just beyond my skin, as if I didn't quite remember how to absorb it. But never mind. Here was the third and final song. With my last chance to impress came a tiny hitch of nerves, but then the gears of the performance fitted neatly together and advanced. My voice knew the correct notes, my face the correct expressions. My feet produced the correct steps.

I waited for the glow that I remembered from all those years of the Siamese Sweets—that perfect alignment of breath and muscle and will, that sensation of warmth pouring off my skin to meet the warmth the audience offered in exchange. But even as I sang and danced, my heart stayed numb. My body was executing the act—properly, ably—but my thinking had separated out into a cold, steady stream. Had the first song been deadly, I wondered? Would the manager make an offer? And how would that work, exactly, with my commitments at the Institute, at school? What if he wanted me to perform on Saturdays, and I started turning up to church with purple shadows under my eyes? What if he wanted me on the schedule right away? My physics teacher had given me until Friday to submit two overdue lab reports. When would I finish them?

I sang my last note and snapped my hands toward the ceiling. This time, whistles studded the applause. I tucked my right toe behind my left heel and bowed low.

Offstage, Mrs. Broom kissed the top of my head. The stage manager, nearly running into us on his way back from striking the stool, told us to get the hell out of the way. Mrs. Broom threaded her arm through mine and led me out the stage door.

"Coming down from the high," she said, smiling knowingly. "It's like plunging into a cold ocean. You don't have to say anything, dear." But that wasn't it at all. I felt a void again, but this time it wasn't Josie's absence I felt, it wasn't a void to my left—it was a void I recognized inside of myself: what pleasure I'd felt onstage had been hollow, meager. No better than singing a hymn on a Sunday at the Institute.

We went out the stage door and came back in through the front. A table had been held for us next to Mama and Daddy's. Daddy nodded at me, his face bright with the same pride I'd seen at the movies, as he'd gazed up at Josie. Mama seemed absorbed in the next act, a man playing the clarinet. When a balding man with bulging cheeks came over to the table and tapped Daddy on the shoulder, Mrs. Broom patted my knee. I spun a coaster on the tabletop. Daddy followed the man into the lobby. A few minutes later he returned, grinning.

So I'd done it: I'd earned my solo act. Satisfaction arrived in a trickle. Daddy pulled me out of my seat and made quick, hushed introductions before we all followed the manager out to the lobby. I glanced back at Mama. To my surprise, she was gripping Mrs. Broom's arm as if she might fall over. She looked stunned.

The words she had spoken in the alcove on our first day in Chicago came back to me in a rush: "It wasn't fair of me. To put you on the stage. You weren't cut out for it." And all at once I understood: She'd assented to my solo act out of desperation. Through all those weeks of rehearsal, she'd been expecting me to fail.

Well, I'd shown her, hadn't I. But through the trumpeting of a pride that I could not distinguish from spite, I heard again Mama's pronouncement—not cut out for the stage—and the words that had seemed so cruel suddenly had the clarion ring of truth. Maybe I was good enough for the Pirate's Den. Maybe I was good enough to get the family out of trouble, maybe I was even good enough to make something of a proper life for the three of us. But being good enough wasn't the same as wanting. The glow had always been Josie's glow. I'd known that from the moment she scooped up that fallen pear in Kalamazoo. The satisfaction I felt now wasn't joy. It was only envy inverted. The thing I had earned—a brief run at a seedy cabaret—was a crumb compared to my sister's stardom.

As Daddy and the manager discussed a contract for my solo act, I thought about the tedium of rehearsal, the stomach churn of nerves, the discomfort of a frigid back stage. How I hated all that! Maybe I'd always hated it. What a price it was to pay for something so fleeting, something so minor, in the end.

I knew, from having heard Mama negotiate so many times, that
Daddy was agreeing to amateur bullshit, that she would never have
put up with half these terms during the Siamese Sweets. But she
was watching him with soft eyes, looking as feeble as a kitten in an
alley. For the first time in my life, I understood that my mother
could be weak. Show business, the harness, the romance of the
opera, my solo act—Daddy had a way of making Mama lose track
of what she thought was sensible. He'd made her forget what she
knew better than anyone: our future was safest in the care of Uncle
Eugene.

"No," I said. Everyone turned to me. I avoided Mama's eye. It
was my choice. It had to be. "I don't accept."

Daddy laughed. He took me by the shoulders and ushered me
out the door.

"She's beside herself," he called back to the manager. "Overwhelmed. She doesn't know what she's saying."

Back down in the dressing room, he dug at his hair.

"Have you lost your mind?" he asked. He sounded as bewildered
as if I'd thrown a punch. But I felt an odd urge to laugh. What a
relief. Not just that I was righting our course but that I wouldn't
have to perform ever again. I could finish my lab reports, be a
schoolgirl, do the things a Wise Daughter did.

"I'm not cut out for the stage," I said. The words came brightly,
clearly. "Mama, you told me that once. Do you remember?"

I turned to her, expecting to see understanding or relief. Gratitude even. But she was gripping the handle of her cane tightly, her
eyes flashing with anger, as if by reminding her of her own judgment
I had transgressed. I turned back to Daddy.

"It's okay, Daddy. We'll go to Uncle Eugene." I knew that I was
hurting him, but there was no stopping now. He would understand.
He'd have to understand. "We'll tell Uncle Eugene the factory is
going under. We'll tell him they're laying men off. I'll tell him. He
won't doubt me. He'll find you another position. He'll take care of
us. Don't you see, Daddy? He'll take care of us."

Daddy gaped at me for a moment and then forced his gaze down to the floor, as if to study the dark trails of moisture that marked the way to the drain.

"She's made her decision," Mama said at last, softly. "You said that, didn't you? That it was her decision to make?" She didn't look at me—only at him. "I'm not sorry you had this time—this goodbye, Lenny. But our lives have a new shape now. After all this time. Couldn't you find some other way to be happy?"

He looked up at her. Some crucial hope was leaving him, the loss so palpable I could almost see it, a white form rising out of his body. And then he left, slamming the door. The walls quaked.

"Lenny!" She followed. I took a step toward the door, but Mrs. Broom grabbed my arm.

"Leave them be, Harriet," she said.

I shook myself free. When I got to the top of the stairs, the stage manager was waiting, red in the face.

"If I hear one more peep out of you lot—"

I pushed past him, out the stage door. Mama was half a block away, Daddy well ahead of her, practically jogging. Holding my dress off the wet sidewalk, respectful of the stolen materials though I no longer needed them for anything, I hobbled after my mother. She stabbed at the sidewalk with her cane. My big toes throbbed. My heel caught between bricks and I stumbled.

As he approached the L station—the way home—Daddy seemed to hesitate. But then he kept going, faster than before.

Mama stopped. When I reached her I put my hand on her shoulder. She didn't flinch, but she didn't look at me either. It was as if I were nothing to her, a ghost whose touch she couldn't feel. Daddy passed through stretches of shadow and pools of light, never breaking his stride, never looking back. Mrs. Broom caught up and threw my coat over my shoulders—her old tattered fur, which I'd been wearing again, with a promise from Daddy that if I made a go of it at the Pirate's Den he'd buy me a new coat to replace the one I'd lost. All at once, I started shaking, as if my brain had only just then comprehended the cold. Mrs. Broom wrapped an arm around Mama's waist.

"He'll get it out of his system," she said, through hard breaths. "And you'll work things out with Eugene. You'll get on with it. You always do."

Mama was silent for another moment. Then she turned toward me, a wildness in her expression I'd never seen before, her body moving with sudden fluidity, a liquid rage.

"What were you thinking? What in God's name were you thinking?" She slapped my face, once, twice, over and over until Mrs. Broom forced herself between us.

"Maude, enough," she cried. I stumbled away from them and lifted a hand to my cheek but couldn't touch it, could only half-shield the tender skin from the cold air. I wanted to shout: *I did it for you. I've given you what you asked for, I am who you've told me to be.* But even as the words scratched at my throat I knew they were wrong, that I'd forced a rupture between Mama and Daddy more serious than any that had come before, and now I didn't know whether either of them would ever forgive me. Mrs. Broom held Mama by the shoulders; their faces moved with furious speech, but my hearing was full of the roar of a train and then the screech of its brakes. I turned from them. For a few seconds longer, I could still see Daddy, the softly lit edges of his shrinking back. Then all I could see were dozens of strangers coming down off the L.

1913

April of 1913: he doesn't know it yet, but the finest year of Leonard Szász's life is about to begin. Maude is pinning old sheets over the windows of their dreary new apartment on Tenth Avenue when she climbs down from the stepladder, clutching her back. Lenny watches from the corner, angry at her for showing off, for not letting him help, for not accepting the reality of her leg and her cane and her delicate condition. The sound she emits is low, nearly feral. Through clenched teeth, she tells him to get Vera.

He runs five blocks downtown, to the sixth-floor apartment Vera shares with a pack of Fleischer's girls. By the following morning, the babies have arrived—babies, two of them—too tiny to be real, a pair of squalling, hairless rabbits.

Vera brings Maude the babies to feed, and Lenny paces outside the bedroom, feeling superfluous, clumsily male. But something is wrong: Maude weeps. All that first day she weeps, and all the next night. Lenny takes a few hard pulls from a bottle every hour or so to keep himself at neutral. He had been the youngest of his brothers. He hadn't understood the violence a baby's arrival enacted on its mother's body. Vera assures him that everything is normal. It's only natural, she says: a period of adjustment.

But on the third day of crying, Vera comes to Lenny, her face tight with what he now recognizes as fear, and asks him to go in, to try talking to her. The bedroom is a cave smelling of milk and blood. The babies are sleeping, both of them at the same time, a miracle, but Maude's face is pale and tear-stained. She can hardly speak for crying until finally the words erupt, the words neither of them will ever refer to, but which will sit between them for the rest of their lives: "I thought this time it would be different."

The next day, the babies are his. Maude needs her rest, Vera says cheerfully, and he carries the bassinet out of the bedroom. The two of them take turns preparing bottles, rocking the girls, bathing them, feeding them, Vera ceding a little more responsibility to Lenny every day. He catches her looking at him with reluctant admiration. He ties the corners of their diapers into tidy little bows. He holds the one that won't sleep without being held, he dangles the pocket watch above the one that likes to look at the pocket watch. Eventually the blur of baby, of perpetually renewing need, divides into two: Harriet and Josephine, each already herself. He sings "Baa Baa Black Sheep" and "Hush Little Baby" and a song his father used to sing about a clumsy glass mouse whose mother has to patch him up with glue.

Vera cooks and carries in a tray for Maude. Lenny eats one-handed, one of the girls always making some claim on the other hand. Mr. Fleischer sends a final check. Lenny trawls their apartment for things to sell. There is no place for him in the theater, not yet, not with his reputation, but he starts to leave the girls with Vera for a few hours at a time so he can bring in some money washing windows or painting houses or hauling trash. He cannot do more than this because he cannot bear to be away from them—not for a full day, not yet, not when they are so little still. Not when their need for him is so absolute.

They grow: six months old, seven months. Lenny is stunned by the way he possesses the facts of their lives. Until the day he dies he will cling jealously to these facts, the private history of his daughters' infancy: the way they hum for hours, one picking up whenever the other leaves off. How their teeth come in at exactly the same time, in exactly the same order. The night he paced for hours on the tar-paper roof until Harriet, sticky with a fever, finally slept against his chest. Josephine's gleeful shriek the first time she thought to bang a spoon against a pot.

On the same day, for the first time, both girls say, "Da." The

next day they say, "Vee." For their mother, to whom Vera carries
them on her better days, and there are more of those than there
were at first, they do not yet have a name.

Three days after their first birthday, Lenny comes home from
pulling up carpets in a mansion on East Eighty-Seventh Street,
hands raw and lungs full of fibers, to find Vera at the stove, frying
onions and beaming.

"Go look," she says, adjusting the flame. And Lenny knows
right then but he still rushes into the bedroom and there is
Maude, bathed and dressed with a girl in each arm, cooing into
their startled faces. Lenny embraces all three of them, as afraid as
he has ever been, though it makes no sense to be afraid. She is
their mother. At the edge of his mind's ability to put into words
the things he feels is his certainty that he will never do anything
better than caring for his daughters. Mothering them. Another
truth he almost grasps as he holds them in his embrace, chin in
the crook of Maude's neck, eyes closed tightly: He has been father and mother both, and now Maude is claiming what is hers,
and that is her right, that is natural. And he wants that for her—
after the past year, after the past two years, after what he has
taken from her, of course, of course, he will give her the girls. He
must give her the girls. It doesn't feel like a choice; it feels like
sleepwalking off the edge of the earth.

At first they cry for him, reach for him, and Maude weeps
again and says, "Why don't they reach for me?" Her weeping ter-
rifies him. Both because he can imagine her slipping back under
the weight of her sadness, and because he can imagine himself
swooping in, reclaiming what he's given up. So he makes himself
leave. An evening out and then another, a few drinks here and
there, just so they have a little room to breathe, he thinks, so
Maude can get to know her daughters.

Soon, it adds up to the old habit. And trailing the habit
comes the old feeling, that familiar, burning injustice: Why is he
working at odd jobs, a man of his talents? The question feels
larger than its obvious answer, too fundamental to be extin-

guished by a simple accounting of recent history. And larger still for the loss of the girls. Another seething instinct: If he can't have them, can't have the care of them, then he must shine in the world. If Maude will mother them, he must prove himself, at last, in the theater. A man provides. A principle obvious and absolute. He makes the rounds again with new sketches, but it's no, no, and quicker than before. Gone is the polite pretense of consideration. Gone is the encouragement to try again. One morning, after weeks of unanswered queries, he goes to David Belasco's office. One secretary after another says Mr. Belasco will be in touch if he is interested. But Lenny knows if he can only talk to Mr. Belasco directly, Mr. Belasco will recognize his vision. How his talent has been wasted. He waits. Surely Mr. Belasco will leave for lunch, he thinks, a sip of whiskey stinging his own empty stomach. But the noon hour passes, and then one o'clock. Another secretary says she really must insist that he go.

"I'll wait to speak with Mr. Belasco," he says. Her nostrils flare. He knows she is going back to speak to Mr. Belasco herself, to tattle. He loses track of his body, briefly. He's knocked a stack of magazines off a table. A man in a bow tie hurries into the hall. Lenny slumps in a chair.

Three thick-necked men appear, and there is a hand twisting his collar, there are arms wrapped around his chest. They are pushing him out and down the stairs and through a dark hallway, then into the alley where each of them lands a few kicks in his gut or his groin. His mouth fills with dirt and saliva. A shoe lands on his face, and the rough surface of the alleyway grinds against the other cheek.

A few minutes pass before he manages to stand and start the slow walk home. He spits and spits again but cannot clear the grit from his mouth. He worries a loose tooth with his tongue. Sweat stings the tiny lacerations, some still nubbed with gravel, in the alley-side cheek, and the gridded red imprint of the boot. His blood feels brittle. With every step up to the apartment his bottom ribs burn.

When he opens the door of the Tenth Avenue apartment, the girls are standing in the sink. Maude is pouring a cupful of water on Josie's head while Harriet reaches out to catch the falling stream. All three of them are singing the song about the glass mouse. Light shines through the window in a straight, clear beam that falls on the girls, just the girls, and if he were a different man maybe he'd see a halo or maybe he'd just see sun, but because he is who he is he sees a spotlight. It is the light that transforms them. Lenny doesn't do it; he just has the vision to recognize a transformation that has already occurred.

Maude, seeing him, raises a hand to her mouth; he begins to cry. But by the time she is pressing a cold cloth against his scrapes, certainly by the time she stirs fragrant salts into a hot bath, he is calm. He knows the way forward. He understands: The way back to the theater is also the way back to the girls, with whom, in the face of Maude's brisk competence, he has grown so shy. He will build his daughters a world. He will make them an act.

He is sensible enough to wait until his scrapes have healed to ask and even then she says over my dead body. She says leave the past in the past. For two years he pleads. He draws costumes. Wouldn't that be sweet?, he says, the two of them dressed as a cow, one in the front, one in the back, just like you and Vera. He knows it is a risky tactic, but he still trembles with frustration when Maude responds by ignoring him fiercely for four days. He is ashamed of himself—a grown man near tears because his wife will not let him put their daughters in a cow suit and teach them a few songs.

It's Coco Cohen who gets him the message: Coco Cohen, valiant conqueror of his virginity, still dancing at Lippmann's Burlesque Theater on the Lower East Side, has a friend deliver a note to a bar where she knows Lenny will turn up eventually.

"Stella heard your girls are following you into the family business," she's written, referring to a Lippmann's dancer he only dimly remembers, and he is embarrassed that he cannot remember running his damn mouth, that his habits are predictable enough for Coco to have found him here. But then he reads the rest. Stella has moved up to clean burlesque at a theater on Forty-Seventh and Seventh Avenue that is retiring a little upright re-hearsal piano, free to whoever will haul it away.

One morning late that March, Lenny walks to the theater, three blocks over and six blocks up, twenty minutes, a pleasant walk on a cool, bright day, but as he anticipates the walk home his whole body tenses. The sensible thing would have been to hire someone to haul it, but Maude controls the purse strings, as she always has. And what friends does he have, these days, to ask a favor? But it is better this way, he thinks, as he knocks on the stage door. After so many years in the theater, he's learned the power of an entrance.

A couple of men come out of the shop to help him get the piano down the stairs, up the aisle, and out the door. They secure it to a cart with a length of rope and wind a heavy canvas strap through the cart's handle and over Lenny's shoulders and chest. He digs his foot against the sidewalk; the cart creaks into motion. The men wave as he heads east on Forty-Seventh.

One long block and his back is already throbbing, his chest stinging from the drag of the strap; he can feel blisters forming on both feet. Two men emerge from a saloon and watch, curious, as he leans against the cart to catch his breath. The barkeep comes out and hands him a pint of beer, which he downs in a few deep pulls. When he wipes his mouth and starts moving again, the men tag along, making wagers over whether he'll faint. An-other block, and the muscles in his legs feel like liquid fire. A group of boys runs around him in a circle, taunting him good-naturedly. But then the leader of the boys grows serious, barks at his mates to lay off; he runs up ahead, telling folks to clear the way. The last of the long blocks, and Lenny feels as if his right shoulder is about to pop out of its socket, but this must be half-way, he thinks. He eases out of the canvas strap and pushes the cart from behind, turning left. Then back into the strap and he's

moving downtown, the boys running half a block ahead, shouting
for people to make room, the wagering men taking bets from a
couple of others.

At Forty-Sixth Street, a woman emerges from a shop and offers him a doughnut, still warm; a block later, another woman
comes out with a pretzel. The sun is growing hot, and his hands,
curled for so long like claws around the canvas strap, struggle to
hold on to the offerings, which, when he finally chokes them
down, slosh dangerously in his gut. But his entourage continues
to grow: the men and the boys and a few girls now, who laugh
whenever he looks in their direction, and the people pressing
their faces against the windows. For the first time in his life, an
audience. At Forty-Fourth he stops and tries to wipe the sweat
from his face with his shirt, but it is already damp, and when he
puts it down, it is stained pink: his hand is bleeding. When he
starts moving again, the boys whoop.

Three blocks to go. Of all of the exertions his body has
known—hauling set pieces through a blinding hangover, helping
a buddy carry a chest of drawers to a fifth-floor apartment, getting the shit kicked out of him outside a producer's office—the
only physical discomfort to which he can compare his dry mouth
and heaving breath and burning knees and the ringing in his ears
as he passes haltingly over Forty-Third Street and a cop shouts at
him to hurry along is his crossing of the Atlantic, alone, at nine.
During that week, he could hardly keep food down. He rarely
slept, for fear of a man who leered at him from a nearby cot. A
smell rose from his fellow passengers, of blood and shit and sick.
His head was shaved for lice at quarantine, and weak, disoriented, he found his way to his aunt's apartment alone. As he
yanks the piano up over the curb, as an impatient driver zooms
past so close his whole entourage shouts in protest, he resolves
that when he has pulled his girls close again, he will tell them all
about the little boy he was, about the crossing, and about this
morning, about the pain bursting like lightning through his back
that makes him wonder if his muscles have simply split open, if

they'll ever knit themselves together again, about the churn in his stomach that only gets worse when at Forty-First Street a woman runs out of an apartment building with a drink and a camera. But he downs the drink and grins, panting, into the flash. A man makes as if to help him, but he summons a strength he thought he'd already spent and shakes his head no. It's up to him: the last half block. Lungs seizing, a purple brightness splotching his vision, the pressure behind his eyes so intense he thinks maybe they will bleed, maybe they are bleeding, maybe it is blood he feels rolling down his face and not sweat, he pulls. And then he is on the sidewalk below the apartment. He tries to call up to them, but his voice barely makes it out of his throat, and a boy near him echoes his call: "MAUDE! HARRIET! JOSEPHINE!" and the crowd joins him in the kind of booming unison that rarely happens except on a stage: "MAUDE! HARRIET! JOSEPHINE! MAUDE! HARRIET! JOSEPHINE!" Lenny slips out from under the straps, staggers a couple of steps so he can lean against the piano itself, his legs starting to buckle under the weight of his body as he wills them to come, wills them to look. At last: the curtain brushed aside, and Maude's face in the window, one girl sitting on her hip and the other peeking over the sill, and even though he is three stories beneath them, even though he is bleeding sweat into his eyes, as the crowd cheers he is certain he sees something in his wife's face—a softening, an invitation, a pleasure she has stopped trying to thwart. He knows in that moment that she loves him still, and that his girls will live inside his love. He knows he will have his act.

PART FOUR

CHAPTER

17

IT WAS A FRIDAY AFTERNOON IN FEBRUARY OF 1931, TWO
months after the Pirate's Den. In the kitchenette down the hall
from Uncle Eugene's office, I set an egg timer for nine minutes and
then pressed my forehead against the cool, rain-streaked window to
wait. Behind me on the counter sat a tray that held the tea, steeping
in its pot, two cups and two spoons, and a plate of the Hydrox cookies that Uncle Eugene's secretary kept stocked in a cupboard above
the sink. It was my second Friday in the kitchenette, my second time
preparing Uncle Eugene's tea, but already it was all growing less
strange: the view from the fifth floor, the arrangement of the tray, a
pair of shiny new shoes, a new bed with crisp new sheets, new rou-
tines and responsibilities.

On the morning after I refused my solo act, I'd come downstairs
and found Mama sitting at the kitchen table, still in her blue dress.
Without a word, she carried her coffee out onto the back steps, even
though it was a bitter morning, the sky low and gray, old snow eddy-
ing around the yard. She didn't go to work, and I couldn't bring
myself to go to school. All day, a single fact seemed to permeate the
air between the two of us, flooding my lungs every time I took a
breath: Daddy hadn't come home.

At nightfall, Mama made me put on my coat and boots and
trudge beside her up and down State and Clark and Wells, scanning
the faces of the men who shuffled out of flops and cheap hotels and

dance halls with their hats pulled down low. Every day for the rest of
the week she called in sick. She left countless messages for Bert
Koster, finally taking me to the opera house, where the shop manager refused to let us through the stage door. On Sunday, she sent
me to church with instructions to tell Uncle Eugene that both she
and Daddy had the flu, and to thank him for his prayers.

The following week, Vera—I was suddenly allowed to call her
Vera, as if the crisis had inaugurated me the rest of the way into
adulthood—managed to lure Bert over to her place. Mama and I
came into her sitting room, where he was waiting.

"I see," he said, ruefully, removing a sprig of mistletoe from his
lapel.

"Where's Lenny?" Mama asked.

He gestured for us to sit, but Mama didn't budge, and neither
did I. He closed his eyes, as if against a sudden sharp pain.

"I don't know, Maude."

And then with a sigh, he told us what he did know, filling in the
gaps around Daddy's half-truths about the end of his employment
at the opera: He hadn't worked at Ravinia that summer, not that
he'd been paid for, anyhow. His contract in the fall had only been
part-time. A few weeks into the new season, he had cornered Mary
Garden in the elevator and tried to make her accept a portfolio of
his designs. She had fired him on the spot. Of more than that Bert
was not sure, but he thought Daddy might have borrowed some
money from a man he played cards with, maybe a few times. Maybe
he'd done a little work for the man, to try to pay it back.

"A pretty rough guy, Maude," he said, letting the brim of his hat
slide through his fingers. "If I'm being honest."

For a few nights after that, Mama sat at the foot of the stairs,
staring at the front door, clutching a rolling pin like a weapon. I
claimed Daddy's last sketchbook for a diary and for the first time in
ages wrote prayers, a few to God, but mostly to Daddy himself,
apologizing for having ruined everything and begging him to come
home, though by then I understood what Mama could not yet
admit: he was gone for good. I wrote poems, too, as I had after

Garth disappeared, and though I burned most of them out of sheer embarrassment, I felt a certain power every time I picked up my diary and pen: the possibility that I might arrange the chaotic facts of my life into some sort of order. That I might press something true into the world.

On Christmas, Vera came over with a bottle of gin, which she and Mama emptied while I baked a ham. A few days later, Mama kept watch while I lugged a few suitcases into a cab. Leaving the landlady to discover the house abandoned, we hunkered down in a basement apartment a few blocks closer to the slum, where Mama took the bedroom and I slept on a brown couch that smelled of cats. If we opened the windows, fumes from the gasworks stung our eyes.

Mama no longer spoke to me of Daddy, though she went to Vera's a few nights a week and came home snappish and pale. She finally returned to work and started coming to church again on Sundays. When Uncle Eugene asked after my father, she invented bright stories: new responsibilities at the factory, progress toward conversion.

I stuck to a tight circuit: school, and home, and Vera's on Saturday to do my chores, and the Institute for Junior Altar Guild and Bible Study and services. When Josie's second picture, *Fallen Angel,* came out, I added the Division Street theater to my routine. It was there I stopped one blustery afternoon in February, to break up my walk home from school. When the picture ended, I wasn't ready to face the cold, so I stayed put and watched it through a second time. Josie had a supporting role, but every scene she was in seemed to spark. The reviews had singled her out for praise; some had hardly mentioned the proper star, Velma Clifford. Watching her that afternoon, I couldn't decide whether the pressure that collected in my chest was loathing or pride.

I arrived home to a dark apartment. Mama was sprawled on the brown couch, dead drunk, one of Daddy's whiskey bottles empty on the floor beside her. She was clutching a telegram. I pried it out of her fingers. It had been sent care of Vera, collect.

"IN LA PROSPECTS GOOD FOR H MODELING DANCING STUNT WORK SEND FUNDS IF ABLE LOVE=L"

I covered her with a blanket and went to sleep in her bed. When I woke in the morning, the scent of bleach assailed my nostrils. I came out of the bedroom and found the apartment scrubbed clean. Mama was hunched over the stove, drying her hair.

"Put on your pink dress, with the sash," she said, sounding almost like her old self: brisk and businesslike. "You're going to see your uncle."

She brushed my hair, and curled it, and tied my sash in a fat bow, all the while feeding me a script as long ago she had taught Josie and me songs, line by line. But when I repeated it back to her she frowned.

"It's not right," she murmured, rubbing her hip and studying me through narrowed eyes. She went to our trunk of clothes and pulled out her own gray suit. When I had changed into it, she pinned my hair back and pinched a little color into my cheeks. We stood together at the chipped mirror above the kitchen sink.

"There," she said to my reflection, tapping my spine to remind me to stand up straight. "See? You graduate in the spring. You're not a little girl anymore. You're a bride-to-be."

I drew in a sharp breath. In the mirror, Mama's face was pale, the skin slack around her mouth and eyes. But her gaze was clear, the movement of her fingers sharp as she plucked a stray hair from my shoulder. My sense of responsibility rose like a tide in my chest. Daddy was gone; he wasn't coming back. Mama wasn't waiting for him any longer. And in his absence, a good marriage was no longer simply an advantage Mama hoped to extract from my uncle on my behalf, but an urgent duty. Through marriage—not a solo act, not some achievement tantamount to Josie's stunning career—I could secure the family's future. Mama's future. When I was married, with a house and money in the bank, Mama wouldn't have to scrape or hustle or worry about landladies or debts at the grocers. She wouldn't have to cross her fingers and humble herself before Uncle Eugene.

Most of what I said in Uncle Eugene's office that morning was true: Daddy had run off, Mama was afraid to tell him. If I left out the Pirate's Den, if I fuzzed the timeline, that didn't change the fundamental fact: we needed his help. I brought him back to the apartment and led him into the bedroom, where Mama was sitting up against a pillow, a smooth sheet covering her legs, face bare, hair loose and shining, the Bible he had inscribed for her open in her lap. She closed it, her eyes growing wide.

"Eugene," she murmured, pulling her cardigan shut against her throat.

"Leave us, Harriet," he said, softly, tenderly, and I thrilled with the certainty that whatever Mama told him he would believe.

A few days later, a troop of missionaries-in-training came in a van to help us move into a fine new furnished apartment in Streeterville. Uncle Eugene gave Mama a raise and sorted out our debts. As part of the new arrangement, I was to go to his office every Friday afternoon for tea and a chat: a capstone to my Christian education, he said. A preparation for the next stage of life. Wife School, Vera called it, when she came to see the new apartment. I blushed, and she apologized for teasing, but really what I felt was resolute. In a year, maybe, I would be a wife. Mama and I would be safe.

The egg timer dinged. It had been waiting on the counter when I'd arrived that afternoon for my second Friday afternoon chat, Uncle Eugene having set aside the tea I'd prepared the previous week with a sympathetic smile, declaring it a bit weak. "Nine minutes ought to do the trick," he'd said, patient in a way that drew attention to his patience, the virtue of it. I fished the tea bags out of the pot, hoping this time I'd gotten it right, and carried the tray to his office.

He stood as I came in, rapping his desktop lightly with his knuckles. I set my tray on the table beneath the window and poured the tea, and then waited anxiously while he took his first mouthful. He made no complaint, just asked after my mother's health and my own, and how things were working out in the new apartment, before passing into current events. I'd glanced at a paper on the way over, and I was able to express a polite, intelligent interest in the topics he raised. Mostly I concentrated on taking small bites and not getting Hydrox stuck between my teeth. Eventually he stood and, with hands folded behind his back, took a few steps toward the center of the room.

"Beloved, I wish above all things that thou mayest prosper and be in health, even as thy soul prospereth," he said, turning back to face me, his voice swelling, as if he'd stepped behind a pulpit before a few hundred people. "I wish to speak this afternoon of soul health, Harriet. John hopes for his friend all sorts of prosperity: prosperity in material things, prosperity in his body, prosperity in his spirit. But how does a soul flourish? What does it mean to attend to the health of a soul? Think back a couple of months, to your poor mother, stricken with that flu."

I nodded uneasily. He listed what he supposed to be her symptoms and compared them to the condition of an ailing soul: a loss of appetite, like the absent hunger for God's word and for the company of other Christians that keeps a man from church; a shortness of breath, like when prayer that is "the Christians' vital breath" becomes an empty duty; a fever that fires in the brain false visions and foolish ideas, like the lies that entice a Christian from what he knows to be good.

"Now, Harriet," he said. "What do we do to heal the body when it is sick?"

For my every suggestion—call the doctor, take an aspirin, rest—Uncle Eugene spun a metaphor about the recovery of soul health. But he kept glancing at the clock. At quarter to five, as if on cue, he abruptly asked how I was faring at school.

"Oh, very well, thank you."

He studied me a moment.

"I would think by now you would know you can trust me with your troubles, Harriet."

"Sir?"

"Your mother spoke to me."

I sat very still, my heart tripping forward, as if I'd just been struck by stage fright. A few days earlier Mama had marched into my bedroom, my fall grade report in hand. When it had arrived back in December, in the immediate aftermath of the Pirate's Den, she'd set it aside without comment. Now she waved it in my face, something almost gleeful in her reprimand. During our week and a half in the new apartment, she'd buzzed around with unfamiliar domestic energy, as if she might exorcise what remained of her grief over Daddy by arranging the tasteful furniture Uncle Eugene had secured for us, by ordering fresh flowers and trying to cook, and by working to make sure I ended up the sort of girl who could stay the course and build on the gains she'd made. She still didn't speak about Daddy; she hadn't even said a word about the telegram she must have guessed I'd read. Between us, there were only the hard, plain facts of the present and the project of my future.

I assured her that there was nothing to worry about; since the start of the new term, I'd hardly done anything but study. Already I was on track for the honor roll.

"Your uncle won't mind bad grades, per se," she continued, as if I hadn't said a word. "He doesn't need you to be a scholar. But it's the convention. The order of things. He won't help with the next part until you've graduated from high school. He's been very clear about that. I'll think on it."

She left, and I glowered at her back, irritated that she hadn't listened to me, that I hadn't been able to make myself understood.

But it hadn't occurred to me that she would rat me out to Uncle Eugene. Now he leaned against the edge of his desk, legs extended, supporting himself against his palms, as if to signal he was a friend as much as an uncle, an adult who knew how to relate, and I understood why she had done it—Eugene Creggs the White Knight, never happier than when he was called upon to assist a lady in distress.

"You must remember, Harriet, that mind health is soul health: The mind is your system of moral germ defense, your teachers are assistants to the Great Teacher of man. And there is no more shame in asking for help with your studies than there ever is in asking for His help."

I started tidying the tea tray, needing to channel the agitation I felt coursing through my hands.

"Shall we pray on it, Harriet?" he said gently.

I put down the napkin I'd been folding and turned to him with what I hoped was a grateful smile.

"I'd like that, sir."

We knelt side by side in front of his desk. He thanked God for scattering the clouds of ignorance with the sunshine of knowledge; he prayed that I might be equipped with every tool I needed to succeed in the useful purpose the Lord envisioned for my life, and that my education would not merely fill my head with facts but invigorate my spirit and strengthen my character. As he continued, his prayer grew vague, circling back over the same territory. I opened my eyes just long enough to see he was looking at the clock, frowning slightly. He went on like this until, finally, there was a knock at the door.

"In your name we pray, Amen." He stood, dusting off his knees. "Come in!"

The door opened, and in came Ruth. I scrambled to my feet. She wore a pointed felt hat and wide-legged black wool trousers, though the Institute dress code strictly forbade pants for women. Uncle Eugene took a few steps toward her, then abruptly stopped, as if he were afraid of spooking her. The silence swelled.

"Harriet, do you remember your cousin?" he finally asked.

As I shook Ruth's hand, she all but winked. I looked down at the floor, praying Uncle Eugene hadn't noticed, and that he didn't notice the color I felt flooding my cheeks.

"Ruth has been studying on the South Side," he hurried to explain. "And of course, it isn't convenient for her to come all the way up here, to see her father preach, or to visit as often as she would like. But she has agreed to come once a week to help you with your schoolwork. So we can be sure you stay on track the rest of this term."

"Thank you," I said, embarrassment spreading through me in hot, slow waves as I saw myself through Ruth's eyes: playing the goody-goody, the Institute girl, the Wise Daughter. The very part she'd refused. "That's very kind."

Whose idea had it been, I wondered—had her father asked her to tutor me? Or had she surprised him by responding to one of his letters with the suggestion? How long had it been since they'd met face-to-face? A few minutes later, we all walked out together, having agreed that Ruth and I would meet in one of the Institute classrooms the following Tuesday afternoon. Uncle Eugene's car was waiting downstairs. As Ruth got in, she grimaced at me from behind her father's back, as if to make sure I understood she was making a sacrifice. I clung to the strap of my purse, forcing a smile. Uncle Eugene climbed in after her. The car pulled away from the curb. I'd never noticed the strong resemblance between the two of them until that instant—the car's window framing a family portrait as they both waved goodbye.

ON TUESDAY AFTERNOON, she swept into the classroom wearing the same pointed hat, and trousers again, this time bright blue, as if she wanted to make sure her father noticed her flouting of his rules. Her cheeks and the tip of her nose were red.

"I wanted to see how it turned out," she said, smiling and peeling off her gloves. She breathed warmth into her palms. "After I saw you last. Not murdered, I see." But there was a tenderness in her expression that made it plain she knew something of what had happened since we'd seen each other back in November, at least something of the version Mama and I had reported to Uncle Eugene.

"Not murdered."

"Well, that's a relief." She followed my gaze back over her own shoulder, to the open door and the hallway beyond. "Hmm. Yes. This is no place to have a proper conversation. Shall we?"

She started to turn. Panic flooded my chest.

"But what if he comes by, to check in on us? What if someone sees us go?"

She looked at me for a moment, her gaze curious and steady. And then she shrugged.

"I'll tell him the change of scene was conducive to our work."

"I don't know, Ruth, I don't want—"

"If we're going to be friends, you'll have to trust me to manage him," she said, and I was braced by her authority—the same authority she'd displayed as a little girl playing school—and by that word: friends. How clear she was about it.

It had been raining earlier; now frozen drops like glass beads spangled branches and railings and the domed tops of trash cans. Ruth bought me a bag of hot chestnuts from the man at the corner, diligently, as if she were filling a prescription, then set off along a street I'd never been down, even though it was only a few blocks from the Institute. When our conversation faltered, she gestured up and down the block like a tour guide.

"This is Towertown," she said. "The village. Bohemia." She pointed out a few of the ramshackle shops and restaurants and galleries that lined the street, their signs and awnings vivid against the gray afternoon. "I used to sneak away from the chapel or a class or Junior Altar Guild or some other bullshit that he had roped me into and wander around here. It was like I had this shadow life, where I'd been to all these places, when really I'd just walked past them, and either they were closed because it was Sunday, or I was too frightened to go in, because my father was nearby, and I wasn't where I was supposed to be. People say it's past its prime, and I suppose that's true. But it's still my favorite part of the city."

I nodded, stunned into silence by the fact that this place had existed here all along, blocks from the Institute, within a mile of any place I'd lived in Chicago, and yet I'd never explored it. On Goethe Street, Ruth led me down a half-flight of steps to a tearoom called Aunty's with a bright green door and a curtain of colored lights in its cracked window. Inside, lumpen candles dripped wax onto bare tables, few of them occupied; pen-and-ink cartoons papered the walls. Ruth ordered us a plate of flaky pastries and small porcelain cups of black coffee as thick as syrup, which we carried to a table in the back, near a low, empty stage.

"All right," she said, gesturing to my schoolbag. "Let's have at it."

We went through my schoolwork, class by class. She hunched

over each textbook, looking up at me to fire off questions, scribbling notes. In the end, she sat back in her seat and crossed her arms, one corner of her mouth lifting.

"You don't need my help at all," she said. I smiled down at the sludge in the bottom of my coffee cup, embarrassed by how it pleased me to hear her say it. She went on in a softer voice. "You know why he asked me to do this, don't you?"

I shook my head.

"He wants you to keep an eye on me. To influence me. To save me."

"Really?" I knew she couldn't be entirely right—she hadn't seen my fall grades, and I resolved then and there that she never would. And I'd heard the skepticism in her voice, the mocking note. But I couldn't help but feel pleased by this, too; it was a good sign for my future prospects if Uncle Eugene already thought I might be a good influence on his own daughter.

"Oh yes. He thinks I'm a reprobate. He used to rant about all of you—your life upon the stage. Your mother was Auntie Cautionary Tale. Everything a woman shouldn't be: immodest, ambitious, faithless. I think he blames her somehow, for my having turned out the way I am." She said this frankly, without bitterness. She took a bite of pastry and brushed crumbs from the front of her blouse before continuing. "My mother admired your mother, you know."

"She did?"

She nodded. "She never said so, not in so many words, but she would tell me stories, and I could tell. I think she thought your mother was brave."

We filled the next hour with talk of school and of home, of books we'd liked as girls and ones we'd read of late. All at once I felt a dart of shame.

"Ruth, when we came to Toledo. Your hair. The gum. I'm sorry. We were horrid."

She looked down at the table for a moment. When she looked back up she was smiling.

"You were," she said, matter-of-factly. "But I wasn't so pleasant myself, in the end. It was all so long ago." She was quiet for a moment, and then went on with a sly smile. "Did you see that bit in *Hollywood Spy*? About Velma Clifford."

I had: The leading lady of *Fallen Angel* was allegedly telling whoever would listen that Warner Brothers had managed things badly by releasing *Sister's Keeper* first, setting Josie up for more than her share of attention. We laughed: my sister, Ruth's cousin, the subject of Hollywood gossip.

It was pitch-dark when we left Aunty's. I knew Mama would be expecting me home, but we wandered for a little while longer, stopping in at a couple of galleries and browsing at book stalls, where Ruth pressed books into my hands, and I pretended I'd heard of their authors. We agreed that next time, we'd meet at Aunty's instead of the Institute. We'd tell Uncle Eugene we were studying at the library.

IN THE WEEKS THAT FOLLOWED, it was as if we'd always been friends, always in the habit of each other's company. We stopped in at Towertown tearooms and secondhand stores and galleries. We spent Saturdays at museums and movies and took rambling walks over the North Side. We'd dropped the pretense of tutoring, but I had no doubt Ruth was advancing my education. She complained that the Dil Pickle Club was overrun with slummers, but she took me there anyway, for a lecture on sexual reform presented by a homosexual German doctor, and another on prison riots. She borrowed a friend's car and drove me to see a talk on Shakespeare's heroines at the Evanston Women's Club. Together, we pored over the "Where to Go" section of *Golden Book Magazine*, ranking the places we'd most like to visit. We were having coffee at Aunty's one afternoon when she told me about a reading Edna St. Vincent Millay had given at the university her freshman year.

"She was magnificent," Ruth said. "Like a celestial being ported to earth." She flushed slightly and rubbed some lipstick from the rim of her coffee cup. "I've been trying to write poetry ever since. Sonnets, because she writes sonnets."

"Me too," I said in a rush. "Not sonnets. But I've written some poems too."

She told me about a café near the university where a group of famous poets held meetings, rattling off their names like an evocation—Gladys Campbell, Elder Johnson, Jun Fujita—and I nodded along as if I had any idea who she was talking about. A few days later, I took the L down after school and met her there. We took turns reading our poems out loud in slightly raised voices, as if the poets might hear us and recognize our talent and invite us into their group. No one paid us any attention, except a waitress who smirked from behind the counter, but Ruth analyzed my poems as if she'd been assigned them in one of her university classes.

"Who is he?" she asked, looking up from a page.

"Who?"

"The boy. Have you had your heart broken, Harriet?" she asked, serious and thoughtful, her dark eyes pressing with the weight I remembered from Toledo. I shrugged, and she didn't ask again. Before we parted ways she gave me a folder full of her old syllabi. I brought it to the library that weekend along with a list I'd jotted down in my notebook of references she'd made that I'd wanted to look up: the Haymarket Affair, Dada, primitive art, Dora Russell, Havelock Ellis.

For Uncle Eugene, I invented a report Ruth had helped me revise and flashcards she'd made to test me on French verb conjugations, startled by how fluently I was able to lie. I pretended not to notice his desire to hear more about her life, knowing he wouldn't disturb the delicate pretexts of our arrangement by asking directly. Mama did ask, though she was mostly concerned about my behavior—she wanted to make sure I hadn't been indiscreet, that I wasn't giving Ruth anything unsavory to report back to her father. When I shared with Mama only the most wholesome bits of what I knew of Ruth's life, the ones even Uncle Eugene couldn't have objected to, I told myself I was protecting Ruth, though I knew that wasn't quite right—Ruth was exactly herself always, whoever she was with, and as long as my relationship with her served my interests with Uncle Eugene, I couldn't imagine Mama balking at any fact about who she had become or how she lived. Eventually, I realized: it was Uncle Eugene I was protecting. It was his reputation—his authority—that would be damaged if Mama learned how he'd failed to form his own daughter into the sort of girl he thought she should be.

ONE EVENING EARLY THAT MARCH, Ruth and I emerged from a gallery on Wabash to discover snow falling thick and fast, with several inches already accumulated on the sidewalk. Traffic was stopped behind a spin-out at the corner. We trudged to the L platform, where Ruth looked with dismay at the massing crowd: workers hurrying to make it home before the trains stopped running, or trying to reach the Loop, where they would be hiring men to shovel the streets.

"Why don't you come to our place?" I said, forcing the words through a sudden wave of shyness, though we'd been practically inseparable for a month. "You can stay the night."

We were stamping the snow off our boots by the front door when Mama came around the corner. At the sight of Ruth, she froze. The transformation happened too quickly for Ruth to notice, but I saw: the straightening of the shoulders, the smoothing out of a cross expression. Her greeting was high-pitched and energetic. She ushered us out of our coats and into the living room, where she plied us with hot cocoa and made bright, nervous conversation from the kitchen until she called us in for dinner. As we ate, Ruth stared at Mama intently, but every time Mama asked her a question Ruth had to ask her to repeat it. In my bedroom, later, after we turned off the light, I could sense Ruth in the cot beside my bed, not asleep though she wanted me to think she was.

We woke the next morning to frost-spangled windows and branches bowed under inches of snow. There was no hope of getting to work or school. Mama burned eggs and hovered until Ruth and I managed to escape into the blank, glittering world, where Ruth seemed, at last, to relax. We trudged through knee-deep drifts until

we found an open cafeteria, where we sat in a booth, eating sandwiches and drinking coffee and reading the paper.

From behind her section, Ruth whistled low.

"What?" I asked.

She lowered the page and glanced over it at me. And then she
spread it out on the table. Across from the movie listings, there was
a full-page advertisement for yet another new Josephine Wilder
picture: *The Defense Rests*. Josie was pictured in a wide-brimmed hat
that cast half her face in deep shadow. The movie was to open on
April 6. Our eighteenth birthday.

"'One of Hollywood's finest young talents, in the most anticipated dramatic picture of the year,'" Ruth read. She looked up, prepared to laugh, but then her expression softened. I ripped the crusts
of my sandwich, embarrassed to think she had seen my flash of envy.

"Pie?" she said, brightly, and waved the waiter over without waiting for me to answer. She ordered us each a piece, à la mode, then
leaned toward me, hands folded.

"Did I ever tell you about Cecil?" she asked. "That was who you
saw me with. At the opera. My date. Cecil Gunn."

He had been her professor, she told me. He'd had a wife, in Bos-
ton or somewhere like that, but she'd thought for a long time that he
was telling the truth when he told her his marriage was over. He'd
even obtained for her a birth control device from the Netherlands,
she said, watching for my reaction.

I knew she'd told me about Cecil to right the scales. Shared
something private because she'd stumbled upon a private feeling of
mine.

The waiter delivered the pie. Ruth arranged a neat bite on her
spoon, pie, sauce, and ice cream.

"I stopped believing him, eventually, about the divorce," she said.
"But he'd promised to help me get a scholarship, and that I believed
for a very long time. Foolish me."

I let a bite of ice cream melt in my mouth.

"You know the boy in those poems I wrote?" I finally said. Ruth
nodded.

I told her everything there was to tell about Garth. She didn't flinch. Then I told her about the solo act, filling in the whole truth around the scaffolding we'd presented to Uncle Eugene, which he'd presented to Ruth when he'd written her, asking if she might help with my studies, never expecting her to agree.

"You've really done a number on my dad, haven't you?" she said, smiling.

I started to object, but she shook her head.

"No," she said. "Don't be sorry. He deserves it."

"He's been kind to us." I was embarrassed by my instinct to defend him.

"He wasn't so bad, when I was little," she said, after a moment, in a measured tone. "I think he liked being a father, when I was just a moldable lump. When he expected to succeed at the molding. But then when Mother died, I hated God. If He was real, He was a monster. And my hatred burned my belief away. I know exactly the moment it went: on Easter Sunday when I was fifteen. I was sitting in church, and all at once, it was like this structure that had always existed in my heart turned to ash. For a moment it was terrifying. But then I laughed. Right in the middle of my father's Easter sermon, I laughed out loud. He was furious, afterward. He thought I was being deliberately provocative. And then it was as if his seeing me that way, falsely, made me become it. For the first time in my life, I was defiant. I told him I wasn't sorry. That he could make me go to church, but he couldn't make me pray. He couldn't make me believe."

When she was sixteen, in the fall of her senior year of high school, the rupture between the two of them had deepened. She'd had her heart set on Smith College. She had even arranged, with a teacher's help, to take the entrance exam, but Uncle Eugene had told her she could attend the ladies' training program at the Institute or stay at home for a year and, if she behaved herself, apply to Hamilton Bible College for Women downstate.

The battle consumed them for months. He took her out of town on a lecture tour to prevent her from taking her exam. In retalia-

tion, she refused to eat or speak for four days. When she fainted at
a reception of the faculty of the Pittsburgh Theological Seminary,
he partially relented: She could apply to any school she liked as long
as she continued to live at home. She applied to every college in
commuting distance, was admitted to all of them, and chose the one
farthest from her father's house. Then she picked another fight,
and, grudgingly, he made another compromise, allowing her to
board with a widow of his acquaintance, who she was convinced
spied on his behalf. Then last spring, despite Cecil Gunn's failure to
help, she'd won her scholarship; she'd used the tuition money Uncle
Eugene had given her to move out of the widow's house and into her
own apartment. He had been furious when he'd found out, but he
hadn't stopped sending her a monthly allowance.

"I don't know why he doesn't just give up on me," she said.
"Sometimes I convince myself it's fatherly love, simple as that.
Other times I'm certain it's all a game he's determined to win. That
he wants to reestablish control. But my conscience is clear. He
knows how I live. I graduate this spring, and I'm getting a job. And
when I have enough saved up I'm moving to New York, and he
won't have anything over me."

She leaned toward me, a pucker between her black brows.

"Have you ever thought about it, Harriet? New York?"

"Thought what about it?"

"Going there?"

I dipped the corner of my handkerchief in my water glass and
rubbed it over a sticky spot on the table.

"I was born there," I said, lightly.

"But being there. Living there."

"It might be fun, sometime," I said, concentrating on the spot.
"If my husband wanted to."

I folded my handkerchief and looked up at her. She was studying
me, sympathetic and curious. After a moment, she changed the subject to a date she'd been on the week before, which she'd already told
me about, and soon we were laughing, well clear of the strange and
dangerous territory into which we'd accidentally veered.

RUTH STAYED IN OUR apartment that night and the next, sleeping on the cot, dressing from my closet. As Mama flitted around, making her anxious display of some other woman's version of motherhood, Ruth grew less shy. Mama's performance irritated me, but Ruth seemed amused. By Sunday morning, the trains were up and running. Ruth walked with Mama and me as far as the L, where Mama asked if she wouldn't come with us to the Institute.

"Sorry, Aunt Maude," she said, shrugging. "I'm not a churchgoer."

As Mama watched her climb the stairs, I saw that the full reality of the situation had dawned on her at last: all along, Ruth had been the Foolish Daughter. As we walked on she was silent, and I knew she was trying to decide how to use that information to our advantage.

IN THE WEEKS THAT FOLLOWED, Josie was once again inescapable: There she was on posters, on signs, on a billboard that loomed high above the intersection of Clark and Diversey. She was named one of the WAMPAS Baby Stars of 1931. A snap ran in *Photoplay*: Josie on a celebratory ski trip with her fellow WAMPAS Babies Barbara Weeks and Marian Marsh and even Velma Clifford, the shared honor having apparently smoothed whatever feathers *Fallen Angel* had ruffled. They all wore Nordic sweaters and grasped cups of hot chocolate adorably, beneath perfectly lipsticked smiles, everyone in mittens that the caption claimed Josie had knitted herself. I rolled my eyes. But I pasted the picture in the scrapbook. I wondered if Josie had really learned how to ski.

One morning, I sat at the kitchen table, reading yet another article about my sister, while Mama did breakfast dishes. Offhandedly, the reporter mentioned a car accident Josie had been in on the last day of filming. She had escaped unscathed, though an unnamed companion had broken both his legs. A "mechanical error" was blamed. The reporting was oddly chipper, as if this were simply more grist for the movie promotion mill: "Miss Wilder called the smashup 'the most terrifying experience' of her life, but added: 'My Aunt Alice always told me, Josephine, when the horse bucks you, you get back on the horse.' Lucky thing Miss Wilder's new contract with Warner Bros. makes her the highest-paid woman in Hollywood: the horse—in this case her beloved fire engine red Duesenberg Model J—has already been replaced with a new model in royal blue."

"Do you want to then?"

"Hmm?" I asked, looking up. Mama turned from the sink.

"Go see it. On your birthday. After Vera's." She waited for my answer with her jaw clenched, leaning wearily against the counter, as if her desire to see Josie's picture were somehow a wrong I had done her.

"Oh. Sure."

Without responding, she turned to rinse her coffee cup. Before she could turn back, I stuffed the newspaper into my satchel and hurried to leave for school.

ON SATURDAY NIGHT, MAMA and I went to Vera's, where we celebrated my birthday with sardines on toast and coconut cake, and then we set out for the early show. At Mama's suggestion we went to the Chicago, same as on the opening night of *Sister's Keeper,* and for the first time in months I felt a spasm of grief for my father. I wondered if Mama still missed him, if she'd brought us to the Chicago in his honor as much as Josie's. She'd been quiet all evening, and as soon as she finished buying the tickets her silence became absolute. She refused Vera's offer of candy with a quick toss of her head. In the auditorium, she trained her eyes on the screen, leaving Vera and me to talk over her lap.

Josie played a waitress falsely accused of murdering her husband. Her acting was even better than in her first two pictures, every layer of the character brought to brilliant life: the heat and tenderness of her love for her husband, the tough exterior that made her a plausible suspect, the slow unfolding of her trust in the defense attorney assigned to her case, the deepening of that trust into love. They had her in a long dark wig, and until the very end of the picture, her costumes were simple, even dowdy, but that somehow only made her face brighter and fresher, her beauty irrepressible.

It was raining when we emerged from the theater. Mama stood under the marquee, leaning against the brick wall of the theater, clutching her bag to her chest, while Vera hailed a cab. On the ride home, she rested her head against the window and stared out at the bright, blurred lights of the city. Vera came up to the apartment with us, hovering at Mama's back as if she'd just had a surgery. I stayed long enough to find an umbrella, and then told them I was meeting Ruth, braced for some objection. But Mama looked at me vaguely, as if I'd just woken her from a nap.

"Fine," she said. "Of course." She turned and drifted into her bedroom. Vera went to put on the tea kettle.

I met Ruth at Le Petit, where we sat by the fireplace. She gave me a birthday gift—Edna St. Vincent Millay's new collection of sonnets—and spiked our coffee with brandy from a flask. Afterward, we went out to walk. The rain had stopped. The scent of cedar and tar rose up off the wet street, along with the softer perfume of little green things trying to grow in the cracks in the sidewalk and dirt strips between buildings. We walked up Rush, where street by street we passed back and forth from the Gold Coast to bohemia, in one block chauffeured cars idling at the curb and society people pouring out of hotel dining rooms, and in the next, dark second-hand furniture stores, or long-haired, corduroy-clad boys smoking their way through intermission outside little theaters. We cut through Bughouse Square, where the speakers had mounted their crates and were already making a lively din.

"You didn't say. How was the picture?" Ruth asked.

I thought a moment.

"She wears a wig. It's a very bad wig."

"But she's not bad?"

"She's all right," I said, tucking my scarf more tightly into my jacket. "It's a silly story. A melodrama. Her bread and butter, you know."

"I don't know, actually. I've never been to one of her pictures."

"You haven't?" I asked, warming with a pleasure that made me ashamed. "My my, whatever happened to family loyalty."

"In fairness to myself, I met the girl one time and she wasn't exactly a kindred spirit."

I laughed, but at the same time I was struck by an earnest longing: I wanted them to know each other. For Ruth to know Josie, the real Josie, the one I had loved, and for Josie to know Ruth as I'd come to know her, and if that was impossible, then I wanted Ruth's take on Josephine Wilder, the same as any other cultural phenomenon or event in my life. We weren't a ten-minute walk from the Division Street theater, and all at once I wanted Ruth to know her, too: the girl I was when I climbed the fire escape.

"Come," I said. "This way."

When she saw the marquee that bore Josie's name she clapped her hands. I dragged her past the ticket booth, her confusion delighting me, and made a great show of turning down Dearborn, of insisting when she hesitated at the alley's dark edge. At the bottom of the fire escape I jumped a few times, head still a bit clouded from the brandy we'd drunk at Le Petit. Then I remembered.

"You have to make me a stirrup," I said.

"A stirrup?"

"Like this!" I showed her with my hands. "A boost. I've done this a thousand times, you know." She tried, but kept collapsing beneath my weight, which made us both laugh.

When a man turned in to the alley, she screamed and ran.

"Ruth!" I hiked up my skirt and ran after her. When we came out of the alley I stumbled into her, laughing, and let my forehead fall against her arm.

"Look, he's just standing there, smoking a pipe. He thinks we're lunatics," I said.

"Or maybe he's the lunatic, waiting for us to return so he can slit our throats," she said. "Why don't I just buy you a real ticket? A birthday present."

We went back around to Division. Ruth bought the tickets, but then I led her through the lobby as if I were giving her the grand tour of the family estate. The picture was already about a quarter of the way through. We sat in the first open seats, closer than I usually liked, but it seemed right, somehow, that Josie should loom right over us. Ruth kept whispering in my ear: What a silly line of dialogue, could the leading man be more wooden, the second female lead sure had a voice ill-suited to sound. When someone shushed us it only made me feel closer to Ruth, nestled more deeply inside the particular facts of our friendship. Our secret connection to the girl on the screen.

But she didn't say anything about Josie herself until afterward, when we were walking toward the L. Saturday night was, by then, hurtling rapidly toward Sunday morning, and that meant the Institute and Uncle Eugene. It was colder now, the streets quieter. Instead of lingering, people hurried indoors or into cabs.

"She was good, Harriet," she said, gently. "Really good."

"I know," I said. And it was both I'm sorry and congratulations, thank you and god damn it.

I waited with her until her train came, and then I started toward home. Despite the late hour, I felt alert, agitated even. It was still our eighteenth birthday, for a few more minutes. Josie's and mine. As I walked back past the theater, my legs seemed to carry me of their own volition, to know where it was I had to go. It was even darker in the alley than it had been before, and I ought to have been frightened. I'd never come so late at night, I'd never turned in to the alley off such an empty street. But fear was light in me, a sweet, bubbly thrill. This time, I remembered the broken rake: right where I'd left it months before, behind the trash can. The ladder clattered down. I slipped off my heels and climbed. The window was a little stiff, but I leaned in with my shoulder and up it went. The storeroom was dark. I made my way carefully across the floor, managing not to bump anything, and listened at the door. Safe. I tiptoed through the hallway and down the stairs. I could hear the strains of the score over the credits: the late show had just begun.

I slipped into the auditorium. As I made my way toward the back, I was conscious that the soft light illuminating the way up the aisle was my sister's light, the glow from an image of her face and body as her character unsuspectingly said goodbye to her husband for the final time. I hunched low in a seat near the back. Third time through, I could anticipate the small shifts in her expression, the subtle modulations of her voice, the turn of the coffee cup, the rough swipe of a hairbrush. As she finally persuaded her defense attorney of her innocence, the camera cut close to her face and then his, back and forth, and I felt each beat just a moment before it registered on the screen: her desperation, his recognition, her relief, the first hint of love.

In the next scene, there was a shot of Josie leaning on her forearms over a sink full of dishes, face glistening and irritated as she listened to her nosy neighbor try to persuade her to take a guilty plea. As I watched, something shifted: some quality of the light, of the texture of the image. It seemed as if my vision were stretching back as well as forward, as if the picture were somehow expanding to contain new volumes of information, though nothing about the actual shot was any different than it had been the two other times I'd seen it that evening. The camera cut close to Josie's face and I understood: I was seeing her. Josie. Not her character, not her acting, just Josie, as if I could look around the edge of the film and glimpse my sister as she'd been that day on the set, in her life. A girl of nearly eighteen pretending to be a woman of twenty. Frail and agitated. And lonely. Oh, it struck in my chest like a bell, the clear, sharp fact of her loneliness. And it had something to do with the car accident I had read about in the paper, with the strange way it had been reported. The story hadn't been complete. I knew as surely as if the old cradle telegraph had whirred back to life.

I wanted to reach through the screen. To take her hand, to pull her home, to safety. And then it was as if we still had the power to trade feelings and she'd passed me her unhappiness. It filled me: a heaviness in my bones, in my skin, down to the ends of my hair and the bottoms of my feet.

The camera cut to the neighbor playing solitaire at the kitchen table, but the heaviness remained and I knew then it wasn't simply Josie's unhappiness. It was also my own.

I scowled into my lap. How could I think I was unhappy? Uncle Eugene had saved us. I was satisfying my responsibilities at home, at school, and at the Institute. And at the same time, I had Ruth. A life in parallel tracks, everything I could want or need. All tidy, all under my control.

The next time I looked at the screen, Josie's character was appearing in court, her eyes wide with fear, her lip trembling. When I tried to peer around her, I detected nothing but the cold fiber of the screen. The portal, whatever it was, had closed. And then I realized I was calm again, relieved of the weight I'd felt. Maybe I'd been mistaken. Maybe the unhappiness had been Josie's all along.

I watched a little while longer. With each shot, the figure on the screen seemed less and less like my sister, and more like an actress, a star who bore a passing resemblance to someone I used to know. I wished her a happy birthday anyway. And then I stood, ready at last to go home.

I GRADUATED FROM WALLER IN JUNE WITH A DECENT ENOUGH grade point average that Mama and Uncle Eugene declared Ruth's tutoring a success, though I knew I'd have done better if I'd spent more time studying and less running around with my cousin. Uncle Eugene gave me a job in the Institute's Correspondence Office, where I typed answers to the letters Mama sorted up the hall. He often asked after Ruth. She had graduated herself, a few weeks earlier, moved into a Towertown studio fitted into an old stable, and started work as an assistant in the research department of "WCFL, the voice of labor." I answered his questions cautiously, letting him believe the extent of our acquaintance was the occasional coffee or lunch; once he asked whether I thought she might make it to church some Sunday, and there was a fragility in his expression that made me answer, gently, that I hoped she might.

He didn't know that I knew he still sent her a monthly allowance; he didn't know that I'd already spent many evenings in her studio, where she tracked her savings on a piece of paper tacked to a wall beside her bed, with "New York" and a figure written at the bottom of the page. Mama asked me about Ruth too, warily, and I knew she was less confident than Uncle Eugene of which cousin was influencing the other. But she saw that Uncle Eugene liked our being friends, and didn't interfere.

We were at Ruth's place one evening that June, frying potatoes, when the window slid open and a man tumbled through.

I screamed, brandishing the spatula. Ruth laughed.

"Stand down," she said. "That's just Morris Dack!"

He parted a curtain of red hair to reveal reddish-brown eyes with lashes so light they almost disappeared into his ivory skin.

"Sorry for having frightened you, madam," he said. He draped his long, slim body along the edge of the picnic blanket we'd spread over the floor and plucked a wedge of potato off a sheet of brown paper.

Morris had been a classmate of Ruth's, it turned out; he and two friends were living for the summer in a studio around the corner, which was mostly full of an old printing press, which was the reason for his call. He wanted to print a little magazine, the collected works of the village crowd: poems, essays, and the like. Morris had come to ask for Ruth's help editing and putting the thing together. She assented at once and volunteered me to help.

"Harriet is a poet," she said, and I looked down at the picnic blanket, embarrassed. But Morris seemed to find this entirely plausible.

When we'd eaten all of the potatoes, we went up to the roof. The heat was soft that night; the roof smelled of the laundry someone had hung out to dry. We stole a sheet from the clothesline and lay down on it, three in a row. Morris was moving to New York City at the end of the summer to teach at a college, and Ruth peppered him with questions: where he would live, how the subway worked, whether it was true you could see shows for free if you worked as an usher. The two of them began to make plans for when Ruth lived there too. Museums they would visit, famous people they would befriend, parties they would throw.

"What we should do is get apartments in the same building," Ruth said.

Morris laughed.

"We can fit a pully between the fire escapes," he said. "Send messages up and down."

Feeling a pang of loneliness, I let my ears close to a conversation I wasn't really part of. At the gauzy boundary between the city's glow and the dark part of the sky, I saw, burning dimly, the constellation Garth had renamed for Josie and me in his bedroom nearly two years earlier. She had another picture out already, a romantic comedy called *Lady at the Helm,* which I'd seen with Ruth. During one scene, I had been certain I was once again seeing around the film to something true: a real-life romance between my sister and Dougie Taft, her costar. But the portal had only stayed open for an instant, and then it was just another amusing movie, one I was content to see a single time. I knew Mama had gone as well—I'd found her ticket stub in the china plate on her bureau where she put her rings at night. Every now and then, when I went to paste a review or an article or a photo in the scrapbook, I would find a copy there already, the page still tacky with glue.

Morris bolted from the sheet. Ruth followed, laughing. From the clothesline, he pulled down a man's denim work shirt and a pair of overalls, which he tossed to Ruth. She put them on, giddy, as he shimmied into a woman's slip, and the two of them hid behind the remaining laundry on the line. A moment later, they pushed the laundry open like a curtain and stepped through it, arms linked.

"How glad the many millions, of Anabelles and Lillians, would be to capture me," Ruth sang, taking the man's part of "I've Got a Crush on You." Morris chimed in with the woman's part. They improvised a dance as they sang. I leaned back on my elbows. My loneliness melted away. What an easy pleasure it could be, singing and dancing. Here we were, my friends and me. At the edge of our future lives, but for now, together, on the same roof, warmed by the same food and drink. When they finished the song I scrambled to my feet and cheered. Ruth took my right hand, and Morris my left, and, together, the three of us spun beneath the same stars.

WE SPENT THE SUMMER collecting magazine contributions from the village: poets jockeying for an invitation to a Harriet Monroe party (a name I pretended to know for weeks before I learned she was the editor of *Poetry* magazine); students who bunked at the Three Arts. A colleague of Ruth's, who had once taken us to a forum on labor issues and then afterward for borscht at the Russian Workers' Co-op, gave us a series of interviews with Chicago schoolteachers who had gone months without pay. Eunice Tietjens gave Morris a poem and her blessing. On an August evening, light still at eight o'clock, Ruth and I arrived at Morris's studio, proofed pages under our arms. The next night, there would be a party at Aunty's. Ruth would read one of her Millay-inspired sonnets; Morris would read a short story and give a speech. I refused to get on a stage, but I thrilled to know that one of my own poems would appear in the magazine, under the name Harriet Shore.

Morris greeted us in his undershirt, pink all over. Outside it was ninety degrees; the studio was a sauna, even with the windows wide open, even with Morris's friend Ben running an electric fan over a huge block of ice. The humid air kept gumming up the works of the press, which was an antique abandoned by a previous tenant that no one was entirely sure how to operate. Soon Ruth and I were down to our slips, ink smudged all over our arms. My mouth stung from cheap wine. I was breathless from laughing. Friends of Morris kept stopping by to check on our progress. One brought a cherry pie from P&E. Another brought a whole chicken dinner from the Blackthorn Tavern, courtesy of a contributor who'd written a comic sketch about the waitressing life. We had printed a hundred copies when Ben noticed an error on the first page. Ruth and I chased him around the studio, threatening to stab him with a fork if he dared notice another. She and I left at two in the morning, sweat-drenched with aching shoulders, the finished copies packed into crates, save a short stack Morris was using for a pillow.

In the morning, I dressed for work in a sensible skirt and blouse, and carried in a shopping bag the dress I planned to change into for the party. Every time my toe bumped the bag beneath my desk, it pleased me to know I had smuggled this evidence of my other identity into the Institute. When the clock struck five, I shepherded a few stray paper clips into their bowl and hurried upstairs, eager to get through my Friday chat so I could make it to Aunty's on time. In the kitchenette, I laid out the cookies, I aligned the spoons, I timed the tea.

But when I got to Uncle Eugene's office, he was holding his briefcase, ready to leave.

"You turn right around and put those things away," he said, smiling playfully, as if he were in possession of a delightful secret.

"Is something wrong?"

"Not at all," he said. "A change of plan. A little surprise."

"Oh!" I said, brightly, disciplining my gaze away from the clock but unable to keep from wondering how long this surprise would take.

"Don't worry. Your mother approves."

I smiled, as if Mama's permission were exactly what I'd been worrying about, and went to dispose of the tea I'd just made, the tea he had surely anticipated my making and might have stopped me from making by waiting for me in the kitchenette instead of his office, or simply by leaving a note. At the sight of his car out front, I blanched, but what choice did I have but to get in? After whatever was about to happen had happened, I would hurry to Aunty's. It was only just past five.

But as the driver turned onto Sheridan, I knew that what was happening was that we were going all the way out to Uncle Eugene's house in Evanston. I pictured Ruth and Morris waiting, wondering when I'd turn up and what was keeping me, then finally realizing I wasn't going to come at all. My contraband costume change, in a bag on the floor between my feet, felt surplus and embarrassing.

Uncle Eugene's housekeeper, Hilda, led us into the parlor, where Mama was wearing a high-necked black dinner dress with a full skirt—her widow's weeds, she called the dark clothes she'd been wearing since Uncle Eugene's rescue, which she'd once told me were a way of making an indecent situation look more like a decent one. He left to change, and Mama told me my own best dress was waiting in the guest room.

"And comb your hair, Harriet," she said.

Hilda showed me the way upstairs. I put on my dress, a midnight blue satin crepe, and freshened up, leaving my useless Towertown party clothes in the guest room along with the skirt and blouse I'd worn to work. Back in the parlor, I sat down beside Mama but couldn't meet her eye.

"You were pleasant on the way over?" she said.

"Of course," I said. But I was thinking of Ruth and Morris, guilt thumping in my stomach.

"Well, you're scowling now, Harriet. Your uncle thought we should give you some warning, but you know how you always get. We didn't need nerves to contend with on top of everything else."

"And what is everything else, exactly?"

But Uncle Eugene returned to the parlor before she could answer, and not long after that the doorbell rang. Mama patted my knee. Her wide, stiff smile transported me into the hallway before any of a hundred auditions—Mama cleaning my cheek with a spit-damp thumb, reminding me that everyone was counting on me to be brave.

Hilda came in, trailed by a young man. Uncle Eugene shook his hand, gripping his shoulder warmly.

"Welcome, son, welcome," said Uncle Eugene. "Mrs. Szász, Miss Szász, may I introduce Mike Jennings?"

He took my fingers limply in a bony hand, looking just above my eyes instead of into them. I wasn't sure if I said my hellos audibly, if I was exerting any control over my face. A man. They were presenting me with a man.

We all sat.

"And how is the senior Mike Jennings?" Uncle Eugene asked.

The younger Mike Jennings offered an earnest report that touched on his father's health (an allergic cough a few weeks back but that was much improved), the market (buy now, sir, that's my father's motto; you know it's a matter of patriotism with him), and his father's struggle to find honest laborers to finish the renovations on his house in New Buffalo (frankly a surprising problem, sir, in the current climate, but some people just don't want to work). Mama plucked invisible lint from her knees and gazed intently at young Mike Jennings, as if to convey to him, should he happen to look in her direction, that he was exquisitely interesting. But he didn't look at her, or at me, and when Uncle Eugene extended the bounds of the conversation to include the two of us, Mr. Jennings's voice rose in pitch, and red splotches crawled up his neck, which was already speckled with razor burn.

Hilda brought in lemonade and glasses on a tray, and Uncle Eugene gestured for me to pour. The pitcher was slippery with condensation and heavy for its size, while the glasses were comically small, like doll cups. I splashed plenty on the tray.

I handed Mr. Jennings his glass. His face was slim and waxen, his eyes wettish, a dull brown. He smiled as he thanked me, revealing a finger's width of damp gum. Not quite on purpose, I imagined kissing him—those long fingers grasping at me, my lips close to those gleaming gums. Blushing, I turned back to the lemonade tray.

The lemonade was unpleasantly sweet, but I quickly emptied my doll's cup, and then I had to squeeze my fingers into a fist to keep myself from taking too many salted peanuts from the silver dish that Uncle Eugene was explaining his grandmother had brought over from Scotland. He and Mama made some stilted conversation about weather and traffic, and then, as if according to a script they'd worked out together, Mama asked Uncle Eugene if I'd told him about my latest lamb cake.

"Why, no, Mrs. Szász," he said, beaming.

Mama clasped her hands.

"Oh, just this week Harriet made a darling angel chiffon cake in the shape of a lamb for one of the little neighbor girls. She frosted it so beautifully, it was almost too pretty to eat."

My blush deepened. The story was a lie; it repurposed a cake I'd helped Minnie make for Easter back in the boardinghouse days, which I'd broken trying to force it from the mold, and then frosted while it was still hot, so that when I brought it out to the table one of the boarders had laughed and said hadn't we better shoot the poor thing and put it out of its misery. I listened, astounded, as Mama explained that all the neighborhood children asked for my cakes, and I just couldn't bear to disappoint any of them. I was an angel, really, Uncle Eugene said, to keep up with all the orders. Mama reached over to squeeze my forearm.

Hilda called us into the dining room. Uncle Eugene took the head of the table and Mama the foot. I sat between them, across from Mike Jennings. The grandfather clock in the corner showed a few minutes after seven. The reading had begun; Ruth and Morris knew for certain that I'd let them down. Hilda brought out fruit cocktail topped with marshmallows and Uncle Eugene said grace. As we ate, he prompted Mike Jennings to share with Mama and me that he would graduate from Michigan State in May with a pharmacy degree. Over chilled celery and grapes, Uncle Eugene explained that Mr. Jennings's father owned the JenMart chain of pharmacies.

"How interesting!" I said, and at my first contribution in many minutes, Uncle Eugene nodded approvingly, as if my silence had been evidence of girlish diffidence and not uncharming, though it was also a fine thing that I had managed to overcome it.

We worked through a salmon loaf and a platter of French-fried potatoes, and then returned to the parlor for chocolate cake and coffee, which I managed to pour with a steadier hand than I had the lemonade. It was quarter to nine when Uncle Eugene finally put Mama and me in his car and said goodbye.

Mama made light conversation on the way home—she didn't trust Uncle Eugene's driver. But I felt the intensity of her expectation, her readiness for the discussion that would come when we were alone. I answered in grunts, wondering whether anyone was still at Aunty's, willing the traffic to thin. Outside our building, I made a show of digging in my purse rather than going in right away. Mama waved the driver off. I waited until he turned the corner to speak.

"There's somewhere I need to be." I was taller than Mama now, but the way she fixed her expression made me feel as if she were looking down.

"You'll have to drop that Ruth business eventually. You know that, right?" She said this as if it were obvious—as if of course I should already have known—but at the same time she seemed to take a cruel satisfaction in saying it out loud.

"How could spending time with his daughter possibly be—"

"I'm not a fool, Harriet. You know as well as I do that if he knew the half of what the two of you got up to—"

"He doesn't, though, does he? And he won't. She understands, she'll never tell, and he likes the idea of our being friends, he thinks I'm a good—"

"Yes, yes. He's full of praise for you. The other day he called you 'conscientious and even-tempered.'" She tipped her head to one side with a wry smile, as if to invite me to laugh along with her at his bad misunderstanding. I stared at her blankly. Her expression cooled. "He's offering you real advantages, now. Access to his world. Better than we could have ever hoped."

"I know that, Mama."

"I won't have you throwing it all away. Do you understand?"

"I understand," I said, but I made no move to go in. At last, she turned, greeting the doorman with all the warmth that had been absent from her final words to me.

I ran to Aunty's. The girl who worked behind the counter was locking the door; she told me the crowd had moved on to Seven Arts. At Seven Arts a girl I half knew said I'd just missed them, but she thought Morris and some others had gone to the Green Mask Inn. I stumbled in, damp and out of breath, and there, at last, I found him, sitting in a booth in the back, close to a thin boy with longish black hair, whose cheeks and lips were rouged. They made room for me to slide in.

"Oh, I know you," said the black-haired boy, Arnold, when Morris introduced me. "You're the Sunday school girl." Even as I laughed I was struck by a tumbling grief. It was a feeling continuous, somehow, with my irritation at Mama and the discomfort I'd felt when Ruth had asked if I'd ever considered moving to New York. And it was the same feeling as my regret at having missed the reading, which was the same as the humiliation of having carried a Tow-ertown dress to the Institute and lugged it to Uncle Eugene's house, then back out again, into its natural environment, but still in a bag. It all added up to a falseness at the core of things, the sense that I couldn't quite hang on to the different stories I told about myself. With Garth, I'd managed to split myself so tidily in two. Even when I'd been working on my solo act, it had been easy enough to keep my worlds, my responsibilities, separate. Now everything seemed to be in a constant state of collision.

I apologized and Morris forgave, dabbing at my tears with his handkerchief. He made Arnold forgive me too. When I asked where Ruth was, the two of them exchanged a look.

"She went home after," Morris said softly.

At her studio, I knocked and called out, but she didn't answer. I tried to go through the window as Morris had, on that lovely night in June. But I couldn't get it to budge. I went back inside and won-dered, for a frantic minute, if I could pick the lock on her door, but the only lock I knew how to pick was the one on what had once been Josie's diary. And what madness, that I was contemplating breaking into Ruth's apartment on the very night Uncle Eugene had finally produced for me a prospective husband, which meant I'd succeeded, I'd proven myself a Wise enough Daughter to deserve one.

I sat and slumped against the wall. Shouldn't Ruth understand? Ruth, who had come to know me so well? Who knew her father? Didn't she see that my circumstances were different from hers, my talents more limited, my family in greater need? All at once, her disdain for conventionality seemed tiresome. Smoking on street corners, speaking audaciously of sex, saying "shit," her political meetings, even, all of those fevered discussions with people she seemed so eager to impress, who made me feel embarrassed about my shabby education and lack of conviction—how little it all cost her! I glared at her door as if she were to blame for the fact that I'd missed the party, as if she were to blame for Mike Jennings and his horrible gums, and for Mama and Uncle Eugene plotting and watch-ing their plot unfold.

The lock rattled. The door opened, and there she was, still wearing the green satin dress I'd helped her choose for the occasion, but under a robe, her feet in slippers, makeup gone save the smudges beneath her eyes, which fixed on me with a hardness I remembered from Toledo: Ruth with her mangled hair standing beside her mother, who trembled with anger at culprits she knew would go unpunished.

"The top hook's stuck," she said, her voice clenched. "I can't get it off."

I scrambled to my feet.

"I'll get it," I said.

We looked at each other. Her chest rose and fell. And then the hardness in her expression dissolved. With the smallest smile, she nodded and turned. I closed my eyes, all of the horrible things I'd thought as I'd waited rinsed away by a sweet rush of relief that threatened to turn into tears. When I was sure I wouldn't cry, I followed her inside.

T HAT MONDAY AFTERNOON, I WAS AT MY DESK IN THE Correspondence Office, typing a letter, when Uncle Eugene came in. Miss Sullivan, the supervisor, stood at once to greet him. A murmur traveled among the girls as he made his way up the aisle between the rows of long, heavy desks. He stopped at mine.

"Harriet," he said. "If Miss Sullivan can spare you, I was hoping you would join me for a walk."

We set out at a leisurely pace, Uncle Eugene with his hands folded behind his back, his face turned up toward the sun, as if we were strolling beside the seaside, the air light and fresh. But the day was humid and thick with the scents of the city. I longed for the dim of the office and the little electric fan one of the girls had installed on her desk, which spat a warmish draft in my direction at the end of each rotation.

"And what do we have you working on today?"

I told him about my efforts to implement a new organizational system for the correspondence archives, and about the letter I had been drafting when he arrived. After two months in the Correspondence Office, I was trusted, now, to author my own responses, hewing closely to the templates, of course, but exercising my judgment in all the particulars: which template was required, whether the letter ought to be passed to the radio production office to possibly be read on the air, whether I ought to make a request for a donation and if so to which campaign, whether I ought to send the correspondent any literature. It pleased me to watch a thick stack of pages accumulate in the tray on my desk, ready to be folded and stamped, and even more so to be given a special assignment by Miss Sullivan.

"Very good, very good," he said. "Our girls in Correspondence do the organization a great service."

We turned the corner.

"Your mother mentioned an invitation?"

A flush crept beneath the pink, damp heat that had already begun to collect in my cheeks. On Saturday afternoon, Mike Jennings had called and asked if I could join him for lunch the next day after church. I had been stunned into silence, mortified on his behalf. The night before, Ruth had pelted me with questions about the man her father had introduced me to—the mark, she had called him. She'd taken notes with blue chalk, right on the cracking plaster wall, pros and cons, until the cons towered dramatically over the pros and we both dissolved into laughter. As I tried to find the words to refuse Mike Jennings, it seemed as if he ought to know already that what he'd suggested was impossible. Finally, I stammered out some excuse and then rushed past Mama and into my bedroom, where I locked the door to keep her from asking any questions.

A man huffed past us on a bicycle. Uncle Eugene didn't look at me, didn't press for a response. His quiet eventually became a void I needed to fill.

"I'm sorry."

"Oh dear me, no need for apology." He stopped and looked at me, brows gently furrowed, as if he were wounded at the thought he might have wounded me. I smiled back weakly. He pulled a handkerchief from his breast pocket and, with a starch-sharp corner, patted his forehead. We started walking again.

"I simply want you to know that it pleases me to think you take this matter seriously," he said. "Not every girl, thinking of marriage, understands that she is contemplating her life's great work. A wife studies her husband until she understands him better than he understands himself: his needs, his flaws, his little moods and preferences, his weaknesses and his strengths. The masculine ego can be so fragile, but a good wife knows how to protect her husband's, to bolster his confidence. She makes herself attractive and agreeable, yields where she can so her husband's home is always a refuge, and in this way she secures his affection and care."

He was gazing forward, as if at some distant and lovely vision.

"Oh, of course, a husband must also work to understand his wife. He must also compromise, think of her needs. But you see, the wife is the emotional heart of the marriage. The work of a wife is work only a woman can do. It will satisfy you, Harriet, like nothing else save the work that is its ideal complement: that of motherhood. But make no mistake. It will challenge you too. The choice ahead of you—the choice of a partner in marriage—is the most important any young person will make."

Damp and thickheaded from the heat, uncertain of how to respond, I waited for him to continue, but he seemed satisfied that he'd made his point. He asked whether Mama had had a chance to read the book he'd recommended, which he suggested I try when she was finished, and then he asked about the latest efforts of the Altar Guild.

Back at the Institute, students were reading in the shade of the courtyard, sitting on benches, or sprawled across blankets on the grass. The traffic was quiet, and I could hear the buzz of cicadas. Uncle Eugene folded his hands behind his back, something double-edged in his smile.

"It does my heart good, to see the faith you place in your mother and in me," he said, and I knew we'd returned to the subject of marriage, and the choice he'd told me was so important and mine alone to make. "I have every confidence that you will act prudently, in accordance, always, with His will."

He put a hand on my shoulder and led me inside.

AFTER THAT, EVERY FEW weeks, he introduced me to another mark: A soft-spoken boy, cheeks still rosy with pimples even as his hair receded back from his forehead, primed to take over the family business, something to do with corn. A former college football star, Northwestern '26, now in cement; he had high hopes for the fourth quarter. An accountant with long pale fingers that made me think of spiders. The dinners all followed the same script: the oversweet lemonade, until Labor Day, when we switched to ginger punch. The tiny crystal cups, the peanuts in the silver dish. Mama and Uncle Eugene exchanged anecdotes that showcased my charms, the lamb cake in frequent rotation. At some point, Uncle Eugene would prompt the mark to describe his schooling and professional achievements. I would lean forward, projecting my avid interest. Over pork chops or celery salad or hot buttered beets, I would ask questions to draw him out.

Whenever the cab dropped Mama and me off at home, I went right back out again, to Ruth's. Mama didn't object. I think she had calculated that I needed to talk things through with someone, and that I might rather it be my friend than my mother. Maybe she thought Ruth's spinsterhood offered a useful contrast to the superior life she and Uncle Eugene were trying to arrange for me. Sometimes I came home again to an empty apartment and a note from Mama saying she'd gone to Vera's, and then I felt rebuked, as if she had only gone out to remind me that she too had friends in whom she could confide, that when she was young she'd had her own taste of bohemia, that there was nothing I might try that she hadn't already done.

When a call came on a Saturday or a Sunday afternoon, and the mark invited me out—to lunch after church, or a ball game, or a Wednesday evening Bible study—Mama would hover, listening, expectant. And I wanted to say yes: I wanted to yield, if not to His will, then to Mama and Uncle Eugene's, to prove I was a good daughter, equal to my responsibility. Uncle Eugene and I had stopped meeting on Fridays, but on the occasional afternoon walk he would remind me that I needn't rush. The reminder always felt weighted in a way I couldn't quite interpret: Was he issuing a correction to some inappropriate eagerness he perceived on Mama's part? Or was it all pro forma, an insistence that the decision was mine alone when really he shared Mama's disappointment that I hadn't made progress with any of the fine prospects he had offered up?

It didn't matter. Every time I stood beside the hall table, clutching the receiver, the mark's breath filling my ear as he waited for a response, the latest postmortem, blue chalked on Ruth's wall, would slam into my memory. And it would become impossible then to do anything but demur. To hang up the phone and hurry out the door. To go for a fast walk beside the lake, as if I might outrun my own galloping sense of responsibility.

ONE NIGHT LATE THAT October, Ruth and I were at her place, each in a pair of her pajamas, lounging on cushions on the floor and playing gin rummy, having quickly dispatched the evening's mark— a professor of Greek and Latin with a sparse reddish beard who couldn't stop laughing at his own puns.

"Hello there," came a voice from the window. It was Morris Dack's friend Ben. "What are you doing? Say you'll come with me to the Coal Scuttle?"

Ruth put down her cards with a snort.

"The Coal Scuttle? Next you'll ask if I want to pay seventy-five cents for a bus tour of bohemia."

He leaned the rest of the way through the window, hooking his elbows over the sill.

"We're not staying long. We're meeting some very silly people who are taking us to a party."

"What sort of party?"

"A birthday party, I think. In Lake Forest." Ruth gave him a skeptical look. He smiled back. "Now, Ruthie, surely it's a boon for the revolution if you redistribute to yourself some of the capitalists' food and drink?"

She turned to me, ready to roll her eyes, but then her expression shifted—I followed her gaze to the wall where she'd recorded the professor's pros and cons.

"Okay," she said, slowly. "Why not?"

An hour later, Ruth was climbing after a girl named Clara and I was climbing after Ruth into a big silver car parked outside the Coal Scuttle. Clara squished up against the driver's side and a boy whose name I had already forgotten climbed in after me and slammed the door, crushing the four of us in tightly together. Ben got in front with the boy who was driving—Paul something. The men were in white tie, Clara in a peach silk gown with voluminous sleeves, but when we'd met in the club Clara had threaded her fingers with ours, squealing as she looked us up and down: Ruth had wrapped her hair in a turban and put on a long, loose black dress and a silly beaded vest she'd picked up in a secondhand shop on Goethe Street, and I'd changed back into the modest rust-colored taffeta I'd worn to her father's house hours before. Clara had told us that we were a couple of dolls, that she couldn't wait to show us off.

As soon as the car pulled away from the curb, the boy whose name I couldn't remember fell asleep. Clara starting quizzing Ruth about her life in Towertown: Did she know any dopeys, any lesbians? Was everyone frightfully artistic and sex-mad? Did they all go in for the interpretation of dreams? Soon, the city was a soft glow receding in the rearview mirror. Paul was guiding the car around the black curve of the lake, Ruth telling an elaborate lie about working as a nude model, when Clara reached over and grabbed my arm.

"You know who you look like?" she said, leaning over Ruth and pressing her face close to mine. I froze. "The girl from that dreadful movie. What was her name?"

"You know her name." The boy to my right had snapped up, irritated. "Three months ago you wanted to join her fan club."

"*Grandpa Wants a Wife,*" said Clara.

It had been Josie's first real flop. For weeks I'd been carrying the words of the unkindest reviews around with me, like stones settled at the bottom of my gut. I thought I felt the pressure of Ruth's elbow against mine, but I couldn't tell whether that was simply because we were all squeezed in so tightly together or if she'd done it on purpose, to reassure me. Would she even think to reassure me in that way, or was that just a comfort I remembered from harness days, something particular to Josie and me?

"It wasn't much of a picture, but Josephine Wilder is a fine talent," Ben said seriously, turning from the front seat. He squinted at me, tipping his head back and forth, as if trying to decide whether he agreed with Clara's assessment.

"If you say so, but that was the most dismal picture I've seen all year," Clara said. "Anyhow, from this angle there's a resemblance."

"Nonsense," said Paul, the driver, who hadn't said a word since our brief introduction at the club. In the rearview mirror, he caught my eye. "Josephine Wilder isn't half as enchanting as our Miss Szász."

Clara leaned back in her seat with a humph. Paul's face was friendly, full, his round cheeks pebbly with freckles, hair reddish-brown and thick. He wasn't handsome, not exactly, but when we'd met up at the club I'd been struck by his solidity—his breadth and mass, which made it seem as if at any moment he might pull away his tuxedo and reveal a football uniform—and now, as he held my eye in the mirror, the warmth of his expression stirred something in me. He glanced quickly at the road and then back at me, his brown eyes disappearing into slits as he grinned.

The boy to my right nudged my elbow. He was holding out a flask.

I looked back at the mirror. Paul had returned his attention to the road. I accepted the flask, took a sip, then handed it down to Ruth. She gave me a tender look, but I half shook my head, preferring to leave behind the strange, alarming moment of Clara's near-recognition and to focus instead on the present that had displaced it. The possibility of another glance in the rearview mirror from Paul.

"Did you say a dollar a day?" Clara asked Ruth, reaching for the flask. "Were you posing nude the entire time?" Ruth gave me one last lift of her eyebrows and then turned back to Clara.

"Generally, yes," she said.

I half-listened to her lies, from time to time letting my eyes flick up to the mirror. Twice more, I caught Paul looking back.

In a leafy neighborhood full of grand houses, he turned up a long driveway that ran through a flat front yard dotted with topiaries, past a reflecting pool, emptied for the season and guarded by a sculpted faun. Every window in the vast, symmetrical brick façade of the house was brightly lit. The foyer was laid in black and white marble. A staircase curved grandly toward the second story, around a sprawling chandelier. We handed our wraps off to some sort of servant—a maid? I didn't know the terminology, and I was as embarrassed by my own lack of ease as I was by Clara's surfeit of it.

Ben, Paul, and the boy with the flask went off to fetch the rest of us drinks, but Clara threaded her arms between Ruth's and mine and pulled us deeper into the party. She explained that the parents of the birthday girl, Ramona, were in Argentina. That she was being supervised by a grandmother, who was very dear and very old and very likely asleep upstairs at that moment, having been persuaded by Ramona to leave the young people to their fun and given a nice portion of brandy to make sure she continued to mind her own business.

"She's an absolute gem. Ramona, not the grandmother. I'll introduce you."

A crowd was gathered around a grand piano, singing a song I'd never heard before but which all of them seemed to know, every last word, a string quartet sitting nearby, idle, its members drinking coffee. Their voices followed us through crowded rooms with wood-paneled walls and high ceilings, mingled with chatter and laughter and the clink of glasses. Every man was in patent leather shoes, every woman in slippers that looked as if they would be ruined if they touched a city sidewalk. Grim-faced waiters circulated carrying champagne on trays. Clara dragged Ruth and me from group to group, introducing us gleefully, as if we were specimens she'd obtained on an anthropological expedition: one proper bohemian, one model of middle-class propriety. At first I tried gamely to be friendly and polite, to apply everything I had learned from Emily Post. And then I reached out to shake hands with one girl.

"My word," she murmured, her eyes widening with malice.

I flushed deeply, uncertain what my error had been. Ruth glared at the girl. After that, when Clara's friends gushed or gawked, I managed only to nod. Something had turned in Ruth, too; she answered their questions about village life succinctly and honestly, until Clara grew bored and wandered away, her promise to return, we knew, a lie.

"Are you having fun?" Ruth asked, squeezing my hand.

"Loads," I said, brightly. She let herself smile. We made our way into a vast room with a row of tall windows set into the back wall. A buffet was laid out over a long white-clothed table.

"Ben's right. Might as well enjoy what's here," said Ruth.

"You go ahead. I'm not hungry." She set off for the buffet, and I went to wait beside the window. In the dark, I could see the outline of a garden to one side, and to the other, a smooth, flat stretch of grass. At the bottom of the yard, a bonfire shot sparks into the sky, dark silhouettes clustered around it. Through a gap between trees in the thicket beyond, I could just see a silver shard of lake.

"Well, there you are." My heart clenched and released. It was Paul, at my elbow. I looked over to the table. Ruth, picking something off a platter, hadn't seen him. "I want you to know that we gentlemen did return with the promised libations. But the three of you had run off. So what was there to do but drink them ourselves?"

He was very close to me, suddenly, smiling down at me. I backed into the window; the panes were cool through my dress.

"Not a thing. You did what you had to do."

He lit himself a cigarette and offered me one. I shook my head, too nervous to smoke. He pointed with his chin over my shoulder.

"Care for a tour?"

I checked Ruth: still working her way up the buffet.

"Why not?" I said, trying to be light, gay. To match whatever idea he had in his head of a girl worth describing as more enchanting than a movie star.

Outside, I thought we'd go right, toward the yard and the fire, but instead he led me left, into the garden. The sky seemed to stretch forever; pale dustings of stars appeared behind and between the sharper, brighter stars that I could only sometimes see in the city.

"Chilly?" he asked, and before I could answer he'd taken off his jacket and draped it over my shoulders. He led me along paths laid in stone, through cold, dark beds piled with leaves and bound up in net for winter. I snapped a dried blossom off its stem and scattered the petals. When I was married, I decided, and had a home of my own, with things of my own, nicer even than what Mama and I had now in our fine little apartment, I would have a garden. Oh, not like this garden, I understood full well. There were different degrees of comfort, different kinds of right people. For a fleeting instant, I imagined the prospective husbands I'd be meeting if Mama's brother-in-law had been some fabulous industrialist or Four Hundred type. Men like Paul. Names in the social register. Or maybe I wouldn't be meeting anyone at all; maybe a certain Christian belief in redemption and reform had been necessary to make me marriageable, even with most of my history shorn away from the story the marks heard, even with Uncle Eugene describing the origins of my father's name, to one wary man, as "European."

I tossed away the stub of the dried flower, relieved Ruth couldn't read my mind. It landed on the leaves with a soft sound. I wondered if she'd discovered me gone. How she was entertaining herself alone.

Paul put his hand lightly on my back. Something deep in my body seemed to open up, like a hinge unbending. He guided me off the garden path and into a little green surrounded on three sides by an even hedge. At the center of the green was a gnarled tree, and in its branches, a tree house.

"I practically lived in this thing the summer I was nine. I was best friends with Ralph that year."

He didn't explain who Ralph was, and I didn't care. Ramona's brother, I guessed, and then I imagined that Paul had once been in love with Ramona. But I didn't mind that either. I liked it, somehow, stepping for an evening into the drama of these people with their elegant shoes and reckless fun, who lived as if there were no Depression, as if nothing would ever be expected of them other than good grooming and lively conversation.

Paul went up the ladder of two-by-fours and pounded the trap-door with his fist until it loosened. I hiked up my dress and climbed after him, breathing deeply, taking in the mossy scent of the tree. As I grabbed for a rung near the top, my knuckle rubbed sharply against the bark. No blood, but a scrape, a warning that for an instant shook me out of the dream of the last several minutes. For weeks I'd been saying no, no, no to nice boys proposing wholesome outings in ser-vice of respectful courtship overseen by my mother and uncle. And now here I was, following a stranger up a tree, after hardly any urg-ing at all.

I reached for the next rung, scowling into the dark. And why not? In a year I'd be serving my husband dinner, sharing his bed. Studying his moods, protecting his masculine pride. But for now. For now! There was a quickening in those words, an urge that felt somehow holy. For now the fact of the desire coursing through my body seemed reason enough to keep climbing.

Paul reached down through the trapdoor. I grabbed his hand and let him help me the rest of the way up. As soon as I got to my feet, I kissed him. He wrapped his arms around me and his stomach pressed mine, warm and soft. He nudged his jacket off my shoul-ders. It landed on the floor with a quiet thud. I wriggled from his grasp and reached around to loosen the ties on my dress. The sleeves slid from my arms; cool air rushed against my skin. He grinned and then started kicking a path clear through the clutter on the tree house floor, all of it silver in the moonlight: an old tea set, a teddy bear, a tin can radio. When I laughed, he kicked harder, making a show of it. I sat in the space he'd cleared and leaned back on my palms. He knelt over me and kissed me to the floor. The boards snagged my hair, surrounding me with the scent of dirt and damp. He pulled down the straps of my slip and brassiere and then reached around and struggled to unhook it, giving up, finally, with an exag-gerated groan. I did it for him. I wanted him to trace a line down between my breasts with his finger, to mark the smoothness of my skin with his own touch, but he just looked, and I liked the feeling of his looking. In the moonlight, I was just as silver as anything else, the color of pale skin on a movie screen. Goosebumps spread across my chest and shoulders.

He yanked off his jacket and vest and tossed them aside. I nudged off my shoes and wriggled out of my stockings and bloomers. His pants caught at his ankles, and he laughed as he kicked his way out of them.

I thought I knew what to expect, but when he pushed himself into me I cried out, startled. He pulled his face back from mine, grinning; he'd taken my shock for ecstasy.

"You know, half an hour ago I would have sworn you were a virgin," he said, amused, but also slightly abashed, as if he weren't entirely sure whether I'd like his saying it. I kissed him so I wouldn't have to decide.

He moved, steady as a metronome, his face buried in my neck, his breath seeping into my hair. His shirt grew damp where I clutched at his back. A leaf crunched beneath my head. After a minute or two, my sensation thinned and flattened. Soon I realized I was waiting for it to end. But I didn't mind that, not exactly. I gazed up at the ceiling, satisfied by the story I narrated to myself: An assignation in a tree house! With a man whose desire I'd managed to stir with a glance in a rearview mirror. Paul's sweat collected on my belly. Where, minutes earlier, I'd felt the urgent tug of desire I now felt only a soft warmth. But somewhere beyond my body I was thrumming, electric with a sense of my own achievement. The fact of what I'd done.

When it was over, Paul rolled away and started whistling that song they'd been singing around the piano. He folded his jacket into a pillow and tucked it beneath my head. We lay on our sides, facing each other and smiling. He pressed his hand flat against mine, as if to compare sizes. There was a kink in his middle finger. I pressed mine against it.

"I was seven," he said. "Fell off the roof of the greenhouse. But I didn't tell anyone for ages because I wasn't supposed to be up on the greenhouse in the first place and I didn't want to get in trouble. The thing healed crooked, and then I wouldn't let them break it to set it straight again."

We were kissing again when I heard Ruth's voice from below, hissing my name. I sat up, heart pounding.

"Just a minute," I called down. Paul hid behind his hands, then parted his fingers, grinning sheepishly.

"Is it good night then?"

I nodded.

"I'm sorry to hear it." His cheeks colored slightly. "I suppose I shouldn't—you'll want to go down without me, I suppose?"

"Oh. Yes. Right." I hadn't thought, until that moment, how it might look: to climb down from a tree house, trailed by a man. He leaned back on his elbows and watched me dress. When I had myself in order, he lifted the trapdoor. Away from the edge, out of sight, he kissed me a final time.

"Thank you for a charming evening, Miss Szász."

Was I supposed to thank him in return? It was a scenario Emily Post had not addressed. In the end, I pecked his cheek and started down the ladder.

Ruth handed me my wrap, smirking.

"I got us a ride back to the city. But she wants to leave now." There was a thud above us as the trapdoor closed. Ruth glanced up, and then back at me, still grinning at first, and then softening with concern as she pressed her hand lightly against my elbow. "Hey, are you—"

"I'm fine," I said, and smiled to prove it, but under the force of her worry and Paul's consideration of my reputation, the lovely sense of achievement I'd felt minutes earlier had begun to crack.

Traffic was light on the drive back, but our driver, tipsy, proceeded slowly, gripping the wheel, eyes fixed on the road, keeping up a steady monologue so she wouldn't drift off—lists of things she needed to buy, a long, involved story about her mother's secret first marriage. When she ran out of stories she began to recite: the

Gettysburg address, Give me Liberty or Give me Death. I stared through the window, the evening's pleasure scabbing over with worry: Paul had been thoughtful there at the end. But what might he say to his friends, later? Who were his friends? If he told Ben, that would be one thing—an embarrassment, but one quarantined in bohemia, no threat to the other portion of my life. But what if Paul knew someone who knew someone who knew Uncle Eugene? There were different kinds of right people, yes, but right people of all sorts overlapped. Why hadn't I thought of that before? How as I'd walked through that dark garden had I been so dumb, so in the thrall of my body? Right people met in civic groups, on ladies' committees, in smart department store restaurants. What if some Institute busybody heard Paul say my name? That would be all it took: a name spoken with a curl of the lip, a certain tone. All his grinning and ease—maybe he was exactly the sort of man who seduced women and then made them into jokes. In a sermon, Uncle Eugene had once compared a woman's reputation to a stained-glass picture, which, once cracked, might be glued together again but whose flaw would always be apparent when the sun shone. So much was at stake for Mama and me. How had I been such a fool to hand a strange man a hammer?

And then there was the most dire consequence, the one that would expose me even if Paul kept quiet. The possibility flickered like a shadow at the edge of my thinking. Why hadn't I bothered to worry about letting myself be ruined? Destroying Mama's hopes alongside my own?

Ordinarily I drew comfort from the closeness of the city streets, the steady flow of people, but now the brightness and activity seemed to collect into a mass that weighed against my chest. When, at last, we pulled up in front of my building, all the more immediate worries tumbled into my mind: it must be nearly three o'clock in the morning, and I was sure I smelled of liquor. Maybe Mama would be able to detect the rest, as she'd always been able to detect misbehavior and lies on my father.

I squeezed Ruth's hand and said good night, conscious that she was watching after me as I hurried away, able to picture her worried expression: brows pulled together, corner of her mouth drawn in. For the doorman, I tried to project the image of a wholesome girl who had just attended some unusual but appropriate entertainment: a concert, a church dance. In the elevator, I held myself carefully upright.

I braced myself as I stepped into the dark apartment. But after a couple of seconds, I breathed out in relief. The place was empty; Mama wasn't home. The note was waiting in the usual place: "At Vera's."

I took a hurried bath in a few inches of scalding water, scrubbing at myself with soap. I wasn't so ignorant about the workings of my body to actually believe that was any protection against the dire consequence I was still refusing full entry into my imagination. Vaudeville had offered me plenty of unseemly knowledge; Ruth had completed my education. Weeks earlier, we'd laughed together over the diaphragm Cecil Gunn had bought her, which she kept beside her bed in a biscuit tin. I wondered if that made the sin extra sinful— having an ungirlish understanding of its mechanics and consequence. The water was still hot, but I began to shiver. I had the odd sense that the empty apartment was watching, collecting evidence against me.

Like a child afraid of the dark, I ran to my room with my eyes closed. I pulled on my nightgown and lay in bed, still damp, heart racing. Somewhere outside, a car backfired; a dog barked. I heard movement in the apartment above. After a while, my heart calmed. It was an omen, I decided, that I had come home to an empty house. It meant there needn't be any other consequence, dire or otherwise.

But when I got up for a glass of water and saw that it was half past four, I grew worried again. She'd never been so late getting home from Vera's. I telephoned, but no one picked up. I climbed back into bed, assuring myself that she wouldn't disappear, as Daddy had—she couldn't. But where was she now? Was she hurt? In trouble? Was it my fault? I wondered. Was this punishment for my sin?

An hour passed, and then another. Finally, I heard the door

opening and the sound of her keys, dropping in the dish in the front hall, and then her uneven gait. It was morning, too late to try to sleep, but I rolled onto my side and shut my eyes, relieved and angry, as if I were the mother and she were the daughter who had stayed out all night.

The door to my bedroom swung open. An instant later, she'd tugged the curtains with such force that the rod slipped its hook.

"Mama?" I squinted into the brightness. She stumbled toward me.

"Up," she said, yanking away all of my covers. She took a few steps back, as if to get a better look at me, or to make sure I could get a good look at her. "Get up, Harriet." Her voice was thick with drink.

I stood, crossing my arms against the cold. But how could she know already? When she'd only just gotten home herself?

"How many has he introduced you to? Three months, and not one man worth a second look? Not one?"

I glanced at the clock, as if it might hold some explanation.

"Please, Mama, it's—"

"I've been patient, Harriet, but you have a part to play. You can't just dillydally, you can't be half committed."

My head was throbbing.

"Uncle Eugene says that the choice of a partner in marriage is the most—"

"Enough!" She pounded her cane against the floor. "What is it you're waiting for? A grand romance? A fairy tale? Your father and me, that was a fairy tale. And see how that worked out."

Sorrow corkscrewed through my chest. I sank back onto my bed, half-listening to the first words she'd spoken to me about Daddy in the better part of a year: He had been the greatest mistake of her life. If she'd been fortunate enough to have had a mother who'd watched out for her, like she watched out for me, she wouldn't have thrown it in her face. I was spoiled, that was the problem. I didn't appreciate what other people did for me. I was like my father: Oh, I thought I was so clever when I drank and did god knew what else with who else, sucking on peppermints, claiming women's troubles, but did I really think I could keep it from her? After all those years with him.

The account she made of her life with Daddy seemed to drape like a thick blanket over what I remembered of the truth. In a surge of anger, she rushed to the side of the bed and crouched down, so her face was close to mine. Her words rang out, bright and clear, as if she'd pronounced them from a stage.

"If you're not careful he'll see you. He'll see you're no better than your father, than his own daughter. And if he sees that, Harriet? We're sunk."

SHE STAYED IN HER ROOM all Saturday. I didn't see her again until Sunday morning, when it was time to leave for the Institute, where she only looked at me when Uncle Eugene was paying attention, and then it was a hard, opaque look from which I could extract no information.

In the days that followed, I waited for her to grow more specific in her anger, to say "Lake Forest," or "party," or "man," to forbid me from seeing Ruth. But she didn't. Vera came over for dinner, and when Mama was in the other room, I probed, casually, for clues about what might have kept her out so late that night, and what might have set her off, if not what I had done. I thought, maybe, I saw a twitch at the corner of Vera's mouth, some sign of strain. But she just shrugged and asked me to change the record to something less morose.

That weekend, Ruth and I went to an exhibit of new American paintings and sculpture at the Art Institute. Late in the afternoon, we sat together in the museum cafeteria. Concentrating intently on her half of our ham sandwich, she mentioned that there was a place right on State Street, across from the Chicago Theatre, that was just like an ordinary doctor's office, sanitary and professional, with real nurses in white caps, where a friend of a friend had just walked right in and gotten an abortion.

I was shocked and grateful in equal measure. And just as grateful when, quickly, nimbly, she changed the subject.

A few days later, my period arrived. I decided I needn't think any further about my night in the tree house with Paul. It had simply been proof of a possibility. Now I had that proof. I could get on with what was required.

*

ON CHRISTMAS DAY, MAMA AND I CLIMBED THE STEPS OF Uncle Eugene's house just as the streetlights flickered on, fog twining around their dark necks. A pine wreath hung from the front door; pine boughs were draped along the window boxes, and bright red bows tied to the porch railings. Mama rang the bell, and then reached over and smoothed the towel wrapped around the warm pan of gingerbread that Vera had dropped off at the apartment.

"You're looking pale," she said.

In the two months since the party and Mama's strange outburst, she had rarely spoken to me except to criticize: my dress was too tight, I'd talked too much about myself at dinner, if I stayed up reading I'd ruin my eyes and then we'd have glasses to cope with on top of everything else, besides which she hated to think I was becoming a show-offy intellectual type like that cousin of mine. I pinched my cheeks to draw up some color. Uncle Eugene hadn't introduced me to a mark for several weeks. Mama had said, more to herself than me, that we shouldn't worry, that it was a busy season for the Institute, but when he'd invited us for Christmas, she'd seemed relieved. Now, as I turned to her, displaying my freshly pinked cheeks, she nodded, but with narrowed eyes, her mouth bunched, her scrutiny indistinguishable from disappointment.

The door opened.

"Merry, merry, merry Christmas," Uncle Eugene cried, his cheer belied by a weary look in his eyes. We followed him to the parlor, where we were met by a fresh waft of pine from the tallest, fattest Christmas tree I'd ever seen anywhere but a stage. All around the room, white candles were twinkling. Ruth sat slouched beside the fireplace, knees to chest, on a little chair I had seen a dozen times before but only now recognized as a piece of the children's furniture from her old playroom in Toledo. Uncle Eugene watched with a thin, tight smile as she stood to greet us.

A few days earlier, we'd drunk gin in her studio and plotted, getting our stories straight: how much time we spent together these days, what, exactly, we did. Evidence of my improving influence. Her accepting her father's invitation seemed to belong to that category. She teased that she was only coming because she wanted to see me in action at his house, and, as gaily as I could, I told her she'd better behave herself, so he didn't start to wonder whether Harriet the Institute Girl was all an act.

She kissed Mama's cheek.

"Merry Christmas, Aunt Maude." Her voice quavered slightly. She was wearing an ill-fitting brown velvet dress I didn't recognize. I wondered if it was out of her high school wardrobe. If her father had made her change when she arrived. For the first time, I considered the fact that somewhere in that house there was a bedroom that had once belonged to her. Maybe it was still a time capsule of the girl she had been, full of that girl's clothes, her books, a coterie of china dolls in pastel dresses, their hair a little faded but still as smooth as silk. A Smith pennant.

"I can't wait for you both to try Harriet's gingerbread," Mama said, brightly. "Her own special recipe."

"I'm looking forward to it," Ruth said, smiling even as she gripped one arm with the other hand.

I went to put the gingerbread in the kitchen, expecting Ruth to follow. But she just sank back into the little chair. When I returned to the parlor, Mama and Uncle Eugene were keeping up a bright conversation while Ruth stared into the fire. I sat beside Mama on the couch. We spoke of the day's services at the Institute, the first of which Mama and I had attended, the second of which, in Mama's telling, we'd listened to on the radio while I made the gingerbread. Ruth said little. At one point, she rose, and from a table in the corner fetched a cast-iron nutcracker shaped like a squirrel.

It was too whimsical an object for Uncle Eugene, and I knew it must have been Aunt Marion's. I saw her hand, now, in all the room's festive touches: the red glass beads on a string, hung along the mantelpiece, the paper Santas, the cut tin creche. So often at Uncle Eugene's I'd been aware of the game of replacements: how Uncle Eugene stood in for Daddy, Mama for Aunt Marion, I for Ruth. Now there were more of us than there were parts to fill, but somehow that only made the gaps seem more vast. How many Christmases had it been since Ruth's last Christmas with her mother? If she were still alive, would Mama and Aunt Marion be slipping out of their mother selves now and into frantic, girlish fits of laughter, as they had in Toledo? Would Mama seem suddenly depleted, and insist on going upstairs to lie down? If Daddy hadn't left us, would he have consented to come to Christmas at all? Uncle Eugene was describing plans for a cafeteria the Institute would open in the New Year to serve forgotten men, and I wondered if Daddy ate in places like that now, or if he too had found his luck in California. Though luck was fickle. Josie's latest picture, *Hard Cases*, had been another flop.

Ruth fed the squirrel nuts, cracking them by raising and lowering its tail. Sometimes she ate them, and sometimes she just tossed the meats and the shells alike into the fire. When the clock chimed five, Uncle Eugene invited us to serve ourselves from the dishes Hilda had laid out on the sideboard earlier in the day. Turkey and dressing and candied yams, stuffed celery, onions baked in butter, three molded salads, wedges of toast topped with creamed shrimp and avocados cut to look like mistletoe leaves. Ruth took my usual place at the table; from the marks' seat, I watched her push her food around her plate. I ignored Mama's disapproving look when I went to fill my plate a second time. From the head of the table, Uncle Eugene told long stories that felt like sermons and explained facts and ideas in his puffed, persistent way, as if his discourse were a gift the rest of us were fortunate to receive. But it was Ruth he looked at most often. He wished she'd eat more, I saw that. But he also wanted her to react to him: to laugh at his jokes, to glow with admiration, to defer, to show she knew he was brilliant and wise. His need was as plain to me as my parents' need had always been, and though I'd often felt overwhelmed by that need, unequal to it, I had always understood that it was the path through which goodness lay. It was different with Uncle Eugene and Ruth, somehow, I could see that, though I couldn't quite see why it should be different. But I understood: If she acted as he wished at Christmas, he'd only want her to come to church on Sunday, and then he'd want her to move back home and marry well. If she gave any of herself he'd want her whole self, and to give him that would be to destroy herself. He started explaining President Hoover's proposal for economic relief, which I knew Ruth knew inside and out, having written a brief on it for work. I saw a flash of irritation cross her face and suspected Uncle Eugene had gotten something wrong. I wondered if he even knew what her job was. She took a small bite of dressing. My relief that she hadn't corrected her father felt like a betrayal.

After dinner, Ruth and I went to the kitchen to assemble coffee and dessert, alone together at last. Her familiarity with the contents of every drawer and cupboard made me feel like an interloper. While the water boiled, she leaned against the counter, closing her eyes.

"It's miserable in there. I'm miserable in there. I shouldn't have come."

"I think he's happy you did," I said, arranging slices of gingerbread on a tray.

"Oh, Harriet, I'm rotten, but somehow that's the worst thing about it. You want?"

She'd taken a flask from her pocket. I hesitated only a moment before nodding. When I handed it back, she tipped generously into two of the coffee cups she'd laid out on a tray.

Back in the parlor, I passed around slices of gingerbread, and Ruth distributed the coffee, and in spite of myself I felt a flash of jealousy: how easy they came to her, the gestures of a hostess, which she disdained and which I'd had to wring out of a book. Uncle Eugene brought Mama and me gifts from under the tree: for Mama a daily devotional with a moss green cover, and for me, a set of tea towels, monogrammed with a single initial, "to be completed on a happy occasion to come."

"Thank you, Uncle Eugene," I said warmly, running my fingers over the embroidery.

Ruth snorted into her coffee cup.

Uncle Eugene went very still. My heartbeat was frantic as I waited for him to cast her out, right there in front of Mama and me. If he even scolded her, it might all come undone—the delicate web of half-truths and self-delusion that allowed me to have my cake and eat it, to be a good Institute girl and Ruth's best friend.

He smiled firmly. He lifted his fork and took a bite of gingerbread, letting his eyes flutter shut as he swallowed.

"Now, this is a fine gingerbread," he said. "Your mother used to bake gingerbread, Ruth. Do you remember? It will be a lucky man who takes for a wife a woman who can make a gingerbread like this."

Ruth dropped her plate. It hit the floor and shattered. She looked sharply at her father, her gaze throbbing with a hurt that seemed to have been waiting all evening behind a shutter, and now the shutter had been thrown open, the hurt was shining through. I felt the fragility of the moment, the need for patching over, and almost echoed Uncle Eugene's praise of the gingerbread, before I remembered that I was meant to have made it myself. In the end, it was Mama who, too brightly, too shrilly, agreed with Uncle Eugene, while I hurried to gather the white shards from the floor.

ON NEW YEAR'S EVE, RUTH AND I WENT TO A PARTY WHERE I kissed a strange man at midnight. That would be the last of it, I resolved. It was 1932. The year I would marry.

But the pace of Uncle Eugene's matchmaking remained slack. Out loud, Mama blamed the weather. Bitter, lashing rains that over-night turned into heaps of snow, gray days when dusk came before it ever got properly light. On a frigid evening when Mama and Vera and I were holed up in our apartment, eating popcorn and playing pinochle, Mama told Vera it hardly mattered that the city's taxi drivers had recently gone on strike, that everyone was hibernating anyhow, as if Vera were the one who needed reassuring.

At the end of the month, Uncle Eugene introduced me to a wid-ower with a gray beard, whose nine-year-old daughter reached under the tablecloth to poke me in the thigh with her fork. The next night, Ruth and I went to a burlesque interpretation of the book of Genesis presented at a hole-in-the-wall theater on North Clark, and then to a party of the company, where after a few drinks I slipped into a supply closet with one of the performers, who slid his hand up my skirt and made me feel what Paul had failed to make me feel in the tree house.

But the one didn't have anything to do with the other. Mama was right: winter was a lean season. That was natural. I hadn't shown Uncle Eugene a thing to object to. I was the daughter who had stayed, who had seen my duty through. My husband would turn up in the spring, I decided, along with the robins, along with the groaning open of the ice-locked lake.

In February, Uncle Eugene produced a missionary, freshly returned from the Far East, who recalled his work in an uninterrupted monologue from peanuts and punch straight through dinner. Before I had a chance to pour him a cup of coffee he got a bloody nose and went home. I didn't bother mentioning him to Ruth. She had started taking on extra jobs—copyediting, translations—that swelled the tally of her savings so rapidly I had to stop looking at the page on the wall. She read me letters from Morris Dack detailing his adventures in New York, and I knew it wasn't enough to express admiration, or even jealousy, that she was fishing for something more—a concession, a promise, some share of my future. Sometimes, I left her place early, out of patience for reasons I didn't want to investigate. Sometimes I spent the night, intimidated by the bite of the wind, or simply unable to tolerate the idea of going home to my mother.

My fourth winter in Chicago turned—haltingly, through spells of bitter cold and late flurries—into a dismal spring. It was chilly on my birthday, raining off and on. That afternoon, Mama and I had lunch with Vera, who said she'd heard the Lindy baby had been found, but the afternoon's papers said otherwise, which made the whole day seem foul and disappointing. That evening, on our way to Uncle Eugene's, I stared through the cab window at a sky that gleamed light gray behind thready dark clouds that threatened to mass and pour, freshly annoyed with Mama for having accepted an invitation from Uncle Eugene on my birthday, when she knew Ruth and I had made plans. Ruth had said not to worry, that I could just come over to her place after. But it felt like another betrayal on my part, a nick in our friendship.

As we turned onto Sheridan, we passed a worker pasting a new poster up over one advertising *Turkish Delight*. Josie's latest flop. I glanced at Mama, who, to my relief, didn't seem to have noticed. The picture had been banned as indecent in seventeen states. Religious leaders across the country had issued statements denouncing it as evidence of Hollywood's degradation of traditional Christian values and an attack on the moral and spiritual welfare of America's children. Uncle Eugene had read his statement over the radio, ending with an appeal for donations to a new Campaign for Morals in Cinema.

The cab stopped at a red light. Mama leaned her head back and closed her eyes, the last of the faint daylight sparking on the white threads in her hair. A year earlier, I might have enjoyed watching Josie's face disappear under Norma Shearer's. Now I thought of an article I'd read earlier in the week, which claimed Josie's unpredictable behavior on the set of her next movie, *Shiver Me Linda,* had led to costly reshoots. Already it was supposed to be one of the most expensive pictures ever made. Josie played a socialite, kidnapped by pirates; there were dance numbers filmed at sea, in Technicolor. When I remembered the article's last line, it seemed somehow to be as much about me as it was about Josie, as if her faltering career were the public expression of my failure to find a husband: "This reporter is forced to ask: Has the starlet once known as the Neatest Sweet Tomato gone splat?"

When Hilda delivered us to the parlor, Uncle Eugene was sitting at a small desk, staring glumly out the window at the rain that had just begun to fall, pen poised over the hardbound notebook in which he drafted his sermons. A long moment passed before he turned to greet us. Mama and I sat on the couch, and he took his place across from us in one of the armchairs. His conversation was clipped, absentminded, as if he were still focused on his sermon, or the rain. It seemed plain that he didn't want us there, and I felt freshly annoyed at Mama and him both for having disrupted my plans with Ruth.

After a little while, Hilda called Uncle Eugene to the telephone.

"I'm afraid Mr. Hockelburg will be late," he said when he returned, a small, stiff smile hardly masking his irritation. "A minor crisis at the office."

When Mama pressed him for details about Mr. Hockelburg, he provided them succinctly: he'd just taken a position working for his grandfather, who owned real estate downtown. His father was the minister of the First Presbyterian Church in Lake Forest and on the board of the college there; his mother was from one of the fine Chicago families, the middle of five daughters. The others had been society darlings in their youth, but Mrs. Hockelburg struck him as a solid, sensible woman.

Hilda brought in the peanuts and punch. I distributed them in the usual fashion. But after a minute, Uncle Eugene put down his punch glass. He went to a cabinet in the corner, where he turned a key, opened the door, and pulled out a bottle.

"Sherry," he said, in a clear, sharp voice. "A gift from a member of the board." He carried the bottle back along with three small glasses. I looked to Mama, hoping for guidance, but she was staring, wide-eyed, at the bottle from which Uncle Eugene had begun to pour as if it were the most ordinary thing in the world. He handed Mama and me our glasses and raised his own.

"To Harriet, of course," he said. "Our birthday girl. Many happy returns." As he drank, he closed his eyes and smiled, as if returning to a long-forgotten pleasure. When neither of us followed suit, he gave Mama a quick, impatient nod. She let the liquid touch her lips and then set her glass down as if it were poison. But I couldn't make myself drink in front of Uncle Eugene. I couldn't. He didn't seem to notice, or to care, as if it were sufficient that Mama had obliged him. He raised his glass a second time.

"And to my wife," he said. Mama went ashen. Uncle Eugene drank deeply, then threw another log on the fire, sending up a spray of sparks. He leaned against the mantel. Yellow light flickered against his face, pooling in the troughs beneath his eyes.

"Today is our wedding anniversary," he said. And then he turned to Mama, his smile brittle. "Do you remember Edison Day?"

"Of course," she said. She watched him cautiously, sitting up very straight, her hands folded tightly over one knee.

"Our town was the very first where a city hall was built wired for electricity, if you can imagine that," he said to me, noticing my untouched glass on the table and swallowing a small, approving chuckle. "Mr. Edison sent the chandelier that still graces the front lobby. For many years there was a festival every spring. Oh, small towns always find a reason for a festival, and that was ours. Each year the children fought over who would get to carry the banner at the front of the parade. Maybe they still do. Your mother must have been—eight, nine?" She nodded, still wary. When he turned back to me she emptied half her glass. "And Marion a few years younger than that. My mother was in charge of the parade that year. In the end, she chose the two of them. The Foster girls, everyone called them."

"My mother made us white dresses, and stoles." She spoke haltingly, as if she were easing out onto an icy pond she wasn't certain would hold her weight, and though the explanation was for my benefit, she was looking at Uncle Eugene so intently it was as if I weren't even in the room. "Mine was green and Marion's blue."

"It was that morning that I busted a tire on my bike, just up the road from your farm. Do you remember?"

"Yes." She drank again, but this time she looked up at him with a girlish smile. "My father came down to help you repair it. Marion and I watched from behind the fence. You were already so impressive then. All the children in town knew your baseball records."

He laughed and lifted the bottle of sherry toward Mama. After a moment's consideration, she held out her glass. He topped her off and poured a little more for himself.

"The first time I saw your mother, Harriet, she was a tiny girl with scabs on her knees, her hair in braids, holding out a bouquet of violets from the field in back of my father's church."

"The hours we spent in the field! And in the graveyard."

"Marion. She was the one, wasn't she? On Halloween?"

The two of them told the story together, in turns, as if they'd done it that way a thousand times before: One Halloween the children of the town gathered in the Presbyterian graveyard to tell ghost stories, and Uncle Eugene's father came upon them, waving a switch and shouting that they were signing their own tickets to Hell. They all ran off, but Marion tripped and fell behind. When Old Reverend Creggs caught her by the arm, she looked right up at him said, "I'm not thcared."

They laughed until Uncle Eugene had to wipe his eyes with a handkerchief. He finished telling: his father had carried Aunt Marion back to the house, but left the punishing to Mrs. Creggs, who gave Marion a piece of pie and sent her on her way.

"Oh, your mother's gooseberry pies!" Mama cried. "She had such a light hand with a crust."

Uncle Eugene beamed, the tips of his ears turning pink.

"She was particular about the fruit. How she used to pick over a bushel. I'd sit beside her, eating the discards.

"James and I used to row down to that bend in the river, just south of the bridge, to find berries for her. We found a patch there no one else knew about."

Silence fell over the room like a damp cloth dousing a flame. Mama's gaze hardened. Uncle Eugene cleared his throat and stood. He walked toward the fireplace again, hands behind his back. My heart fluttered. I regretted not having drunk any of my sherry.

"James is my brother," Uncle Eugene finally said. "Much my junior. Closer to your mother's age."

"What do you hear from James these days?" Mama asked, her lightness effortful, conspicuous. Uncle Eugene described the restaurant his brother operated, and the dispensation of his children to various relations after the death of his wife. Patches of color collected in Mama's cheeks.

The doorbell rang. Uncle Eugene collected the bottle and glasses and locked them in the cabinet. The two of them arranged their faces, straightened their bodies, assumed the proper form, but I wondered if Mr. Hockelburg would detect the tension in the room and suspect something strange had happened just before his arrival.

The parlor door opened. For a moment, Hilda was blocking my view of the mark, but even before I could see his face, I recognized something in the way he moved, the easy grace with which he carried his height. Mr. Hockelburg was Paul. Paul from the Coal Scuttle, Paul from the tree house was the son of a minister, a man apparently even closer to my uncle than I'd feared. Paul, a mark. His eyes lit on me. I braced myself for the telling smirk, the remark that would shine a light on the crack in the glass. But Mama and Uncle Eugene were still locked in the strange mood summoned by the mention of Uncle Eugene's brother, and if they noticed the startled lift of Paul's eyebrows, it didn't seem to register as anything out of the ordinary. He greeted Uncle Eugene, and when Uncle Eugene introduced Mama and me, he said hello as if I were a stranger, received my own stammering pleasantries with only the slightest grin.

Hilda called us in to dinner right away. The conversation unfolded as it usually did, Mama and Uncle Eugene following the familiar script, but they remained distracted. Paul didn't often look right at me, but I sensed his awareness of my presence in the way he held his shoulders, and in his voice, booming and self-conscious. When he did meet my eye, something pulsed in the air between us. He plied Mama with questions about my gingerbread, which had replaced the lamb cake as proof du jour of my baking skills.

"Perhaps you'll have the good fortune to try it someday," she said at last, ending the line of inquiry with a dull smile. He turned his attention to Uncle Eugene, asking about his seminary days, where he had nearly but not quite overlapped with Paul's father. Uncle Eugene kept his answers short. Several times he looked at the clock.

"Your father mentioned you've recently returned from Europe?" Uncle Eugene said, seeming less interested in Europe than in letting someone else be at the center of the conversation.

"That's right, sir. I was there for a year. Just got home in October."

Paul looked at me then, making the word "October" a reminder of what we knew that Mama and Uncle Eugene didn't. I snapped my eyes down to my plate, my stomach swirling. Mama and Uncle Eugene asked halfhearted questions about Paul's trip, which he answered with stories about visits to museums and cathedrals, assessments of the quality of hotels, sober reflections on the political situation in Spain. But beneath all this I detected a message in code, a secret story just for me signaled in the occasional extraneous detail—a peacock strutting outside the Vatican, a woman in a full face of makeup buying bread at eight o'clock in the morning—or the way he shook his head when he mentioned a particular friend, or a slightly cocked eyebrow, or a too-long look over the table. I knew he wanted me to imagine gay nights out, absinthe and dancing and even romance. He was telling me he was, like me, split. That he performed for his family like I performed for mine. That if we were ever alone together, he would tell me the rest.

He tried asking me questions about my studies and my work at the Institute, but I could only choke out half-answers. How could I speak in front of Mama and Uncle Eugene to this Paul—Paul, the son of a minister, Paul, employed in his grandfather's real estate business, Paul the mark—when every time I closed my eyes I remembered Paul half-dressed in the tree house, and myself, half-dressed beside him? I resolved to do better, only to drop a forkful of riced potatoes on the tablecloth. I swept them up in my napkin. Paul hid behind his own napkin to smile.

When Hilda brought out a birthday cake for me, Paul pretended to be indignant.

"If only I'd known it was a birthday party," he said, and I felt myself flush from head to toe, certain that this time Mama and Uncle Eugene must have heard the insinuation in "birthday party," that they must be seeing the smirk Paul pressed around his first bite of cake. But they were concentrating on their own cake and coffee, as if the work of consuming it were utterly absorbing. It was still early when Mama said hadn't we better. Uncle Eugene called us a cab. Paul and I said good night, and just like that, it was over.

On the drive home, rain speckled the windshield in faint bursts; the tires buzzed along the wet road. Mama gazed out her window, quiet, remote from me, which I didn't mind: I was trying to hold on to everything I wanted to tell Ruth, all my surprising new knowledge about Paul, which I wanted to dissect with her, as we'd dissected every mark in the beginning. I'd tell her about Mama and Uncle Eugene's reminiscing too, the strange turn their mood had taken when Mama mentioned Uncle Eugene's brother. Maybe she would know the story there. He was her uncle, after all. And her father with that bottle of sherry. Oh, how she'd laugh!

We were a few blocks from home when Mama turned and grabbed my wrist.

"You're a good girl, Harriet. You know that, don't you? You always have been. You've always done as I've asked."

"Okay, Mama," I said, trying to pull my arm away. Her grip only tightened.

"And I've stuck by you, haven't I? Haven't I always done what a mother ought?"

Her eyes looked very small and pink. Before I could think of any response she began to cry. She made no sound, but her nose turned red, just as mine did when I cried. She didn't pull out a handkerchief or blot at her face with the sleeve of her jacket, as if as long as she behaved as if nothing were happening, nothing would be happening. When the driver pulled up to our building, he shot a worried look over his shoulder, but she shook her head and thanked him brightly, and then hurried out and waved him away.

"Ruth must be expecting you," she said, and her voice hardly cracked as she beamed, as if she loved nothing more than my going to Ruth's. "Have a splendid night." And before I could say anything, she started toward the door. "Oh," she turned back, "and happy birthday!" And then she trilled good evening to the doorman as she hurried inside.

IT WAS JUST THE SHERRY, I thought, as I walked to Ruth's. Sherry and reminiscing, the company of Aunt Marion's ghost, and whatever sad story they hadn't quite told about James Creggs. I wondered what Paul had thought, coming into the room, seeing me there. Had this version of me disappointed him? Was I less than he remembered?

Ruth opened the door, waving a crepe paper streamer from each hand and blowing a noisemaker. I let her pull me in and seat me on one of her floor cushions, where she served me a jam jar full of rum punch and a slice of applesauce cake, chattering brightly about her day.

"Listen," I said, interrupting her. "You'll never guess who the mark was tonight."

"Who?"

"Paul. From Lake Forest."

It took her a moment to remember.

"Tree House Paul?"

I nodded. Her laughter struck like a volley of tiny arrows. "Lord, how ridiculous! My father. Christ." She turned suddenly sober. "Hey, he didn't—"

I shook my head.

"He was a perfect gentleman," I said.

"Phew," she said. I frowned into my jar of punch. I hadn't meant Paul to be a joke. But Ruth had already launched into a story about shopping for the punch ingredients, her talk driving my voice, my impulse to tell, down deep into my chest. When I emptied my jam jar, she filled it again. If she noticed I'd grown quiet, she made no sign. She went on chattering: about punch, about cake, about an essay she was revising to be published in a friend's magazine, until the nervous energy that had been flowing beneath her conversation all evening sent her, practically skipping, over to her bed. She pulled an envelope from under her pillow.

"Open it," she said, thrusting it toward me. "It's a birthday present." She sat across from me on an egg crate and watched.

The envelope was full of newspaper clippings—apartment listings. It took me a moment to realize they were all from New York papers.

"Morris sent them. I'm going. I have the money saved. Oh, now what's that face? You've known all along that was the plan."

Ruth. Leaving Chicago.

"When?" I managed to say.

"That depends." She stood and paced, hands folded behind her back, looking exactly like her father when he was working up to a point. She stopped, finally, facing me. "You know the college Morris is teaching at? The tuition is free. Once you told me you wished you'd had the chance to go. Do you remember that?"

"Maybe."

She knelt down and looked me square in the eye.

"So why don't you? Come to New York with me. Take a class or two. See how you like it. Or just get a job. Let's have an adventure."

I stuffed the newspaper clippings back into the envelope. My hands were trembling. I went to the sink and started scrubbing a dirty bowl. Ruth followed.

"How many men has my father rounded up for you?" She leaned against the sink, pressing her face close to mine. "If you wanted to get married, you would have done it already."

"It's not like shopping for a hat, Ruth." Through the window came a sharp, damp breeze and the sound of laughter from someone passing on the street. "Uncle Eugene says there's no more important choice than—"

"But what do you say?"

"Stop it, Ruth, you're being—"

She took the bowl from my hands.

"Listen. When I first met you, when we were little girls, I was insane with jealousy. I couldn't believe your lives. Vaudeville? My god. The way you spoke and acted. It was as if you'd grown up just slightly askew, not quite feeling the ordinary things, not quite know-ing what was expected. And that made you free. I couldn't have put it that way then, but you were the freest girls I'd ever known. Josie of course, but you too—you were just more deliberate about it, more aware of what it meant to use that freedom. And now I meet you again, and you're running toward everything I've spent my whole life figuring out how to escape. And it's just—I know you, Harriet. I know you. It's not what you want."

A pain was collecting just between my eyebrows, the seed of a headache. I turned away from Ruth. I wanted to sit in a chair, a deep, comfortable chair, but there were only crates and cushions and the lumpy pallet bed, and all at once, I hated it. Ruth's studio, and all of Towertown, home décor in the village: kitchenettes that had once been feed stalls, everything low to the ground and draped in some dusty fabric, everything smelling of smoke and fried onions.

I retrieved my purse from the bed and fumbled in it for a cigarette.

"You seem to know an awful lot about what I want," I said, lighting it.

"I just want you to think for yourself. To choose for yourself."

"I do choose. I have chosen."

"Have you? A true choice, one you've made freely and without—"

"Jesus, that's all so easy for you to say. Free choice, free love, to hell
with convention. You can afford all that. You have no idea what it's
like to be poor, to be responsible. Your father sends you an allowance,
Ruth! After all you've done! I think you could run off and do a strip
tease in a lesbian circus and he'd still put that check in the mail. You're
his daughter; his real daughter. But I have to earn my keep."

"Is that what you call it? Showing up at my father's house to play
the timid virgin, then turning around and necking with half the village."

I smashed my cigarette against the chipped saucer she used as an
ashtray. For a long moment, I couldn't make myself speak.

"That's a lousy thing to say."

"It's a lousy way to be." She was flushed and wide-eyed, every
muscle taut, the corners of her mouth lifting, as if with the pleasure
of being about to clinch the argument. "I don't give a damn if you
want to go to bed with someone, Harriet. I wish you would. It's the
lying. And for what?"

"Did you ever consider that I might really want to get married?
Does it really seem so sickening to you? A husband? A family? A
position?"

"If you found someone worthy, someone who could make you
properly happy, I'd sew your goddamn gown. If it was what you
wanted—"

"It is what I want."

"You're more than a meal ticket, Harriett."

"What the hell is that supposed to mean?"

We faced each other. My chest rose and fell. She was perfectly
still, her eyes bright and clear.

"Your mother uses you." She said it forcefully, but the triumph was gone from her voice. There was only resignation, as if to an unpleasant truth. The duty to deliver the fatal diagnosis. "She doesn't see you. She doesn't understand—"

"You have no idea what my mother sees or doesn't see. You have no idea what it's like between us. You couldn't possibly know."

Hurt filled her eyes slowly, the meaning of my words taking a moment to unfurl: the thing I hadn't quite said, but had said just enough of to make her hear it. How could she know, when she didn't have a mother of her own? She took a single, ragged breath. I followed her gaze down to the floor. She was barefoot; I worried, suddenly, stupidly, that she would get a splinter.

She looked up again, calm. A moment before she had reminded me of her father; now, more than anyone, she resembled Mama.

"I'll say this much for your sister," she said. "She knows how to think for herself."

The possibility of our having anything more to say to each other disintegrated then; it was like how Ruth described the end of her faith in God, a structure turned to ash. I put on my jacket and walked out the door.

The rain had started up again. A spring rain, gentle and cleansing despite the chill, and though some people put up umbrellas or held newspapers over their heads, no one seemed to be in a hurry to get out of it. On the corner, a boy climbed up and swung around a lamppost, making his friends laugh. Two men sat beneath a café awning, playing chess. From open windows came the sounds of argument and music. I felt as if I were moving very quickly, but somehow, everyone else seemed to be passing me: people walking alone, people walking in pairs, groups that split to get around me and then formed again. Young people, creative people, political people, daring people, love nesters, painters and poets, sinners of every stripe, and those who came from all corners of the city to gawk at them. Ruth had brought me into their company. I'd enjoyed it. But she had known, from the beginning, that I couldn't settle here. That I had responsibilities. What she had suggested—it wasn't just that I should abandon Mama, it was that I should abandon everything I understood about myself. Everything that remained of that understanding after Josie had robbed me of part of it, Daddy of another part. Ruth claimed to know me, to defend me, but wasn't she just bossing me about being bossed? Still the tyrant she'd been as a little girl presiding over Josie and me with her yardstick.

When I got home, Mama was shut in her room. I crawled into bed without changing out of my wet clothes. In the morning, I woke to Mama's voice, calling me to the telephone.

"Hello?" I said, cringing through a sour, thudding headache.

"Well, you certainly sound as if you had some more night after we parted ways." Paul's voice was as cheerful as a whistle. "Care to tell me about it over lunch?"

THERE WAS RAIN ON THE MORNING OF MY WEDDING, A drenching rain that made rivulets of shadow in the patches of colored light that fell from the stained-glass window onto the laps of the people in the front pew of the Institute Chapel. When Paul said, "I do," his grin seemed wolfish, and I was grateful that Uncle Eugene had already turned to look at me. He read my vows in the same urging, didactic tone in which he'd prayed on Friday afternoons, when we'd knelt side by side in his office. When I answered with my own "I do," my mouth and throat felt numb; it was only Uncle Eugene's approving nod that convinced me I'd actually said the words aloud.

On the drive to Lake Forest, the sky brightened. When we arrived at Paul's parents' house, the crew hired for the occasion was spreading tablecloths and wiping off chairs, and Uncle Eugene and Mama and Paul's father all said how magnificent it was, that the weather had decided to cooperate. Paul's mother, her gray taffeta managing, like all her clothes, to look both expensive and dowdy, gazed out at the sparkling lawn with a grim satisfaction, as if she'd arranged for the change in the weather herself.

Paul and I received our guests. The luncheon was served. Afterward, I stood in a ring with the handful of people save Vera who belonged mostly to me, and not to Uncle Eugene or Paul's family: Polly and Ula, a few girls from the Correspondence Office, a mis-

sionary's youngish wife with whom I had once served on a commit-
tee. I concentrated on keeping my shoes from sinking into the damp
earth, conscious every time my eyes spun around the circle of the
absent face.

TWO MONTHS HAD PASSED since my birthday. Two months since
Ruth and I had fought. At first, I'd been occupied by Paul: lunches
and then dinners and dancing, though we maintained a strict ten
o'clock curfew, giggling to each other at our performance of propriety. The first time he joined Mama and me in our pew at the Institute, I wanted to run straight to Ruth's studio and tell her everything,
but I wanted just as badly to continue to punish her with silence, to
stay furious, to wait for her apology as I collected the facts of Paul
without offering her any share in interpreting them. He'd already
told me about his family, but that afternoon, after church, as we
walked beside the lake, eating hot dogs from a cart, he told me again,
more personally this time: his mother played preacher's wife as if
she were born to the role but never let his father forget that she'd
married down. His oldest brother, the minister, already had a plum
pulpit in San Francisco and a pretty wife and two curly-headed children. The next brother, the doctor, had been a star athlete in college, was devastatingly handsome, popular wherever he went.

"And then there's baby Paul," he said, grin tempered by old hurts.
His parents, alarmed at the way he'd loafed around after his gradu-
ation from Yale, had sent him to Europe hoping he would find some
way of occupying his time equal to the upbringing they had provided him.

"I suspect they also just wanted a break from having me around.
From having to explain me to their friends," he said, chucking the
end of his hot dog into the lake. And as I watched it travel in a long
arc, I felt a surge of pleasure at the athleticism that rippled beneath
the soft layers of Paul's body, the same way sharpness flashed through
the gentle gaze he turned on the world. "Of course, I didn't manage
to impress them abroad any better than I had at home."

He told me some of the true Europe stories I had imagined on the night of my birthday, though it was all a little less glittery, a little more sordid than I'd guessed: a great deal of drinking, a debacle involving a friend who had gotten a girl pregnant. He alluded delicately to a failed romance of his own. Home again, he'd slipped back into the groove of his old life—bridge parties, nights out, long lunches at the Casino. At last, his parents had insisted: the job at his grandfather's bank. Then the dinner at Uncle Eugene's.

"They've given up on my ability to get myself settled, you see. So they're doing the settling for me," he said, sitting on a large rock and letting his feet dangle over the edge.

I sat beside him. He knew that Mama and I were on our own, that Uncle Eugene looked after us. I hadn't told him about my history in show business. I hadn't even mentioned Josie. A few days earlier, I'd read in the paper that she'd dropped out of her latest picture due to ill health. An unnamed friend assured the reporter she was doing just fine. "Early to bed and a beefsteak a day should have her back to her old tricks in no time!" the friend promised. The sky over the lake was a pure, cloudless blue; the gulls soaring against it were like white kites. Weak spring sunlight fell on the edges of waves and fractured. What was there to say about Josie now? How would I even begin to tell the story? A cold gust blew across the water. I clung to my hat.

"I guess we're both just a couple of strays," I said. For the first time since the tree house, he kissed me.

The next day, I went by Ruth's. When I pressed my ear to the door, I was certain I heard movement inside, but I knocked three times and she didn't answer. I went back a few days after that. No luck. A couple of weeks later, the morning after Paul and I agreed to marry, I tried again, bringing with me the copy of *Black Beauty* I'd stolen from her in Toledo, which her mother had inscribed. I scrawled a note of apology and tucked it into the book, which I left leaning against the door. When I returned a few days later, the book was gone. But Ruth didn't answer my knock.

I told anyone who asked that I'd always wanted a June wedding.

That Paul and I couldn't bear to wait a year. He and I were in cozy agreement: we were leftovers, strays, entrants into the marriage market with significant liabilities that made each family consider it a lucky match. The great joke, for the two of us, was everything we knew about each other, the shared memory of the tree house. We knew we were the ones getting away with something.

I sent Ruth a wedding invitation. Every day, Mrs. Hockelburg and I zoomed around the city in a chauffeured car, packages piling in the trunk. When we weren't shopping for the wedding, we were shopping to furnish the apartment Paul and I would share when we returned from our honeymoon. Over lunch, she asked sharp questions and issued corrections, polishing the rough edges off my manners. At home, Mama plied me with unfamiliar affection. She told me I had been very clever to wait for a proper society man. And even though that wasn't what I'd done, I basked in her praise. I was pleased to think that with Paul's help I would keep Mama in finer circumstances than she could even have hoped. He tried several times to discuss with her arrangements for after the wedding. Did she want to move into a new place, something smaller, perhaps, something closer to Paul's and mine? Until, of course, the happy future event, by which point we would surely have a house of our own where she could join us. When she demurred, saying there was time to discuss all that later, I was annoyed: Wasn't all that the whole point? I didn't want to wait to see the fruits of my conscientious daughtering.

The same day our wedding announcement ran at the top of the society page, a note arrived in the mail, an RSVP. Ruth was terribly sorry she wouldn't be able to attend. She sent greetings from New York, where she hoped she would have time to see the two of us if we ever made our way out east.

NOW, AS I STOOD in a ring of other girls, only approximately my friends, my awareness of Ruth's absence summoned the gloom that all day had pressed up against the boundary of my pleasure, that had been ready to assert itself whenever I sank too deeply into my own thoughts or whenever the joyful bustle slowed.

"Do you have plans for a honeymoon, Harriet?" asked one of the girls from the Correspondence Office.

"We'll leave tomorrow morning for Lake Louise," I said, though I'd answered the same question so many times that my words no longer felt like a true, spontaneous statement so much as a line from a play.

"How romantic!"

I nodded, trying to make my face bright, to invite further questions. But someone asked Ula about the missionary work she would undertake in China in the fall, and Ula launched into a recitation of her itinerary. Soon I found the conversation in the circle had stitched itself shut and that I was outside the seam. I let my eyes wander across the lawn, to where Paul was standing with his mother and some of his mother's friends. He caught me looking and winked. I felt a flutter of excitement. That night, we would stay at the Drake Hotel, where we could do again what we hadn't done since the tree house. In the preceding weeks, the matter had been addressed by each of the adults in my life: Mama had left an Institute pamphlet on my pillow. Vera had pulled me aside and whispered that if a husband wasn't happy at home, he'd get happy somewhere else, and that I might as well enjoy myself too. Even Mrs. Hockelburg had straightened her shoulders and put down her teacup, lifted her chin, and gazed over my shoulder as she explained that there were duties in marriage that I might understandably find distasteful but that I must remember, were all part of the Lord's plan. When I read the Institute pamphlet, I wondered if I had doomed us: if my virginity had indeed been designed by God as a seal on my marriage. As Ula described her language studies, I wondered what any of the girls in the circle would say if they knew what I had already done. Had any of them felt temptation, I wondered? Succumbed to it? Maybe one of them had. And I was struck by a sudden, desperate sadness. How little I'd let myself know them, how little I'd let them know me. I wondered who Ruth knew in New York. If she had already made proper friends.

I mumbled an excuse no one was listening for and went inside. In the kitchen, I asked one of the waiters for a cup of tea, which I carried through the halls until I found an empty room. I stood at the window, hidden from my wedding guests by a thick red drape. My reflection wavered on the surface of my tea.

"Harriet Hockelburg," I said to her. And then I leaned against the window frame and let the minutes tick by, conscious of my inattentiveness to the party, my failure in the first duty of my married life.

"It's time to cut the cake." Mama was standing in the doorway, looking pretty in a parchment-colored gown we had purchased according to Paul's mother's specifications, on Paul's account.

"I had a headache," I murmured. "I was just—"

Mama held up a hand.

"You don't need to explain, Harriet," she said, gently. I had to work to keep from scowling. What business did she have being gentle with me now?

I let her lead me back to the party. On the patio, on a lace-covered table, the cake stood—three tiers topped with sculpted sugar birds, Paul waiting beside it. When I took my place next to him, he touched my back. I flushed as I smiled up at him.

"Shall we?" he said. Together, we lifted a knife and cut a piece from the cake's top tier. It broke in two as I slid it onto the plate. I flinched, sensing, from across the garden, Mrs. Hockelburg's lack of surprise that I hadn't quite pulled it off. But there was a murmur of approval as Paul took a bite and then I did.

Then quiet fell over the yard. When I turned from Paul, I saw that the crowd was dividing, as if someone were drawing a zipper through it. When the split reached the table where we stood, there, with that empty space unfurling behind her, as if she'd traveled along it up a red carpet, was Josie.

For the first time in three years and four months I looked into my not-quite reflection: a face like my face but brighter, plucked and buffed and lotioned to a pearly sheen. Sharper, too, its lines more forcefully carved, its shadows statelier and more dramatic.

Calmly smiling, even as I felt my own expression twist with shock. She wore a dress of gray crepe, with wide, fluttery sleeves, the skirt slightly flared; golden red curls clustered along her jaw like bunches of marigolds, in striking contrast to her wide, flat blue hat.

"My sister, the bride!" she said, her voice so clear and booming it must have reached every ear in the yard, though she had delivered the line most directly to the man who was trailing her with a large camera. "Oh, Harriet, dear Harriet. The happiest of days!"

Before I could say a word she was behind the table, taking my hands in hers and pulling me away from Paul. She kissed my cheek and the camera clicked, and for an instant, all I saw was flash.

UPSTAIRS, IN THE BEDROOM WHERE I HAD FRESHENED up before the reception, Paul leaned against the windowsill, smoking a cigarette. I sat at the vanity, listening through the walls as his mother berated his father and Uncle Eugene. Their voices occasionally punctured her monologue, low and meek, before she firmly reasserted control. She'd excused herself from the party minutes after Josie's arrival. Josie and her cameraman, whom she'd introduced as Justin St. John, had left not long after that, taking Mama, who had seemed bewitched by my sister, unable to pull her eyes from Josie's face. Josie had kissed me briskly and told me there was a car for me out front, that I should take my time so it didn't seem too odd, but that when I was ready, they would be waiting for me at Mama's. Her voice had sounded remote and alien, as if she'd borrowed it from the Warner Brothers lot. Not long after that, the guests had seen themselves out.

Paul cleared his throat.

"Well, I stand by it: you are more enchanting," he said, the first words either of us had spoken since we got upstairs. Both of us laughed, but then his face clenched, and he looked down at his cigarette. I fingered the bottle of perfume he had given me the evening before.

"I'm sorry I didn't tell you."

"I wish you had," he said, his voice cracking slightly. He didn't look up. "But I suppose you've been in the habit of—not telling people."

"You aren't people."

"I didn't think I was."

A door slammed, and then there was the sound of Mrs. Hockelburg striding up the hall. Paul held his breath until she'd passed.

"Mommy's on the warpath," he said.

"What will she do, do you think?"

"Oh, it depends on how the scandal shakes out. How her friends respond. She always dispenses justice as she sees fit. I suppose we have our whole lives to see how that works out in our case."

The weight of his smile seemed to press the air from my lungs. I turned to the mirror.

"She isn't a part of my life, you know," I said, running a brush through my hair. And then I was struck by shame—for not having told him, for turning from him now, for wanting so badly to get through the conversation so I could get to Josie.

I made myself go to him. I took both his hands as I had that morning at the altar, hoping he didn't notice how slick mine were, or how they trembled.

"It's almost as if I forgot to tell you because she doesn't matter. These past few weeks—these happiest of weeks—I haven't even thought of her. We won't see her. Our life will have nothing to do with her." I let him kiss me. But when he pulled me in close and traced a finger along my clavicle, I leaned away, trying to keep my smile soft, wifely, reminding myself to be Pleasant, Patient, Positive, suPportive, as that Institute pamphlet exhorted wives to act in "those little spats that inevitably afflict even devoted Christian couples."

"But now that she is here," I said, very gently, "I need to go, Paul. I need to see what she has to say."

He turned from me, but not before I saw the hurt that passed over his expression. And then there was something in his bearing, in the way his shoulders rose and fell with his breath, that all at once made me feel his authority, as if he were preparing to remind me of the vow I'd made hours earlier: to love, honor, and obey. But when he turned back he was smiling again. And in the end, he agreed that I should go. He gave me a final kiss and walked me down to the car.

WHEN I ARRIVED AT Mama's apartment, Josie was sitting on one of the living room sofas, Justin St. John flat on his back on the other, snoring softly.

She crossed the room and we embraced. She smelled like powder and lilacs and whatever chemicals made her hair that color. Her dress was soft beneath my chin, her arms bony against my back. Her heart made its rabbit patter against my own breastbone. There was no distinguishing the love I felt for her from the hate, the relief from the rage. I pulled back to look at her. Her eyes were skittish, hard. I could have spanned her wrist with my thumb and forefinger. Her fingers felt like cold twigs in my palm. Her nails were painted a witchy green, but she had chewed her cuticles raw. When she saw me noticing, she snatched her hands away with a nervous laugh. As pretty as she was—and she was impossibly pretty, pretty in a way that seemed to explain irrefutably why no one ever mistook me for Josephine Wilder, the movie star—she also looked exhausted, as if she hadn't slept through the night since she left home.

"I'm sorry, darling," she said, in something closer to her natural voice. "I guess I can't help making an entrance."

"Well, look at the two of them." Justin St. John had stood. He was tall and lean, his eyebrows thick black feathers, his skin sun-baked. He shook his head, flashing a white smile. "A picture!"

"Thank you, Justin darling. But now I must ask you to leave us. I need to explain everything to Harriet and Mother. I want the three of us to be together."

"Of course, JoJo."

He kissed her cheek. She watched him go.

"Is Justin your—" I wanted to say "lover," but that didn't seem right. Boyfriend? Companion? Or maybe he was her husband now. I thought of all the men she'd been coupled with in the papers and felt a surge of hope that she had long since shed Raymond Fish. She laughed.

"You sweet thing. He's my press man and he's queer as fruit cocktail." My cheeks colored. "Have I shocked you?"

I shook my head, wishing I could explain exactly how un-shocked I was. But the words jammed in my throat. I recognized a nervous energy shuddering through her body and knew she was going to lift a hang-nailed finger to her mouth. She managed to stay herself, shoving her hand into her pocket.

"Pockets in a dress. How darling," I said.

"I have them put into all my clothes, so, you know." She waved her chewed-up fingers at me.

Mama came in from the kitchen, teapot in her free hand. I knew if I tried to take it from her she would brush me off, but it pleased me to think that when she came to live with Paul and me, a maid would do that sort of thing. "Did Mr. St. John—"

"He had to go," Josie said, shrugging.

I sat in the spot Justin St. John had abandoned. Mama sat across from me, and Josie took the armchair in between. Mama poured tea. No one spoke until the tea was fully distributed, as if we'd all agreed to wait, as if those were the terms of the parley.

"Something has happened," Josie finally said. She blinked a few times. "I have not been faithful to my husband. I have never been faithful to my husband. At least not for a long time. Harriet, you spoke to him once—maybe you're not surprised."

Mama looked at me sharply. I sloshed a little tea in my lap and hurried to blot it up. Josie went on, not seeming to notice that the revelation that I'd spoken to Raymond Fish had made any ripple between Mama and me. Something tightened in my heart—god, how reckless she always was with her words.

"Ray was the one who insisted, years ago, that no one could ever know the truth about our family. He said we were a joke, that no one would hire me if they knew my history. Eventually I realized that this wasn't quite true. I don't think anyone would have minded,

really, about our little act. The bigger problem was my age—
I wouldn't have gotten the work I got if the studio had known I was
a minor. But that's the thing about Ray—he has a way of making the
truth feel so slippery. As if you've missed the point, and he's being
very patient about your terrific stupidity. It took me a while to see
this because at the beginning it was so much fun. I was making us
rich. We were happy."

"Were you?" I asked before I could stop myself, ashamed that the
question wasn't fully motivated by pure sisterly concern but by
something coarser—the nosiness of a fan. She shrugged, twisting a
bracelet around her wrist.

"As happy as anyone, I suppose."

Mama leaned over the arm of the sofa and touched the arm of
Josie's chair, as if she didn't quite dare touch Josie herself.

"Go on," she said.

Josie took a long drink of her tea.

"Things soured for us some time ago. But Raymond always said
that if I tried to leave him he would expose me as a liar, report the
work I did underage, and destroy my career. I believed him, so I
stuck around. And for a while, we seemed to have an understanding.
But my latest indiscretion has been indiscreet, and now Raymond is
on a tear. It doesn't help that I'm not as bankable, at the moment, as
I have been in the past. I assume you've seen the papers." She smiled
bitterly. "A year ago, the studio would have smoothed everything
over for me. But things are more complicated just now."

She put down her teacup and straightened her spine. I had a vision of her rehearsing this speech as she must rehearse her film
roles, mapping out every gesture, every shift of expression.

"Two days ago, a friend of Mr. St. John's, a reporter, telephoned.
Raymond, it seems, has a diary of mine. He's trying to sell it, along
with all the rest: the Siamese Sweets, my affairs. Some other girls
might make hay out of this situation, but I'm a little boxed in, I'm
afraid. I'm not even supposed to be married. He liked me making
news with those men, you know, at the time. Flirtations were very

charming for Josephine Wilder, single girl. Less so for Mrs. Raymond Fish." She brushed her hands over her pointy knees, as if to
say, that is that.

"It was Mr. St. John's idea for me to come here. You see, Harriet,
your wedding really couldn't have come at a better time. My sister
getting married to a man from an upstanding family, and Old Uncle
Eugene officiating? I wish he and I had had a chance to talk—the
two of us are in the same business, really." She laughed. "But it's all
so very wholesome, you see. It puts a different spin on the situation."

"How did you even know?" I asked.

"I've kept tabs on you, sissy. Shit." She looked down at her thumb.
She had scraped away a nub of skin; a red bead of blood was bloom-
ing beside the nail. I handed her my handkerchief, which she accepted without a word, without a shift in her expression. "That
picture of us will run in the papers tomorrow. And we'll do an interview first thing in the morning with Mary Pancake on WGN. *The
Stars Speak*. You know the program? We'll scoop Ray, explain the Siamese Sweets before he can. And I've already done an interview
about my impending divorce, which will come out in next week's
Hollywood Spy. The reporter's a friend. So if Ray tries to come after
me, he'll just look like a big bully peddling old news. I'll already have
the public on my side."

"Josie, tomorrow morning—"

"Don't worry about a thing. Justin has the whole interview plotted out. We'll go over the points. And I'll do most of the talking."

"But Josie, I'm leaving in the morning. For my honeymoon."

"But you can't." She frowned. It was as if she had never considered the possibility of my refusal. As if as far as she knew, I was still
a meek girl, waiting for my sister to write, to telephone, to give me
permission to resume my life. "I need you."

Mama leaned a little farther over the arm of the couch, toward
Josie. "Josephine, what you're asking your sister—"

Josie stood and faced her.

"Is it more than you asked of me?" she asked, her voice oddly flat, as if she'd played the moment in her imagination too many times, draining it of its intensity. "A little girl, who couldn't have said no if she'd wanted to?" Her jaw tightened and her nostrils flared slightly. Mama looked tired as she gazed at Josie, pressing a fist into her bad hip. Finally, Josie's lips twitched with something like a smile. She turned to me. "Harriet, I just need an hour of your time, then you can run off with your husband and forget all about me, if that's what you want."

"Of course that's not what I want," I said, indignant, as if I hadn't said as much to Paul an hour earlier. I took Josie's hand. It was cold and stiff, and I could see the seams in her makeup, the exhausted, yellowish skin underneath. My desire to say yes to her, to meet her need, pulled like gravity. I glanced at Mama, expecting resistance, expecting an admonition not to risk everything we'd just won, but she was still looking at Josie, transfixed, like the Foolish Daughter Uncle Eugene had once described, who had allowed herself to be enticed by sin. I didn't know if helping Josie was sinful. I suspected it was foolish. But marriage was permanent—that was exactly the point. I'd gained for us the freedom to take risks. Paul would understand.

"I'll change my ticket."

Josie took a deep breath through her nose and let it out with a sigh.

"I suppose I should send for Mr. St. John," she said. "He can go over everything you need for tomorrow, and I can get out of your hair—"

"Wait." Mama stood. "Won't you—stay for a while. We've heard nothing of your life—of the years—" She pressed the back of her hand against her mouth and fell back to her seat. *Stay,* I echoed Mama's plea, fiercely, silently.

Josie was quiet for a long while.

"I suppose I could use another cup of tea," she said at last.

She told us stories, formed things, glittering and practiced. The slightly racier versions of anecdotes we might have read about her in the fan magazines: madcap nights with names we knew, jokes at her own mild expense—daffy things she'd said in front of important men, the time she'd gotten lost on her way to a party at her own house. But eventually, we began to speak of the past. The life we'd shared. Josie claimed not to recall half the stories Mama and I told about our time on the road, but now and then she lit up, assented to our having been at a particular theater in a particular town with a particular lineup. Sometimes she added a detail or two, often seedier or sadder than the details at the front of my own mind but undeniably and satisfyingly true. A few times, she recalled something about the act so sharp-edged it threatened to split the surface of our reunion, to expose the stark facts of our family and its failures. But every time, the three of us recovered; it was as if we had all decided that the time we had together would be nice, that we would make it nice. Whenever Josie and I made the same gesture or said the same word in unison, I felt a deep, sweet pleasure.

Mama produced a bottle of champagne, and a second, from a case Vera had sent over earlier in the week, not knowing the wedding would be dry. Eventually, light flooded the window, thick and red-rimmed. When it faded, Josie and I went from table to table, turning on the lamps. I thought guiltily of Paul, alone in our suite at the Drake. When we got hungry, Mama apologized that she had so little on hand and offered to scramble some eggs. Josie got on the phone and forty minutes later, two black-clad waiters pushed a feast on carts into the apartment. I remembered only then that I'd hardly eaten at my wedding luncheon. Impossible to think that it had happened only hours before. Josie shook a few pills from a little silver box—vitamins, she said, coolly—and then watched while Mama and I ate our fill, pleased, it seemed, to preside over our comfort. The phone rang twice. We didn't answer.

It was after ten when Mama emptied the last of a third bottle of champagne into Josie's glass and asked, "Do you ever see your father?"

Josie widened her eyes theatrically. "Mon dieu."

"It's a simple enough question." Mama placed the empty bottle on the coffee table.

"I have seen him."

Mama waited. Josie emptied her glass and gave her hair a shake.

"He turned up a year ago, on the lot. He was living in an appalling little place on San Julian Street with, I don't know, a pack of feral dogs. He smelled like a still. It seems he had sent some letters, which it seems I had ignored. That afternoon he made a scene with the guards. Raymond and I decided it would be better to meet with him than have him running his mouth."

"Well?" Mama said. She stared at Josie as if I weren't in the room.

"He wanted help. Connections in the business. Raymond thought we'd better give him what he asked for. Raymond thought he was shaking us down, and maybe he was. It's hard to say."

"And now?"

Josie brushed invisible crumbs from her lap.

"He's a special effects man for Paramount," she said, lightly. "You'll see him in the credits as Larry Salt. But I don't see him at all, by agreement, and he doesn't try to see me." She stood then and stretched, the wide sleeves of her dress fluttering like wings. "It's late. We have an early start tomorrow. I should get back to the hotel."

The phone had just finished ringing again. I stood up and turned on my ankle. I had to reach out a hand to steady myself.

"That was Paul, I'm sure of it," I said. "I should go too."

"Can't I have both of my girls under the same roof, for one night?" Mama said.

Josie ran her fingers along the back of her chair, looking as if she didn't particularly trust Mama's display of sentiment. But then she shrugged.

"I could have my driver bring over my things," she said.

"But Paul—"

"He'll make do," Mama said.

And maybe it was the champagne, maybe it was the weight of a long, strange day, but I wanted to say yes, to submit to this rendering of our family: the three of us, together again. Maybe my staying in Mama's apartment was as correct and inevitable as my marriage to Paul had been, as Mama's choreography had been in the prime of the Siamese Sweets.

Josie insisted I borrow a pair of her pajamas—pink-and-white striped, made from the smoothest silk I'd ever felt.

"Are you scared?" she asked, when I turned off the bedroom light. "Of Paul?"

"Scared of him?"

"Consummation. The marital act."

"Oh. That." I heard the smirk in my voice, and Josie did too. She swatted at me. I wished then that we had said good night to Mama hours before: already there was an ease between us we hadn't managed with Mama in the room. But my eyelids were heavy now; morning already felt so near.

"Aren't you a surprise! Is he the only one?"

My cheeks grew hot. I felt as if I ought to tell her such things, ought to want to tell her. But she'd been gone so long.

"How would you like it if I asked you something like that, Josie?"

"Oh, my affairs have all been in the papers. Some of it's true. Enough of it. Besides, I've been a married woman for quite a while."

"Was it dreadful with Raymond?"

"He has moles on his back. Big, lumpy black moles. I used to pretend they were connect-the-dots, to pass the time. I think he thought I was being sexy."

"Josephine! That's revolting."

"But that hasn't been part of things for a while."

"That's good, I guess."

"Yes." She was quiet for a bit. "I'm in love with someone, though."

"Who with?"

"Dougie Taft."

"Ha!" I sat up and clapped my hands. "I knew it! In the bakery scene in *Lady at the Helm,* where you're rolling that dough and there's that cloud of flour and when it settles you're kissing. I could tell, I could just tell. I even told Ruth, I think my sister really is in love with Dougie Taft. She said you were just actors, that you were acting. But I knew."

"You go to my pictures?"

"Of course I do, Josie."

She smiled down at the quilt. I waited for her to ask after Ruth. The silence grew long.

"Is that who you're leaving Raymond for?"

"I suppose. In theory. But he wants me to retire when we have children, and I think I'd go out of my skull. No offense."

"Why exactly should I take offense to that?"

"Oh, Harriet, so touchy! I only meant because you're married now. On the cusp of the domestic bliss that women in this family have historically failed to achieve. Good for you."

"Not Aunt Marion," I said, wanting, again, for her to ask about Ruth. For a long while, we lay there, not talking; but neither of us went to sleep.

"You know she had another baby, right?"

"Aunt Marion?"

"No. Mama."

"Ha ha," I said. She shifted to look at me, resting her head on her bent arm.

"It's true. A baby boy. Before I left I looked through her things. I was looking for money. But I found this photograph of a man who looked just like you. I knew we had to be related. His name was on the back: Robert Lodge."

"Oh. Right." I remembered the photograph I'd found when Josie had returned all my letters and I'd snooped through my parents' things. "I found that picture too. I thought he looked like you. That's Mama's son?"

I didn't realize how loudly I was laughing until Josie swatted my arm.

"You'll wake her."

"I thought it was her boyfriend."

Now Josie laughed. I tried to catch my breath, but as soon as I managed, Josie sputtered, and whenever she got herself under control, I started laughing again.

"How did you find out? About our brother?" The word "brother"

made us laugh some more, our laughter threaded with a bright fila-
ment of grief.

"If you have money you can always get information," she said
when we'd calmed. "A few months back I was—I don't know, bored,
or lonely. And that name came back to me—Robert Lodge—and I
decided to track him down. I hired a private investigator. Of course,
her name wasn't in the records, but I put the pieces together. That
was why she left home. Why she never talked about those years. She
would have been fifteen." She picked a loose thread in the quilt,
then spoke with great excitement. "Oh, and guess who arranged the
adoption?"

"Who?"

"Uncle Eugene. So you see? He was our brother's father. That's
probably why Daddy hated him so much. And why Aunt Marion
was such a bitch."

I concentrated on the blue square of moonlight stamped on the
wall, remembering my birthday, Mama and Uncle Eugene's reminiscing, the sudden shift in the mood. I was certain that Josie was
right: Robert Lodge was our mother's child. But I was just as certain
that James Creggs had been the baby's father. That Uncle Eugene
had stepped in and taken responsibility where his brother had failed.

It was too delicate a story to tell Josie. I missed Ruth with sudden fierceness.

"I don't think so," I said at last, pulling the quilt up over my
shoulder.

"You were always such a goody-goody, Harriet. You never wanted
to believe that Mama or Daddy could do anything bad."

I wanted to tell her she was wrong about them, and wrong about
me. I wanted to ask her if that's why she'd gone—to punish them. If
there was anything I could have done to make her stay. If she was
sorry. But I also wanted to be the steward of Mama's secret. What
was left of it. Even if that meant letting Josie hold on to whatever
idea of me she'd projected forward in time from the girl she'd known,
however little that idea had to do with the person I'd actually become.

We passed several minutes in silence.

"Thank you for tomorrow, Harriet."

"You're welcome."

"You'll follow my lead?"

"Of course."

"We need to get this right."

"Don't worry."

There was another long quiet. I began to sink under the weight of sleep.

"Justin thinks we should sing."

"Oh?"

"Just a little. Casually. Mary Pancake will ask if we want to. It will play like we're doing it on the fly."

"I see."

"Justin thinks people will really like it."

"Hmm."

"Do you want to try it now, Harriet? Just to see if we still can?"

I sat up. She was wide awake, staring at me, her gaze reminding me so much of Daddy's—the need in it—that my breath caught. She reached toward my right hand with her left, spreading her fingers in our old sister salute, and then she tapped her fingers against mine, one, two, three, four, five.

Behind my breastbone, an old desire turned like a key. I tapped back. She smiled with what appeared to be all the love I'd ever wanted from her and hummed a note. I matched the pitch. We didn't even need to nod. The old intuition was ready, the private telegraph humming. We sang softly, the same song we had sung the first time Daddy put us in the harness:

"The cat has his cradle, the fish has the sea, I've got my sister, my sister's got me."

Our quiet voices spun together, formed a perfect, shimmering thread. The bedroom, the apartment, Mama, my wedding day— they all fell away. We sang for each other and to each other. The song was like an event outside of time, a kink in the universe that resurrected my five-year-old self, granted for the first time a share of my sister's breath and muscle, and my almost-sixteen-year-old self, who didn't know she would never feel it again. I'd seen Josie act. I knew her affectionate, grateful expression could be a performance. But I didn't care. It felt real.

"We go together," we sang, "like coffee and cream!"

As the last note stopped ringing, ordinary time reclaimed us. I slipped back into myself, into the dim blue light of the bedroom, into the soft swaddle of my borrowed pajamas. Josie reached over to the nightstand for her little silver box and selected another pill, which she swallowed without water.

"For sleep," she said, and lay back on her pillow. She was quiet a moment. "You're a good sister, Harriet."

The silence grew long. Finally, I forced out the expected answer.

"You are too, Josie."

But what did I mean? Not those words, not really. Maybe only this: as I'd made Josie wait to hear them, I'd felt the prick of her indignation in my own heart.

Her breath was soon steady with sleep. But I was wide awake, watching the hands of my alarm clock hurtle toward tomorrow. I tried to picture the rest of my life, as if it were a film and I could speed up the reel. It ought to have been possible. I knew the script; the cast was set. But my mind was blank. I couldn't picture going on the radio with Josie in the morning. I couldn't summon the feeling of Paul's kiss, I couldn't imagine his warmth beside me in bed, let alone the rest that I knew must follow: the home we would make together, the child, the children.

Sometime after midnight, I slipped out of bed and tiptoed down the hall. I pulled Mama's trench coat over my pajamas and grabbed my pocketbook, thinking I'd just step outside a moment, have a cigarette, clear my head. But when I got downstairs the doorman was asleep, the street was quiet, the night warm and smooth. It was easy to feel invisible. To move.

I coursed empty streets, thinking of Josie at fourteen, sneaking out of that hotel in Berwyn to follow Mama. How exhilarating it must have been: violating all the rules that had never been a source of comfort to her, the way they had been to me. I thought of Mama somewhere up ahead of her, unsuspecting. What had she wanted, when she slipped away from a hotel in a strange town? To catch her breath? To shock herself briefly out of the reality of her life? I wished I could know.

My routes through the North Side were etched deep into my muscles; before I knew it, my feet had carried me the mile to Vera's. The music hall had closed the year before and the street was lifeless save at Vera's house, where the attic light burned. It had been months since I'd gone over, and there was something strange about the place—the light on in the attic, the rest of the house dark. Vera crossed in front of the alcove window, her fists digging into her back as she stretched. It was only then that I noticed the sign in the lawn: the house had been sold.

The door was locked, but the spare key was where it had always been kept, behind the loose brick in the front path. I let myself in. All along the dark hallway, doors opened onto empty rooms. There was a crate where the registration desk had been, waiting to be nailed shut. Upstairs, on the bathroom door, there was a dark square where the sign had hung, informing guests they were entitled to one bath a week.

I opened the door to the attic.

"Hello?"

She screamed, and then she came out of one of the rooms off the plywood hallway that cut through what had once been our apartment. Her hair was wrapped in a cloth and she wore rubber gloves up to her elbow.

"Jesus Mary and Joseph. Is it just you?"

"Yes."

She looked at me as if I were made of glass, as if I might shatter if she breathed wrong.

"Come on down," she finally said. "We'll talk. You carry that bucket for me and maybe I'll forgive you for scaring ten years off my life."

In her sitting room, she pulled a tarp off a couch and went to put on a kettle. The shelves were stripped, the walls bare. She returned with a half-eaten box of chocolates, a pot of tea, and a bottle of whiskey.

"Slim pickings," she said, sitting down next to me. "So you're not with your husband." She didn't sound surprised.

"What's going on? You sold the house? Does Mama know?"

She poured the tea.

"You go first. What happened with your sister? Where's Mr. Hockelburg?"

I explained, as quickly as I could, all that had happened since Josie turned up at the wedding. "Now you."

She stirred whiskey into her teacup with her finger, watching me anxiously.

"Your mother wanted to wait," she finally said. "She was going to write. She didn't want to risk spooking you. When you were so close." She studied my face. "You know, you look so much like your mother. When she was your age."

"Josie does," I said. "Josie's like Mama."

She shook her head.

"It's something about your eyes. The way you look when you concentrate."

"What was Mama going to write about, Vera?"

She sighed.

"My husband died. In the fall. There are some friends of ours—Fleischer's girls, from the old days—who live in Boca Raton. A little pink cottage on the beach. I always knew that someday I'd sell this place and join them. After your father left, your mother decided she would come too. She just needed to see you set up first."

So that was why Mama had come home so upset that night in October; that was why she had grown so impatient about my choosing a husband. Mr. Broom had died, making the prospect of her own freedom suddenly, tantalizingly near. I looked down at my lap, unable to bear Vera's gentle, searching expression. How foolish I had been, to imagine Mama meekly trailing Paul and me into our new lives together. She had never needed taking care of. About that much, Ruth and I had both been wrong.

"Did I ever tell you how we met?" Vera held the box of chocolates out to me. I took one, conscious that Vera was about to tell me a story from Mama's blank chapter. Something Mama hadn't wanted me to know. She seemed resigned, as if the small betrayal of her friend were worthwhile in service of a larger goal.

"She was younger than you are now. Only fifteen. Running away from home. We were at the train station in Cleveland. I liked her right away. You just know about a person, sometimes. She bought me a doughnut because she was afraid I was getting bored. But I wasn't bored. I never have been."

She went on. She told me about how Mama had shown up on her stoop a few months later, and how a few months after that she was going to class and learning to dance, and already, everyone could see she was something special. She told me stories Mama had told her about her girlhood and her own parents. She told me about Daddy, too—his journey across the Atlantic, his rise in the theater, stories he'd told her when he saw that becoming Vera's friend would help him win my mother's affection. She told me about their courtship, and it pleased me to think that whatever had happened between them, they'd had a proper love story. Vera told me about the accident that had left Mama lame. She told me it had been Daddy's fault. That she thought Mama would never have forgiven him, if she hadn't had to because of Josie and me.

They didn't know there were both of us, of course, until we came. Mama had run away from Daddy, gone to Ohio, to stay with Aunt Marion and Uncle Eugene and baby Ruth. Daddy had gone to retrieve her. Carefully, gingerly, Vera told me about how after our birth, Mama had been sick. Unable to care for us. How for a year, Daddy had been like father and mother both. When Mama got well again, Daddy had struggled. She told me about the day he pushed the piano to our apartment, and there Vera's stories knitted with the feathery tissue of my own memories.

She never mentioned Robert Lodge, but I could slot him in, between that train station encounter and Mama's arrival in New York. A child she hadn't wanted. A child from whom she'd fled, leaving

Uncle Eugene to clean up the mess and for the rest of their lives to possess her most painful secret.

The storytelling had run its course. For a while after, we sat in silence, drinking cold tea. When I stood, Vera begged me to stay until sunrise, but I kissed her cheek. I said goodbye.

Back on the empty street, I turned Vera's stories over in my mind. Other bits and pieces, details and moments I'd collected over a lifetime of eavesdropping and snooping and paying attention, adhered to them. I wondered how Mama had felt, discovering she was pregnant for the second time. Was there part of her that wished she could have given Josie and me away, as she had Robert Lodge?

But she hadn't given us away. She'd been a mother to us. Maybe not the mother I'd have chosen—I saw that now, that I'd always been grasping at something she hadn't been equipped to give. I'd married grasping for it, as if she would have spent the rest of our lives showering me with affection and praise because I'd been so very good, because I'd done exactly as she asked. But for Mama, my marriage had been a simpler matter. A contract satisfied. She'd fulfilled her responsibility, given me what she thought I needed. Ruth had been right about that: Mama hadn't understood me. But I believed—needed to believe—she'd done her best. We'd both done our very best.

My sense of what I owed my family seemed to fall apart and reconstitute itself. I couldn't save anyone, couldn't make anyone do anything. But I could hold on to their stories. I could know them. And I could be someone, among them—add my own stories to the family record.

But what would my stories be? It was the question that had driven me out of bed hours earlier. And still, I didn't know the answer.

I sat on the steps of a shop and lit a cigarette. The darkness over the rooftops seemed tender, precious, as it always did in that last hour or so before it would loosen with dusk, give way to the inevitability of tomorrow. The hems of Josie's lovely pajamas were damp where they'd dragged along the sidewalk. As I filled my lungs with smoke, I thought of Garth: that first cigarette, in the park, after the rain. I thought of Josie. Asleep in my bed, expecting to find me there when she woke, ready to sing with her on the radio. And then I thought of Paul, dear Paul, waiting for me at the Drake. Waiting for our life together to begin. My husband. Finally, I thought of Mama. Maybe she was dreaming of Florida. Maybe she had gotten up to do some packing, too excited to sleep. It pained me to think I would never know the version of my mother that Vera knew. But I was glad, at least, that Vera knew her. That someone did.

With sudden, stinging clarity, I understood what I had to do. What I wanted to do. I stubbed out my cigarette and ran to Clark Street, where day and night were continuous, where the lights were always on and people always out and about, where cabs made steady rounds. I hailed one—the first time I'd ever done it on my own, but I knew exactly how, it was as easy as breathing. When the driver asked me where I was going, I started to laugh. He stared at me in the rearview mirror, and I knew I must look deranged, in Josie's pajamas and Mama's coat, laughing wildly. That only made me laugh harder. I couldn't stop. I didn't want to. I felt as if a soft, good substance were filling my chest, pressing against my ribs. It was happiness, but a happiness that felt nearly like grief, so thick was it, so thick I could hardly breathe.

"Look, lady, I don't have all—"

"Sorry, sorry," I said, patting the wet corner of my eye with the back of my hand. "Take me to Union Station."

EPILOGUE

LINDA DELANEY TURNS OFF THE TAPE RECORDER.

"You went to Ruth?"

I nod. "I had our honeymoon tickets in my purse. I traded them for a seat on the New York Special."

"What about your husband?"

"Oh, that was easy. An annulment. His mother pulled strings to move the paperwork along. He was a good sport. Poor Paul."

"And Josie?"

"I never saw her again."

"Never? Did you talk on the phone? Did you write?"

"I went to her pictures. I read the magazines." Like any other fan.

"So," she says, with a little sigh. "The end."

I lean toward her.

"Or the beginning."

She smiles indulgently.

"Endings, happy or otherwise," I go on, shaking my head, needing her to understand. "It doesn't work that way. My life—it's been like any other. Closed chapters and false starts, minor victories, regrets great and small. Love. Its absence. Loneliness, and stretches of blinding grief. Happiness too. But, you see, it's all added up to a life I chose. A life that belonged to me."

For a moment, she holds her pen over her notepad, chewing

thoughtfully on the edge of her lip. Then she smiles. She puts her pen and notepad in her briefcase and starts to break down her tape recorder.

I sit back, deflated. After all these hours, I haven't gotten through. I have no doubt, now: in Miss Delaney's telling, I'll be nothing but the dull sister left behind. My life blotted out by the incandescence of Josie's. So what now? How do I hold on to the truth of Josie's unwitting gift, her clearing of the stage? The truth of those years in Chicago and all that came after?

We shake hands at the door. Back in the study, I watch through the window as she hurries up the road, as if she can't wait to get to work, as if she can hardly keep up with her own abundant expectations. And despite my disappointment, I feel a rush of tenderness, for Miss Delaney and for the girl I once was—to be so young. So near, still, to the beginning of things.

When she's out of sight, I cut Josie's obituary from the paper and give her headshot a kiss. I put it away in the trunk, along with my parents' stories. Back at my desk I close my eyes so I don't have to look at the morning's failed writing, still sitting in the typewriter. I'll rest a bit, I decide, and then I'll call Ruth at the office. A decade has passed since she moved into this house: joining forces in our dotage as we did in our youth, though that distinction doesn't mean much in her case. She refuses to retire, and is out half the nights of the week: meetings of the board of the women's clinic, poetry group, peace vigils in the square.

Yes, I'll call Ruth, and I'll ask her to stop by the video store on her way home and pick up a couple of Josephine Wilder classics: *Lady at the Helm*, perhaps, and *Don't Tell Father*. And maybe that last one, if she can find it, that made-for-TV thing. *Killer Hornets from Space*. I laugh, remembering. Josie, facelifted within an inch of her life and shellacked in makeup, stung to death fifteen minutes in. But she was having a hell of a time. I could tell. I could always tell.

Maybe Ruth can get some ice cream too. I'll pour whiskey. It will be a memorial. A last goodbye. Or maybe just the last note of the same goodbye I started saying all those years ago in Union Station, famished, bleary-eyed, wearing my sister's rumpled silk pajamas. I'll finish saying it, and then I'll live the rest of the story. Here—as I drift toward a nap, it's beginning again: the loudspeaker crackling "all aboard" and a puff of air beneath the carriage. My heartbeat as strong as the chug of the train as we pull out of the station, into the blinding afternoon.

ACKNOWLEDGMENTS

AMONG THE MANY SOURCES I CONSULTED IN WRITING this book, the following were of particular importance: *The Gold Coast and the Slum,* by Harvey Zorbaugh; *Opera in Chicago,* by Ronald L. Davis; *American Vaudeville,* by Douglas Gilbert; *Dining in Chicago,* by John Drury; and *John Sloan's New York Scene.* Ned Wayburn was a real person (though as a character in this book he is pure fiction), and his 1925 book, *The Art of Stage Dancing,* was an invaluable resource.

Some of the ideas and examples in Eugene's sermons come from *The Great Friendship and Other Sermons,* by John W. Holland; *Doran's Minister's Manual,* by G. B. F. Hallock; and *"Billy" Sunday: The Man and His Message,* by William T. Ellis. (Eugene's background as a baseball player was also inspired by Billy Sunday.) His explanation of marriage comes from *The Adventure of Being a Wife,* by Mrs. Norman Vincent Peale. While the Institute for Bible Studies is a fictional creation, some of the details of its operations and radio broadcasts come from the archives of the Moody Bible Institute.

For answering my questions about trains, thank you to Ken Hough. For answering my questions about twins, thank you to Sarah Corney (and thank you to Addison and Andrea for the example of your teeth). For answering my questions about piano moving, and for sending me an inspiring photo of a vintage cart, thank you to Mark Ripatti of Beethoven Pianos. And for answering my questions about mail service in the 1930s, thank you to Baasil Wilder, librarian at the National Postal Museum.

*

I'M SO GRATEFUL TO WHITNEY FRICK, WHO FROM THE FIRST had such a perfect and intimate understanding of this book that her questions sometimes made me feel as if she were thinking with a better version of my own brain, and to Rose Fox, whose brilliant suggestions have made this book immeasurably better. A dream team! Deepest thanks to Rebecca Gradinger for her patience, wisdom, and insightful readings of many drafts, and for the great care and skill with which she's shepherded this book into the world.

Thank you to Muriel Jorgensen and Ted Allen for their attention to all the details, and to everyone at the Dial Press.

From my earliest childhood, I was extraordinarily fortunate to have learned from incredible teachers. A lifetime of gratitude to Rossann Baker-Priestly, Leo Ramer, Chris Waters, Alice Gambel, Judith Hurdle, Virginia Oram, Dan Bourne, Ansley Valentine, Peter Havholm, Deb Shostak, and Jeff Roche.

Thank you to Aria Sloss and MJ Wesner for wonderful writing workshops that came just when I needed them.

The Iowa Writers' Workshop changed my life. I will be forever grateful to Sam Chang, who is a national treasure, and to all of my teachers there: Ethan Canin, Marilynne Robinson, Ayana Mathis, Andrew Sean Greer, and Julie Orringer. Thank you to Jan Zenisek, Deb West, and Kelly Smith for keeping the place running. For many years, every time I got into a pickle Connie Brothers was the person who got me out of it. I love her dearly and will never be able to thank her enough.

Thank you to all of my classmates and Iowa friends, from whom I learned so much. For their many kindnesses, particular thanks to Alexia Arthurs, Carleen Coulter, E. J. Fischer, Christa Fraser, Rafael Frumkin, Jorge Guerra, Yaa Gyasi, Ellen Kamoe, Carmen

Machado, Paul Maisano, Ben Mauk, Dina Nayeri, David Owen, Jen Percy, Margaret Reges, Helen Rubinstein, Susannah Shive, Kevin Smith, Tony Tulathimutte, and Jamie Watkins.

Thank you to the Truman Capote Foundation for making that vital time possible.

I'm grateful to all of the incredible students who have made teaching one of the great joys of my life. For giving me the chance to teach, thank you to Stephen Lovely at the Iowa Young Writers' Studio. At the Magid Center, I'm grateful to Danny Khalastchi and Alli Rockwell. And at Sackett Street, many thanks to Julia Fierro.

Huge thanks to everyone at Prairie Lights, especially Jan Weismiller, Karl Catlin, Terry Cain, Kathleen Johnson, and Victoria Walton, for making it one of my favorite places in the world (and for letting me work there—the best job I ever had!). And to the café crew, especially Sam Caster and Caitlin Bradford—thank you for putting up with all my loitering.

I am ever grateful to my DESCO (and DESCO-adjacent) pals: thank you Drew Ashwood, Aidan O'Connor, Eugenie Kim, Tyler Poniatowski, Kari Elassal, Erik Simpson, Sarah Richardson, and Brenna Mead. Special thanks to Judd Merrill, who read an early draft of this book. Thank you to Eddie Fishman and John Rustum for being great bosses.

Thank you to Matt Matros. Thank you to Lindsay and Indy Wilczynski. Thank you to Ryan Hontz and the Wine and Shine crew.

Thank you to all the Weisses, Parkers, Hayfords, Johnsons, and Jacksons. I'm especially grateful to my parents, Drew and Deborah Weiss, for never questioning (out loud) the series of increasingly impractical life choices that made it possible for me to finish this book.

My grandmother, Paula Weiss, was this book's biggest cheerleader. My great aunt and uncle, Arlene and Jerry Gross, made me feel like a real writer when I was just a kid. I miss them terribly and wish so much that I could have shared the finished version of this book with them.

Julia Weiss and Elizabeth Uzelac are my sisters; I would be lost without them.

Riley Johnson: you made every word of this book better and truer, and you make every moment of my life richer, warmer, and more beautiful. Lucy: you've made the world new again. I love you both with everything I am.

THE
SISTERS
SWEET

ELIZABETH
WEISS

Random
House
Book Club

Because
Stories Are
Better Shared

TM

A BOOK CLUB GUIDE

A LETTER FROM
ELIZABETH WEISS

Dear Reader,

I first learned about vaudeville at the age of eight, when I performed in a children's theater production at the old Orpheum Theatre in Galesburg, Illinois. I loved everything about that place: the ornate proscenium arch. The scent and heft of the curtains. The grungy dressing rooms, bearing many years' worth of nicks and stains. The ghosts—oh, there were definitely ghosts, who sent an unmistakable shiver down your spine if you happened to find yourself backstage alone. A decade ago, when I started researching *The Sisters Sweet,* memories of the Orpheum came rushing back, brought to new life by every detail I learned about this bygone era.

But the more I wrote, the more my curiosity was drawn by what lay beyond the glitz and spectacle—the real human stories that played out after the curtain fell—and questions that, as time wore on, began to feel more personal: How might a family be shaped by life on the stage and on the road? What would it feel like to watch a dream you'd been striving for your whole life slip through your fingers? And what if that dream had never really been yours in the first place?

Harriet Szász, the protagonist of this novel, lacks her mother's talent, her sister's charisma, and her father's hunger for glory. But she is nevertheless a product of her upbringing in the theater, where she and her sister, Josie, pose as conjoined twins in a vaudeville act. When Josie exposes the fraud and runs off to Hollywood, the rest of the family retreats to Chicago, where Harriet has to figure out what it would mean to live life on her own terms and decide whether she dares to try.

In telling Harriet's story, even as I turned toward the past— reading about Depression-era Chicago and early 20th century stage dancing, studying old sermons and cookbooks and high school curricula, watching pre-Code movies—I found myself looking more deeply inward, drawing on my own experiences of sisterhood and familial expectations and performance and failure and friendship and love. I hope the result is a book that will draw you fully into another world, bringing to life a cast of complicated women who must navigate the constraints of that time and place, and at the same time illuminate the struggles we still go through to know ourselves—to discover, and fight for, our own dreams.

WITH GRATITUDE,
Elizabeth Weiss

DISCUSSION
QUESTIONS

1.   While *The Sisters Sweet* is largely about Harriet's journey to discover her own dreams, it's also a novel about sisters. Why do you think Elizabeth Weiss decided to write Harriet and Josie's story solely through Harriet's perspective? How does focusing on Harriet's viewpoint influence your understanding of the sisters' relationship?

2.   Weiss writes, "Just beyond my pride there had been something else, the awareness that my mother was as real as I was, that the boundaries of her experience extended somewhere beyond my view." Discuss the relationship between Harriet and her mother, Maude. How well do you think we can ever know our mothers?

3.   In the first half of the novel, Harriet understands her identity primarily through the eyes of her parents: "But now it was as if Mama had altered the past as well, erased everything I had always understand to be true about myself." How do you think Harriet's parents shaped her identity? How does her sense of self evolve throughout the book? And how deeply do you think we allow our parents to define us?

4.   Performance is a major theme in the novel. What types of performance did you notice, both literal and metaphorical?

5.   Josie was the one who left. Harriet was the one who stayed. Or as Weiss writes, "She had run because she was Josie, and I had stayed because I was me. We'd already had our catego-

ries." How else do you see characters conform to their seemingly predefined categories in the novel? Why do you think we tend to define ourselves in relation to other people?

6.   In some ways, *The Sisters Sweet* is about what we owe our families and what we owe ourselves. Where do you think that distinction lies for Harriet? Where does it lie for you?

7.   What did you think of Lenny? Do you think he is the villain of the story, or did you find him to be a sympathetic character? How was he different as a husband and as a father?

8.   At one point, Harriet muses, "Maybe I had learned that rules could be changed, but rules still pricked something in me, they still marked clear, useful edges." How do themes of obedience and rebellion play out in the novel?

9.   Ambition is another pivotal theme in *The Sisters Sweet*. How does each character struggle with their ambition? Did you notice any parallels between characters?

10.   If you could write a different ending for Harriet and Josie, would you? What would you change?

VAUDEVILLE
SISTER ACTS

From the 1880s to the 1930s, singers, actors, dancers, pianists, trombonists, fiddle players, quick-draw artists, magicians, female impersonators, fire eaters, stripteasers, jugglers, contortionists, and performers of every imaginable stripe appeared on vaudeville stages from coast to coast, delivering variety entertainment to the masses. For many of those vaudevillians, as for Harriet and Josephine Sweet, work was a sisterly affair.

THE CHERRY SISTERS

ACCOUNTS VARY AS to why the Cherry Sisters—Ella, Effie, Lizzie, Addie, and Jessie—first decided to step away from their hardscrabble farm life and put on a show. Their debut concert was in 1893, at the Daniels Opera House in Marion, Iowa. A decades-long career followed, with the sisters, in various combinations, singing, playing, acting, and reciting, often works of their own composition. They won a following, but not for the reasons they might have preferred: billed as the "World's Worst Sister Act," they were met by audiences with jeering, tossing of projectiles (rotten produce, rocks, cigars), and a general spirit of outrage that all became part of the show.

BESSIE AND NELLIE McCOY

THE TWIN DAUGHTERS of pedestal clog dancers Minnie McEvoy and Billy McCoy, Bessie and Nellie were nine years old when they finagled their way onto the bill of one of their parents' shows and performed an act of their own devising (or so the story goes). After a successful kiddie run, each attempted a solo career, but Bessie was the breakout star, becoming known as the "Yama Yama Girl" after her signature 1909 performance of a song of that name.

THE DUNCAN SISTERS

ONE OF THE most successful sister acts of the early twentieth century, Rosetta and Vivian Duncan became known for their musical comedy take on *Uncle Tom's Cabin,* in which Vivian played Eva, and Rosetta, in blackface, played Topsy. (Vaudeville contributed its own chapter to America's shameful racial history. Blackface and minstrelsy were foundational to the development of the form, and racist tropes and ethnic stereotypes were commonplace on vaudeville stages.) The Duncans resurrected their Eva and Topsy routine during every phase of their careers, until Rosetta's death in a car accident in 1959.

THE DOLLY SISTERS

BORN IN HUNGARY, twin sisters Rosie and Jenny Dolly were teenagers in 1909 when they made their vaudeville debut in a tandem dance routine. They later posed as conjoined twins in the Ziegfeld Follies and eventually earned the record for the longest run by a sister act at the Palace Theatre in New York, vaudeville's top stage. The Dollys became true celebrities, their love affairs and Jazz Age lifestyle overshadowing their artistry. A car accident in 1933 left Jenny gravely injured and initiated the tragic last chapter of the sisters' lives. Jenny died by suicide in 1941. After her own suicide attempt in 1962, Rosie died in 1970 at the age of 78.

THE GUMM SISTERS

BORN INTO A family of entertainers—their father was a singer and their mother played the piano, and together they operated a theater in Minnesota—Mary Ann, Dorothy, and Frances Gumm were destined for the stage. Little Frances was only three when she started performing with her sisters, but she quickly distinguished herself as the star. After the family moved to Los Angeles, the girls continued to tour and appeared in some short films while they waited for their big Hollywood break. In 1934, at the age of twelve, the baby of the family was spotted by an MGM scout. By then, she was going by her stage name: Judy Garland.

DAISY AND VIOLET HILTON

DAISY AND VIOLET HILTON were born in 1908, conjoined at the hip. Their mother abandoned them to the care of a midwife, who exhibited them in a pub and later forced them to appear in circus sideshows. Under the constant threat of their adoptive mother's abuse, Daisy and Violet learned to play instruments and to sing, their talent proving as much of a draw as their physical anomaly. Eventually, under the management—and strict control—of a man named Meyer Meyers, they became the highest-paid act in vaudeville. They were in their twenties when they gained legal freedom from Meyers and the right to their own earnings, but by then, vaudeville was in its decline, and in the coming decades, the sisters struggled to find their footing in the shifting entertainment landscape. They died in poverty and obscurity in 1969.

SOURCES:

No Applause Just Throw Money, by Trav S.D. | *American Vaudeville: Its Life and Times,* by Douglas Gilbert | "The Shaming of the Cherry Sisters," by Jack El-Hai | "Time Machine: The Cherry Sisters" | "Bessie McCoy Davis" | "The Dolly Sisters: Vaudeville's Most Famous Duo," by David Soren | "The Dolly Sisters: Alike as Two Peas," by Trav S.D. | "The Duncan Sisters, Topsy and Eva," by Trav S.D. | *Bound by Flesh,* film directed by Leslie Zemeckis

ELIZABETH WEISS earned an MFA
from the Iowa Writers' Workshop, where
she was a Truman Capote Fellow. Her
nonfiction has been published in
The New Yorker online. She has taught for
the University of Iowa, the Iowa Young
Writers' Studio, and the Sackett Street
Writers' Workshop, and is a mentor for
the Minnesota Prison Writing Workshop.
She lives in Minneapolis with her family.

Instagram: @lizjweiss